NEWTON'S CANNON

Greg Keyes was born in Meridian, Mississippi to a large, diverse storytelling family. He received degrees in anthropology from Mississippi State University and the University of Georgia before becoming a full-time writer. He is the author of the 'Age of Unreason' tetralogy, as well as *The Waterborn*, *The Blackgod*, the *Star Wars* 'New Jedi Order' novels, and *The Briar King* – Book One of 'The Kingdoms of Thorn and Bone'. He lives in Savannah, Georgia.

'A dazzling tale'
Realms of Fantasy

'Colourful, intriguing and well handled'
Kirkus Reviews

Novels by Greg Keyes

The Chosen of the Changeling
THE WATERBORN
THE BLACKGOD

The Age of Unreason
NEWTON'S CANNON
A CALCULUS OF ANGELS
EMPIRE OF UNREASON
THE SHADOWS OF GOD

The Psi Corps Trilogy
BABYLON 5: DARK GENESIS
BABYLON 5: DEADLY RELATIONS
BABYLON 5: FINAL RECKONING

Star Wars®: The New Jedi Order
EDGE OF VICTORY: CONQUEST
EDGE OF VICTORY: REBIRTH

The Kingdoms of Thorn and Bone
THE BRIAR KING

Greg Keyes

NEWTON'S CANNON

Book One of
The Age of Unreason

TOR

First published 1998 by Del Rey
an imprint of The Ballantine Publishing Group, New York

First published in Great Britain 2004 by Tor
an imprint of Pan Macmillan Ltd
Pan Macmillan, 20 New Wharf Road, London N1 9RR
Basingstoke and Oxford
Associated companies throughout the world
www.panmacmillan.com
www.toruk.com

ISBN 0 330 41997 8

1 3 5 7 9 8 6 4 2

A CIP catalogue record for this book is available from
the British Library.

Printed and bound in Great Britain by
Mackays of Chatham plc, Chatham, Kent

For My Father
John Howard Keyes

Acknowledgments

My thanks to:

My readers.
Pat Duffy, Nell Keyes, Heli Willey, Nancy Ridout Landrum, Joe Sheuer, Tracey Abla.
Ken Carleton—for general eighteenth-century minutia. Dr. Thomas Poss—for ironing out the Greek passages. Maitre d'Armes Adam Adrian Crown—for his expert opinions on eighteenth-century weapons and fencing.
Any mistakes herein are not theirs, but mine.
Kuo-Yu Liang, Amy Victoria Meo, Richard Curtis, and Marga de Boer for support and encouragement; Veronica Chapman for working harder than an editor ought to; Martha Schwartz for doing the hard things; Dave Stevenson, Min Choi, Alix Krijgsman, and all the other folks who make books read and look like books should.

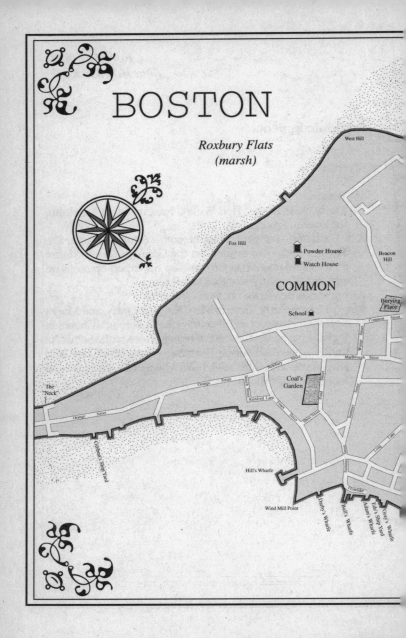

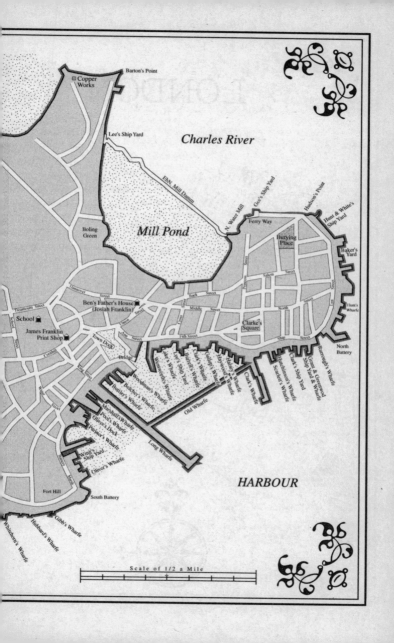

Barton's Point

Copper
Works

Lee's Ship Yard

Charles River

F&N Mill Damm

Gee's Ship Yard

Hudson's Point

Hunt & White's
Ship Yard

Mill Pond

N. Water Mill

Ferry Way

Boling
Green

Burying
Place

Baker's
Yard

Treamount Street

Street

Ben's Father's House
(Josiah Franklin)

Back Street

Salem Street

North Street

Hunt's
Wharfe

School

Middle Street

Clarke's
Square

James Franklin
Print Shop

Fish Street

Ship Street

Town Dock

Ann Street

North
Battery

Cornhill

Bridge

Woodman's Wharfe

Gee's Ship Yard

Scarlett's Wharfe

Clark's Ship Yard & Wharfe

Grant & Greenood
Ship Yard & Wharfe

Burnop's Wharfe

Clark's Wharfe

Walker's Wharfe

Gibbs's Wharfe

Hutchinson's Wharfe

Hill's Wharfe

Hayes's Wharfe

Clark's Wharfe

Dolbeer's Wharfe

Butler's Wharfe

Marshall's Wharfe

Poole's Wharfe

Oliver's Dock

Old Wharfe

Turner's Wharfe

Wing's Ship Yard

Long Wharfe

Oliver's Wharfe

Fort Hill

South Battery

HARBOUR

Whitebon's Wharfe

Hubbard's Wharfe

Gibb's Wharfe

Scale of 1/2 a Mile

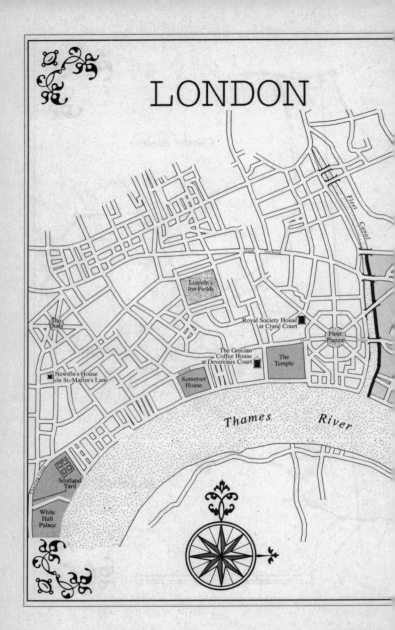

... it may also be allow'd that God is able to create Particles of Matter of several Sizes and Figures, and in several Proportions to Space, and perhaps different Densities and Forces, and thereby to vary the Laws of Nature, and make Worlds of several sorts in several Parts of the Universe.

SIR ISAAC NEWTON, *Opticks, Query 31*

Contents

Contents

Part Two

THE CANNON

Prologue

1681
Jupiter Flying on His Eagle

Humphrey wiped the sweat from his forehead and paused briefly in his working of the bellows. He glanced nervously at Isaac, who was staring into the red maw of the furnace with all of the intensity of a lover—or a madman.

"Isaac, should you not rest?" Humphrey pleaded. "How many *days* have you been at this?"

Isaac did not even deign to glance at him. He stepped instead to the worktable and emptied the contents of a mortar into a beaker. Then, he attacked his notebook with pen, scribbling furiously. "I do not know. What day *is* it?"

Humphrey stared at his friend, whose stained shirt clung to his emaciated frame like parchment. "And how long since you have eaten?" he persisted.

"Work the furnace, Humphrey," Newton growled. Humphrey had seen him like this before, going days without eating or sleeping, utterly consumed by thoughts that even other scholars could only vaguely guess at. If Isaac were merely deluded, Humphrey would not stand here pumping the bellows like a slave, but Newton was not insane. He was that rarest of creatures. He was a genius. Holding the coveted Lucasian professorship at Cambridge at the age of thirty-nine, Newton was virtually without peer.

"Now," Isaac muttered, gripping up the iron tongs from his bench. He flung open the furnace. A blast of greater heat rushed out into the room, so that the last of the cool breeze wafting

1

through the open windows was banished. Newton squinted against the heat, but his hand was sure as he reached in with the tongs and withdrew the effulgent crucible.

With a more considered motion, Isaac tilted the stoneware cylinder over a thick beaker. Humphrey winced, expecting a molten fluid to pour spattering from the spout, but instead a small silvery sphere tumbled out. He had a glimpse of it before an acrid cloud of steam erupted from the beaker. As Humphrey coughed into his handkerchief, Isaac calmly reached over and closed the furnace.

As the heat diminished, the room was momentarily still. With the shuttering of the furnace, everything suddenly seemed quite *ordinary*. For the past ten hours, Humphrey had felt engulfed by an alchemical nightmare.

"Now," Isaac muttered, "we shall see. We shall see if Jupiter rides his eagle."

Humphrey was not well versed in the arcane hermetic language of alchemy. He knew, though, that jupiter was a metal of some sort, said to be useful in producing philosopher's mercury—the original, truest metal of all, the source of all other metal.

Newton peered into the flask. "And the menstruum carries it up," he said, quite matter-of-factly. Humphrey watched Isaac dash off a few notes.

"May I see?" he asked.

Newton nodded impatiently, biting the end of his quill.

Humphrey ventured to gaze into the flask. A sphere of some metal rested in what remained of the yellowish fluid. He recognized the smell now—the sharpness could only be ammonia. But what was that swirling, those flashes? The latter suddenly increased dramatically.

"Isaac," he began, when suddenly the flaring redoubled, tripled. He staggered back from the workbench. A tree trunk of lightning suddenly grew up from the beaker, passing through the air where his face had been. It grew, fluorescing between red and blue, and shuddering the room with thunder. Humphrey screamed and turned his back on the terrible flame. He could not see; brightness etched across his eyes like acid spilled on copper. He tripped, sprawled, fell over a table.

Strong arms pushed up beneath his and lifted, and he opened his eyes. The light was brighter still, the flaming sword of an archangel, and he squealed once more with terror before fainting.

Humphrey came to himself lying on cool grass, the spots before his eyes fading. Dazed, he looked around. He lay in the garden just outside of Isaac's laboratory. Overhead the heavens were mild and blue, cottony with clouds. Isaac sat a few feet from him, writing furiously in a notebook. The air crackled with a sort of tearing sound.

A serpent of flame rose through the roof of Isaac's shed and writhed high into the sky beyond sight, a Jacob's ladder.

"What?" Humphrey groaned, pleased that he could hear his own voice again.

"And the menstruum carries it up," Newton explained, as if to a child. "But how could I have known? This changes *all*."

"That lightning—"

Newton nodded his head furiously. "Yes! Yes! It is the air, decomposing. Lux, liberated by the true mercury! The very aether is exposed, Humphrey. We have touched the nature of matter. Do you understand what this means?"

"Yes," Humphrey replied, faintly. "It means that you need a new roof."

1715
The Angel of Kings

Louis flinched at the faint rattle of musket shots he heard through the thick glass. Following them, the mob suddenly erupted in renewed shouting. At the window, Phillipe began to wail.

"Come away from the window, Phillipe," Louis told his eight-year-old brother. *What if one of the balls were to find its way into the Palais Royal itself?*

Phillipe turned a tear-streaked face toward him, his dark eyes wide with terror.

"Louis, they are going to kill us!" he moaned. "They will burn the palace down and they will— *Where* is Maman?"

"Mother is about the royal business," Louis said. He strode across the gallery and took hold of his younger brother by the sleeve.

"Come," Louis insisted, "your king commands you." He said it with as much authority as he could muster.

It worked. It *always* worked, if people knew in their bones that you were the king. The trick was in *convincing* them of that. Especially with Cardinal Mazarin around, always telling him what to do. Mazarin thought *himself* king.

As Phillipe came away from the window, Louis took a quick glance outside. He saw the mob below and the ghost of his own face on the glass, the pale image of a ten-year-old monarch. Was it set and determined enough, or did his eyes, like Phillipe's, parade his terror?

His features *seemed* composed. He remembered the set of his mother's lips, the brave light in her eyes, and copied it as best he could.

"Here, Phillipe," he said sternly, "come beneath my arm. I will protect you."

"Where is Maman?" Phillipe repeated. "Where are the soldiers?"

"The soldiers are guarding the doors."

Louis remembered the terror in the eyes of the handful of guards. He remembered what they had said to his mother. *"We shall all die at your doorstep."* Perhaps they had meant to sound brave, but they had sounded defeated. Louis doubted that they could be counted on should the mob burst through the doors.

"Who will guard us?" Phillipe asked.

Louis drew his sword. It was a tiny thing, a toy. But gesture was more powerful than reality. He took Phillipe under one arm and held the little rapier with the other. "Your king will defend you," he promised. "Now, let us go to one of the rooms without windows."

They made their way into a darkened salon lit by a single lamp. There Louis sat on a gilded settee and drew his little brother against him. "Here we shall be safe," he said, knowing it was a lie. "And should the mob come through the door, they will learn how a king defends his brother."

"God is with us, is he not?" Phillipe asked, trying to sound brighter but only managing to sound pitiful.

"God is with us," Louis assured him.

"Then why is Monsieur Cardinal dressed in gray?"

Louis bit back a retort. He, too, had seen Cardinal Mazarin forsake his red robes for gray, anonymous clothing. What a fool! What a coward! But to Phillipe, he said, "The cardinal knows what he is doing. Hush, and think of more pleasant things."

"I will, Louis," the younger boy promised.

More faint reports, and Louis battled once again with his own fear. It was all coming apart around him, but he was the king. Had he no control over his kingdom? How could Paris be rising up against him?

How he hated Paris.

"I will build us a great palace," he told Phillipe idly, "in the country, far from here, from these mobs."

But Phillipe was asleep, and Louis realized that he spoke to comfort himself.

And now shots rang closer—they were in the hall! The thud of boots and the clamor of rough soldiers' voices were outside. Louis tightened his grip on his toy sword. If he behaved the king, he *was* the king, *was* the king . . . He repeated it, saying it to make it real.

Now the door burst open, and there stood John Churchill, the duke of Marlborough, ruddy face haughty above his adamantium breastplate, long black coat swept around him like raven wings. Marlborough, the thrice damned, the devil, come here to burn Versailles around him.

But this *wasn't* Versailles. It was the Palais Royal, and he was only ten, and Versailles only barely a dream.

"Your Majesty," Marlborough smirked in his heavily accented French. "Your Majesty may put away his toy." He did not even bother to raise the barrel of his *kraftpistole*.

"Get out of my palace," Louis demanded, but Marlborough only laughed. He saw through Louis, knew him for a fraud . . .

This was all wrong. Louis ran, the laughter echoing behind

him. A shriek tore from his lips, and a wave of humiliation flooded him.

He wanted to wake from the nightmare . . .

Louis XIV, the Sun King, awoke in the seventy-second year of his reign to a reality far more bitter. Pain flamed in his leg, coursing through his groin and belly, seeking his very heart. Though his bedclothes and person had been doused in flower-scented perfume, the sickly corrupt smell of gangrene lay heavily in his nostrils. He was, he remembered, in Versailles—in that splendid country palace he had dreamed of in his youth. He could see that he was surrounded by his family and courtiers, even now, on his deathbed.

"His Majesty is awake," someone whispered. Louis recognized the voice of his dear wife, Maintenon. Her tone made it clear that she had not expected to see his eyes open again.

"Sire? Is there aught we can do for you?" That was Fagon, his physician.

"Indeed, Fagon," Louis managed. "You can preserve my life."

The elderly doctor's voice trembled. "Sire, if there was anything I could do . . ."

"My dear family, my friends," Louis began. He drew a shuddering breath. "It is good that you are all here now. It is strange, for I had resigned myself to death. I was willing to meet my God. My confession has been received, and I have said my good-byes." He could see Maintenon's face, thickly caked with powder, the tracks of her tears channels upon her cheeks. Despite that and her seventy-five years, she was still beautiful, still the woman for whom he had given up all other mistresses. The sight of her encouraged him to continue.

"But now, you see, I know I must not die. Marlborough has returned, bent on our destruction. I cannot leave my young heir with that burden. I cannot leave *France* with that burden."

A general gasp arose. So they knew, too. They had been *keeping* it from him. With Marlborough leading the allied armies, France would fall. "Fagon, bend near," he commanded, feeling his strength already ebbing. "In the *cabinet du Roi*, there is a bottle . . ."

"The Persian elixir?" Fagon whispered, incredulous. "May I remind Your Majesty that even if this dubious potion should have any effect, it may endanger your immortal soul merely to *think* of resorting—"

"I am your king, commanding you," Louis replied, trying to keep his voice pleasant. "Do as I bid."

"Majesty," Fagon murmured, and limped from the room.

Maintenon bent close now. "You have sent for the elixir presented you by that horrible little man from Persia?"

"He was the ambassador of the shah of Persia, Madame."

"That wretched, ill-formed man? His other gifts—what were they, some blemished pearls and turquoise? What makes you believe that this elixir has any more worth than those pitiful baubles?"

Louis felt a bubbling in his throat, an acid taste in his mouth. "Because—" He gasped. "—my scientific philosophers have tested it. It is effectual."

Maintenon stared down at him in dismay. "You did not deign to mention this to me?"

"To what purpose?" He lowered his voice to a whisper. "I had decided *against* using it. I was weary of being king, Maintenon, weary of everyone I know dying. I hoped, at least, to precede you to the grave. I hoped to see my dear niece again, my brother . . ." Maintenon's face was suddenly obscured by a dark fog. Her voice piped like an oboe, but it carried no sense to him as he drifted back down into oblivion.

He hoped that his decision had not come too late.

Louis dreamed again of his childhood years just after his father died, when he himself was like a mannequin, brought out to play king and then returned to its dark box. Whole days passed without anyone speaking to him; his own servants scoffed at his commands.

In this dream he was drowning in a garden pool. He could not swim.

He reached the side easily enough, shouting now, but no one answered his calls. He began to cry out of humiliation. No one cared in the least if he drowned.

Now, in his dream, someone lifted him from the pool. Warm winds enfolded him and dried his clothing, whispering to him.

"Who are you?" he asked.

"Hush," a voice told him. "There are angels who protect kings, and I am such a one. And you shall be the greatest king of all."

"An angel who protects kings," Louis repeated. In his dream he was warm, happy, and the pain and fear of a moment ago were fleeing. In his dream, he slept and he knew peace.

1716
A Miracle

Benjamin Franklin was ten years old when he saw his first miracle. Cold fingers of wind had been groping up the narrow streets of Boston all day, and as night fell they clenched and tightened their grip. The sunset burned like a furnace, but it was empty bluster. The equinox had come and gone, and winter had an early hold on the Massachusetts colony.

Ben was only just beginning to recognize the chill as he stood on the Long Wharf, watching the tall, sleek lines of a sloop as she sailed into port. He was worried less about the cold than about how to explain to his father where he had been and why it had taken him so long to get a loaf of bread. He should not lie to his father—that would be a terrible sin, he knew. But with his brother Josiah so recently run off to sea, his father would not want to hear that Ben had been watching ships again. He did not want to lose *two* sons to the waves and wind, that had been made abundantly clear. Ben wondered if there were some way to frame the truth so that it was not incriminating. He could argue that his love of ships was just a love of well-crafted things. But he *did* long to follow his brother to adventure— whales and pirates and unknown realms. The *truth* was, he could not stand the thought of remaining for his entire life in

Boston, not with the promise of grammar school and college snatched away from him.

His mood now bleak, Ben turned down Crooked Lane, hoping to shave a few moments from his journey back home. The narrow alley was almost entirely dark, as stars began bejeweling the indigo sky above. Here and there the halfhearted flame of a candle gave life to a window. The candles brought Ben no comfort, reminding him instead of what he would be doing tomorrow: boiling tallow to *make* the wretched things. And the day after that and so on, until he was an old man.

Halfway up the lane he saw a light that did not flicker. At first he thought it a lantern, but even the illumination of a lantern *wavered*. This shone as steadily as the sun. Ben felt a little chill that had nothing to do with the marrow-freezing air. The light was peeping through half-closed shutters of a boardinghouse.

His decision took only an instant. He was already late. This light seemed so unnatural, he knew that it must be some trick. Perhaps the flame was encased in a paper lantern. He moved through the yard as quietly as he could, until he could see the light itself: a pale, bluish, egg-sized sphere. He immediately understood that this light was not a flame. But if not flame, what?

A spark from flint and steel had something of the quality of this sphere's light, yet sparks lived briefest of all. His young mind could find nothing else to account for what he saw. Besides, he knew in his bones that this was alchemy, magic— *science*, the king of magics.

If there was magic, there must be a magician. He crept closer to the house until his eye was almost pressed against the thick pane of glass.

The sphere was the only source of light in the room. There was no fire in the hearth, but the window was warm to the touch. Ben wondered if the magic light gave off heat as well. If so, it could not be very much heat, since less than a foot away from the glowing sphere a man sat, reading a book. The sphere, Ben now saw, was actually *floating* above the man's head, so that his wig and brows shadowed his face. His wig cascaded in ringlets to his shoulders. His blue coat resembled a uniform of some kind. He was leaning over the table, tracing the characters in his book. So clear was the light, so legible the characters, that Ben could make out that the book was written neither in English nor in Latin. The characters were all swooping curls and curves, as beautiful as they were enigmatic.

The man was not having an easy time reading the script, Ben thought. He was puzzling at it. Ben could see this because the magician traced his finger over the same line several times before moving on.

How long he stood there, Ben did not know. Nor was he afterward certain why. But what Ben thought was, *That could be me. That could be me reading that book, commanding that light.*

There were no whales or pirates in Boston, but there were books. The three years of school his father had been able to afford had provided Ben with the skills he needed to read and understand what he read, and he had long ago devoured most of the books his father and uncle owned. None of them were on magic, but if there was such a thing as magic, there must be books on it. And now that he *knew* there was such a thing, his future suddenly seemed brighter. He would become more than a tallow chandler.

Indeed, when he tore his gaze from the window and went at last home, he realized that if one flameless lantern could be made, then so could another. And if enough were made, neither he *nor* his father would be in the candlemaking trade for long.

Tiptoeing away he spared one look back, and in that instant the magician looked up from the book and rubbed his eyes. It was an unremarkable face, but it suddenly seemed to Ben that the man *saw* him from the corner of his eye, as if he had known Ben was there from the very beginning. Then the magician's features were in shadow again, but his eyes seemed to catch the light, reflecting red like those of a hound. Ben abandoned all efforts at silence and flew home with what speed his short legs could command.

"I told you, Josiah, the world is changing faster than we want," Uncle Benjamin maintained, propping his elbows on the table. "I'd heard tell of these flameless lamps in England two years ago. And now one has come to Boston." He shook his head wonderingly.

Ben's father frowned at his brother. "I'm not so concerned with these new devices as I am with my son's moral well-being. In your excitement, I wish you would at least remonstrate with your nephew for spying."

Ben felt his face burn. He looked about him to see if anyone else had heard, but the hubbub of conversation produced by Ben's siblings—eight of them were at home tonight—was enough to drown out the three of them. Ben, his father, and Uncle Benjamin often fell into conversation after dinner, especially now that Ben's older brothers James and Josiah were away. The remaining Franklins rarely cared to join them in their usually bookish discussions.

Uncle Benjamin took his brother's soft-spoken comment to heart. He turned to his nephew and namesake. "Young Ben," he said, "what betook you to spy on this man? Is spying a habit you nurture?"

"What?" Ben asked, astonished. "Oh, no, sir. 'Twere not an act of peeping but of investigation. As when Galileo trained his telescope on the heavens."

"Oh, indeed?" Ben's father asked mildly. "Your observations were purely scientific, then?"

"Yes, sir."

"And you felt no impropriety at peeking into someone's window."

"It was an *uncovered* window," Ben explained.

"Ben," his father said, frowning, "you argue well, but if you do not take care, you will logic yourself straight into hell."

"Yes, sir."

"Come, Josiah," Uncle Benjamin said. "If *you* had seen such a strange and unnatural light—"

"I would have passed it by or knocked to inquire, preferably at a reasonable hour," Ben's father finished. "I would not have sneaked across the yard and peeked into his window." He glared at them both.

"Only this one time, eh, Ben?"

"Yes, Uncle," Ben affirmed.

Ben's father sighed heavily. "I should never have named the boy after you, Benjamin. For now you rise to defend his every misdeed."

"I'm *not* defending him, Josiah. What he did was wrong. I'm merely making it clear that the boy knows he did transgress." He did not wink at Ben, but his glance seemed to contain one.

"I *do* understand," Ben assured them both.

His father's face softened. "I know that you are perfectly adept at learning your lessons, Son," he said. "Did I ever tell you about that time he came home tootling on a pennywhistle?"

"I have no recollection," Uncle Benjamin admitted. Ben felt another blush coming on. Would his father ever cease to tell this story? At least James—who never failed to taunt him cruelly about his mistakes—was not here. Though he would never say it aloud, Ben could scarcely be sorry James was 'prenticed in England.

"I'd given the boy a few pennies," Ben's father explained, "and he came home with a whistle, well pleased. Such a din he made! And I asked him what it cost and he told me. Then what did I say, Son?"

"You said, 'Oh, so you've given ten pennies for a whistle worth but two.' "

"And he learned," his father went on. "Since then I've approved of all his purchases—not that he makes many."

"I know what he saves his money for," Uncle Benjamin said, patting Ben's shoulder affectionately. "Books. What are you reading now, Nephew?"

"I'm reading *Grace Abounding to the Chief of Sinners*, by Mr. Bunyan," Ben answered.

"Ah, so *The Pilgrim's Progress* pleased you, then?"

"Very much, Uncle Benjamin." Ben pursed his lips. "And speaking of such matters . . ."

"Yes?" his father asked mildly.

"Since I won't be going to school anymore, I'm hoping to pursue my education, here, at home."

"And I encourage you to."

"Yes, Father, I know. Your encouragement is my sword and

shield 'gainst ignorance. It is— The short of it is, I want to educate myself in science."

His father settled back in his chair, face thoughtful.

"What will that profit you, Ben? I've never told you not to read anything, I've always encouraged it. But I wonder about these new philosophical machines. They seem worrisomely close to witchcraft to me. You know that, too, or you wouldn't have asked me whether you could learn of them."

"They don't say so in London," Uncle Benjamin interposed softly.

"Or in France," his father shot back, "but you know what deviltry they've put this 'science' toward there."

"Bah. The same could be said of such an honest invention as a musket. It only profits us to know the mind of God, don't you think?"

"Indeed. But is it the mind of God that makes stones glow and float in the air?" Ben's father lifted his hands. "I don't know, and neither do you. Neither does Ben, and it's *his* immortal soul I worry about. Not to mention his pockets, for books are not cheaply had."

"Father," Ben said carefully, ordering his words in his mind, "you ask how it will profit me. I ask you, When every man in Boston has a flameless lantern, who will buy candles?"

The two older men turned to stare at him, and he was secretly pleased at their dumfounded expressions.

"Say that again," Uncle Benjamin whispered.

"Well, suppose these lights are easy to make—"

"Suppose they are *expensive*," his father interrupted.

"Yes," Ben persisted, "suppose they cost ten times—thirty times—the price of a candle. But suppose also that they never burn down—need never be replaced? Would not the wise man then invest in the more expensive item so that he could save in the long term?"

His father was silent for a moment. His uncle sat equally quiet, observing the exchange between father and son.

"We don't know that they last forever," Josiah finally said. "We don't know that they are not even more dear than thirty times the cost of a candle."

"No, Father, we don't," Ben said. "But if you give me your leave, I can find out."

"Do what you think best, Ben," his father at last acquiesced. "And when you are not certain what is best, then you speak to me. 'One leak will sink a boat: one sin will destroy a sinner.' You see, I, too, have read your Mr. Bunyan."

"Agreed, Father."

"Now then, here is another thing that touches on your bookishness. Where were you *before* you spied on this magician? You took a very long time after a single loaf of bread, even with some espionage thrown in."

"Oh. I . . ." He had forgotten about that. He picked at the grain of the table wood with his thumbnail. "I went down to the Long Wharf. A New York sloop was coming in. I heard some boys talking about it."

Ben's father sighed. "Why do boys so pine for the sea?" he asked.

"I don't pine, sir—" Ben began.

"I wasn't asking *you*, lad. It was a question for the Almighty. Ben, I know that if I try to keep you in the chandler's trade, you will treat it badly or run off like your brother Josiah. So here is my thought. I will try to find you a trade more suited to your talents, and in turn you will remain here in Boston, at least until you've reached a proper age."

Ben hesitated. "What trade did you have in mind, Father?"

"Well, I must apprentice you, so here is my thought." He leaned forward and reached across the table to clasp Ben's hand. "Your brother James is due home soon from England. He has just written me that he has purchased a press and some letters. James is going to set up a printing shop right here in Boston."

Ben felt a sudden, almost giddy hope. Was his father going to send *him* to England, too, to serve an apprenticeship in the printer's trade? That was more than he had dared hope.

"Yes, I thought you would like this idea," his father exclaimed. "Brother, what did I tell you?"

"It will please him well," he replied, but his eyes were watching his nephew carefully.

"It's settled then, if James agrees," his father said, eyes shining.

"When your brother returns, you shall be 'prenticed to him. That should bring you in touch with those books you seek, give you a trade that will bring you pleasure, and keep you here in Massachusetts."

Ben felt his happy expression freeze. Be apprenticed to James? What a horrible thing *that* would be. The thought of becoming a printer was interesting. It was the years of servitude to a brother that worried him. *Father* telling him what to do was one thing, but being under the command of James was quite another.

Ben reached his bed that night with a feeling of both wonder and resignation. Though he could hardly dispute that things had taken a turn for the better, it seemed that something was slipping away from him. And at the very edge of sleep, he realized it was the floating light and that strange, curling text. The shadow of James and the future he brought with him dimmed hope of that alchemical light.

That can *be me*, he thought again insistently. *I will find every book in Boston that tells of science and magic, and I shall make my own devices. I shall profit from inventing them, too, and Father will be proud.* But something about that rang false, so that when sleep at last found him, it found a fitful and unhappy boy.

Part One

_____

REASON AND MADNESS, 1720

1.

Versailles

Louis awoke to the clatter of Bontemps, his valet, putting away his folding bed, as he did every morning. A frigid wind blustered in through the open windows of his bedchamber, and Louis greeted it with none of his former pleasure. Once, it would have invigorated him. Now, he imagined the wind as death's frustrated caress.

Another metallic click, a sigh, and he heard Bontemps retreating. Louis arranged in his mind the day to come. The order in his days was his only remaining comfort. He had made Versailles into a great and precise clock, and though he was king, he was carried along by its mechanisms as surely as his lowliest servant or courtier. More certainly, in fact, since a servant might slip briefly away and steal a private moment, encounter a mistress, take a nap. This was *his* only private moment, in bed, pretending to be asleep. It gave him time to think and to remember.

The Persian elixir had given him new life and a body that felt younger than it had in thirty years, but it had robbed him of everything else. Gone were his brother Phillipe; his son Monseigneur; his grandson, the duke of Burgundy, and his wife, the duchess Marie-Adelaide, whose death had broken his heart. It was as if God were sweeping clean the line of Louis XIV. The dust had also claimed almost all of his old friends and companions. But worst of all was the loss of his wife, Maintenon.

Now he had only France, and France was a restless, thankless mistress. He knew—though his ministers tried to keep it from him—that there were whispers against him now. As the years passed and he grew stronger and more full of health, those who had hidden their wishes that he would die and make way for a new regime were allowing themselves snide asides. They were plotting. There were even some who whispered that the real Louis *was* dead, and he the devil's proxy.

He had returned to Versailles to show them he was king and to restore the image of glory to accompany his renewed health.

In the antechamber outside, he now heard the subdued chatter of the ever-present courtiers, awaiting their chance to see him. He heard footsteps entering, and he knew without opening his eyes that the *porte-buchon du Roi* had come in to light the fire in the fireplace.

The gears of Versailles creaked on. More footsteps as the royal watchmaker entered the room, wound Louis' watch, and departed.

Yes, he had been right to return to Versailles. Five years ago, when he was dying, his chateau of Marly—comfortable, pleasant, intimate Marly—had seemed the place to spend the remainder of his days. Versailles was drafty; it was an instrument of torture that cost a sizable fraction of the treasury each year to maintain. But Versailles was splendid, a fit dwelling for Apollo. The nation needed him here.

A shuffling from the side door was his wig maker, bringing his dressing wig and the wig of the day.

That meant he had a few more moments. Beneath the covers, he stretched, and was gratified to feel muscles respond to his commands. Since his brush with death, his body felt fresh and alive. All his old appetites were returning to him. *All* of them, and some would not be denied gratification much longer.

Why, then, if his body was again sound, did a feeling of dread still hound him? Why did his dreams grow persistently darker? Why did he fear being alone?

The clock struck eight. "Awaken, Sire," Bontemps said. "Your day has begun."

Louis snapped his eyes open. "Good morning, Bontemps," he said, attempting a smile. He shook his head, gazing at the lean, fiftyish face looking down at him.

"Are you ready, Your Majesty?" he asked.

"Indeed, Bontemps," he said. "You may admit whom you wish."

* * *

The morning *lever* continued. His doctors came in and inquired about his health. When the chamberlain admitted the first of the courtiers—the ones who had earned invitations to the *grande entree* through diligence—Louis found himself dreading their presence, their fawning submission, their requests.

He felt that way until he saw Adrienne de Mornay de Mont-chevreuil among them.

"Mademoiselle," he exclaimed, reaching to embrace her. "To what do I owe this exquisite pleasure?"

Adrienne returned his embrace and then curtsied. "I am well, as I always am in your presence, Sire." Her smile was as flaw-less as a perfect ruby. "I hope Your Majesty is well."

"Of course, my dear." He smiled and cast his eyes over the remainder of the courtiers, all young men, all with that hopeful light in their eyes, all wondering what advantage they might be able to extract from this dear girl.

Adrienne wore the uniform of Saint Cyr, the simple gown with black ribbons that showed she had achieved that school's highest rank—just as she had always dressed when she was his late wife's secretary. Louis generally disapproved of such in-formal dress, demanding that the ladies wear the *grand habit*, but Adrienne's clothing suited her as the clothing of the court ladies did not. It matched her thoughtful features and wide, in-telligent eyes. She wore the uniform, he suspected, as a badge, a quiet proclamation that she had attended the school and had passed all of its tests. It meant that she was as educated as any woman in France, and more so than most. Louis was suddenly suspicious that she wore the gown also to remind him of how dear she had been to his wife. What was she about, this young woman?

"It is good to see you," he said. "Your letters comforted me greatly after the queen's death." That would let her know that he had been reminded, and she would now press the advantage she believed she had.

Adrienne continued to smile, a faint grin not unlike that on the *Mona Lisa*, which hung across from his bed. "As you know,

Sire, I have taken up residence at the Academy of Sciences, serving the philosophers there."

"Ah yes, Paris. How do you find it?"

Her smile broadened. "As you do, Sire: stifling. But the work of your magi is most fascinating. Of course, I understand little of what they do and say, but nonetheless—"

"I, too, find their theories incomprehensible, yet their results are to my liking. They are a great resource to France—as are those who serve them."

She bowed her head. "I shall not waste Your Majesty's precious time, but I will tell you that I did not come to ask a boon for myself. There is a member of your academy, a certain Fatio de Duillier. A most remarkable man—"

"Near to your heart?" Louis asked, a trifle coldly.

"No, Sire," Adrienne replied quite strongly. "I would never bother you on such an account."

"And what does this young man desire?"

Adrienne caught his shifting mood, his growing impatience. "He has tried for many months to receive an audience with Your Majesty and failed," she said. "He wished only that you receive a letter from him." She paused and looked him in the eye, something that few dared to do. "It is a short letter," she finished.

He considered her for a moment. "I will receive this letter," he said at last. "This young man should know how fortunate he is to have your favor."

"Thank you, Sire." She curtsied once more, understanding that she was dismissed. A sudden thought struck Louis, and he summoned her back.

"Mademoiselle," he said, "I am planning a small entertainment on the Grand Canal several afternoons hence. I would be pleased if you would join my company on the barge."

Adrienne's eyes widened slightly, and an expression he could not identify crossed her face. "I would be pleased to, Sire."

"Good. Someone will instruct you in your attire."

He then turned to the other courtiers, listening politely while they each expressed some sentiment and asked some favor. When they were all dismissed, he stepped out of bed, preparing to dress, to keep his appointments. But he paused to receive the letter that Adrienne had passed to Bontemps. He broke its seal. It was, as the demoiselle had promised, brief.

> *Most Reverent Majesty.*
> *My name is Nicolaus Fatio de Duillier. I am a member of your academy and a former student of Sir Isaac Newton himself. I tell you in all sincerity that if you speak with me but a moment, I can tell you how to win the war against England, with great finality.*
>
>

Your humble and most unfortunate servant,
> *N. F. de Duillier.*
>

"Why have I never heard of this de Duillier?" Louis complained to his chancellor, the duke of Villeroy.

Villeroy's face was drawn beneath his plumed hat. The powder on his face did little to hide his surprise at Louis' statement.

"Sire?"

"I have a note from him. He is one of my philosophers."

"Yes, Sire," Villeroy replied. "I know of him."

"Has he approached you as well?"

"This de Duillier has radical, unworkable ideas, Sire. I did not want you bothered with them."

Louis gazed down at Villeroy and the other ministers, intentionally letting the silence expand to fill the gallery. Then he said, his voice quite low, "Where is Marlborough now?"

A general murmur arose among the other ministers. Villeroy cleared his throat. "News came late last night that he has taken Lille."

"What of our fervefactum? How can an army take a fortress defended by a weapon that boils its blood?"

"The fervefactum has grievously short range, Majesty, and is too massive to transport. The alliance uses long-range shells, many of which have been taught magically to seek their targets. In fact, they have instructed such shells to seek our fervefactum when they are in operation. They also—" He grimaced. "At Lille they used a new weapon: a cannonball that rendered the fortress walls into glass."

"Glass?" Louis shouted.

"Yes, Sire. Transmuting the wall and shattering it simultaneously."

"What does this mean for the future of the war?"

Villeroy paused, obviously pained. "Our finances are strained," he began softly. "The people suffer from taxation and hunger. They are weary of this war, and now the tide has finally turned against us. In three years we have scarcely won a battle. And now Marlborough is moving toward Versailles, and I fear we cannot stop him."

"So my chancellor and minister of war has no proposal for staving off our imminent defeat."

Villeroy looked down at the table. "No, Sire," he whispered, shaking his head.

"Well," Louis exclaimed, "have any of my other ministers any suggestions?"

Muttering died to silence before the marquis de Torcy, the minister of foreign affairs, voiced what they were all thinking.

"Have we given no thought to a treaty?"

Louis nodded. "As all of you know, I have thrice entreated the alliance against us to conclude a peace, and have each time been cruelly rebuffed—even when I came perilously close to betraying my grandson and surrendering Spain. These people do not want peace with France, they want to *destroy* France. They fear our might, and they fear our command of the new sciences. Did you know that two members of my Academy of Science have been assassinated in the past year? For that reason I stationed a company of special corps to protect them. I will now move them to Versailles; Paris is too dangerous."

"What of Tsar Peter of Russia?" asked Phelypeaux, secretary of the royal household. "He has defeated Sweden and the Turk, securing his own power quite beyond question. Could we not entice him into an alliance?"

"The tsar has more to gain by watching Europe weaken itself than by taking sides. Accepting his aid would be allying with the wolf to battle the hound. Our enemies are at least civilized nations. If we were to ally with Peter, we would soon find dancing bears occupying my gardens. Worse, we would have to join with him against the Turk, and the Turk is our best weapon against Vienna."

Villeroy grimaced tightly. "And yet Peter stands only just behind you in the numbers of philosophers he employs. When Gottfried von Leibniz flocked to Peter's standard, many followed."

Louis waved that away. "I wish to summarize what has been said here today, rather than to discuss Tsar Peter. We are losing the war for want of proper weapons. You, Villeroy, have just pointed out that I have the greatest philosophers in Europe under my command, and yet England annually produces more effective artillery. How can this be?"

Villeroy straightened his hat a bit. "Your Majesty, England has Newton and his students. We have *more* philosophers, it is true—"

"And yet—" Louis allowed his voice to rise. "—we have *one* of Newton's students here, who tells me in a letter that he had to *smuggle* to me that he has the means to bring us victory. And no one thought I should be troubled with this?" He swept his glance about the room. "Monsieurs, I am not myself an adept, and I do not read widely. I am the king, and it is mine to judge the fate of our nation. I want to see this Fatio de Duillier, and I want to see him tomorrow, in the Cabinet des Perruques."

Plumed hats nodded like a field of poppies in the wind.

Fatio was a nervous, pinched-looking man in his midfifties. His face was dominated by a nose like the upturned keel of a boat, behind which lurked evasive, light brown eyes. His lips were continually pursed, as if he had just tasted something bad. Louis regarded him for a moment, and then took his seat in an armchair.

"Let us come to the point quickly, Monsieur," Louis stated. "I want only to ask you a question or two before hearing what you have to say about the audacious letter you sent me."

"Yes, Sire." De Duillier's voice was unexpectedly pleasant, if a bit high. Fatio was awed in the presence of the king and entirely at a loss for what to do or say. That was good, Louis felt.

"You are, I take it by your accent, Swiss?"

"Indeed, Sire."

"And you were a student of Isaac Newton?"

"Student and confidant, Your Majesty. I have brought my correspondence with him to confirm this."

"What I chiefly want to know is, Why are you no *longer* his confidant?"

"We had—" Fatio drew what seemed to Louis a shaky breath. "—a falling out. Sir Newton is not an easy man; he is prone to harm his friends."

"*Harm* them?"

"Yes, Sire. He can be quite harsh, and when his favor is withdrawn from you, it is gone forever."

"I see. So Newton cast you out."

"Not for any lack of scholarly ability, Your Majesty. His correspondence shows quite clearly that he had nothing but admiration for my skill as a mathematician."

"Do not presume, Monsieur de Duillier, to try to guess at my intentions."

"Forgive me, Sire."

"Was your quarrel with him of proportions sufficient for you to betray him? For are you not here to offer to pit some magical weapon of yours against his?"

Beads of sweat stood clearly on Fatio's head as he answered. "Majesty, I care not what happens or does not happen to England. But upon Sir Isaac Newton I wish revenge. The weapon I will detail for you will accomplish both your aims and my own. In prevailing over England, I will also show Newton that he was wrong to shun me."

"Tell me of this weapon," Louis commanded.

Fatio cleared his throat and drew forth a sheet of paper that he unfolded with trembling fingers. "Well, the principle is rather simple, but the mathematics have still to be worked out," he said. "It involves merely the creation of a certain set of affinities, but as Your Highness may know, the proofs required to actualize such—"

Louis leaned forward, frowning. "This is not what a king wants to hear," he whispered. "Kings do not care where your ideas come from. They want only to know what your work will *do*."

"Oh . . . well—" He paused and lowered his voice. "—it will destroy London, Majesty, or any other city you care to name."

Louis stared at him, dumbstruck.

"What do you mean," he asked finally, "*destroy*?"

"As if it never was. Not one brick shall remain."

Louis regarded him for a long moment, careful to keep his mask in place.

"How?" he asked softly.

Fatio told him, and the king's eyes widened. Then he stood and went to the window, staring out at his gardens for one quarter of an hour before turning back to where the man awaited, twisting his paper in his hands. "Monsieur de Duillier, you are a scientific man. Perhaps you can tell me this. Why do the shadows lie so long in my garden, though the sun stands at noon?"

"It is winter, Sire," Fatio replied. "The earth has tilted such that the angle of the sun is from the south. In the summer the shadows will scarcely be seen."

"Let us hope, then, Monsieur de Duillier, that God grants us another summer, for I mislike this long light. As of tomorrow you have my leave to pursue this. Your budget will triple, and I will place a staff at your disposal."

Fatio fought to keep his features under control but failed.

"Go, with my blessing," Louis said.

Fatio left, clearly on the very edge of flight, nearly tripping on his own shoe buckles.

2.

The Printer's Apprentice

"Are you certain that permission has been given for this?" John Collins asked, blue eyes dubious.

Benjamin Franklin straightened his battered tricorn and glanced sidewise at his friend. "Permission? By whose permission does one exercise the natural powers and liberties God has given him? Come, we're harming no one in this, and greatly improving ourselves. And by improving ourselves, how can we not improve our country? This is, in the end, a *patriotic* endeavor."

John snorted. "I've heard that speech before! How old were we—ten?—when you convinced me and the rest to 'improve' the millpond by building a quay out into it, the better to catch minnows? Never mind that the stones we used were stolen from a pile intended for building a home. You argued *then* that we were performing a civic service, and with no more justice."

Ben shrugged. "Yes, I admit an error in judgment. Our ends were honest enough; 'twas only our means that were questionable."

"Yes, questionable as in my father laid rod to me when the workmen complained of us," John reminded him.

"John, John." Ben sighed, clapping his companion on the shoulder. "I am four years wiser now, and full acquainted with the concept of private property. I've made arrangements with the 'prentice."

"But as you well know, a 'prentice has no say in such things, so what is the word of this 'prentice to us?"

"His word is gold to me, for he offers what I want," Ben replied, becoming irritated.

"Now there is the mark of a *reasonable* man," John shot

back. "He can always find *reason* to justify what he wants to do."

Ben pursed his lips in growing annoyance. There were few people in Boston—man or woman, young or old—who could best him in an argument, but his best friend was one who could.

The two boys made their way down across the fields that lay between Queen Street—where he worked in his brother's printing shop—and School Street. The sun was bright in an afternoon February sky. They trod a path worn well by other children too impatient to make the square turns of the streets.

They were a study in contrasts, Ben with his chestnut hair above a plump face and sharp chin, John more nearly towheaded, with high cheekbones and a jaw as blockily solid as an anvil.

"See here, John," Ben resumed, "if you have become too *timid . . .*"

"I never said that," John replied. "It's just that you led me to believe that we had the word of Nicholas Boone the *master*, not Thomas Perkins the *'prentice.*"

"I never said such, though I apologize if you thought it. What you must understand is that 'prentices have an economy all of their own. That is why I can trust Tom's word."

John grunted. "The economy of slavery, perhaps. I can do without the pretty welts and bruises you wear under your shirt, thank you."

"Well," Ben muttered after a moment, tasting acid on his tongue, "all apprenticeships are not like mine. But he is my brother, and we should not speak ill of him."

"I *shall* speak ill of him," John shot back. "I shall speak ill of him who beats you for no other reason but that you have more of wits in one finger than he has in both clenched fists."

"Very eloquent, John. Perhaps you should be a scribbler of poetry rather than a mathematician."

John glared at him but persisted stubbornly. "It is far from poetical to observe simple facts," he insisted. "And where *is* your lord and master, that you wander so freely in the daylight hours?"

"Filling those two fists of wit you mention with ale at the

Green Dragon," Ben replied, "for at least another hour and not much more. And so we should make haste."

"I thought we were not to speak ill of James."

"Speaking the truth can hardly be considered ill," Ben replied. And then he added, in a quieter voice, "James is well intentioned. He has always had a temper, and it might be that I am too provoking."

"Yes, I should think so," John agreed. "But I should also think one's brother might have more charity. He merely loathes to be outstripped by a boy eight years his junior."

Ben thought so, too, but he dismissed the suggestion with a diffident wave of his hand. "Well," he said, "the business of printing suits me, for the time being. I'm not likely to find a better trade in Boston."

"Oh, aye, in *Boston*," John agreed, and they shared a brief, conspiratorial glance. They both ached to see what lay beyond the horizon. James made it all the worse when he spoke of London, where *he* had apprenticed. Sometimes Ben was sure his elder brother did that just to rub it in, knowing that Ben could not honorably break their contract: that he was bonded until the age of twenty-one.

"Well, we've nearly arrived," Ben said. "Are you in with me, or not?"

John raised his hands helplessly. "My mother has always told me I am destined to end with bad company," he said.

They were now at the bookstore owned by Nicholas Boone. Ben and John stumped up to the door and glanced around, trying not to appear furtive. Ben stepped up and knocked.

The door opened to reveal a young man of about nineteen years with reddish, disheveled hair and glasses. His white shirt was smudged with printer's ink, as were his blue knee breeches.

"Oh, so it's young Franklin and Collins," the fellow said, his voice low despite his obvious cheer at seeing them. "What could bring the two of you here?"

"We've come for the Freemason meeting, Tom," Ben replied. "What did you think?"

"Oh," Tom said. "Then I hope you know the password."

Ben held his hand up solemnly, as if swearing to something, and chanted, *"Ostium aperite blockheado magno."*

"Hey!" Tom replied, indignantly. "I'm not much for the Latin, but—"

"That means 'Open the door, great friend,' " Ben translated.

"I somehow don't believe that *blockheado* is Latin for 'friend,' " Tom returned. "And here I was about to do you a favor."

"And much do I appreciate it, Tom."

Tom nodded good-naturedly. "Come this way, then. As I said, I think Mr. Boone will not miss a volume or two over the space of a few days."

The two younger boys followed him through the shop. After a few moments of searching through books on the shelves, Ben turned innocently to Tom.

"Didn't a ship come in from England, not two days ago?"

"Yes indeed. I'll be unpacking the new shipment this afternoon."

"I wonder if we could look at those."

Tom looked suddenly uneasy. "The new books? I don't know, Ben. Surely there must be something here that strikes your fancy."

"I was hoping for something of a more scientific bent," Ben explained.

"Scientific." Tom returned to scanning the shelves.

"I might make a guess that there is such a book in those boxes," Ben said innocently.

Tom grimaced. "But if you borrowed one of the new books, I would have to have it back early in the morning."

"What a fine suggestion," Ben said. "Thank you for your understanding, Mr. Perkins."

Tom looked confused for a moment—probably trying to understand how loaning out a brand-new book had suddenly become his idea—but then turned to the crates. One by one, he lifted out the precious new volumes while Ben stood over him, hardly able to contain his impatience.

"That's it!" he breathed, as Tom hefted out a particularly weighty tome.

"*The Principia Mathematica?* Sir Isaac Newton's book? I thought you had read it."

"This is the amended version," Ben explained. "The one with the new alchemical treatise."

Tom continued to hesitate as he stared at the red-bound volume. "I don't know, Ben."

"Did I tell you," Ben asked, "that I brought you a present?"

"Truly?" Tom brightened as Ben reached into his coat pocket and withdrew a folded sheet of paper.

"I *hoped* you would bring me something," he exclaimed. "Is it the *London Mercury?*"

"Only the first sheet, I'm afraid," Ben apologized. "But that news you now hold is only a day old."

"A day old, all the way from England," Tom wondered, unfolding the sheet. "Your brother James was a genius to think of this."

"His brother, the king's *arse*," John snarled. "Using the aetherschreiber to send that paper from London was *Ben's* idea, not James'."

"John—" Ben began.

"James would never even have bought the machine if Ben hadn't convinced him to."

"That's an exaggeration, John."

"Really? Your idea?" Tom asked.

"Please, Tom, don't go repeating that."

"But was it really your idea?"

Ben blew out a breath and then quirked his mouth, a mockery of a grin. "It might have been."

John snorted. "*Might* have been."

"Well," Tom said, "I used to wonder if all of this science would find a practical purpose, but that aether-scribbler changed my mind about that. To be able to write across the Atlantic in an instant—"

"That," Ben said, holding up his borrowed book, "is why I read Newton."

"That was a right lucky guess, Ben," John observed as they made their way back to Queen Street.

"No guess at all, John," Ben replied smugly. "It so happens that I knew one of the leading citizens of our town had implied in a letter to Nicholas Boone that this volume would be well appreciated and quickly purchased were it to be ordered."

"And how did you come to see this letter?" John asked.

Ben grinned slyly. "I wrote it," he replied.

Ben knew he was in trouble when he saw his brother's shop door was open. The open door probably meant that James was home early.

"*There* you are," James snarled when he entered.

"I—" Ben began, turning, but then he saw the expression on James' face. He bit back his reply and deposited his book on a nearby bench.

"I thought you would be setting type," James went on, more quietly.

"I was just about to begin that," Ben said. "I was only out for a walk."

"Certain that you were. But where do you walk this time of afternoon? Perhaps down to the water to see the pretty ships?"

"Not today," Ben replied.

"I see. Well, as you know, I, too, understand the attraction of the waves, little brother. But let us not forget that you've signed your indenture, with Father and God as witness."

"I wouldn't forget that," Ben replied, but the statement seemed feeble, somehow overpowered by the iron presses. Ben thought about breaking his indenture almost every day.

"That's good," James said. He sank heavily into an oaken chair, then ran ink-blackened fingers through his tousled auburn hair.

"I can be a hard man, Brother. I don't mean to be. But Father taught us right and wrong, and he's entrusted you to me. You understand that, I know."

Ben lowered his eyes, gulping down arguments.

"I'll set that type now," he murmured.

"Be still. You'll set the type when I tell you to." James clasped his hands together. "Father has raised seventeen of us, Benjamin. *Seventeen.* Now he deserves that his burden lighten, especially

now with his business so poor. I'll not tolerate you running back
to him with your complaints."

"While *you* are the very exemplar of filial concern!" Ben
heard himself sarcastically blurt. "You would never *dream* of arguing with Father yourself, would you? You *so* despise to see him
agitated. As the other night—when you called him 'fearful' to his
face on account of his distress over the new scientific cannons—
I'm quite certain you were as respectful as Isaac in your heart!"

"Ben."

"You only wish that Father not know how you beat me!"

"Father has never been one to spare the rod himself," James
snarled. "Though I can think of *one* child he spoiled."

Ben felt his face burning. "You always say that," he snapped.

"Spare me your bookish speech," James answered wearily.
"You were and always will be his favorite. We all know that,
and most resent it none. But the rest don't have you 'prenticed
to 'em, and *I* do. So you settle down, and don't you worry Father. For whatever he says, for these nine years you are mine,
and by *God* you will be a proper man and printer at the end of
them."

Ben clamped his teeth on another retort, for James was
watching him carefully, waiting for his excuse. He had already
been hit once today.

"In any event," James went on, "I hope you had a fine holi-
day, for it will cost you tonight. I'm expecting another install-
ment of the *Mercury* over the aetherschreiber, and someone must
stay up to set it. So whatever that is you've brought to read, you
can plan on returning it unread." James quirked his lip a bit and
continued. "What would Father think of this habit of yours of
thieving books?" He directed a crooked finger toward where
Ben had placed the *Principia*.

"It isn't *theft*—" Ben began angrily.

"Oh, it isn't? You are a printer, Ben, or apprenticed to be.
How is it that we printers make our money?"

"By selling what we print," Ben answered.

"By selling how *many* of what we print?" James pressed.

"As many as we print, we hope," Ben answered.

"Precisely. And how many would we sell if my apprentice were to lend a copy of each broadside and paper to be passed around town?"

"I take your point, but it isn't theft because I give the books back."

"Do you give the words back and what you learned from them?"

"But I can't afford to *buy* such books," Ben complained. "If it weren't for my reading, for what I know of things scientific, *you* would not have the fine business you are about to enjoy—" He stopped abruptly when James bolted from his chair. His sleeves were rolled up, and the sinews of his arms bunched dangerously. Ben closed his eyes, preparing for the blow. But the blow did not land, though James continued to stand close enough for Ben to smell the sour scent of ale on his breath.

"Open your eyes, little brother," James commanded.

Ben did so, to find James gazing down at him with an odd expression—something different from the fury he had expected.

"Why do you provoke me so? Why must your mouth always get the better of both our senses?"

You are the one who always begins the arguments with Father, Ben thought. *You are the provoking one.* But, "I don't know," is what he said. *It is just so easily done.*

"You made a fortunate observation about the aetherschreiber, Ben. I admit that, though I would have seen the possibilities, too, given time. I have much to worry about and less time for idle thought than you. It is I, remember, who must pay our bills. Bills that will not be paid if we don't publish. And this scheme of ours has yet to prove itself. We shall be the first to deliver the *Mercury* to Boston on its printing date, but others will quickly imitate us. We must be prepared to offer more."

"What do you mean?"

James laid a hand on his shoulder. "Are you ready to discuss business with me respectfully and put away your boyish pride?"

It is you who are too proud, Ben thought.

"Yes, sir," Ben said, trying to put a little enthusiasm in his voice.

"Very well. Have a seat, Ben.

"I have settled on two things," James said. "But I'll hear what you have to say of them. The first is that I want you to write a few more of those Grub-Street ballads of yours. The one about Blackbeard's grand escape made us a few shillings and was generally pleasing."

"Except to Father," Ben replied carefully.

For once it was the right thing to say. James shook his head. "Our father is a wonderful man—and no son could love his father more than I—but he comes from a different time. Remember that I tried to convince him to quit the chandler's trade when I returned from London? Already candlemakers were going bankrupt when I was apprenticed there."

Ben remembered that he had made the suggestion to Father, the night he'd seen the flameless lamp, but it would not do to bring that up. Ultimately James was right; their father, unconvinced that the new alchemical lanterns would become popular, had continued making candles. But then Cotton Mather himself had endorsed the scientific lights, and the major thoroughfares of the town were already lit with them. The new town hall had not a single candle in it. More than one disastrous fire had plagued Boston, and many saw the lanterns as a godsend.

"More ballads, then," Ben relented.

"You needn't sound so excited about it," James said dryly, and Ben suddenly realized that his brother had actually been trying to *please* him, give him something interesting to do for a change—although something he hoped would profit them.

Ben tried to brighten, though he felt not at all cheery. "Yes," he said. "Perhaps I can write a poem about Sir Isaac Newton."

James smiled condescendingly. "What dry stuff *that* would be. I was thinking of Marlborough—something military, that's what people like."

Ben shrugged and nodded.

"The other thing," James went on, "is that I wish to use the aetherschreiber to find other news—perhaps from the continent."

Ben looked at him blankly. "What?"

"Oh, not the way we do from England, where we have my friend Hubbard to send us the *Mercury*. But we can get other things, can we not? Dispatches, conversations?"

"Well," Ben began, "that would be a fine idea if the aether-schreiber worked in such a manner. But it does not."

James frowned. "I know how they work, Ben. Between my machine and the one in England there exists a sociable quality which binds them together. It is the same sort of affinity as gravity or magnetism."

"Yes," Ben acknowledged. "But Newton's point about affinity is that they are of different specificities."

"Don't *think* to lecture me," James cautioned.

"I'm only trying to explain why your idea won't work."

James regarded him coldly for a moment and then nodded. "Go on, then."

"Affinities are a kind of attraction between similar objects. And the more similar the objects, the more powerful the affinity. Gravity is the most general affinity, because the only similarity it requires is that the objects in question both be composed of matter.

"And you also know that magnetism is more specific, for it only affects certain metals. That's why a magnet will draw up iron even in defiance of gravity.

"Well, the affinity that allows the aetherschreibers to write to one another across the ocean is much more specific. The chime—that crystal plate in the aetherschreiber—is twin to the one in England. But what that means is that these two machines can *only* speak to each other. The crystal is poured by a glassmaker and then cut in two. No two objects in the world are as similar."

James frowned. "There must be some way to find the affinity of some other crystal."

Ben cocked his head. "I don't think—" But then an idea struck him. "The book I have over there is the revised *Principia Mathematica*. If what you wish can be done, it is probably in there that I shall find the means to do it." He then waited breathlessly.

Finally, James sighed heavily. "Stay up tonight and transcribe the rest of the *Mercury* when it comes in. Lay out the sheets, and *I* shall set type in the morning and delay waking you for an hour. That will give you time to read this book, will it not?"

Ben nodded.

"Because my muse tells me that I am correct in this, Ben. And if I am, our future will be assured."

Your future, you mean, Ben reflected.

"Finish today's type, and then you are free to read. Hubbard won't begin sending until eleven o'clock or so. As for myself, I have other matters to attend to." He rose and dusted his knees with the palms of his hands. "We accomplish the most, Ben, when we work together without bickering. Sometimes you give me hope, little brother." He donned his cinnamon coat and left the printshop, doubtless headed back to the Green Dragon.

It took only a few moments for the little elation Ben felt to evaporate. He had succeeded in gaining permission to read his book—something he would have found a way to do anyway—but he had also implied that his brother's idea might be possible. The fact that James even came up with the notion demonstrated that he knew little if anything about Newton's laws of affinity. How could he ever explain to his brother—without getting hit—that what he wanted was simply impossible, if not laughable?

3.

Adrienne

Adrienne paused in midstroke, frowning, unsure whether she had really heard a faint scratching at her door or merely the echo of her own pen on paper. When the faint rasping repeated itself, she deftly lifted her pages of calculations and slipped them into the drawer of her desk. As she rose, she glimpsed her face in the mirror and read the conflicting emotions there: anger at having to hide her work, shame, and beneath all of that, a furtive sort of glee. It was the face of a sinner who loved too well her sin.

Not that her devotion to the scientific was a sin—it was just not what a young woman did. But the concealment—that was another thing, especially when she dared not speak of it in confession.

She approached the door hesitantly. Scratching was what passed for knocking at Versailles, but this was not Versailles. Had someone been sent from the court? "Yes? Who is it?"

"Fatio de Duillier," a muffled voice answered.

"Monsieur, it is only in Versailles that one scratches for admittance," she called. "Elsewhere, one knocks."

"Yes, of course," Fatio answered. "I wonder if I might speak with you."

"You might if you are accompanied by a chaperon," she answered, making certain to tinge her voice with regret. "Otherwise I fear what might be whispered of me."

"Oh, dear, of course," the disembodied voice replied. "One moment, Mademoiselle."

She stepped back to her desk to make certain that everything was as it should be. Her mouth pulled in a sardonic grin when she realized that the *Principia* lay open on her bed. She had concealed a fish but left the whale in plain sight. She pushed it beneath her mattress.

If her interests in mathematical subjects ever became general knowledge, she would find her position at the Academy of Sciences terminated. Only her former appointment as the queen's secretary had made it possible for her to be here in the first place. Only by preserving the illusion that her interests were confined to music, mythology, and needlework could she remain close to the truest love of her life: the sublime precision and balance of equations. Furthermore, if attention were attracted to her skills and knowledge, it might lead to broader inquiry into how she *attained* her intimacy with science, and that could endanger persons other than herself.

Though lately she wondered if she even cared about *them* anymore, as they seemed to no longer care for her.

Fatio probably wished to thank her for her intercession on his behalf with the king. He owed her more than he knew; she had unfortunately attracted the attentions of Louis when he had doubtless forgotten her. The king had heroic appetites in all things, and the Persian elixir had clearly revived many of the king's vital juices. Yet with Maintenon alive, Louis had always been gentlemanly, fatherly even, to Adrienne.

In their last meeting, she had sensed less paternal sentiments. What attracted him to her she could not imagine. The meaning of beauty was still a mystery to her. When she looked at herself in the mirror she saw tresses a single remove from black, skin that bore the dark tint of her Spanish grandmother, eyes like ripe olives. She saw a figure that—even at the age of twenty-two— still retained a sort of adolescent awkwardness. It seemed to her that her nose was too big.

Nevertheless, the king found her attractive, and though she hated to admit it, a part of her was flattered. After all, he was the king. There had been very short, very guilty moments when she had daydreamed of being his mistress. But being his mistress, she had come to understand, could be more a curse than a blessing.

This time, there came a knock at her door, and with a sigh,

she returned to it. She knew that Fatio was also attracted to her, but she had even less interest in him as a suitor.

"Yes?" she inquired.

"Excuse me, Mademoiselle," Marie d'Alambert, the matron of women at the academy, replied. "Monsieur Fatio de Duillier wishes to speak with you."

"Thank you, Madame," Adrienne answered, and opened her door. "I would be delighted to receive the gentleman."

Fatio sipped his coffee with enjoyment. "Dear lady, you have been of incalculable service to me. The king not only received me, but he has provided me with a staff and a budget to pursue my project."

"I am delighted to hear that," Adrienne answered. De Duillier was not a bad sort—somewhat lacking in social graces, perhaps, but a fine mathematician. Her investigations into his work showed that he had been a student of the great Isaac Newton in his youth. And de Duillier seemed untroubled by using her skills with books to his advantage. This allowed her to use the king's library without suspicion. In fact, de Duillier called on her services so frequently, she was virtually his personal secretary. This permitted her to observe lectures from distinguished scholars, even to attend meetings, all without raising the hackles of those around her. She had only to pretend to find it all so *dreary* . . .

Of course, it also meant keeping de Duillier's hopes up, something it rankled her to do but which, fortunately, was not so very difficult.

"Though I do not understand your work, it seems fascinating," she told him.

"You could come to understand it, my dear, if you wished," Fatio assured her. "You are not an unintelligent woman. In fact, you have more intelligence than many members of the academy."

Adrienne raised her hand to her mouth. "Please, sir, do not say such things," she gasped. For Madame d'Alambert sat no more than twenty paces away and she could transmit gossip like a plague.

"Ah, I have embarrassed you, and I did not mean to," Fatio apologized. "But I have not come here merely to thank you and to flatter you. Rather, I have come to offer you a position."

"Monsieur?"

"I have been furnished with funds to hire a staff. I need someone to correspond with my colleagues through the aether-schreibers. Have you ever worked with such devices?"

"Yes," Adrienne said, blinking. "I was Madame de Maintenon's amanuensis."

"And you have some facility with English?"

"English? Why, yes, some."

"I offer you the post. Will you join my staff?"

"This seems very odd," Adrienne told him. "Won't my lack of knowledge concerning your project prevent me from performing satisfactorily?"

Fatio shook his head. "You need not understand what you send—in fact, in some ways it is better that you do not."

"Well, then." She sighed, trying to sound reluctant. "I will try to accede to your expectations. But the instant I fail to give satisfaction . . ."

Fatio stood, taking her hand. "Mademoiselle, I feel certain that you will never fail to give satisfaction. If you would come by my laboratory in the morning—perhaps at ten o'clock? We can begin this business."

"Very good," she replied. She ached to ask exactly what that business was, for she did not know what project he had presented to the king.

"Tomorrow then," Adrienne said politely, but inside she was crowing. For a woman of noble birth there were only two options in life: marriage or the Church. And yet, in Adrienne's mind was a faint idea of a third path, a narrow, strange course that had beckoned to her since childhood. Now, finally, she saw how she might at last set her feet on it.

She could not let her triumph show, however. The instant Fatio was gone, she caused her face to fall, and she sighed heavily.

From where she sat, Madame d'Alambert chuckled. "You

should have seen that coming, dear. The one thing they did not teach you at Saint Cyr was the nature of men."

The next day Adrienne made her way to Fatio's workrooms. She found him bustling among two desks layered in papers and books and a worktable scattered with beakers, crucibles, and piping. Fatio greeted her warmly and escorted her toward a pale young man of about twenty whose body was lean and attractive, but whose eyes glittered like blue ice. She did not care for those eyes; they seemed to see nothing when they looked at her.

He favored her—or perhaps Fatio—with a narrow, passionless grin when they approached.

"Monsieur," Fatio said to the other man, "I would like you to meet the lady de Montchevreuil, of the school of Saint Cyr. She was instrumental in our acquisition of the king's favor."

"Enchanted, Mademoiselle," the young man replied. His voice was soft and melodious. Though she could not identify his accent, she felt certain that it was Teutonic—perhaps Swedish.

"And, Mademoiselle, this is my assistant, Gustavus von Trecht."

Adrienne curtsied. "*Guten Tag*, Herr Trecht," she said.

Gustavus merely smiled and shook his head. "I am actually a Livonian and speak only rudimentary German, Mademoiselle."

Adrienne was trying to remember where Livonia was—north, she remembered, either a Swedish or a Russian possession. She wondered what business this strange, exotic man had in Paris. She would learn, but she would do so without asking.

"Mademoiselle will be assisting us," Fatio explained. "She is well acquainted with the library and with the operation of the aetherschreiber."

"I am confident she will prove invaluable," Gustavus remarked, and Adrienne was almost certain she detected skepticism in his tone.

"And what is your area of expertise, sir?" she asked Gustavus.

"Calculus is my principal interest," Gustavus answered, "especially its applications in altering the affines of ferments. I am also greatly interested in the motions of the heavenly bodies."

"Monsieur, you already have me quite at a loss," Adrienne

replied, but what actually struck her was how closely that paralleled her own interests. "Perhaps some day you could explain—in the simplest terms, of course—precisely what that *means*."

"Of course, Mademoiselle," he replied, but his tone held out little hope.

"It is to do with *changing* things, my dear," Fatio gallantly supplied. "And with bringing them together or pushing them apart."

"Oh. Like the aetherschreiber?"

Fatio's eyes danced with admiration. "Yes, yes, how astute. You are certain you have not read upon this subject?"

"Oh, no," Adrienne lied. "I only meant—well, the aetherschreiber brings words from one machine to the next, does it not?"

Fatio nodded. "Yes. I will show you."

He led her across the room to an uncluttered table on which three aetherschreibers sat. At first glance they were a confusing melange of gears and wires. But most of the apparent complexity was in the clockwork mechanism that drove the writing arm that protruded over the small surface on which the paper was placed. When the schreiber was receiving correspondence, the gears whirred and wire tightened and loosened, as the arm wrote whatever the machine was being sent.

"This is the heart of it, here," Fatio said, jabbing his finger past the mechanical devices to the center of the machine, where a torus of silvery metal surrounded a crystal plate. The metal was faintly luminescent. "Are you familiar with music, Adrienne?"

"Yes," she replied, noticing that he had suddenly used her Christian name. "I play the harpsichord and the flute passably, and I was taught to read music."

"Then perhaps I can explain by analogy," Fatio said. "That crystal there is the *chime*. In a sense, it can be made to vibrate like the string of a harpsichord—the vibrations are aetheric rather than in the air—but don't let me confuse you. Just think of it vibrating like a harpsichord string."

"Very well."

"Now imagine that the note is, say, middle C. If you had a harp nearby, which also has a string tuned to middle C, what might you observe when you play that note on your harpsichord?"

"The C string on the harp would sound," she said promptly. That was the most elementary aspect of musical theory, one that a well-educated lady could be expected to know.

"Yes, yes!" Fatio exclaimed. "And so it is with the aether-schreiber. The mate to this machine has a crystal tuned in precisely the same way as this one, so that when this one vibrates, its mate does, too. That is why we must have three schreibers here—we are corresponding with three other scholars."

"But, Monsieur," Adrienne said, "a string can be tuned to different notes. Why not these devices?"

"Ah, well, there the analogy breaks down, Mademoiselle. Just rest assured that aetherschreibers work only in pairs and cannot be 'retuned,' as you put it."

"What a pity. Then we would only need one of them."

"Yes, but think of this: Since no machine other than its mate can receive what is written on this one, it is a perfect device for relaying secret information. The letters cannot fail to arrive at their destination; they cannot be intercepted or read by the enemies of France." He lowered his voice. "The mates of two of these, you see, are in England. We pass messages with no *chance* of discovery."

"I see," Adrienne said, nodding. "Then it is better this way."

"Oh, indeed. At least for our purposes."

"Well," Adrienne replied, "if it suits your purposes, my dear Fatio, I am quite content."

Fatio beamed and then shrugged. "It is the wonderful fact about science that we can make the world as we *will* it."

Adrienne nodded, and from the corner of her eye she caught the expression on the face of Gustavus. For an instant, the polite, slightly bored façade had slipped aside and behind was a ferocious scowl of contempt—even hatred. It was gone so quickly that she was uncertain she had even seen it.

4.

An Ingenious Device

"I'm not certain what this has to do with aetherschreibers," John Collins said, dubiously eyeing the odd apparatus that Ben was tinkering with.

"Perhaps nothing," Ben murmured, checking the thing he had just finished for flaws. "Though I used part of an old one to make this."

"What is it?"

"If God is kind, it is a philosopher's stone."

"If God is kind, perhaps he will cure you from having been struck too many times on the skull."

Looking back at his device, he certainly had to admit that it did not resemble a philosopher's stone. What he had built looked more like a cross between a fishing rod and a coffee grinder, with a set of crystal goblets thrown in for good measure.

John sighed. "I'm a degree or two better than you at mathematics, but I have to admit, I don't see any connection between what we proved out on paper and this thing."

"Let's see if it will work," Ben replied. "Then we can sort out later why it did. If it doesn't—"

"Then the same," John said. "Though it might be easier to explain to your brother why what he wants simply cannot be done."

"Explain to the storm why it cannot cross the harbor, and you would enjoy greater success," Ben replied. "And yet, it is often the obstacle that invents the circumvention."

"What?"

"I mean that James might be right. He forced me to consider

the impossible, and I may now admit that what he asks might be done."

"Oh, not you, too!" John exclaimed.

Ben shrugged. "Forty years ago no one would have believed in flameless lamps or adamantium armor or blood-boiling guns—and then Newton invented the philosopher's mercury. Let's just see."

John held up his palms in surrender. "Start it going, then."

"Help me carry it over there by the water."

The two boys were at the edge of the millpond, facing the leaden expanse of the Charles River. The air was tinged with a brackish smell and the tang of the copper works' furnaces some quarter of a mile to their left. Hammers and hoarse men's voices carried from the nearby shipyard. They carried the machine to the pond. Ben then tilted down the long copper tube until it was just in contact with the surface of the water. He wet his fingers.

"Turn the crank," he told John.

"Oh, of course, *I* turn the crank," his friend muttered.

The crank moved a shaft, on which were mounted eight glass hemispheres of varying sizes. Ben touched his wet finger to one, and a clear tone sounded—the same sort of sound one got from a crystal goblet by stroking its rim.

Ben watched the water expectantly, counting to one hundred and twenty. Then he touched a different hemisphere, and a higher note sounded. He held it for the same length of time.

"I'm impressed," John said, sarcastically.

Ben pursed his lips and tried a third note. He had been holding the third note for one minute when he heard John gasp. Looking at the water, he laughed excitedly. John cranked with a will now, and the note sang out. When John tired of cranking they switched places. They finally stopped, both breathing heavily, to admire their work.

"I don't believe it, Ben," John said, wiping tears of laughter and triumph from his eyes.

Around the copper rod, for a space of nearly three feet, the millpond had frozen solid.

* * *

"I still wonder how your experiment can be applied to changing an aetherschreiber's mate," John said, after the glow of their victory had begun to dim. Having left the device in the millpond, they now sat nearby on a small jetty, legs dangling over the water. Ben absently watched a boat cross the river, sail burnished copper by sunset.

"To be honest, I'm not sure," Ben answered, "but I feel that this is progress in the right direction."

"What you built is a miniature fervefactum, but reversed. It turned water into ice."

"I didn't finish the experiment," Ben said. "Let's try it again."

The two of them almost ran back to Ben's device. The mass of ice had begun to thaw, but a fair-sized chunk still clung around the rod. Once again, John cranked the handle as Ben sounded the notes. The fourth did nothing, but the fifth caused the rod to glow an eerie pink color. When he sounded the sixth note, the result was spectacular: The ice hissed and exploded, stinging them with minute shards. John cried out and let go of the crank. They both stared at the unmistakable plumes of steam rising from the end of the rod.

"I call it a *harmonicum*," Ben stated.

John wiped his face and then turned to Ben angrily. "What if our *blood* had boiled, Ben Franklin, you blockhead? If one of us had been near the end of the rod, the water in our bodies would have gone straight to steam, just as the ice did. What if the area affected had been greater?"

"But it *wasn't*," Ben pointed out reasonably.

"But it *could* have been," John retorted, though Ben could tell he was already trying to sort out particulars of what had just happened. "So now it *is* a fervefactum," he went on in calmer tones. "But I've never heard of one that also *freezes* water."

Ben nodded. "I must admit that this experiment turned out somewhat different—better—than I expected. But let's sort it out."

John quirked his mouth a bit, then, almost shyly, said, "You *are* something of a scientific man—more so than me."

"But your skill in mathematics is greater," Ben pointed out.

"Without your help, I wouldn't have guessed this could be done." He paused a bit awkwardly and then said softly, "I need your help, John."

John's face retained a dubious cast. "Explain it then," he sighed, "until I see what my figuring did."

Ben shrugged. "We know that matter is composed of four elements, do we not?"

"Damnatum, lux, phlegm, and gas," John agreed. "I didn't say to treat me as an imbecile."

Ben nodded. "I'm sorry. Tell me what you do understand about matter."

"I have read the *Principia*, and *Optics*, and Robert Boyle's book on the foundations of alchemy," John said, somewhat pompously. "I know that all substances are formed by combinations of the four elements in various proportions and configurations."

"And ferments?"

John nodded. "Ferments are the patterns or molds in the aether that matter resides in."

"A simplistic accounting, but true."

"Don't tell me *you* understand all there is to know of aetherics," John retorted.

"No, you're right, I don't," Ben admitted. "And I didn't mean to slight your explanation. It *is* aether that gives matter form, and the analogy of a mold isn't a bad one. But these 'molds' are built of affinities, like gravity, electromagnetism, sociability."

"Understood," John said, "but now you begin to reach the limits of what I know."

Ben plunged on with his explanation. "When we say that there are molds in the aether, we do not mean whole things—like houses or chairs or men—are there. We mean that the shapes of the compounds—iron, lead, gold, *water*—are there. I prefer to think of these ferments as self-weaving looms—that's the analogy Newton uses—each of which knows the design of a different tapestry. Each takes the four elements and weaves them together to create its own particular design."

"That's why part of the formula we worked on required a matrix," John stated.

"Exactly. You see why I like the loom analogy better. Thus we can think of a copper ferment weaving copper from damnatum, lux, and a small amount of gas."

"Yes."

Ben liked playing teacher to John Collins, a boy who had thus far outdone him in debate, writing, and mathematics.

"In any event," Ben continued, "the warp of the loom and the *plan* by which matter is woven are formed of various kinds of attractions and in unique combinations. Each compound, each ferment, has its own peculiar harmonic, or vibration."

"I'm still following you," John said. "That's how aether-schreibers work—the mated pairs have identical harmonic qualities."

"Yes, exactly. As does iron or glass or—" He paused significantly. "—*water.*"

John stared at him. When he spoke his voice seemed almost strained. "You changed the ferment so that the matter in it was rewoven from water to ice."

"Yes!" Ben crowed, clapping John on the back. "Of course, it is a very minor change, one that occurs naturally. After all, anyone can boil water—"

"But only by applying heat, thus changing the ferment in a cruder fashion. Your harmonicum does it directly."

"As do any number of devices," Ben reminded him. "The flameless lanterns operate by causing air to release lux. As you said, my device is a smaller version of the French fervefactum. Ever since Newton discovered the philosopher's mercury—the substance that can transmit vibrations into the aether—we have found ways to alter the states and composition of matter."

"But this machine of yours is different?"

Ben smiled. "I think so. Because it can do two different things."

"Freeze *and* boil water."

"Yes. Most devices are made to mediate only one kind of change. My machine translates the vibrations of sound into aetheric ones—there is a small amount of philosopher's mercury in its heart, which I got from a broken aetherschreiber. All I had to do was provide a number of possibilities—"

"Wait," John said, holding up his hand. "This was strictly hit or miss? You had eight notes. What if none of them affected the ferment? Or what if the effect had been— It could have done *anything*."

"No," Ben averred. "I didn't think of this all by myself. An inventor named Dennis Papin designed most of the device. In fact, he used it to run a small boat. This device only affects water, and water has only three states—liquid, solid, vapor. By making the glasses different sizes, I thought the chances were good I could produce at least one change of state."

"But this Papin's machine did not use glasses?"

"No. His doesn't use sound at all. He derived the proper vibrations of the mercury—and thus the aether—in the more usual way, by using an alchemical catalyst to set up the proper harmonics."

John looked at him with what might have been awe. "By God, Ben, whatever made you think of using glass?"

Ben pursed his lips. "I don't have the faintest idea. No, wait, that isn't true. It was something my father said. He plays the fiddle. Usually he plays well, but the other night he was having difficulty finding the notes. And he joked, saying, 'I have but to hit all the notes to find the proper one!' and then he ran his finger down the string, sliding from one tone to the next. And something in here . . ." Ben tapped his skull.

"Something in there has a serious genius," John finished for him.

"I had no real reason to think it would work, until you proved it on paper," Ben confessed. "And then I reread books so that I could explain it to you if it *did* work. I've learned more this last week by experimenting than in three years of reading."

"' 'Hands learn quicker than eyes,' " John quoted, " 'and quicker by working than sloth.' " His eyes narrowed in suspicion. "You already knew it would work because you've already experimented!"

Ben allowed himself a sly grin. "You have me," he said.

"And then you pretended not to know that it would work."

John was getting angry as the implications sank in. "Ben Franklin, were you trying to fool me for fooling's sake?"

"No, John," Ben said, feeling his face color. "It's just that . . . what if it *had* boiled my blood? I didn't want to risk my best friend in such a way."

John's face changed; the anger blew out of it, replaced by confusion and mock severity. "Oh, well . . ."

"It's time we got going," Ben observed. "Could you help me carry this thing home?"

"Why glass, Ben? Why not a fiddle string?" John asked as they walked past the bowling green lugging the awkward device. A handful of people playing at ninepins stopped to stare curiously.

"I tried that first, and it didn't work, though I'm not certain why. Bear in mind that the crucial element is the philosopher's mercury, because only that transforms my musical notes into aethereal ones. I don't know *why* it does that, I just know it does. Perhaps the sound must come from crystal, or perhaps the tones generate some other kind of harmonic in the glass—which in turn affects the mercury." *Despite all of my fine talk,* Ben thought to himself, *I really don't know what it is I've done.*

"I wonder why it glowed pink on that one note?"

"Another thing for you to help me explain."

"At least I see the relevance of the experiment to aetherschreibers now," John allowed. "If you can use sound to change the ferment of water, you can use it to alter the ferment of the chime in the aetherschreiber. And if you could alter it gradually—like your father moving his finger down the violin string—then you should be able to match it to the ferments of other aetherschreibers."

Ben nodded. "That's what I'm hoping."

"Have you tried that yet?"

"No, I want to try it tonight. And I was hoping—"

"Hoping what?" John asked, when Ben stalled.

"Hoping that you would help me write up the math so we can send this somewhere—perhaps to Sir Isaac Newton himself!"

" 'Collins and Franklin on Harmonic Affinity,' " John said. "That sounds good."

" 'Franklin and Collins' sounds even better."

They were just launching into a debate when Ben caught a motion from the corner of his eye. From the shadows of Hillie Lane, a man in a brass-buttoned blue coat was watching them, a broad-brimmed hat pulled low over his face. From beneath the brim of the hat, Ben thought he saw the fellow's eyes flash like red fireflies—like the man he had seen reading, under the flameless lantern four years ago. Ben quickly glanced away, feeling a rush of fear tingle up through his feet. As they made the final turn onto Queen Street, he looked back once more, but the strange man was nowhere to be seen.

"I'm going to bed now," James said. "Mind you that you cover the light when you're done."

"I will," Ben assured his brother, though he wondered *why* the light had to be covered. The flameless lantern would continue producing light whether it was covered or not.

The aetherschreiber was nearly done with the page. Ben poised to feed it another, admiring the machine, the grace and precision with which it wrote. It wrote, in fact, in the handwriting of a man an ocean away—that thought sent goosebumps along Ben's spine. At this moment, Horatio Hubbard sat at his machine in London, his hand moving the pen and the metal arm on which it was mounted.

Of course, to keep it writing *here*, Ben would have to stay up half the night, changing the paper and winding the clock key that provided the arm with motive power.

And he needed to solve the puzzle of tuning the schreiber. The triumph of the day remained with him, but it was subdued now by fatigue.

His thoughts kept tracing the same circle—like a two-legged dog, his uncle would say—and when the last sheet of the *Mercury* came off, Ben still had not managed to solve the problem. What he needed was a way of changing the ferment of the crystal the way he had changed that of water—and he needed to be able to change it in a gradual but *consistent* manner—the way his father varied pitch on his violin string. Ben had already begun to think that his use of sound to create analogous changes might be a dead end, because he could imagine no way to vary the pitch of a glass crystal continuously, the way one could a string. If only wire worked!

The other problem was that water was a very simple compound, and the Star Regulas glass that composed the chimes was not. The mathematics of the water ferment had been deduced long ago, but the structure of most compounds was still a mystery to science.

He shook his head blearily. Maybe if he had a *look* at the chime. What was it John had said about hands thinking better than heads? That certainly had to be true of him tonight. He *knew* he could do it. What other man, at the age of fourteen, had made such a discovery as he had today?

Unless, as he was beginning to worry, the discovery had been made long ago and discarded. In which case Isaac Newton would only laugh at John and his paper when it reached him.

Unless it reached him by aetherschreiber, Ben thought, defiantly. He *was* made for more important places than Boston, and he would prove it.

The chime was a strip of Regulas-laced glass two inches long and half an inch wide. It was bolted to the housing that contained the mercury—or rather, philosopher's mercury, which was a very different substance than what came in thermometers. With a pair of pliers, Ben undid the screws until at last both pulled free and he was able to handle the strip of crystal.

Unfortunately, several moments of staring at it brought no revelation. With a sigh he replaced the plate in its housing and began to tighten the screws. It might be that he *was* in over his head. He knew just enough about these matters to understand his fantastic luck this morning and to know that there was much he did not understand. In a few years he might, especially if he could find the right tutor, but now he might best admit that he was licked.

A tiny *snap* caught his attention then, and his blood ran cold. His mind had been wandering, but his hands had tightened the screws too far. The chime had fractured. And though he did not know *everything* about aetherschreibers, there was one thing he *did* know. In fact, at the moment there were two things about this particular aetherschreiber that concerned him greatly.

The first was that an aetherschreiber with a shattered chime would not work. The second was that James was going to *kill* him when he found out.

Which meant he had less than a day to fix what he had broken.

For the first time in almost a year, Ben put his head down in his hands and wept.

Ben woke up after a few fitful hours and gazed out his window at the waking town. A gray haze filled the streets, enshrouding all but the tallest buildings.

What was he going to do? James would not know the machine was broken until this afternoon, but then what?

With a heavy sigh, he rose, doffed his nightshirt and traded it for a pair of knee breeches, a shirt, and his gray coat.

Perhaps he should go and *see* Father—tell him of James' unfair demands. Perhaps that would serve as sufficient cause to break the indenture.

Tiptoeing down the stairs, Ben crossed through the print shop, spared the aetherschreiber a despairing glance, and creaked the door open. The chill of the fog struck him full in the face. Ben hunched into his coat and began walking. His footsteps thunked on the new cobbles.

He realized that he wasn't going to his father's house when he found himself turning left onto Treamount Street. If he went to Father, it would be admitting defeat and would ultimately make more trouble. James was stubborn, argumentative, and rebellious. He and Father would fight; there was no sense in causing yet more strife between them.

So he was walking in the fog, hoping that when it lifted the one in his brain would lift as well.

Off to his left, where Cotton Hill rose, a few dogs began barking. The dogs probably belonged to the Frenchman Andrew Faneuil, whose enormous house was murkily visible upslope. Ben quickened his steps a bit without knowing why. It was something in the tone of the dogs, perhaps; they sounded nearly hysterical.

His brisk stride brought him quickly to the Common, a vast

meadow bounded by Boston on one side and Roxbury Flats—
the marshy, brackish backwaters of the bay—on the other. And
next to the Common, the burying ground, its scattered head-
stones vague and more sinister somehow. Ben paused. Out on
the Common, cows were beginning to low, their lackluster
trumpeting the perfect herald for a day that was certain to be
the most miserable in his life.

Ben was trying to decide which way to go when he heard
hushed footfalls coming his way, weirdly regular, like the ticking
of a clock.

Ben knew instantly who it was by the broad brim of his hat,
by the set of his shoulders. For a moment Ben stood, watching
the stranger approach, gripped by a sudden fear. It was the same
magus he had spied upon four years ago, he was sure, the
man who had watched John and him carrying the harmonicum
home yesterday. Was the man following him or merely out for a
stroll?

Ben pretended to be gazing out at the Common. The metro-
nome steps continued to approach. Ben held his breath, caught
by an almost paralyzing fear. Of course the man had stopped to
stare at two boys carrying such a bizarre device. Who wouldn't?

Then a last heel clacked down. Ben stood, shivering. Behind
him he heard a small, polite cough.

"Good morning to you," a voice said as he turned. The man,
only a yard away, regarded him with a faint smile upon his
rounded features. His accent was from the north of England.
His mouth was grinning, and his cheeks were dimpled. But his
eyes were gray and unsmiling, with the hard look of glass.

"Good morning, sir," Ben managed, conscious of the quaver
in his voice.

"Benjamin, isn't it? Benjamin Franklin?" The man stuck out
his hand. Ben just stared at it dumbly until the fellow raised his
eyebrows and said, "I'm Trevor Bracewell."

"Ah, yes, sir," Ben said, finally reaching out his own hand to
shake that of the stranger.

"Walk with me for just a bit, Benjamin?" Though phrased
like a request, Ben sensed that it was not. He nodded as the

stranger laid a hand on his shoulder and directed his steps out toward the Common.

"Excuse me, sir, but how is it you know my name?"

"Boston is no large place," the man observed. "It is not difficult to find the name of the boy who peeps into your window."

A flush crept up Ben's face, quickly replaced by fear. Where were they going?

"I . . . I'm sorry, sir," he stuttered. "I was younger then, and . . ."

"And you had never seen science in operation before. Yes, I understand, Benjamin. I know the attraction of these things."

Benjamin felt a small flare of courage at that. "Are you a philosopher, then?"

"No," the man said. "No, as you know by now, items such as my light can be purchased. I fear I do not possess the intellect to master this new science. What's more . . ."

He stopped and looked around, and then slipped his arm farther around Ben's shoulder. He increased his pace so that suddenly they were almost running across the Common. Ben shrieked, but something seemed to snatch his voice from the air. Suddenly he could no longer keep up, was stumbling and finding himself being *dragged* along. Now he began to struggle, but the man had shifted his grip to his arm, and the fingers dug into him like steel bands. He was completely helpless, and in his belly he knew he was going to die.

5.

Of Carriage Rides and Cabals

Adrienne followed the smooth motion of the machine's writing arm with some pleasure. The mathematical symbols—interspersed with lines of Latin, English, and French—told a fascinating if incomplete story. Fatio had asked her to send part of a formula to their "colleagues"—whoever they were, for none signed their responses, as she had been cautioned not to sign Fatio's, save with the letter F. This was the response of M. Three. Adrienne liked M. Three better than MM. One and Two—as she had named them—because he seemed brighter. He did not, however, seem to have the answer that Fatio—who was peering restively over her shoulder—was seeking.

"That won't do!" he snapped.

Adrienne wished she knew why. She understood most of the correspondence; it was about the motion of large masses. It was clear to Adrienne that some sort of movement was being calculated, almost certainly orbital motion. But the present correspondence concerned an alchemical formula dealing with affinity. Yet she could not guess *what* affinity. It did not seem to be gravity, magnetism, or simple sociability, though it did seem to be an *attractive* rather than repulsive affinity.

"It's like shooting at a single pigeon in the dark," Fatio complained, stamping across the room toward Gustavus. "I should never have told the king we could do it! 'All I lack is the mediating formula,' I told him. All! I will lack it until doomsday, at this rate!"

"I don't even see how we can know we are correct," Gustavus replied.

"We *must* know we are correct before we implement any-

thing," Fatio said. "And yet, in a month it will be too late! What am I missing? The answer must be simple, I know it is!"

"We will find it," Gustavus assured him.

"I hope so. I told the king—" but then he broke off short, as he remembered Adrienne was present.

If I only knew what you were trying to do, you fool, I could probably help, Adrienne groused inwardly. That was really the largest piece of the puzzle for her. If she only understood the relationship between the calculations of motion and the incomplete alchemical formula, she could do the calculations and pretend it had come from M. Two, who used several different secretaries to do his schreibing.

A sharp rapping sounded at the door. She would have to answer it and likely miss a part of what was being written. She had just changed the paper, so she had no excuse not to answer the door. Once the formula was off the desk, however, and replaced by a blank sheet, Fatio would snatch it up so that he and Gustavus could ponder it, and she would not get a chance to see it again.

She opened the door to a young page boy. He bowed to her.

"Pardon me," he said, "but do I have the honor of addressing Mademoiselle de Montchevreuil?"

Adrienne was astonished, for callers here were almost always for Fatio, occasionally for Gustavus—*never* for her. Then she suddenly remembered the king's invitation. "Indeed, you do."

"In that case, I have the honor of escorting you to the king's carriage. He requests your presence at Versailles this evening."

"This evening? But . . . the king's entertainment is tomorrow."

"Yes, my lady," the page replied. "I have been told to wait until you have finished your immediate business."

"I—" She turned helplessly to see if Fatio and Gustavus had followed this exchange and found them both staring at her.

"Of course you must go," Fatio said softly.

Adrienne turned back to the page. "I must finish something first—a matter of a few moments. Would you please wait?"

Adrienne returned to the aetherschreiber, wound it again, and nervously waited for the message to finish.

* * *

As Adrienne approached the carriage, she realized that it was occupied already—the man inside of it was, in fact, stepping out. She recognized him as he swept off his tricorn hat and bowed low to her.

"Demoiselle de Montchevreuil," he said, "how wonderful to see you."

"And I am delighted to see you, Monsieur Minister," she replied, though she was in fact quite intimidated by Jean-Baptiste Colbert, the marquis of Torcy and the king's minister of foreign affairs. Torcy was in his midfifties, but he carried his years well. The solid bones of his nearly square face refused to let his flesh droop, and his carriage was that of a young musketeer. Only his eyes and the corners of his mouth showed his true age and the weight of his responsibilities. Like so many at court, the marquis had a charming exterior, but his smile hid dragon's teeth and his dark eyes the fatal glance of the gorgon.

At the moment, however, he was charming, kissing her hand and making certain that she was comfortably seated in the carriage before sitting next to her.

"It happened that I was in Paris when the king sent his carriage for you," Torcy explained, "and I begged for the pleasure of accompanying you to Versailles."

Adrienne looked down, wondering how Maintenon would have replied to that. "You are too kind," she finally settled upon—perhaps the most conventional response possible.

Outside, the dark and dreary streets of Paris passed, though they traveled in the pool of light cast by the sorcerous lantern that adorned the coach. She could make out faces, stroked briefly golden, watching them pass, and see the expressions of the Parisians as they recognized the king's coach. Some—the hungriest and meanest of them— scowled openly, though most expressed more controlled disapproval or, occasionally, awe. The general sentiment of Paris toward the king was one of brooding tolerance. After all, Louis almost refused to admit that the great city existed. But their ire sprang from the effects of decades of war. Even the splendor of the new era of science could not eclipse suffering and hunger. She understood that; though her family was counted among the nobility, they were also destitute, and as a child she had missed more than one meal. It had been Madame de Maintenon and the king who had saved her when they had accepted her family's petition to admit her to Saint Cyr at the age of seven. Saint Cyr only received girls whose families were both noble *and* impoverished.

Most Parisians were impoverished, but few had noble blood. This gave them very little hope of ever gaining *anything*. To Adrienne this seemed dangerous. The king was wrong to ignore Paris, for in Paris he might see France; in Versailles he would only see himself.

"How does Mademoiselle find the Academy of Sciences?" Torcy asked.

"I am most content there," she replied. "Everyone is kind to me, and my work is interesting. And, I must admit, I have enough leisure to devote to my own interests."

"And what might those be, my dear?" Torcy asked with a flicker of a smile. His eyes seemed almost on the verge of closing, as if her answer could hold no interest for him.

"Music, predominantly," she answered, "and also writing. I hope to compose a history of the academy someday."

"How very interesting," Torcy exclaimed. "And how laudable. You are aware, then, that it was my uncle who was instrumental in founding the academy?"

"But of course," Adrienne said. "How could one not know that?"

"You are too kind." He turned to look at her. "You know," he said, his tone still more than amiable, "that when the academy was founded, twelve *women* were nominated as members?"

Of course I do, she thought bitterly, but what she replied was, "No? Really?" She hoped she sounded convincingly surprised.

The marquis smiled. "Those were different times," he murmured. "Yet my uncle had a very high opinion of women: He believed that they were capable of scientific scholarship. Of course, none of them had their nominations confirmed, and none have been nominated since. But, as I said, those were different times."

"They must have been," Adrienne agreed, flashing her own

bright smile. "But I wonder if women are truly suited to such endeavors. It does not seem complementary to our natures."

"Oh, but there are many who would disagree with you, my dear. In fact, I have always wondered why *you* chose to find a position in the king's library, when you might have taken the veil at Saint Cyr. Or rather, I wonder *how* it came to be that you were placed there."

A little chill stroked her heart. Did Torcy know about her and the others?

Beneath the wheels of the carriage, stone pavement had given way to dirt, and the stench of the city was being replaced by the scents of the countryside. "I don't know, Monsieur," she replied. "I had expressed my interest to Madame the queen before she passed on."

"Yes, which I can hardly believe she approved of. Madame Maintenon had as little use for science as for vice."

"But I explained to Madame that my interests were not in science," Adrienne told him.

"Yes, and I am sure that she believed you, just as I do," he replied ironically. "What you must understand, Mademoiselle, is that I do not care *what* your interests are, so long as they do not endanger the king."

Adrienne frowned, amazement at Torcy's implication transforming into anger. "Sir," she said steadily, "I am quite certain that I do not know what you are insinuating."

Torcy nodded, all traces of joviality swept from his face. "Very well. Let me be candid," he said. "I remember you. You were an excellent secretary to Madame. You are intelligent, and you know how to hide things. But when the king takes an interest in someone, *I* take an interest in that person. And when I took an interest in you, do you know what I found?"

Adrienne could only stare at him, smiling to hide her panic.

"I found that you had been given your position by the duke of Orléans."

"What?" Adrienne managed in stunned disbelief, for that was not at all what she had thought he would say.

"Yes, it is true. Do you understand the implications of this?"

"Monsieur, I . . ."

"Come, come. You were Madame's secretary for an entire year. You *cannot* be that ignorant of the intrigues of the court, even if you are innocent of its vices."

Adrienne struggled for some response. The duke of Orléans? If Torcy were fencing with her, now would come the kill. She heard herself answer, almost as a stranger talking. "I understand something of them. I know that the duke of Orléans is a possible heir to the throne."

"He might be regent, if the king were to die now, but the little dauphin, the king's great-grandson, would be king. And after that would come King Philip of Spain—also a legitimate descendant of the king. In fact, the royal will even places the duke of Maine—His Majesty's bastard by Madame Montespan— ahead of Orléans."

"If Orléans is not a plotter for the throne," Adrienne managed, "why then are you so concerned that he might have done me some favor?"

"I never said the good duke was not plotting to take the throne," Torcy said. "The dauphin is only ten years old. And if France should ever conclude a peace with her enemies, they will never allow Philip to sit both thrones. *And* if the king were dead, his will would be set aside by Parliament. They would never allow a bastard to rule in the place of Orléans, who is a legitimate prince. So you see, the duke *could* be king—if the appropriate accidents were to occur."

"What are you saying?" Adrienne asked. "Are you saying that Orléans is planning to kill the king and the dauphin?"

Torcy now revealed one of his true smiles, a hard, cold thing totally unlike the amiable façade he had presented earlier. Adrienne found that she liked this one better; it was real.

"I would never *say* that, Mademoiselle. Nevertheless, the duke is the son of the king's late brother, and I need not tell you of the strife that existed between them. Worse yet, he is the son of that *German* woman, the Princess Palatine."

"I know that there was never any love lost between the princess and my late mistress," Adrienne said. "But what has all of this to do with me?"

Torcy examined her squarely. "I do not know," he replied.

"But if *you* know, you had best tell me now. Do not let me discover through spies that you are dissembling."

Adrienne returned his gaze frankly, though her lips trembled. "Before God, I do not know, sir," she said, "though when you find out I would be very pleased if you told me."

Torcy gazed out the window. After a moment of silence, he let down the glass and called for the driver to shutter the lanterns. An instant later, the coach was plunged into complete darkness. Adrienne felt the hackles on her neck rise and a sudden terror of what the marquis might do gripped her. And yet, after a few moments, as nothing happened, the darkness became less black as the natural light of the stars and half moon dusted the landscape argent. In the pearly glow, Torcy's face was as that of a marble statue. "I wonder sometimes," he said, so softly that she almost did not hear, "if these new lights we have created do not blind us to what is real."

Adrienne remained silent, and after a moment, Torcy chuckled.

"I will take you at your word, Mademoiselle, but I encourage you to keep your eyes and ears open. Do not doubt that some game is being played in which you are a piece. Whether you are a queen or a pawn I do not know, but either may check a king—and I will deal with either in the same way."

"I understand," Adrienne replied. "I have no desire to be a queen and no small disdain for pawns."

6.

The Sorcerer on the Common

As abruptly as he had begun, the man stopped running. He stood, holding Ben's arm, staring without apparent passion down at him as he struggled.

"Let go of me, damn you!" Ben managed to gasp. "What do you want? What have I done?" He choked down another scream, overcome by terror. The man dropped him, and Ben fell sprawling facedown on the damp, cold grass. He lay, eyes clenched, waiting for the blow, the knife—whatever was coming.

"Sit up," Bracewell said quietly. Shaking, Ben pushed up with his palms, keeping his eyes on the ground.

"Look at me."

Ben reluctantly turned his gaze upward.

"Now, Benjamin, I want you to listen to me," the man said, squatting down on his haunches so that their eyes were more or less level. He reached over and mussed Ben's hair. "Listen and remember. What you did the other day, with your machine— you are *not* to do that again, is that clear?"

"Ga-w-what?" Ben gagged.

Trevor Bracewell leaned closer. "Or anything of the kind. Do you understand? Leave things be, Benjamin."

"I don't understand." Ben tried to sound defiant but failed. "God curse you, I don't understand."

Behind Bracewell, Ben saw something rise. It looked like the fog but thicker, darker, a sheet of smoke with a dull ember of flame glowing inside, resembling nothing so much as an eye.

"Yes, yes," Bracewell snapped irritably. Ben understood that his attacker was no longer talking to him. Then, the apparition vanished. But in that fleeting instant, Ben felt something thrust into him where his dreams lurked. It was a whole vision, fully formed, an answer to a question.

"What was that?" Bracewell snapped, now speaking to Ben. "What did you just see?"

"What?" Ben gaped.

Bracewell took a deep breath, and then with an apparent effort, he smiled again. "It doesn't matter, does it?" he said, his voice calm once more. "It doesn't matter what *they* let slip because you've understood *me*, haven't you? You will build no more devices, experiment no more. Be a printer, Benjamin Franklin. Keep your mind here, on the things of this world, and you will live a long and healthy life."

With that, the man who called himself Trevor Bracewell stood and, without a single backward glance, strode off into the lifting fog.

Back in Boston, the town clock struck the first chime of six. Before the last had sounded, Ben was already back on Common Street, running faster than he ever had. Halfway home he stopped, his belly heaving to expel a breakfast he had never eaten.

Four hours later, Ben's fingers still trembled as he set type. He kept feeling that grip on his arm, kept hearing the words.

Leave things be, Benjamin, leave them be.

What could that possibly mean? What would Trevor Bracewell do to him if he didn't 'leave things be'?

Bracewell had lied. He *had* to be a magus, despite his claim to the contrary. Was that what this was about, some wizardly competition? Was Boston only large enough, in Bracewell's view, to support one magus—himself? Ben knew that alchemists, adepts, and magi *did* dispute with one another. Sir Isaac Newton had his share of opponents and had waged public war on some of them— notably Gottfried von Leibniz, who claimed to have invented calculus before Newton. But these had been battles fought with words, not with fists and promises of murder. What could have driven Bracewell to threaten a fourteen-year-old boy? In this age of miracles, what could so frighten or anger a man about a machine that merely created ice and steam?

That gave Ben pause. Perhaps the man was *not* a philosopher or a sorcerer; perhaps he was one of the old-style Puritans. Perhaps the man was a witch hunter.

Perhaps he was the devil himself. Whoever Trevor Bracewell was, he was a bully, and Ben had too much experience with bullies to remain long daunted by them. James had hurt him far more than any stranger. No, it wasn't Trevor Bracewell that kept his fingers shaking or sickened him to the point of nausea.

What did *that* was the knowledge that he now *knew* how to fix the aetherschreiber. He was not at all certain what he had seen on the Common, but in the instant in which that single eye had touched him, he had asked himself, *What do I really want?* And the answer had not been, "to live," "to escape," or any other such sensible thought. No, it had been, *to fix the aetherschreiber.* And then he had felt an intense involuntary response— followed by equally intense self-anger—and he had known how to do it. It was as if a million pieces of something had joined together in his head.

The door banged open, and Ben jumped, upsetting the entire line of type he was working on. James was stalking toward him, fury only barely banked behind his eyes. In his hand he carried a newspaper, which he threw toward Ben.

"Look at that!" he snarled.

Ben picked up the paper dumbly. *The London Mercury,* it read, and the date was April 7, 1720.

"Yesterday," Ben said. "We set this yesterday. But this isn't the font we set it in."

"Yes, and what do you suppose that means?" James asked.

"It means— Oh, no, not already."

James nodded grimly. "Yes, already. Someone must have gotten wind of our plan."

Yes, Ben thought, *anyone and everyone at the Green Dragon, I should think.* All the printers that Ben knew had mentioned it to *him.* "Did ours sell?"

James nodded. "Ours was on the street an hour or so before theirs, though I had to pay the Lawson boy to run it."

"You told me to work on the aetherschreiber," Ben began defensively.

"Yes, I know that," James snapped. "I'm not laying blame on you. The blame goes to me for allowing you to convince me of this mad scheme." He threw himself heavily into a chair. "Fine," he said, finally. "So what do we have? Have you written any ballads, as we discussed?"

Ben nodded reluctantly. "I wrote one called the 'Siege of Calais.' It's about Marlborough." He hesitated. "It isn't very good."

"Is it as good as your poem about Blackbeard?"

"Probably."

"We print it tomorrow, then. What of the aetherschreiber? Can you change it so that we can receive more sorts of news?"

Ben stared at James, and for an instant he felt a sort of panic.

"Yes," he said quietly. "I am certain that I can."

"Hah!" James said. "Then I *was* right."

"Yes," Ben acknowledged. "But I need something from you."

"What is that?" James asked, a bit suspiciously.

"Money," Ben told him. "I need money to pay a glassblower."

James pursed his lips angrily. "I've already wagered a lot of money on you, Ben. How much do you need?"

"I don't know. If you give me your leave to go now, I shall find out. If the glassblower works quickly, I can have your news—something—by tonight."

James looked skeptical, and Ben's fury suddenly lashed forth. "It was *your* idea," he snarled.

"Don't yell at me! Don't take that tone with me!" And Ben realized, with a cold, sobering shock, that a tear was working down one of James' cheeks. Ben's hand darted to his mouth in astonishment, and he suddenly felt his own tears crowd thickly around his lids.

"Go, go," James hissed, thus saving them both, for Ben had no more than reached the street before his tears poured forth like the hot, wet drops of a summer storm.

"Will it work?" John Collins asked, touching the odd glass surface with the tip of his index finger.

Ben shrugged. "If it doesn't, James and I are in the poorhouse. Father has no more money for either of us, and with everyone in town selling the *Mercury*, we won't feed ourselves *that* way." He sighed in exasperation. "I thought I was so smart, John."

"Well, you can always sell ice," John began, trying, for once, to brighten the conversation. It didn't work; how could James know that Ben had been forbidden, essentially on pain of death, to continue his experiments?

Of course, here he was, at it again. But if Bracewell could see him here—in his own, shuttered bedroom—then what hope was there? His only hope was that his nemesis had no magical scrying device that could spy through walls.

"Well, then, try it," John continued.

"I'm afraid," Ben admitted. Once he began acting on it, the certainty of his vision had ebbed with dismaying swiftness. Now, looking at the thing the glassblower had made for him, he felt faintly ridiculous.

It was two nested glass cylinders. They stood upright and fit together tightly enough that the inner tube could be drawn up or lowered by gentle pressure from the finger but would remain in whatever position it was left in when one stopped pushing or pulling. In the lower tube rested a silvery fluid; a suspension of philosopher's mercury in its near cousin, ordinary mercury.

"And the chime itself—" John began.

"Yes, melted and alloyed with ordinary glass to form the tubes. I went to the mercantile office and found that they had several broken chimes on hand, and they sold me them for next to nothing, so they are included, too."

"It seems as likely to work as anything. How will you sound the crystal?"

"That's the thing—with this arrangement I don't think I'll have to. I guess we'll see."

Ben lifted his odd construction, fitting it into the new brace he had made. The tubes now rested where the former, flat chime had—within the translator housing. He pulled the inner tube as far out as it would come without it coming free.

"Now," he told John, "wind the scribing arm."

John did so. There was already a piece of paper waiting to be written on, and the lead pencil in the arm's grip was sharp.

"Start it," John said.

"It *is* started," Ben replied.

"Oh."

After a moment, Ben pushed the tube a bit farther in, but there was still no result. He pushed farther, then farther still. John gave a disappointed sigh.

The arm suddenly spasmed, and John yelped. Ben froze, his heart pounding, and then slowly eased the tube back up. The arm jumped again, and then, incredibly, began writing in a thick, crabbed hand.

The Yemassee continue in their rebellious ways and have contriv'd to lure away our former allies such as the Charakee to join their cause. It must be admitt'd that they are not without grievance, but it is more the problem that the Spanish provoke them at every turn, giving their warriors solace in the mission at San Luis . . .

Ben felt like shouting in triumph.

"It works," he muttered. "By the Lord God, it most certainly works."

"You must have known it would," John said suspiciously. "Did you try this one without me, too?"

"No, John," Ben assured him, "I wanted you with me this time in case it didn't work, to save me from throwing myself from the window."

"Move it down," John said, his voice nearly choked on eagerness.

Another half inch down and the arm jumped again. This time it wrote in a language that neither of them understood, though the letters were Roman.

"Mark the tube," John said suddenly, "like a gauge. So you can find them again."

"An excellent thought," Ben replied.

The third schreiber they found wrote in Latin, which Ben laid aside to translate later. The fourth was English again, and the boys followed it with great interest, for it was what appeared to be news of the European war.

> ... *threw up three redoubts during the night, but the grena-diers made short work of two of them by midmorning. The fighting was fierce, however, and we were forced to with-draw. A second sally found their line still holding firm; they managed to entrench two, perhaps three of their drakes which spray clouds of molten lead. God willing, we shall have our own warlock cannon situat'd by morning, but the rain and the sorry condition of these French roads delays their arrival ...*

"There is an item for our paper," Ben said happily.

Two more untranslatable communiqués followed—one of which Ben was sure was German and another that might be Greek. They had still not moved their "divining rod" down more than half of its length.

"And these are only those who write at this very instant," John pointed out. "Who knows, ultimately, how many schreibers you can spy upon?"

It had already occurred to Ben that they were eavesdropping.

"We cannot print private communications without permission, I think, unless the public interest be served—as in this dispatch about the war."

"But you can write to them, can you not? You can establish correspondence with people all over the world. *There* is your real stuff, Ben, not in the eavesdropping."

"Yes, I agree," Ben said, again changing the position of the diviner. He stopped when the pencil began writing again.

This time it wrote in the characters of mathematical formulae.

"Here, what in the world is this?" Ben said.

"Mathematicians, exchanging love notes, I would say," John replied. He squinted at the formula, trying to guess what it might have to do with.

It went on for two pages, ending with a brief note in English.

Ye Correspondence is inexact, but today it seems I will do no better. What is lacking, as always, is ye kind and degree of mediation. Ye mechanism is still lacking. Hope for better on ye morrow, my dear Mr. F.

As always your servant,
S.

"How cryptic," John remarked delightedly. "May I take this home and look at it?"

"Of course, John," Ben replied. "For it appears that I have type to set!"

7.

The Grand Canal

Adrienne pursed her lips into a dubious scowl and then gasped as the servant behind her drew tighter on the laces of her bodice.

"What sort of entertainment is the king planning?" she asked the two young servant girls attending her.

"It is a sort of masquerade, I think, on the canal. You are to be dressed as the red savages of America," answered Charlotte, a girl of about twelve years.

"Truly?" Adrienne glanced down at her dress, but saw little of the savage about it.

"You will see when we are done," Charlotte promised, and then giggled. The other servant, a darker, older girl named Helen, only smiled. "You will be lovely, Mademoiselle," she assured Adrienne.

An entertainment on the canal was a fete such as the king had not held in over five years—not since just before his last illness. But Adrienne remembered stories of the lavish entertainments of the past century, when the whole of the court had dressed as sultans, nymphs, and Greek gods. Most of that had ended with the king's marriage to Madame de Maintenon, who had brought the semblance of piety to the court.

But Madame was now dead, of course. And Louis seemed to be returning to his younger ways of extravagant splendor.

Did he plan to take her for mistress, if only for a single night? She actually felt herself blush at the thought. Madame d'Alambert had been right the other evening, when she said Adrienne knew little of men. She was well beyond the age when most girls were wed or had lost their virginity to a seducer. But for Adrienne, piety was no mere fashion. Despite some intellectual

73

arguments she might muster, in her own heart and soul she knew that God and her sainted mother would see her consumed with guilt if she succumbed to sexual temptation. Living in the midst of corruption was no excuse for becoming corrupted.

If the king approached her tonight, what would she do? Could she refuse him? *Should* she?

Her third path—which had seemed so promising a few days before—now seemed a shaking tightrope. She knew that the few women who had walked it before her—the famous Ninon de Lenclos, for instance—had done so by cultivating important lovers but never marrying.

Refusing Louis XIV could be a very unfortunate thing, even weighed against damnation.

It was especially infuriating to have this dilemma now, with the puzzle of Fatio's work so tantalizingly close to her. That was all she really wanted. She desired no part in the court, of the dark intrigues hinted at by Torcy. Why had she come to the attention of both the king and his would-be successor?

After what seemed another eon, Charlotte squeaked in delight and stepped back.

"Am I so hideous, Charlotte?" Adrienne asked ruefully. For answer both girls took her by the hands and hurried her to stand before a mirror across the salon.

For a moment, Adrienne simply could not speak. The woman who gazed back at her from the mirror was too astonishing.

How many times had she lain awake as a little girl, listening to the music of crickets and nightbirds, dreaming of such a gown? Imagining herself the Cinder Girl, with a fairy godmother to clothe her like the ladies of the court? But her family was poor, and though her uncle was a favorite of the king and promised to buy her such a dress one day, it had never come to pass.

Then the little girl had grown up, and grown up in Saint Cyr, where she learned to love a simpler, more austere beauty, and to put childish thoughts away. And yet . . .

Here she stood, in that fairy-tale dress. The black velvet bodice was embroidered with crisscrossing strands of white pearls. In the center of each diamond thus formed winked a *real* diamond. At her waist and hips were layers of ostrich plumes, and they also edged the richly brocaded silver and black skirt. Its train was short, yet as long as that of a marquise—longer than she deserved.

The bodice dipped deeply, but a white marten cape was draped across her shoulders. Her straight dark hair had been swept up into a towering creation wound through with more strands of pearls and surmounted with feathers.

Here she was at last, about to stand before the greatest king in Europe, perhaps the greatest king of all time. And all she wanted was to avoid his attention and return to the life she had worked so long to have: a life devoted to science. She knew that there was more magic in the circumference of a circle than in all of the palace of Versailles.

Louis' sedan chair swayed slightly on the shoulders of the two men who bore it briskly through the corridors of Versailles. He smiled amiably at the courtiers who packed the halls and crowded against the black balustrades of the marble stair to make way for him.

His excitement began to rise when they left the chateau. Sedan chairs streaming from different parts of Versailles began to form a procession. Behind him was the young dauphin, his heir, and trailing him were the various dukes and duchesses to whom he was most closely related and, of course, Adrienne. He had taken the liberty earlier of stopping in to see her and had been almost stunned by her appearance, for she was even more fetching than he had anticipated. The girl from Saint Cyr had grown into the woman he had imagined she might. Thinking of her now in her dress of black and silver, he felt a certain revival of interest in matters feminine. His court would not respect him if he mourned too long. He understood that plotters and schemers— and even those who wished him well—must not think him aloof from their influence.

Perhaps it was time to announce that the way was again open to his bed. Adrienne would be perfect for that; he knew her to have no political desires. She was innocent and compelling, and more than anything, she was the fine and finished product of his late wife. Maintenon had considered Adrienne an ideal young lady, and he had considered Maintenon the ideal woman. He would renew his heart with the child of *Maintenon's* heart.

The sedan jostled a bit as the bearers' feet met the manicured stretch of the Green Carpet, the long avenue of grass that led them toward their destination. Beyond the Green Carpet lay the Apollo Fountain, and beyond that was the Grand Canal, which went on until it met the horizon.

And at every hand courtiers seemed to extend to infinity. He recognized many. Others he did not; doubtless the lazier ones who could not be bothered to wait upon him.

Louis let down the glass window of his sedan to better see his subjects, but as his eye brushed casually across the crowd, an unease grew in his breast. It was an elegantly dressed throng. Many wore appropriate costumes, bedecked with feathers or at least dressed, as he had insisted, in either predominantly white or red. They were laughing, bowing low as he went past. But there was some vital spark missing, some lack of sincerity.

Once all of France had loved him. What had happened?

He felt a tear tremble at the corner of his eye. If only he could *tell* them. If only he could make them understand that they had but to wait a short time and everything would be right again. The forces sapping the vitality of France would soon vie to see which could grovel lowest, to eat the scraps from the French table. And then they would all know what he had done for them. Then they would love him again without reservation.

Louis blinked. They had reached the canal and the great barge that awaited them.

It was, Adrienne reflected, impossible not to be impressed by the Grand Canal. More like a cruciform inland sea with banks of polished marble, it summed up many things about Versailles. It was monumental in proportion, insanely expensive, impossible to overlook, and entirely frivolous.

A gangplank bridged the noisome water, their avenue to the barge. The king was already aboard the monstrous, gaudy vessel, as were the young dauphin, the duke of Orléans, and the duke of Maine. The wives of these latter two men, she was uncomfortably aware, were lined up *behind* her, a bizarre breach of precedence. Last of all came perhaps threescore courtiers on foot, and on all sides were the Hundred Swiss, the household guard clad in blue and silver. On the barge, a small orchestra had taken up a martial-sounding piece she did not recognize. It had a barbaric ring to it, enhanced by the primitive whine of a musette, the small bagpipe so in vogue these days.

The gangplank clopped hollowly beneath the feet of her bearers. A moment later, a footman opened the door of her sedan, and strong hands lifted her to the deck, where she was politely ushered toward her appointed place.

The decor of the barge was very strange, even for Versailles. The vessel was flat and rectangular in shape, little more than a floating island. Two-thirds of the way back from its bow was a pyramid built in four great steps. At each corner of each terrace stood a standard surmounted by the wavy-rayed sun that was Louis' emblem. At the apex of the pyramid was a large throne and a smaller one, and from the back of the largest rose a taller standard with a grander emblem, this one radiating a brilliant golden light. Two other, similarly ornate alchemical lanterns adorned the bow and stern of the barge, and a hundred smaller suns edged the gunwales. The orchestra played from another, slightly raised stage near the bow. Feathers and ribbons festooned each standard and almost every other surface.

For a terrible moment, Adrienne was afraid that she would actually be seated next to the king in the second, smaller armchair. To her vast relief, however, she found herself ushered instead to the third tier. The dauphin, the king's great-grandson and heir, took his seat upon the smaller throne, his boyish face radiant beneath the magical light. He was dressed in a scarlet coat, a waistcoat of deeper crimson, and a headdress with voluminous plumes erupting from it like a sanguine fountain.

Next to him sat Louis, clad in a brilliant white coat trimmed in gold, with gold stockings. His albescent plumes seemed impossibly tall. The rest of the royal family present, she could see, were similarly, if less spectacularly, dressed. Only Louis and the dauphin were seated in armchairs; everyone else rested on the tiers of the pyramid. Adrienne remained standing, at a loss as to what to do.

"Sit, dear," someone whispered, tugging at her arm.

The whisper made Adrienne flinch. The sisters at Saint Cyr had taught her to fear whispers.

Glancing over in startlement, she met a pair of large brown eyes glowing with more than a hint of quiet amusement.

"Duchess," Adrienne acknowledged, bending her knees to curtsey.

The duchess of Orléans quirked her small lips in a sweet smile. She was one of the king's illegitimate children by his renowned mistress Athenais. Adrienne saw his face in hers, especially, somehow, about the eyes and the set of her lips. Adrienne recalled with chagrin that it was her husband—the duke of Orléans—against whom the minister Torcy had so recently warned her.

"My dear demoiselle," the duchess said, as sweetly as her smile. "It is so delightful to have you amongst us on this otherwise dreary day." She lisped slightly, a defect her enemies never failed to comment on.

"Thank you, Madame," Adrienne replied. "I must admit, I am most surprised to be here." Another woman had just seated herself on the other side of the duchess; Adrienne recognized the duchess of Maine, who treated both her and the duchess of Orléans to an icily indifferent glance before turning pointedly away. Behind Adrienne, one tier up, Adrienne was acutely aware of the *dukes* of Orléans and Maine, while below her, on the lowest tier, the threescore courtiers bickered about precedence.

"I should not be surprised, sweet Adrienne," the duchess said. "You are dear to all of us for your service to the late Madame de Maintenon. We were most happy when the king informed us you would be attending." The duchess cast her gaze out over and beyond the barge, and Adrienne, uncomfortable with the conversation, looked out as well. The dark waters of the canal swam with boats: Venetian gondolas; French men-of-war; English frigates; Dutch, Spanish, and even Chinese vessels. They were all perfect in detail but scaled to twenty or thirty feet at largest.

Two of these miniature ships had just pulled alongside the barge as escorts. Adrienne noticed with a start that Torcy stood in the bow of one, wearing an admiral's costume surmounted by a ridiculously lofty hat. He looked uncomfortable.

"Do you understand this setting, Adrienne?" the duchess asked lightly.

"I am not certain that I do, Madame," Adrienne replied.

"This is a representation of the savage American tribe who call themselves the Natchez," the duchess explained. "They live in our colony of Louisiana, and their chief sits upon just such a structure as this."

"Just precisely so?" Adrienne asked, glancing around at the gold, ribbons, and plumes that ornamented the barge.

"Well," the duchess allowed, "I am given to understand that the Natchez chief lives upon a mound of earth, and that it is a good deal ruder than this. Still, of all of those savage nations, it is said that they are the most civilized, worshipping the sun and their chief, the earthly child of the sun."

Adrienne strained to detect any irony in the tone of the duchess, and for a moment thought she heard it. It was well known that the duchess was terrified of her father. If Louis died, it would be her husband who ruled as regent until the dauphin came of age. Five years ago, he had almost had his opportunity; now it would probably never come. Louis showed no signs of dying, and if he survived a few more years there would be no need of a regent. Adrienne wondered how disappointed the duchess had been to see the throne so close to her grasp and then to watch as it quietly withdrew toward infinity.

"And so we are Indians, then?" Adrienne asked.

"Oh, indeed, don't you *feel* savage?" The duchess grasped Adrienne's hand in an apparent gesture of friendliness, clasping it warmly. Adrienne felt something pressed between their palms.

At that moment the deck of the barge shivered, and somewhere a giant coughed, gasped, and began a deep-throated hum. Adrienne turned, so astonished that she nearly broke the grip of the duchess and dropped whatever was concealed between their fingers. She smiled delightedly as she saw a thick white cloud rising up behind the seated king and dauphin.

"My God," she said, "this is a steamboat!" She looked back to the duchess, whose eyes also seemed genuinely merry.

"You," the duchess breathed wonderingly, "are a precious child indeed."

Adrienne felt her smile transform from genuine to contrived, even as the barge heaved sluggishly into motion.

"Dear," the duchess said, "I have just complimented you. How many of the oafs on this ship have *yet* guessed that it is powered by steam? How many could explain the workings of such an engine?" The duchess was leaning very close now, her lips nearly touching Adrienne's ear. How many were watching her at this moment, wondering what passed between her and Orléans? How many of Torcy's spies? What would the minister make of this, when he heard? And the duke of Orléans, who had furnished her appointment to the Academy of Sciences, had he put his wife up to this? But most important of all, what was the duchess implying?

"You certainly overestimate me when you imply that I understand such fabulous, magical engines as drive this boat," she lied.

The duchess shook her head. "It is rare for me to misjudge anyone, most particularly someone I take an interest in, my dear."

"An interest?" Adrienne said, feeling another blush intrude upon her features.

"Don't be so surprised, dear."

"I have no intention of attracting anyone's interest, Madame— *anyone's*."

The duchess of Orléans's face looked sad and tired. "I know that, dear," the duchess said, squeezing her hand once again, "but it doesn't matter, you see?"

"No," Adrienne answered, her heart sinking, "but I am afraid I may learn."

"If I am *not* mistaken," she told Adrienne, "if you do nurse an interest in the scientific, I believe I can easily arrange a tour of the engines for you, after the entertainment is ended."

"I . . ." Adrienne began, thinking furiously.

"I can arrange it so as to excite the interest of no one." She smiled more broadly. "Of *anyone*."

"Thank you, Duchess," she replied. "You are most kind."

The duchess gave her hand one more squeeze and then removed hers. Adrienne tightened her grip on what she held; it was almost certainly a note.

"How are you today, Monseigneur?" Louis asked. For an instant he saw the ghost of the other who had borne that nickname; his only legitimate son, Louis the grand dauphin. This younger Louis—someday to be Louis XV—was the last Monseigneur.

"I am quite well, Your Majesty," the young dauphin replied. "I am most entertained by my new barge." He was a beautiful child, with liquid black eyes and golden curls.

"That pleases me," Louis replied, patting the boy on the shoulder. Below, he could just make out Adrienne, and he frowned slightly. Who had seated her next to the duchess of Orléans? She would hardly be a fit influence on the impressionable girl.

He made a mental note that Adrienne was, in the future, to be kept away from the duchess.

"When shall the dancing start, Majesty?" the little dauphin asked.

"Why, it will begin quite soon, Monseigneur," Louis assured him. "Do you remember your part?"

"Of course, Your Majesty," the dauphin said. "I am to dance the part of the Stung Serpent."

"Very good."

"Are *you* really going to dance, Grandpapa?" the dauphin asked softly so no one could hear the familiarity.

"Is that so hard to believe?" Louis asked. "I used to dance for my subjects all of the time."

"Who did *you* dance as?"

"I danced many times. Once, in *The Marriage of Pelleas and Thetis*, I danced—let me see—six parts: Apollo, of course, and as Fury, a dryad, an Indian, a courtier, and as War." He smiled at his heir. "The costume you wear today is much like mine was when I played War: red, with great red plumes."

"Is the Stung Serpent also War, then?"

"I hear that the savages have two sorts of chiefs: one who is the chief during peace and one who wages war. The Stung Serpent is the war chief."

"And you will dance as the other, the Great Sun?" the boy asked.

"Precisely so, my good Monseigneur.

"Listen to the music," Louis reminded him. "That is your cue, and mine as well. But you must go down first."

The boy smiled and began to rise, a little too quickly, too eagerly. "More slowly," Louis hissed. "Act the king you shall be one day."

And Louis watched, gratified, as the boy slowed, his face regal, and began to descend the steps of the pyramid toward the dance floor where the courtiers waited, divided into two groups: those dressed in red, and those dressed in white.

Adrienne fingered the note nervously as she watched the spectacle unfold. First the dauphin came down from the pyramid, and all of the courtiers in red lined up with him, including the duke of Orléans and the duchess of Maine. They gamboled in what seemed a rather unorganized fashion for some time; then a servant ran among them, passing out feather wands. At that point the duke of Orléans and the dauphin came back up the stairs and pretended to seize Louis and kidnap him.

"Act as if you are asleep," the duchess of Orléans hissed, and Adrienne slitted her eyes, her thoughts on the steady thrumming of the engines. Were they fervefactum driven, or was there a furnace?

"Now!" The duchess shook her and thrust a white-feathered wand into her hand.

"What?" Adrienne asked.

"We must rescue our chief, the Great Sun, from his enemies."

Adrienne stared down at the tableau. The dauphin was now strutting about the "captive" Louis, pronouncing solemnly—in

English— "The sun has set." Was he meant, now, to be George, king of England? Or Marlborough?

She reluctantly followed the duchess, slipping the note she had been given into her waistband.

The courtiers dressed in white began howling and shrieking, and the orchestra had begun banging upon tambours and tin kettles. The din was atrocious and barbaric. White-clad courtiers were daintily striking red-clad ones with their feather wands.

"Come on!" shouted the duchess. Adrienne followed. A young man dashed up to her, struck a fencer's pose with his feather weapon, and lunged clumsily at her. The duchess interposed, poking the fellow in the face. He shrieked in mock pain and staggered convincingly about.

"Lay to!" the duchess cried. Adrienne blinked, and then waved her feather wand at the nearest red-clad dancer, a plump woman who made an easy target. Despite herself, Adrienne felt a bit giddy at the sheer silliness of this nonsense. Grown men and women, fighting with feather war clubs? What would the citizens of Paris say if they saw this?

The king and the dauphin had moved apart from the rest, fighting back to the crown of the pyramid. Below them the courtiers continued their mad dashing about. A rather thickset man wearing a diadem of red feathers struck Adrienne in the breast with his feather. He twitched his feather from breast to breast and then, with emphasis, poked it toward her crotch. Adrienne stood frozen for an instant, mortified and uncertain what to do, and once again the duchess came to her rescue, jabbing her feather into the man's face. The fellow gasped in pain, and the duchess stepped back in obvious satisfaction as he clutched his shin—her attack on his face having only been a feint to distract from a vicious kick.

"Are you injured?" the duchess asked seriously.

Adrienne opened her mouth to answer, but instead, understanding suddenly, clasped her breast and sank to the deck. "Yes, wounded unto death!" she croaked, and fell forward, hoping no one would step upon her. She wondered if she should hop back up, alive again, as she had seen some of the courtiers doing.

Then a terrible heat stepped upon her back, and the air was suddenly choked with screams of agony and the smell of burning flesh.

8.

Silence Dogood

Ben could not help but smile as he read over the note he had just schreibed.

I thank you Most Warmly for the News you send regarding our Brethren in New York, and I shall here endeavor to entertain you by sending forthwith the News of our own Small Colony. But first, as to address your Question of our Native Critics; and of those Skeptics who are desirous of a more Ancient Time than this we presently live in; I tell you that we have none such here as you speak of. For were there those in Boston who, reading the Mercury or this, the Courant, by the light of alchemical lanterns, were then to Criticize both, I would have no recourse but to title them Great Blockheads indeed. It is perhaps to be admitt'd that a few here still raise the hoary cry of Witchcraft, and mutter of the New Fashioned— but it is well known here that they Contrive to be Ridiculous only in order to furnish these our Colonies with an authentic Atmosphere of the Rustic. They thus provide a Service, offering at once Entertainment to ourselves and Assurance to our Brethren in Britain that those of us on American Soil continue to be Quaint, Curious &c. Did I not know this to be the case, I might be convinc'd that Ignorance and Folly are crown'd as Royally here as you claim them to be in your City. I urge you to reexamine the evidence before you, for as you know, it is common to be an Eagle abroad and an Owl at home.

Ben bent back to the letter, summarizing the various news-worthy stories of Boston. This he sent in return for a similar summary he had just received from the new sheet being published in New York. It was an arrangement between himself and the publisher there, arrived at by aetherschreiber correspondence. He had managed to strike bargains with four such correspondents: in New York, South Carolina, London, and India. He acted as an exchange for the news from all of these places, for his remained the only aetherschreiber capable of being tuned. As a result of this, *The New England Courant*—his brother's paper—was as cosmopolitan as any paper from the home country and sold so quickly that it was impossible to print enough copies. Already James had ordered a new press from England. Furthermore, though almost two months had passed since Ben had modified the aetherschreiber, Trevor Bracewell had not put in an appearance to make good on his threat. Nor had Ben seen the man on the streets—which probably meant that he was not in Boston.

Finishing the letter, Ben reached to sign it, and as he did so, his smile broadened even farther. His letter would appear in New York tomorrow, but it would not bear the name of Benjamin Franklin. Instead, he signed it, in a silly, ornate, and swooping hand:

> *Sir, Your Humble Servant,*
> *Silence Dogood*

Ben was not certain what impulse had driven him to adopt the pseudonym, but he *did* know that he enjoyed it. To be sure, it was a way of protecting himself should Bracewell really be out there, watchful. And since Silence Dogood also tended to make fun of certain elements in Boston society, when word inevitably got here from New York that other colonies were chuckling at the foibles of certain Bostonians, it would be best that the letters came from an anonymous source.

The wind freshened, and caught the white triangle of cloth with a firm snapping sound as the boom swung sixty degrees. Ben ducked absently, more intent on John Collins than on the stout wooden bar. He shifted the rudder to make the most of the wind, sending the small boat scudding up the Charles River. Coming from behind them, the wind carried the thick salt scent of the Roxbury Flats, wood smoke from three thousand houses, and the resiny perfume of pitch from the shipyards. It was Boston following them, a ghost sensible only to the nose.

John looked up from the page he was reading. "This is ingenious," he crowed. "Have you set this yet or read it? Shall I read it to you?"

" 'Twas just delivered," Ben replied. "By all means, read it aloud."

"I will summarize parts. But here is how it begins.

"Sir,
It has been the complaint of many Ingenious Foreigners,
who have travelled amongst us, That good Poetry is not to be expected in New-England."

John paused, blue eyes sparkling with amusement. "Then she pretends that she will discover to the world the beauties of our native poetry."

"I can see the need for that, since it isn't readily obvious," Ben commented.

"You'll see. Here, she begins talking about a specimen of 'our' poetry. For her subject she chooses 'An elegy upon the much lamented death of Mrs. Mehitebell Kitel, Wife of Mr. John Kitel of Salem &c.' "

"An apt and representative piece, I would imagine," Ben replied.

"Oh, yes. As she says, 'One of the most *extraordinary* poems ever writ in New England, moving, pathetic, so natural in its rhyme.' Listen, here the verse itself is quoted." He cleared his throat and read, in lamenting tones:

"Come let us mourn, for we have lost a Wife, a Daughter, and
a Sister,
Who has lately taken Flight, and greatly we have mist her,

"In another place,

"Some little Time *before she yielded up her Breath,*
She said, I ne'er shall hear one Sermon more on Earth.
She kist her Husband some little Time *before she expir'd,*
Then lean'd her Head the Pillow on, just out of Breath and
tir'd."

John had to stop reading, for he had begun to laugh. "Sister, *missed her*," he chortled, wiping one eye. "Expired, *tired*!"

"*Very* moving," Ben remarked. "Very pathetic."

"Aye, pathetic indeed," John agreed.

"Because see how cleverly it is written," Ben continued. "To say that we've lost a wife, daughter, *and* sister, is to give the impression that we've lost three women, rather than one, which is *triply* pathetic."

John frowned. "You *have* read this."

Ben shook his head. "Why do you say that?"

"It's precisely what Mrs. Dogood claims, in the next paragraph."

"Oh," said Ben, innocently. "It just seems obvious, that's all. Do go on."

John regarded him doubtfully for a moment. "Well, the long and short of it is, she gives a formula for how one can write one's own elegy."

"What a useful thing to know."

"Very useful. The most important thing is to choose the right person to elegize, it seems; someone who has been killed, drowned, or froze to death."

"Well, of course. We can't go elegizing someone hung for stealing chickens."

"Exactly."

"Nor someone without real virtues," Ben went on, "though I suppose one can *borrow* virtues for the deceased, if they didn't have an appropriate quantity."

John frowned. "You *have* read this, damn you. Why did you let me go on, so?"

"You really think such rude nonsense is amusing?" Ben asked, seriously. "Poking fun at heartfelt verse written by a sincere and grieving man?"

"Grief is no excuse for bad poetry," John returned. "If he cannot grieve eloquently, let him at least do it silently. And yes, I think Mrs. Dogood's criticism *is* witty, wittier than anything else I've seen in that sheet of your brother's. Perhaps it's just that you don't appreciate well-turned irony, is all."

Ben grinned. "I appreciate it more than *you* will in a few seconds," Ben predicted.

"How is that?

"Because *I* am Silence Dogood, you butter-head."

John just stared at him for a heartbeat or so. "*You* are Silence Dogood?" he managed to choke out.

"None other," Ben replied, trying to seem nonchalant, though he knew his almost imbecilic grin must give that the lie.

"God take me for a fool that I never guessed," John swore. "It has your mark all over it! Does your brother know?"

"You should have heard him and his Couranteers trying to guess who slipped her 'correspondence' under their door."

"Whom did they guess?" John asked gleefully.

"Only the most prestigious men of letters were mentioned as possibilities," Ben replied. "Quite flattering."

"How can it be flattering when no one knows it was you?"

"Because *I* know," Ben replied. "If James knew who really wrote those letters, he would *never* print them. This way I can have my ideas flattered and debated without ever suffering an attack to my person." He did not add his worry that such an attack might be a physical one.

"I should want people to *know* that it was me," John persisted. "I should want credit for my thoughts."

Ben shrugged. "That is a pity, since I had thought Silence Dogood might need a partner in debate."

"Oh, she will be debated, worry not about that," John said. "Her jabs are so clearly and often aimed at members of the Selectmen."

"Yes, we've already gotten letters heatedly disagreeing with the good widow. But I had thought rather that the two of us might guide the debate—make it more clever, show the ridiculous elements on either side of the question."

"But I would write under an assumed name?" John asked.

"Come, John Collins. It would be fun, don't you think?"

"Perhaps."

"Think on it, John. I have no doubt it would be great sport."

"I'll think on it. Meantime, have you taken down any more of those mathematical love letters?"

Ben held up his finger. "Ah." He reached up to steady himself on the boom and to prevent its swinging as he turned his head to search behind him for a second sheaf of papers. He came up with a roll of them, tied up with a ribbon.

"A present for you," he said, handing them to John.

"I wondered," John replied. "You have so much to do these days . . ."

"Not too much to do you this favor," Ben assured him.

"Still, I wonder if we shouldn't build a second 'Franklined' device," John went on, as he undid the ribbon and let the letters uncurl in his lap.

"Please don't call it that or spread around that I've made such a thing," Ben cautioned.

"Yes, yes," John answered testily. "But won't you take credit for *anything* you do?"

"Why? If my design is copied, it's right back to the poorhouse for my brother and me."

John wrinkled his brow. "I think that there is more to it than that. Writing under a false name, keeping your inventions secret . . ."

Ben stared hard at John, and it suddenly occurred to him that Trevor Bracewell had seen the both of them with the harmonicum.

"John . . ." he began.

"What?"

"After we went to the millpond with my harmonicum . . . did anything . . . *peculiar* happen to you?"

John nodded almost imperceptibly, and a shadow seemed to fall across his eyes. He sighed. "I was hesitant to broach . . . I wished to ask . . ." His contrived formality broke a bit, and he swallowed before going on. "Did it happen to you as well?"

"Trevor Bracewell?" Ben asked in a very quiet voice.

John's forehead wrinkled in a puzzled frown. "That name rings a bell," he mumbled at last, "though as far as I remember the man in *my* dream had no name."

"Dream?"

John nodded. "After we went to the millpond—later that night I had a dream, the most frightening I can ever remember. I was back down at the millpond, and a man started shouting at me to stop what I was doing, and then he took you by the neck—you were there, Ben—and he began to strangle you. I went to help you, and then . . ." John swallowed hard, and Ben realized that, though his friend was trying not to show it, he was still disturbed by his nightmare.

"Go on," Ben said.

John chewed his lip. "Did you have a dream like this?" he asked.

Ben nodded. "I'll tell you mine in a moment," he promised. "Go on with yours."

John stared down at his lap, not meeting Ben's eyes. "Well, then there was an angel before me, all bright and with a flaming sword. It told me that God had condemned you, but that *I* might hope for redemption. But I . . . I didn't want you killed, so I tried talking to the angel. When that happened, he touched me with his sword, and I—" He lifted his shoulders and tried to smile. "—well, I think I dreamed I was dead. Worms were eating me, squirming out of my scalp. And I was in such a dark place . . ." His smile was very shaky, but he maintained it.

"Well," Ben said. "My dream was not nearly so bad." He related his encounter with Bracewell, but neglected an important point; that *his* encounter had not been a dream. He was certain of this, for the very next day he had seen the spot on the street where he had vomited. But he did not want John to know that.

"Have you had any since?" John asked.

"Dreams like that? No."

"Do you think it was the harmonicum?" Before Ben answered, he went on in a rush. "Remember that pinkish light, which seemed to serve no other purpose?"

"Yes, of course," Ben replied.

"Could that account for our dreams? Could we somehow have attracted nightmares from the aether?" John sounded sincere.

Ben bit back a skeptical remark and considered the question.

"I have read," he began tentatively, "that Gottfried von Leibniz believes that matter resides in something he calls *monads*."

"Yes—his word for ferments," John said.

"No, only roughly," Ben corrected. "And his theory is now largely discredited. Leibniz believed these monads to be alive, conscious—particles of the mind of God, perhaps."

"Newton proposed something similar, did he not?" John asked.

"Not at all. Newton said that space and time are the *organs* of God, through which he perceives our actions. Leibniz held that substances themselves are animated by consciousness."

John pushed back his hair and shot him a wry, skeptical grin. "Are you hypothesizing that those dreams were the revenge that the millpond got on us for meddling with its substance?"

"No, because I believe that Leibniz was in error," Ben said. "Here, throw me that line; I'll want to tack, now."

John did as directed, but the expression on his face made it clear that the conversation was not done. "It's not impossible," John hesitantly offered.

"Not impossible," Ben agreed, "just not very likely, I think. The evidence of science is that the world operates according to laws—laws of motion, affinity, sympathy. What Leibniz suggests is nothing more or less than what the ancients believed— that the world is a nonsensical place governed by the capricious whims of a million petty deities. All the advances man has made in science and magic stand against that."

"Leibniz was no dolt."

"No, he wasn't," Ben agreed. "But he *was* wrong."

John set his mouth in that tight line that indicated he remained unconvinced. "I have heard even you speculate on polytheism before," he reminded Ben.

"I think that perhaps the creator of this universe is too remote to want our worship or care for our needs. I think there might be intermediate stages of perfection between ourselves and God, just as there are between the lower animals and ourselves."

"Yes, arranged in Locke's great chain. But couldn't these ideas of Leibniz fit in with that?"

Ben leaned overboard and, with a deft motion, scooped a handful of water through the air, which spattered onto John.

"Hey!" his friend complained.

"In this water live a hundred kinds of fish," Ben said, "some lesser and some greater—lower down or farther up the chain. But that is not to say that the water *itself* has anything to say. If I had thrown a fish on you, you would know it to be alive, eh?"

"I know only that you've gotten my sheets wet," John snapped, brushing what drops he could from the paper. "And that if you have some better hypothesis, I would be pleased to hear it."

"I don't know," Ben said, suddenly irritated. "You may be right, in that particles from the aether may have made us ill, discomfited our minds so as to make us dream similar dreams."

"And the man in both of our dreams?"

Ben smiled. "True. Then try *this* hypothesis. Let us suppose that there were another magician about, one well schooled in the arts. Might he not have perceived what we were doing, seen us as threats to his livelihood, and sent those dreams to haunt us?"

John nodded but looked unconvinced. "That sounds more like the old-style witchcraft than *real* magic."

"I agree," Ben said. "Science and alchemy are comprehensible because they can be logically and mathematically understood. And yet you were willing to propose as silly and unscientific a reason—"

"It was *you* who brought up these 'monads'!" John snapped.

"To consider them and dismiss them. This is different; simply because you and I have not read of a science of dreams does not mean one does not exist. In France and Spain . . ."

"Or wherever these formulae come from," John added, glancing down at the papers he still held. "This is strange stuff."

Ben was glad that the subject had changed; he did not like deceiving John, but he just couldn't bring himself to admit aloud that his "dream" had been real . . .

Perhaps, he thought suddenly, he *couldn't* tell anyone. That was ridiculous, of course, because he had made the decision himself. And yet, what if John had the same dilemma? What if both of them had suffered real encounters but could only speak of them as if they were dreams? Of course, John's must have been a dream, since Ben himself was in it . . .

He would have to think about this some more.

"What make you of those formulae, John? I've been working hard on my own mathematical skills, but much of this is still beyond me."

"At least *something* is," John grunted. He was scanning the pages, nodding every now and then. After a moment he pressed one out on his lap. "This section is relatively straightforward," he said. "Do you understand this much?"

"It's calculus, describing a body in motion, is it not?"

"It is, but this object in motion is in orbit about some much larger body. My guess is that it is the sun itself."

"And the smaller body is one of the planets."

John shook his head. "I don't know. A lot of this section is missing—they seemed to have solved this part long ago, and now only summarize the argument. What most of this correspondence is about is a problem with affinity."

"What do you mean?"

"They are trying to create a powerful attraction between two objects, a very specific attraction. You see this part here? It's almost exactly like Papin's theorem—the one that made warlock cannons possible."

"The ones Marlborough uses against the French."

"Yes!"

"About which I know nearly nothing," Ben remarked.

"Well, with the cannon, a very specific resonance is set up between the cannonball and the target. When the ball is fired, its trajectory bends toward that target."

"A cannonball that chases you," Ben said.

Collins nodded enthusiastically. "But the cannon are mostly used to reduce walls from a great distance. Spies and engineers are sent to find the quarry from which the stones for the wall were cut. The alchemists then use a sample stone to create a mock affinity in their munitions. They fire these cannon from a great distance. They can rain tons of iron onto a fortress from incredibly far away with remarkable accuracy."

"I see. And this formula is for a similar operation?"

"Yes," John said. "But while they have the equation that describes the ferment of one of the bodies, they do not have that of the other."

"As if they had not found the quarry from which the stone came."

"Well, that's the odd thing," John said. "They seem to have that. What they seem to lack is the ferment of the cannonball."

"Really?" Ben scrunched his face in concentration, trying to puzzle at what that could mean.

"Realize, of course, that this is *not* the formula for a cannon. I only continued to speak as if it were for purposes of analogy. This seeks to alter the trajectory of one object by an increased and specific affinity with another. And the second object is moving, as well."

"A cannonball built to seek another cannonball in flight."

"Exactly. What I have seen of the motions involved is hellishly complicated—and I understand only the broadest strokes—but yes, a formula to bring two cannonballs together in flight would resemble this. But they cannot calculate the affinitive properties of one of the cannonballs."

For a moment the world seemed to spin around Ben, as if he were the boom caught in a sudden whirlwind. Beyond the river, sunlight winked from something bright in Boston.

"In your opinion," he asked, "are these great men at work on this formula? Important philosophers?"

"The mathematics are an order higher than anything I've ever read about," John said. "Much of this is far ahead of anything yet published. There are also hints that the Crown is financing the work." He grinned. "Perhaps Newton himself is involved; all of the letters are unsigned or signed only with initials. Why do you ask?"

"You remember that paper I said we should write?"

"If you mean the one about your 'Franklined' aetherschreiber, yes. I've already worked out the formula. I'm not certain that it's right, but a more experienced mathematician could tell what I'm trying to express."

"Well, John, here is our opportunity," Ben said. "We should send it to these mathematicians."

"Why? To what purpose?"

"Because," Ben replied, "we have the answer to their problem."

John stared hard at him for a moment, and then blew a long, low whistle as he understood. He turned to regard Boston. It lay bunched behind the beacon and the Trimontaine—a scattering of child's blocks, a few steeples, a single windmill.

"It looks small from here," John remarked.

Ben leaned on the rudder; the resistance of the water felt good, but the boat obeying his command felt better. He simply nodded, his mind already racing ahead, away, overseas.

9.

Regicide

Adrienne lay among the damned, her ears stuffed with their wretched shrieks, her nostrils and lungs choking upon more hideous scents than sulfur or brimstone. A man fell against her, arms writhing, his periwig a mass of flame, his eyes sightless. Adrienne was aware of the searing heat along her own back, and she rolled and rolled again, in case it should be on fire. It was not, or at least she decided not. Gasping, she struggled to her feet, and as she did, smoke reached sharp black claws into her lungs. Her vision blurred, then cleared as the barge rocked beneath her shoes.

She did seem to be viewing a painting of hell, a miniature set before her. Centered in the frame, a pyramid blazed. At its base blackened bodies lay heaped like logs, some still burning. Farther from the pyramid, courtiers dressed in soot capered in a strange dance to music that only the devil might find soothing. Adrienne felt faintly surprised to see the duchess of Orléans, who was struggling to her feet, headdress smoking and gown disheveled but otherwise intact. A man near her was not so lucky; he clutched at a face as red as boiled lobster and rocked on his knees like a penitent.

"The king!" the duchess of Orléans shrieked, waving her hands at the flaming pyramid. "The king! Father!"

Of course, the king, Adrienne thought, and took a step toward the flames. Suddenly, the painting seemed to change. It was no longer the Inferno, but mighty Sodom, its towers consumed by the wrath of God. Her last thought as her legs refused to support her was that she had become a pillar of salt. *Stupid,* she thought. *I should not have looked.*

* * *

The next thing she knew was the total shock of cold, and then water in her mouth, stinging her nose. She tried to scream and swallowed a draught of the foul liquid. Arms like bands of steel were wrapped about her waist. She could hear harsh breathing in her ear.

I must not fight, she thought, as panic began to overcome her shock. *I must not struggle or I shall drown us both.* Even though she thought that, the next time her head dipped beneath the water, she began to kick, to lash back with her elbows.

"Stop it," a voice suddenly said in her ear. "Please."

A husky voice, soft and sincere. He was swimming on his back now, holding her above and somewhat to the side of him, his knees and thighs working behind her own. Her back still burned.

With an awful effort, she let her body go limp. The man swam more strongly now, more confidently, and she felt safer. She blinked water from her eyes and saw gray sky; the rim of her vision was the horizon until she strained to look back the way they had come.

The barge was aflame; the two miniature ships nearby had pulled alongside, and Adrienne could make out small figures being hauled from the water. Dully, she understood that the king and the dauphin would not be among them. They had been at the apex of the pyramid, the very seat of the conflagration. Louis XIV and Louis XV were dead.

What had happened?

Below her, the man's legs continued pushing at the water, and she realized, with that odd and pointless clarity that comes with shock, that this was the closest any man had ever held her— save perhaps her father or grandfather, many years ago.

The rhythm of her rescuer's stroke suddenly changed, and then he shifted her, sweeping her up under his arm. She was suddenly almost cheek to cheek with this man whose face she hadn't seen. Nor did she now, save for the briefest glimpse of profile as he turned toward his other hand, grasping at the rim of the canal. At the edge, five pairs of hands reached down, and suddenly several more bodies splashed into the water. She felt herself lifted up and laid gently on the stones. She caught a glimpse of her rescuer—she thought it was he—supported by several of their benefactors, and then, in a crush of bodies, he was gone.

"Is Mademoiselle hurt? Does she need a doctor?" someone asked.

"Mademoiselle is fine." Adrienne sighed.

Suddenly the crowd on the edges of the canal shouted, *"Le Roi vive!"* "The king is alive!" Some sounded jubilant, but Adrienne heard disappointment also.

"Holy Jesus!" Geoffrey Random blurted. He shut his eyes against the glare. When he opened them once more he looked at the musket he held with new admiration.

"Come along, Brown Bess," he muttered to it, looking around once more to make certain no one had witnessed him firing. But what he had been promised was quite true; he was alone in the gallery, and a look outside told him that the sound of his shot had drawn no attention from anyone.

His employer was as good as his word, at least so far. He, Geoff Random, had just killed a king—*two* kings, for that matter. That would please a whole hell of a lot of people, not the least the duke of Marlborough. But without rather specialized help from within Versailles itself no English assassin could have succeeded.

Marlborough could recognize talent, whether it was in a foot soldier or an officer. And, once again, Geoffrey Random had given the duke reason to think well of him.

Hell, he had stopped an entire war! Not bad for a Northumbrian lad.

He shouldered the rifle and gave his uniform the once-over. From now until he was safely out of France, he was an Irish dragoon in French service, with the forged papers to prove it. He descended a stair and crossed several halls, hoping he wasn't lost.

Pandemonium had claimed Versailles. Servants and courtiers were pressed against the windows, pointing and staring at the scene he had created on the canal. Some shrieked, some wept, others . . . He passed two tables of men and women playing cards who seemed to be betting their next hands against the king's survival.

It almost made Geoffrey sad that the war would end with Louis' death. It would have been far better for the world if all of these useless fops were pounded into paste by the magic cannons and good old mortar fire. Versailles—for all of its beauty—made him feel dirty.

But he felt cleaner once outside Versailles, and he reached the stables unhindered.

"What is it? What has happened?" the master of the stables shouted as he approached.

"The king!" Geoffrey shot back, reluctant to say much for fear of revealing his accent. "I must ride."

"Of course. I will fetch your mount."

"Don't bother. I'll get her myself," Geoffrey said, striding back into the darkened stables.

He found Thames by her whicker. "Come along, old girl," he soothed. "We've got a long ride ahead."

That was when he heard the sound of a pistol cock.

"Sir, I advise you to turn slowly," a voice told him. Geoffrey hesitated. His hand was only inches from his own sidearm, and his sword was closer. But he obeyed the command.

When he saw who had the weapon trained on him, he blinked. "Oh, it's you," he said. He could not remember the fellow's name, but he knew they had the same secret employer, despite the fact that the man wore the uniform of the king's own household guard. Geoff grinned at him. "I got him, didn't I?"

But the guard shook his head; the bore of his Austrian pistol did not waver in the least. "No," he said, softly. "I fear that the king survived."

"How could that be? The entire barge went up in flames."

"I don't know; but with the king alive the investigation will be prosecuted much more thoroughly than if he had died."

Geoffrey saw where this was going, but he smiled anyway. "Well, I shall soon be very far from here. Carry my regrets back to our mutual acquaintance. Ah, look, more guards . . ."

The pistol wavered slightly as the fellow glanced over his shoulder, and Geoffrey drew his sidearm and stepped to his right at the same moment. The guard recovered quickly, firing before Geoffrey even had his weapon up. He flinched as splinters sprayed him from a post half a foot away as he brought his own pistol up more carefully.

His French-made weapon roared. The guardsman grunted and pitched back. Geoffrey grinned savagely. Try to cross him, would they?

In another instant he had mounted and was thundering out of the stables into the broad plaza outside.

A guard in blue, scarlet, and silver stood perhaps ten yards away, a pair of pistols aimed steadily at Geoffrey. He cursed, wishing now he had taken a moment to reload one of his own weapons; an empty pistol and an empty musket did him no good at all.

"Dismount, sir," the young guard called, a determined glint in his eye.

"And what if I do not?"

"Then I shall shoot your horse."

"You needn't shoot either of us. I have silver enough to pay for my passage."

"I assume, sir, that you have killed Remy, who was one of my order. I cannot fail to avenge him."

Geoffrey considered that. "You have a sword at your waist," he said. "Are you schooled in its use?"

"That is why I wish for you to dismount, sir."

"Really?" Geoffrey felt a delighted hope. Could the guard be that stupid? He slid down from the saddle, drew his smallsword, and made a few passes with it.

Keeping one pistol out, the guard uncocked the other and returned it to his belt.

"Step away from your horse," he commanded.

Geoffrey did so. The guard was a bit taller than he, but he looked young. Geoffrey saluted him.

"It is really unfair," Geoffrey told him. "I did honorably by our . . . acquaintance . . . and now you repay me thus."

"You tried to kill our king!" the young man said, carefully holstering his second pistol.

"Then lead me before a court. I shall go quietly."

"You killed a member of the Hundred Swiss. You must pay for that, too, sir."

"How noble." Geoffrey sneered. "What you really mean is that you don't wish for me to testify as to who gave me this uniform, forged my papers." And suddenly he was defending himself. He scarcely saw his opponent's colichemarde, so fast was it drawn. Geoff managed to get his blade up in time to meet it, and his footwork came without thought as he retreated from the furious attack. But then, he caught the rhythm of the advance and gave it back, making it work to his advantage. He pretended to be lulled, matching each advance with retreat, each retreat with advance, until they were as regular as a minuet. When the guard made his move, he would find that Geoffrey Random was no fool.

Geoffrey stamped forward, blade here and there. He let the Swiss watch the blade and not the footwork.

Then, predictably, the guard made his mistake, pretending to retreat but then suddenly hurling himself forward in a skip-and-lunge. The feinted retreat was well done, but not well enough, and Geoffrey was ready for the attack, turning the blade away easily and then kicking viciously at the extended and deeply flexed knee of his foe.

Which somehow was not there anymore. Something very cold touched him just under his sternum. He stared down in amazement at the colichemarde buried in his solar plexus. He dropped his blade.

"How . . . how did you *do* that?" he asked the young man. But Geoffrey never got his answer, for in the next moment darkness rushed up, and he fell.

Louis XIV remembered the dauphin laughing, his face cherubic in the glow of the flameless lamp above them. He remembered a brighter light, then quickly, darkness. Louis had the distinct impression of a cloak being thrown about him, of it drawing tight against a world gone mad. How much time had elapsed since then he did not know.

He *did* know where he was. He was in his own room in Versailles. He could even hear the familiar motions of his valet. Was this morning? Had he merely dreamed?

"Bontemps," he muttered, "is that you, Bontemps?"

"Yes, Sire," the man answered from quite near.

"Draw up the shades or light a lamp, then," he said, trying not to sound irritated.

"Sire . . ." Bontemps began. He paused, then continued, "Sire, the room is well lit."

"What do you mean?" he asked.

"Your doctors say that your eyesight is impaired, Sire," the valet answered, his voice somewhat strained.

"Gone? Entirely gone?"

"That they do not know, my lord. It remains in God's hands."

"Am I dying, Bontemps?" He had never said these words; before, he had known he was dying. There had never been any question, until the Persian elixir had trickled bitterly down his throat. Today, he felt fine—he simply could not see. He tried once again to open his eyes, but he understood now that they must already be open.

"Other than your eyesight, Majesty, the doctors assure me that you are in perfect health," Bontemps said.

"Well, send them back in. I want to speak with them."

"I am sorry, Sire," Bontemps said, his voice quavering in a peculiar manner. "They have done what they can, and I have sent them away."

"Away? Why?"

"Because, Sire, I am your foremost valet. I am the head of your secret police and the person to whom your safety is most dearly trusted. And I know of no man whom I may trust at this moment other than myself. Sire, I did not know what better to do."

"What are you talking about, Bontemps?"

"The attempt on your life, Sire. Someone has tried to kill you."

"To kill me? How?"

The voice sighed again. "I was hoping you might know, Sire. All any of us know is that the pyramid upon which you stood suddenly burst into flame."

"The pyramid," Louis repeated, a sudden well opening in his chest, a sudden plummeting of his heart. "Bontemps, what has become of the dauphin? Is he likewise blinded?"

The pause was a long one this time.

"He . . . the dauphin is with God, Sire."

Louis drew a deep breath. "Leave me, Louis-Alexandre," he said at last. "Send the police and the Hundred Swiss about—"

"I have done that, Sire, and I have sent to Paris for your musketeers."

"Then leave me. Go outside until I call for you." He said this quietly, but with all of his authority. There was a moment's silence, and then footsteps retreating.

He fumbled his way out of bed; he meant to pray. But when he had managed to kneel and clutch his hands beneath his chin, he groaned, discovering there, on his knees, that even when eyes were broken, tears could still flow.

"Oh, my lady, your back!" Charlotte exclaimed. Adrienne lay facedown on her bed; the girls had just stripped the beautiful dress from her, and Helen began to rub the burn with butter—or ointment. Adrienne winced.

"There are blisters?" she asked.

"Oh, yes, lady," Helen answered.

"What could have happened?" Charlotte went on, her high voice tinged with panic. "I hear the dauphin is dead."

"Someone tried to murder the king," Helen explained. "They failed, but the dauphin was killed."

"Were you hurt, milady? Other than your back?"

Adrienne pulled herself up sluggishly. It seemed as if she were made of lead. She forced herself to inventory her body. She could not see her back, but she seemed intact. She felt her head carefully, but could find no bruises or lumps. Her throat felt harsh, perhaps from the smoke. "No," she said. "Do not call a doctor on my account."

"I am not certain that I could, to tell you the truth, Mademoiselle."

"What do you mean by that?" Adrienne asked.

"Only that there are two of the Hundred Swiss at your door. We are none of us allowed to go in or out of this room."

"What?"

"They search for the murderer," Helen explained.

"Oh. Oh!" She glanced about and quickly spotted the dress on the floor, where the girls had dropped it. As her eyes lit upon it, Charlotte started guiltily.

"I am sorry, lady," she said. "I was so worried about you that I forgot . . ." she started toward the dress.

Adrienne clenched her fists in the sheets, wondering what to do. If she told Charlotte to leave it be, it would naturally arouse suspicion. Already, Helen favored her with a puzzled look. So she said nothing as Charlotte lifted the dress and the note from the duchess of Orléans fell wetly to the floor. All three women stared at it.

"Helen," Adrienne said tiredly, "could you get that for me?"

"Of course, milady." Helen walked over and picked up the damp, folded paper. Adrienne caught in Helen's eyes, then, a flicker of suspicion, and knew she must take a chance.

"Please read it to me, would you, Helen?" she asked.

"I am sorry, Mademoiselle," the girl said. "I have not learned to read."

"Oh," Adrienne responded. "In that case, my dear, just hand it to me."

Helen did so, curtseying. "Is it from a man?" she whispered, looking back to see that Charlotte was out of earshot.

"It might be," Adrienne said mysteriously, and took it from Helen's long fingers. "And now, I believe, I should like some rest," she said.

Helen nodded. "I will be in the next room," she said, indicating the parlor, "should you have need of me."

Adrienne nodded. When the girl was gone, she unfolded the note.

Had she not been so numb, she might have felt real panic. The unknown and the unexpected had too often been her guests today. A dull, creeping chill was the only sign that Adrienne's world had been upended. She blinked slowly, wondering how best to dispose of the note. She continued to stare at it, at the small drawing of an owl that was its only contents: the owl, sign of Athena, of the Korai.

She suddenly understood Versailles the way the king explained it—as a vast clockwork mechanism whose gears moved irrevocably, indifferent to human wishes. From every side, a different gear now turned to crush her, and she saw no way out of the machine—no way whatsoever.

10.

The Hellfire Club

The door to the print shop burst open with such force that splinters from it struck Ben ten paces away. He yelped and staggered away as a black cloud flowed through the door. He lost his voice entirely as its pulsing heart of flame entered, floating some seven feet off the ground. Beneath the flame strode Trevor Bracewell, a nasty smile on his face.

"I told you, Ben," he said. "I did warn you, didn't I?" He raised a hand that seemed grotesquely misshapen until Ben realized it held a pistol made of a metal so black it appeared to be a rift in the air. Still smiling, he pointed it at Ben's heart.

Ben awoke clutching at his chest; beneath his clawing hand his heart beat unnaturally.

"Oh, God," he gasped, sitting up. "God!"

He stumbled down the stairs, away from the darkness of his room. In the print shop, he unshuttered the lantern and let the buttery light envelop him, hoping it would drive the nightmare back into the cobwebs of his brain.

Unfortunately, it refused to go. It had been a dream unlike any other dream; other dreams were confused, and though they might frighten or excite, it was rarely clear upon waking why they should do so. This dream had been knife-keen, painting-bright. It left no doubts, was confused in nothing. Had John's dream been like this? It had sounded so; more fantastical, perhaps, but not less real.

He moved to the tables, searching frantically for something to do. There stood the aetherschreiber, but he felt a sudden horror at the very thought of touching it. He wondered if that horror had been laid upon him in the dream—another spell, another thing he was forbidden.

What if it was? He would deal with that in time.

Tiptoeing back up to his room, he took from the book where he had left it the latest letter from "Silence Dogood." Returning downstairs, he began setting it into type. Now and then he glanced apprehensively at the door, fearing it would burst inward.

Had he dreamt of Bracewell because he and John had spoken of him the day before? But not a day had passed when he hadn't thought of Bracewell and his strange cloud. It couldn't have been triggered by anything scientific—he had not even used the aetherschreiber that day, much less experimented with any novel devices.

Had Bracewell somehow known that they'd spoken of him and *sent* the dream to him? The thought sickened him. That thing had come into his head once; could it do so at will? By God, was it *always* with him? Could Bracewell kill him in a dream, or only threaten him? Ben fumbled another word into place, placed spacing blanks between. He realized that he had already concluded what John had; that his nightmare was of unnatural origin.

But why now, when it had been so long since he had seen Bracewell? And how could this damned witch know that he had modified the aetherschreiber?

Witch. He flinched at the word, but it seemed somehow more appropriate for Bracewell than *scientific philosopher.* Aetherschreibers, lanterns—even such terrible weapons of war as the French fervefactum—all were things of the daylight, the explicable. Bracewell's sorcery was of night, terror; it was illogical, inexplicable.

How could he fight it?

The best answer, he knew, was not to fight it at all. He should flee Boston, perhaps even flee the Americas. He closed his eyes, thinking furiously. He could borrow the sailboat again—Mr. Dare had said he might use it whenever he wished. He could make for New York, and from there book passage to England, find Sir Isaac Newton or some other powerful British philosopher, ask him to help. Of course, he had no money, but he could earn passage on a ship by working, as one of his brothers had. It was done every day . . .

The front door creaked open suddenly, and Ben's heart climbed mouthward. He could only stare in horror as the portal swung wider.

But it was James, not some necromantic cloud, who stood framed against the gently illumined street.

"Ben?" James asked, his tone puzzled. "What's wrong, boy?" He chuckled. "By your expression, I would say you were up to no good and I caught you at it. But here you are setting type, and I told you that you might go to bed early."

Ben heard his voice rise unsteadily as he answered. "I couldn't . . . couldn't sleep," he said.

James nodded. "I've that trouble myself now and then." He stepped fully into the room and closed the door. His eyes were just a bit glassy and his speech slightly slurred. Ben knew that James had been out at a tavern. "Normally when I find you up, however, it's with a book in your hand."

"I had a bad dream," Ben explained. He wanted, then, to tell James everything, about Bracewell's attack, about the dream just now. If only he knew how to begin it without sounding insane.

"What are you setting there? I thought we were done," James asked, settling heavily onto a bench and stretching his back so that it cracked audibly.

"What? Oh, it's the latest letter from Silence Dogood."

"Ah, the good widow," James said. "I must admit, I wonder who she is. We were just discussing her down at the Green Dragon."

"You and the Couranteers?"

"Aye. Do you realize that she has been published in New York, as well as here?"

"Yes," Ben answered. "I send them her essays in trade for what they send me."

James frowned and wagged a finger. "You should keep me informed of these things, Ben. Else what will I do when you run off to sea?"

Ben puffed out his cheeks. He wasn't prepared to deal with

James' peevishness just now. "James . . ." he began, but his brother waved him to silence.

"Never mind, Benjamin, I was wrong to say that. You've a smart mouth, but lately you've been a good 'prentice, and you've given me no cause to whip you in many a day. What's more, I owe you much, and we both know that."

Beer sometimes made James feel generous, and it sometimes made him mean—occasionally both. "Thank you," Ben said.

"This is a new age, Ben, a time such as has never been in all of history. Everything is being invented anew, reforged, beaten into new shapes!" He emphasized his last point by slamming his palm into the table. He leaned forward, his eyes alight. "Here in Boston, we will take that reshaping in our own hands, Ben."

He reached into a pocket of his coat and pulled out a folded sheet of paper. "Here, look at this!"

Ben took the paper and unfolded it. For an instant, he was puzzled; it was a handwritten layout for the first page of a newspaper, all ready to be set into type. It looked like their own paper, the *Courant*. But then Ben took better notice of the caption:

The Little Compton Scourge
or
The Anti-Courant

"Who wrote this?" Ben asked, his eyes already picking down the page. There was a long essay attributed to "Zachariah Touchstone," surely as fictional a name as "Silence Dogood."

James lifted his hands. "One of the ministers; I suspect the Reverend Walker or Increase Mather, or perhaps several of them. Here, give it back, I want to read you something."

Ben dutifully handed the paper back to his brother, who searched it a moment, and then, clearing his throat, began to read.

"It is most abundantly clear that the advertisements of the Courant *are the scribblings of a nonjuror, and that the supposed Couranteers comprise no less than a* Hellfire Club.*"*

James looked up at Ben, eyes flashing. "Oh, they shall reap the whirlwind for this! We'll set it first thing in the morning."

"You will print that? That libelous attack on your own person?"

"Of course! I gave it out that I would publish anything sent me, did I not? Sure I will show that I am a man of my word." He leaned forward intently. "But then I shall have their words before me, for all the world to see, and I shall vivisect them on the table of my next issue like an anatomist taking apart a dog. We shall see who looks the more foolish in the end."

Ben couldn't help smiling, and he felt a sudden, unexpected pride for his brother. Still, a part of him could not help but say, "The ministers are the masters of Boston. Are you so certain that you wish to provoke them?"

"*They* have done the provoking—calling us a 'Hellfire Club.' Taking issue with my opinions on science and God is one thing; attacking my person and the persons of my friends is another. We are moving into a new age, Ben, and our good ministers belong to the old one." He gestured at the type Ben had been setting. "Silence Dogood believes the same. Even her name is a lampoon against Cotton Mather, taken from his own 'Essays to Do Good.' "

He rose up and stretched, patted Ben's shoulder, and gave it a little squeeze. "These are great times, and we must strive to be great with them. I somehow feel that in the battle to come, Silence Dogood will weigh in on my side," he said softly, and winked. Then, he pushed through the door and off to his room.

Ben sat staring after him, blinking back tears. He ran his fingers blindly over the raised type, feeling there, for the first time, a powerful science, a compelling magic: a spell to shape minds, a knife to stab at tyrants.

It was a science he had never expected to learn from James.

He realized, then, that he had not told his brother about Bracewell, as he had intended; James had too quickly launched into showing him the *Anti-Courant*.

The hell with Bracewell, he thought suddenly. *I won't run from him.*

I have some ideas of how to deal with you, Trevor Bracewell, he thought, clenching and unclenching his fists.

And he had something else to do, as well. Mouth set, breathing hard, he walked purposefully over to the aetherschreiber. He took up the stylus, slid a fresh sheet of paper beneath it, and began to write.

My Dear Mr. F:
Your correspondence on matters mathematical has recently come to my attention. I wish to assure you that I have not intentionally eavesdropp'd upon your conversations, but a new sort of aetherschreiber—of my own design—has allowed me to do so. I believe, however, that you will be less rankl'd by my intrusion into your correspondence when I tell you that I believe I have a part of the solution for which you have been searching so diligently. Though I wish only to serve, my partner and I would appreciate some credit in the publishing of your results when the time comes. If you are agreeable to this, and if you desire my advice, please reply at your earliest convenience. You need only use the schreiber which you receive this on. If you wish me to ever after cease intruding upon your private matters, you need only say so, and I will most happily desist with sincerest apologies.
                                        Your Most Humble Servant,

Here Ben paused. He could not bring himself to sign his real name, not now. So instead, he gripped the pencil more tightly and signed, in precise letters, *Janus.*

11.

Three Conversations

The next day Adrienne was allowed to go to Mass, though she was accompanied at each step by a guard of the Hundred Swiss. In the ornate chapel she knelt and prayed as earnestly and un-affectedly as possible for the dauphin and for the king. She wished to pray for her own safety, but God knew what she was and was not innocent of—he would help her if it pleased him.

As they returned to her apartments, she glanced up at the silent, tall guardsman. He was a young man—perhaps a year or so older than she—with eyes slightly too far apart but otherwise handsome in a lean, rangy way. The gaudy blue coat of his uni-form, with its red facings and silver lace, seemed ill-suited to him. Only his battered scabbard seemed to belong with the rustic accent he revealed only reluctantly, when she forced him to speak.

"You seemed a bit lost in the chapel," she observed quietly as they stepped into the neighboring courtyard. Rain had damp-ened the stone, spicing the air with a gritty marble scent, and somewhere nearby a finch trilled.

"It seems more a cathedral to me," the young man admitted. "I am used to poorer surroundings."

"I'm sure you mean humbler, for no church is poorer than another in the eyes of God," she replied. "But I understand you. To pray at Versailles is difficult."

He nodded and when they had gone a few steps surprised her by speaking again. "I wasn't distracted when I prayed," he said. "I have prayed often in the past day." He glanced at her shyly. "I prayed for *you*, Mademoiselle."

She felt a slight heat at that, but did not look at him. "Really?" she said. "For what reason?"

"You are in my charge, milady."

"As to that, sir," she began, pursuing the question she had begun the conversation to ask, "why are you tasked to follow my every move?"

Now he colored slightly. "To keep you safe, milady."

"Safe? Safe from whom?"

"From the murderer, lady."

"He has not been found?"

"No. We are not, in fact, certain how the deed was accomplished."

"I see." They had by now reached her apartment, and he opened the door for her.

"I shall be outside, milady," the guardsman assured her.

"I do not doubt it," she replied, and to her surprise found that she meant it. She hesitated, for she felt that there had been some question she meant to ask him, but it had now stolen from her tongue. She reluctantly returned to what was clearly a fashionable prison cell.

Perhaps two hours later, there came a scratch at her door, and Helen hurried to answer it. Adrienne was gazing out the tall window. In the sky, the gray pall of the previous day and morning had boiled away. The warmth of the sunlight, however, was an illusion; the window might have been a pane of ice to the touch, and Adrienne drew a shawl tightly over her new *grand habit*. She had asked Charlotte to find her something simpler, but as of yet the girl had not been able to procure anything.

There was a whispered conversation behind her, and then Helen called, "You have a visitor, Mademoiselle. Monsieur Fatio de Duillier."

Adrienne turned in astonishment. She could see him in the doorway, turning a tricorn with both hands, hair disheveled. She strode briskly toward the parlor. "But of course, Helen, let the gentleman in." The door swung wider, and she could see her guard there as well, face carefully blank.

"You may leave the door ajar, Helen," Adrienne said.

Fatio shuffled clumsily forward, reaching for her hand. He kissed it and, continuing to hold it, met her eyes. Above his beaklike nose, his eyes seemed almost miserable with concern.

"Very good, Monsieur," Adrienne said, trying to appear cheerful. "Here in Versailles your scratching was most appropriate. You are learning the manners of the court, I see."

"Ah . . . yes," Fatio muttered. "I had heard you were on the barge. I . . . are you well?"

She patted his hand. "Never fear for me, dear Fatio," she replied. "My back was scorched a bit, no more. By good luck I happened to be lying down when whatever happened happened."

"Very good," Fatio went on. "Still, the shock, the awful shock of *seeing* . . ."

Her breath felt a little quick, a little strained. "I think I shall sit down."

"I'm sorry; I shouldn't have brought it up," Fatio hastened. She was afraid he might weep, and he mustn't, for then *she* would weep. She had not known them, those blackened corpses, but she might have once, if only at a distance.

She hadn't even prayed for them. She had just forgotten— the scene of the dead and dying had leaked out of her mind. But it hadn't leaked far, just to her eyes now. She covered her face with her hands.

"Oh, dear," Fatio said. "I'm sorry; I shall leave and return later."

"No," Adrienne managed through her sobs, "no, stay here, sir, for my sake."

Helen and Charlotte came over and held her, stroked her hair, wiped her face with a damp cloth. A few minutes passed before Adrienne gently pushed the two girls away.

"Pardon me," Adrienne apologized, nearly in control of her voice again. "I believe I interrupted you."

Fatio shrugged. "I don't remember what I might have been saying," he answered.

"Then tell me how you happened to come to Versailles so quickly."

Fatio blinked. "Oh, why, the king sent for us."

"For you and Gustavus?"

"Yes . . . well, no . . . I mean, he sent for *all* of us—the entire academy."

"What?" she said, astonished.

"The academy is being moved to Versailles. All of my equipment will arrive by tomorrow."

"This is . . . that is incredible," Adrienne stammered. And *mad*, she finished inwardly. What would they use for laboratories? "Have you seen your accommodations?"

Fatio nodded. "Our quarters are less than they might be," he confided. "But the rooms for our work are more than adequate. We can begin almost immediately. Of course, I will find someone to replace you, until you are well enough to . . ."

"What? Oh, no, Monsieur, I am well enough, I assure you."

"Adrienne, I could not think of asking you to work so soon after this ordeal. I'm sure—"

"Sir, no!" Adrienne shouted, shocked at herself. "I mean I need to work, Fatio. If I am idle I will only dwell on things. At Saint Cyr we were taught that work and dutifulness are antidotes for any ill."

His eyes searched into hers, as if he stood some chance of finding in them her true desires, and, surely failing, he nodded reluctantly. "Whatever you wish," he said. "But I would not have others say I required you to return too soon."

"They shall not, I assure you. The king has already returned to work, and as you may know, his grief and injury are far greater than mine."

"The king seems . . . distraught," Fatio offered, his careful choice of words making it clear that a more extreme adjective might have been more accurate, if not appropriate.

"You have seen him?"

"We were practically dragged before him. He demanded—" Fatio stopped and made a little grimace she was certain was intended as a smile. "I understand that the king is usually quite polite."

"I have rarely seen him lose his civility," Adrienne agreed, "but these must be considered the most trying of times. What was he . . . abrupt with you about?"

Fatio nodded. "*Abrupt* is a good description. He wished me

to conclude my research quickly. I have promised him great things, you see."

"Which I am sure you can deliver," Adrienne soothed.

"I hope so," Fatio said sincerely. "It's just that I believed I would have a bit more *time*."

"Well, then," Adrienne said, "we should return to work as soon as possible. Is tomorrow soon enough?"

Fatio made a last attempt to protest, but he bowed to her steadfast insistence.

When he had gone, she called the guardsman over to her.

"Monsieur," she said, "tomorrow I shall need to return to my work. Ask whomever you must, accompany me where you will, but I can no longer remain in this room."

Hours trickled by until the shadows lay long and black outside. Helen and Charlotte lit a fire in the fireplace. Adrienne wrapped a second blanket around herself, remembering something that Madame de Maintenon had once said. "For Louis," the queen had remarked, "a draft counts for nothing next to the perfect symmetry of having two doors precisely opposite one another."

It was not yet night when Torcy arrived.

"Mademoiselle," he said, "I am a busy man. Someone has tried to kill the king, and we must all do our part to discover who has done so."

"Is not the king's valet pursuing the investigation?" Adrienne asked.

"Indeed. And he has appointed me to look after certain elements of it."

"I understand," Adrienne said, "and I am thus all the more grateful that you have agreed to see me."

Torcy flashed his predatory grin. "I would have come to see you, Mademoiselle, whether you had asked it or not."

Adrienne stiffened. "I don't understand," she replied.

Torcy answered. "I will be plain. You remember our previous conversation about the duke of Orléans and your appointment to the academy?"

"I do."

"Then you will understand why I must ask you what you and

the duchess of Orléans had to discuss yesterday, shortly before the tragedy."

Despite herself, Adrienne felt a stab of anger. "Pleasantries, sir," she said, "nothing more. I was seated next to her."

"Yes, I know. I seated you there myself, wondering what might pass between you. Now, be honest with me. What did she tell you?"

Adrienne frowned. "Do you suspect the duchess?"

Torcy scowled. "The duke and duchess of Orléans have been suspected before. When the first dauphin died, and the duke and duchess of Burgundy. It was said that they might have been poisoned."

"The king never believed that," Adrienne said.

"Oh? So you defend the duchess then?"

"No," Adrienne said, but was astonished to discover that she *wanted* to. "No, if the duchess conspired to assassinate the king, then I wish only God's pity on her, for she shall get none from me. I simply state the facts: the king never believed that the duke and duchess of Orléans were guilty of murder. In fact, he never believed that there was murder at all, but blamed some strange disease."

"And how would you know this, my dear? You were but nine years of age."

"I remember, Monsieur. The duchess of Burgundy came often to Saint Cyr. Years later, when I was Madame de Maintenon's secretary, those ugly rumors still flourished. But if the *king* did not credit them and the *queen* did not credit them, I don't see why *I* should."

Torcy took a deep breath. She noticed that his hands were clenched and his knuckles white.

"To be truthful," Torcy admitted evenly, "I never believed those stories either. I believe that the three dauphins and the duchess died of a malignancy—measles or scarlet fever, perhaps. But now I must consider every possibility. And I must consider *you*, Mademoiselle."

"I had no part in this murder," Adrienne insisted. "I know nothing except what I witnessed."

"Tell me what you witnessed, then."

Adrienne related everything she could remember, including her conversation with the duchess of Orléans, omitting only the passing of the note and its contents.

Torcy nodded. "You tell me nothing that I did not already know, but I thank you for your testimony," he said. He then bowed and turned to leave.

"Please, Monsieur, one more moment of your time."

Torcy sighed tiredly. "Yes?"

"The king has moved the academy here, to Versailles, I hear?"

"True, and I approve," Torcy replied. "This puts the scientifics more closely under my scrutiny."

"I wish to return to my appointment working for Monsieur de Duillier."

"Impossible, at the moment," Torcy said.

"I am told that the king is most anxious about this particular research," Adrienne persisted. "I wish to do my part."

Torcy glared at her. "If you had any idea what you were asking—"

"You suspect one of the philosophers," Adrienne interrupted.

Torcy's mouth hung open for an instant. "What makes you say that?" he demanded, his voice curiously strained.

"First, you clearly suspect the duke and duchess of Orléans, the only members of the court with any real knowledge of science. Second, anyone with more brains than a jackass—you will excuse me, Monsieur—could see how this murder was committed."

Torcy's face was a rigid mask, and then, suddenly, he laughed.

"What an astonishing young woman," he remarked, smiling. "My general opinion of astonishing young women is that they should be kept in convents or chains. But tell me, my dear, how was the dauphin killed?"

"This is only guesswork, though I know how to confirm what I guess."

"Go on."

"May I please send away Helen and Charlotte? And may the door be closed?"

Torcy did not hesitate; he waved impatiently for the two girls to go.

"Well?" he said, when the door was closed.

"It was the flameless lantern," she explained, "the one above the king's throne."

Torcy made no remark. She lowered her eyes and plunged ahead. "The lantern works by alchemical reaction; the surface of the orb loosens the affinity in the air that keeps lux and gas bound together."

"Go on."

"Air is composed of three atoms of gas in ferment with a single atom of lux and two of phlegm. The lamp liberates the lux atom, so that the remaining compound is an inert gas, harmless. But if you were to liberate a lux atom bound to one of gas, the result would be a discharge of lightning. If you liberated lux bound to *two* atoms of gas, or even, I think, with phlegm in the right arrangement—then, Monsieur, you produce flame."

Torcy narrowed his eyes. "Are you telling me that the flameless lamp was somehow altered so as to *set the air itself on fire*?"

"Exactly," Adrienne acknowledged.

Torcy turned his back on her. He clasped his hands tightly behind his back and paced over to the window.

"Swear to me," he said, without turning, "swear by God and by the soul of your father that you know nothing of this matter save what you have guessed."

"I swear by God and I swear by the soul of my father that what you say is true."

Torcy turned as abruptly as a snake striking and crossed to her in five strides. His eyes burned into hers from two inches away; his breath was hot. "Swear it again."

"Why?" Adrienne asked, her voice as strong and steady as she could make it. "You do not believe me."

"No," he said. "No, but I am about to place my trust in you, and I want to know that if you lie, you will be damned for that as well as for your other crimes."

"Very well," Adrienne answered. It was hard to hold his basilisk gaze, but she managed it. "I swear by God and my father that I had no part in the murder of the dauphin and the blinding of the king."

Torcy held her gaze as if he had impaled her through the eyes with daggers and now twisted them to see what would ooze from her head. But after a moment, he nodded sharply.

"I accept your oath. I will arrange for you to continue your work with Monsieur de Duillier. But I want something more from you." He paused and stepped back. "I want you to discover who did this. Discover it and tell me."

Adrienne's mouth felt like paper. She simply nodded.

"Mademoiselle, if your explanation is correct—that the air itself was ignited—then how could the king have been spared?"

Adrienne tried to swallow, then licked her lips. "He should not have been spared," she admitted. "I cannot explain it."

Torcy nodded sardonically, and without looking back again, swept wide the door and strode out, shutting it firmly behind him.

Adrienne watched the closed door for a moment, and thought of the note with its scrawled owl.

After years of silence, the Korai had spoken to her. The duchess of Orléans was one of the Korai. Which meant, in its own twisted way, that she had just lied to Torcy.

Even as a girl she had been aware that her knowledge would one day exact a price.

She gritted her teeth, remembering what Torcy had said about being a queen or a pawn, and she silently resolved that if *they* insisted on drawing her into this game, she would *not* be a pawn.

12.

Painful Gardens

"Must he stand over us?" Fatio complained, indicating the guard who watched Adrienne from the doorway.

"I believe he must," Adrienne replied. "He has been assigned to me by the king himself, I am told."

"Well, if that is the case," Fatio muttered, clearly unconsoled.

"I would not worry that he understands any part of what we do well enough to spy upon it," Gustavus said, his voice as musical as his eyes were cold.

"Report it to whom?" Fatio asked. "If he works for the king—"

"My guard is not *deaf*, you know," Adrienne put in a bit sharply. It seemed rude to discuss the young man as if he were not there.

Fatio's eyes widened, but then he nodded and shrugged. "Just so," he said. "And in any event, Gustavus and I have much work to do today, for all the good that it may do us."

Adrienne reassured Fatio. "If you think of defeat, you will draw it upon you. Think instead of victory."

Fatio favored her with a wan smile. Gustavus shot her an irritated one. Both men then turned back toward their workbenches. Adrienne yearned to follow them, to peer at the formulae they so puzzled over, but if ever there was a time to reveal her inclinations for the mathematical, this was not it. Enough attention had been drawn to her already, more than enough. A month before she had been a mouse nosing about in the royal library. Now kings, ministers, and duchesses all vied to see who could more quickly ruin her life—all since she had begun aiding Fatio.

She strode back to the aetherschreibers, sighing, then sorted through queries she was to send out. One machine clicked, buzzed, and wrote even as she did so.

She had to learn what Fatio and Gustavus were working on. The king might desire her physically, and Torcy might be interested in her because the king was, as he said. But it was significant that all of Torcy's questions had centered on her position at the academy and the connection between that and the duke and duchess of Orléans. Of course, if the duchess was one of the Korai, then it was the Korai who had arranged for her to work at the academy. But why?

Adrienne's throat felt as if a noose were already being drawn around it. There was vital information she did not possess, and perhaps the most important was the nature of Fatio's work. It must be important; it interested the king, Torcy, the duchess . . .

She reached over to change the sheet in the working schreiber. *It must be a weapon,* she thought. The calculus she had seen suggested a cannon, but she was confident that it was not. And yet what it actually might be eluded her.

Fatio and Gustavus were deep in discussion; they had not noticed the incoming correspondence. Adrienne surreptitiously read the page.

The communication was from M. Two, but it was not in a handwriting she recognized. A new secretary then, she thought, until she read the first line. She read on through the absurd letter, frowning. Who was playing a joke on her—or rather, on Fatio? M. Two had never evinced even the faintest signs of humor before. An aetherschreiber that could communicate with unlinked devices?

A faint scratching at the door interrupted her. Adrienne shuffled the new letter into the sheaf of papers she was to send. She did not glance back to see whom the guard was admitting, but when Fatio greeted the newcomer, the blood rushed from Adrienne's face.

"My good duke!" Fatio exclaimed. "Gustavus von Trecht, let me introduce you to the duke of Orléans. To what do we owe this undeserved honor, sir?" Fatio inquired.

Adrienne slipped a paper into the machine and began writing, trying with all her will to be unnoticeable, a mere secretary.

"I am here to serve *you*, sir," the duke replied. "I have merely come to ask if there is anything the academy can do to make this transition to your new quarters easier."

"Oh, that is very kind . . ." Fatio began.

Gustavus coughed politely. "The observatory."

"The observatory!" Fatio exclaimed. "Quite right! I had nearly forgotten. Gustavus and I will need the observatory soon."

"Will you?" the duke asked, in a tone which arrested Adrienne. *He doesn't know what they are doing either,* she realized. *He's trying to find out.*

"Unfortunately," the duke went on, "the observatory cannot be moved here, as I am sure you are aware. I could arrange for you to have the use of a reflecting telescope. I can have one brought here by carriage."

"Oh," Fatio said, "why, yes, I think that would do."

"Anything else, my good sirs?"

"I don't think so— Oh, my pardon, Duke, I have failed to introduce my other associate. Please let me present Mademoiselle to you."

Adrienne closed her eyes, praying silently for strength. Then, draping a polite smile on her lips, she turned to meet the duke.

He was a man of middle height, stout, mild-eyed. To her surprise, he looked at her seemingly without interest, but bowed perfunctorily. "Most pleased to see you again, Mademoiselle de Montchevreuil," said the duke.

"Oh, you know Mademoiselle," Fatio said, slightly chagrined.

"We met several years ago," the duke replied, "but more immediately we were both unfortunate enough to be on hand at the great tragedy of two days past."

"Such a terrible thing," Fatio said.

"My wife, the duchess, inquires after you," the duke told her.

"Please tell her that I am well," Adrienne assured him. "And may I inquire after her?"

"Like myself, she was somewhat singed," the duke answered. "You seem to have escaped harm."

"My back was burned," Adrienne admitted, "though not badly. This dress pains me, I fear."

"Then for heaven's sake, my dear young lady," Orléans replied, "dress in something more comfortable—a manteau, perhaps."

"I fear manteaux are not acceptable garb at court."

The duke nodded. "This is true, but the king has other things to concern himself with now. I doubt very much that he will notice how you are dressed."

Fatio gasped, and Adrienne froze her expression, wondering if the duke had intended that cruelly indifferent reference to the king's blindness or if it was a horrid misstatement.

"In any event," the duke of Orléans said, bowing once more, "I leave you all to your work. I am greatly interested in all matters scientific, and I would love to discuss what you do here at length someday. I am a dabbler in experiments myself, you know."

"Everyone in the academy is aware of Monsieur's scientific inclinations," Gustavus said unexpectedly. "We are all much gratified to have such august and informed interest taken in our work."

The duke smiled and nodded. "Mademoiselle, gentlemen."

As he left, Adrienne dropped a low curtsey, and the two men bowed.

"I suppose he shall be king, soon," Gustavus remarked softly.

"Please, Gustavus, do not speak such things. I am quite certain the king will recover his wits presently."

Wits? Adrienne thought, shooting a glance at the young guard. To her complete surprise, he nodded sadly.

Returning to the aetherschreibers, she finished the letter and then another. Though her chest was still tight with worry, it appeared the duke had not come to further implicate her in some plot. The guard, who would surely report all he saw and heard to Torcy—or perhaps Bontemps—could confirm that there had been no secret exchange between them.

She sent two more letters, then reached the strange message from M. Two she had hidden—and nearly forgotten. She stared at it, more perplexed than ever, and then, with sudden resolve, moved to the second schreiber.

We shall see, she thought, *if this is a joke, Monsieur Janus.* Janus, the two-faced god of doorways and beginnings.

Adrienne took up the stylus and wrote—as usual, in English.

My Dear Janus,
We are of two faces concerning your offer. One face fears being spied upon, but the other smiles at the possibility of an end to our perplexity. If this is, indeed, the opening of a door, then I can assure you that your thoughts will receive all of the attention and recognition they merit.

Humbly yours,
Minerva

There. If the author of the letter was a joker, he would understand that his joke was accepted for what it was. If it was something other, she would know soon enough.

She rose early the next day, something nagging at the edges of her sleeping mind, something that shouted to be made sense of but refused to resolve into coherent thought. She did have one relief; the girls had managed to obtain her old gown, the modest, dark manteau in the style of Saint Cyr.

She found the guardsman snoring outside her door. An unwilling smile flitted across her face, as she briefly considered trying to steal off without him. Instead she squatted down and poked him in the forehead with her finger.

"Awake, Monsieur," she told him.

"Shit!" he exclaimed. Then he stopped, flushing scarlet. "Beg pardon, milady," he finished sheepishly.

"I am going for a walk," she announced.

He struggled to his feet and adjusted his twisted baldric. "I am already with you."

"I've never understood these gardens," the guardsman admitted. The marble eyes of several Nereids watched them pass a fountain and continue toward the Grand Canal.

"What is there to understand?"

"They are unpleasant. I always thought that gardens should be pleasant."

Adrienne could not hide a broad smile. "Whatever gave you that idea, sir?"

The fellow shrugged. "I grew up in Béarn. There are many vineyards there. We were poor, but my mother always kept a garden."

"And?" she prompted.

"My mother's gardens, the vineyards—I always found them pleasant. I always assumed that if my mother's garden was *nice*, a king's garden would be paradise."

Adrienne nodded. "They are nice from the window or from the hill near the orangery, are they not?"

"They are grand," he admitted. "But here, among them, they are torturous."

"I agree with you," Adrienne replied. Then, changing the subject, she said, "You say you are from Béarn."

"All of the Hundred Swiss are not Swiss," he said. "Even one of our lieutenants is French. My father was a member of the Hundred, and his father was a musketeer in the days of Louis XIII when *they* were the favored household guard. My family has a long history of such service to the kings of France."

Adrienne nodded. "As does mine. What is your family?"

"D'Artagnan," he replied.

She hesitated and then glanced at him. "I am of Montchevreuil."

"I know," he said shyly. "My father knew your uncle well. He spoke very highly of him."

"How ironic. Your father and my uncle, both staunch defenders of the king—friends even—and now you are my *guardian*."

His face reddened again. "Please, milady," he said, "you mustn't suspect that *I* believe you need watching."

"No, of course not," she said, a little more angrily than she had intended. "Who could *possibly* think that?"

They plodded on for another thirty yards, Adrienne struggling to maintain her anger. She finally gave up. "How long ago did you come to Versailles? May I call you by your Christian name?"

"It is Nicolas, milady."

"Good. You must call me Adrienne. And how long ago did you come to Versailles, Nicolas?"

"It's been almost three years I've been one of the Hundred Swiss," he said, a trace of pride in his tone.

"Three years. That's a long time, still not to understand the gardens."

They continued on, the silence growing awkward again, Adrienne trying to think of some polite topic to continue the conversation upon, but to her surprise, Nicolas preempted her. "If you agree that the gardens are not comfortable to walk in," he asked, "why are you walking in them?"

"Because," Adrienne answered, "they are between me and my destination."

"That being . . ."

"The barge. I want to have a look at it. I heard that most of it had been salvaged."

"I'm sorry, milady, but the barge was burned yestereve," Nicolas told her.

"Why was it burned? How could it have been burned without being carefully examined for evidence?"

"I believe that it *was* examined, milady Adrienne. And the king himself ordered it burned."

How can Torcy expect me to find evidence that has been burned? she thought angrily.

But Torcy, of course, was not the king.

"Well, Nicolas, it appears we have subjected ourselves to these unpleasant gardens for no good reason, and so I beg your pardon.

"It's nearly time for me to be in the laboratory anyway," she observed.

Nicolas nodded, then said, "I must admit that I find these gardens less unpleasant than I once did."

"Why is that?" Adrienne asked.

He was silent for a moment, and then unexpectedly laughed. "That was an attempt to be charming and complimentary, Mademoiselle. It is not something at which I excel."

Adrienne returned the laugh with a small but honest chuckle of her own. "No, it is not," she agreed, "but I am stupid in that way as well." To her own surprise, she reached out and patted his arm.

"Besides," she went on, a bit clumsily, "what need have you to flatter me? You and I are inseparable."

He did not take it as she intended. He fell silent. She knew that she had hurt his feelings, but she had no idea how to apologize. She was trying to think of some way to make him understand that she was only joking when she suddenly understood what she had been trying to grasp that morning.

The observatory, Fatio had said. Fatio and Gustavus needed a telescope.

Why?

13:

Harmonic Sympathy

It seemed to Ben that a great spider was probing his eyelids and ears with rasplike limbs. He could not quite work up the energy to be terrified, but he did reach to brush the horrible creature from his face, and in doing so grasped the edge of the waking world. He pulled himself awake, thankful to avoid a second nightmare.

He could still hear the scratching of the spider's legs, though he began to recognize that it was the aetherschreiber downstairs, scribbling away.

Ben bolted up and stumbled down to the press room.

The schreiber chose that instant to cease. Ben managed to reach it and give its key several twists, but the machine remained still.

He recalled that it was still tuned to the schreiber of Mr. F. The clock on the wall told him that about an hour had passed since he penned his own message, and here was the reply. He took up the sheet and as he read, his lips slowly spread into a smile.

They did not believe him. In fact, they probably thought that their regular correspondent had sent the message as a joke. Of course, if their regular correspondent also happened to be near *his* machine they would both have his message, and so they would soon confirm to each other his reality. Not surprisingly, "F" also understood his "Janus" identity and had joked about it at the beginning of the letter.

Whoever these men were, they *must* be leading philosophers, members of the Royal Academy in London. Who was he, a young boy from the Colonies, to have the effrontery to lecture them on what to do?

He was Janus, that was who he was. And if Janus made a fool of himself, no one would ever know that Ben Franklin was Janus.

Ben looked back at the schreiber. At that instant, someone sat at the other end of it, wondering if he would reply. But to be taken seriously, he must explain his solution in the language of mathematics—and John was to deliver their joint treatise tomorrow.

Though the note was clearly in the handwriting of "F" it was signed this time "Minerva"—the Roman goddess of wisdom. But the really odd thing about the letter was its *date*. Today was April eleventh, but the note from Minerva was dated April twenty-second. But he *knew* that the letter had just now been written—the schreiber was instantaneous.

Could "F" be so absentminded as to be eleven days off? He was very tired, and undoubtedly he was missing something.

He took the mystery to sleep with him, but it did not solve itself in the darkness.

The question of the telescope haunted Adrienne all the following day and into the next. Given the calculus she had glimpsed, there was now no question in her mind but that the two men were observing some celestial body, and yet that seemed completely out of keeping with the secrecy and obvious importance of the project—and with the unsolved affinitive equation. The only explanations that suggested themselves were bizarre: Were the two men designing some sort of vehicle for traveling into the outer reaches of the universe?

In the afternoon, the aetherschreiber delivered another message from Janus. It consisted mostly of a formula. When neither Fatio nor Gustavus were looking, she secreted it in her manteau. She did not read it until that night, in her room.

Helen and Charlotte both came running at her small, involuntary cry, but she reassured them and sent them away, turning her unbelieving eyes back to the scrawled formula. There was a certain crudity to it; a few symbols were not used in precisely the right manner, and at points the author was clearly out of his depth. And yet the essence was astonishingly clear, and it was, without a doubt, the answer to Fatio's dilemma. Almost unconsciously she reached for blank paper, a quill, and ink, and went to work. She could see the entire proof in her head. It was so simple it was actually childish; the correct affinity could be found by moving through all the possible affinities. That was certainly the method by which this Janus had modified his aetherschreiber. That was clear because the sliding potentialities he offered to solve Fatio's dilemma were couched in only a single dimension; he had worked out how to make a tunable chime. Fatio needed a formula that could operate on at least three axes. Her pen fairly raced, and twice she actually laughed aloud in delight. She forgot the king, Torcy, the duke and duchess of Orléans, and the terrible ordeal of a few days before. Only the equation mattered, and it was elegant—not a simple proof but an entire *method*.

Well past midnight she finished it, and then she carefully copied it, disguising her handwriting, and signed it with the initials of M. Two. She was smiling when she fell asleep, the equation still singing in her mind like a chorus of angels.

". . . like Prometheus unfetter'd you have brought a new fire to the world, and you may be assur'd that it is a flame that shall burn brightly," Ben read, and broke off to laugh and slap John on the back. "Prometheus we are, John!"

John was trying to be serious, but his glee kept breaking through. "See how they changed it?" he said. "They've done things to it I never imagined, but its still *my* formula—*our* invention. We shall be famous, Benjamin Franklin!"

"When we trade 'Janus' for our own names," Ben reminded him cautiously.

John shrugged. "I'm not even provoked at that. We have the drafts to show we proved this out."

"In fact," Ben said, "I have already mailed a letter to the Royal Academy in London. The postmark on it will show our precedence. It's signed Janus, of course, but I think we can demonstrate that it was our discovery."

John actually skipped for the next several paces, forgetting his dignity. The two of them were walking across the broad meadow of the Commons. "Who do you think they are, Ben? Whom have we written to?"

"Someone important. See, here, where it says that the Crown will thank us?"

"Oh, yes," John said, gesturing as if he were a king bestowing grace, " 'shine his Apollonian light upon us,' he will! Yet we still don't know what they are about, do we? We helped them solve a small piece of some larger puzzle—"

"I should say a very large piece," Ben interrupted. "My impression was that this was their last stumbling block."

"Yes, but what are they stumbling toward?"

Ben shrugged. "Perhaps, some sort of new cannon to use against the French."

"No, it still isn't a cannon."

"I have a better puzzle for you, John," Ben said. "Why is this dated eleven days ahead?"

"What?" John snatched the paper from him, frowning. "It must be a mistake," he muttered.

Ben shrugged. "I've checked; *all* the communications are dated eleven days ahead."

"Eleven? That reminds me of something," John mused.

"I've wondered if it might not be some message to us, but the earlier communications eavesdropped upon follow suit," Ben stated.

"That *is* a puzzlement," John said, kicking at a tuft of grass. "Unless . . . Unless they are following the Romish calendar. It is some number of days removed from our own. It might be eleven."

Ben stopped dead in his tracks, staring at his friend in horror. "Oh, God," he said, "that must be it."

"What do you mean?" John snapped. "What are you being so dramatic about?"

"We've been assuming that this Mr. F is *English*, and that we have been writing to him in *England*."

"He *writes* in English," John pointed out reasonably.

"But that might be because he was corresponding with an

Englishman. John, what if this Mr. F is Spanish, or . . ." He stopped again.

"John," he said quietly, "what if he's *French*? His Apollonian light? God, John, that doesn't refer to King George but to Louis of France!"

"Wait," John cautioned, "just wait, Ben. *You* started this theme of gods and goddesses. You signed as Janus, he wrote as Minerva, called you Prometheus, and so on."

"No Englishman would call King George Apollo. Zeus or Jove, maybe. Louis XIV, the Sun King—that's what they call *him*. Oh, God, John, whatever we've done just now, we've done for the enemies of our country!"

John could only stare at him, speechless.

14.

Renascence

Louis awoke to the sound of his watch being wound. Versailles did not care whether Apollo could see its splendors or not—it would carry him through his day regardless.

To Louis, that was strength. It had saved him from going mad more than once, and it would do so again.

"How are you this morning, Sire?" Louis-Alexandre asked from quite near.

"I am very well," Louis answered, mustering all of his ancient strength. He had never needed to see his own face to understand what it was projecting, to twist this or that nuance into a smile, a frown. Far less so, now, when he was so much more aware of his muscles. What worried him was that he could not see the faces of others, could not read their moods—the unwilling confession of a dropped gaze, the murderous glint of a too-bright smile. He knew that if he could *see* who had tried to kill him, he would recognize him by his look.

Who had it been? Which cabal? He had heard the name of Orléans muttered more than once, but he did not believe that his brother's son had done this. He had a spine of seaweed and no ambition higher than bedding every woman in France.

It might have been, as Torcy and Bontemps seemed to suggest, an English spy. That was certainly the most satisfying possibility, and in many ways the likeliest. There was the Englishman who had been slain in the stables, the one posing as one of his Irish troops, to lend evidence to that theory.

And yet—Marlborough was winning on the battlefield. Why should England run the risk of international disapproval? Unless somehow Albion had learned of the great weapon France and her king prepared for it. What had de Duillier called it? "Newton's own cannon"?

There were other possibilities. It could be the old nobles, those bastards who had engineered the Fronde long years ago. Bit by bit Louis had been destroying them in favor of the more dependable and patriotic lesser nobility.

The remaining choices were unthinkable. The duke of Maine, Louis' illegitimate son by Montespan, had a chance at the throne now that the dauphin was dead. Yet if any of his children loved him, it was Maine. And Philip, his grandson—his *single* surviving *legitimate* heir—Philip was king of Spain, thanks to him, and his ally in this war against the British.

"Louis-Alexandre," he said, as his valet helped him on with his dressing robe. "After I meet with my ministers, I wish to go hunting."

"Sire, it has only been three days since . . ."

"I am aware of the days as they pass, Louis-Alexandre. And I believe that it has been too long since I have hunted."

"The King's Police have not finished their investigation," Bontemps reminded him. "It is far from certain that it would be safe for you to go outside at the present."

"I will not cower here, Louis-Alexandre, waiting for death to find me. Send as many of the Hundred Swiss as you desire— summon the entire company of Black Musketeers from Paris if you wish—but I shall hunt this afternoon."

Bontemps' sigh was all but inaudible. "Yes, Sire," he replied.

At times, Louis wondered if the Bourbons had not somehow gotten the blood of wolves into their line, for nothing woke the fierceness in him as did the baying of hounds, the braying of trumpets. It was almost as if he could scent the quarry, feel its fear and its fierce determination to live.

It was this wolfish sensibility that told him they were upon a stag.

If only he could ride a horse, rather than bump along behind one in the wheeled monstrosity that had been devised for him. If only he could see the courtiers around him.

The dogs were drawing nearer, running the stag in to them; beaters spread out through the woods were funneling the great beast toward his chariot. If only he had a musket—if only he could see to fire one!

Open your eyes, the angel said. The angel had spoken to him often since the dauphin died. *Open your eyes, and I will show you how an angel might aid you.*

Louis opened his eyes, and a grayness dawned where before there had only been night. To his astonishment, the world quickly grew lighter, until he could make out the slender saplings and thicker, hoarier trees.

His driver pulled the carriage to a stop and waited, cocking an ear attentively to the approach of the dogs. Without thinking, Louis stepped onto the forest floor.

The driver looked odd to Louis; his coat and boots were clear and detailed, but his face was a sort of featureless oval.

"Sire?" the driver inquired. Louis recognized the voice immediately.

"Bertrand," Louis said, naming him. Almost instantly the visage sprang into focus, becoming Bertrand's long, red face complete with drooping mustache. Louis looked around, wondering at the forest. The trees were as clean of line and regular as the colonnade at Versailles, as if they were carved of marble. Perhaps twenty courtiers on horseback gaped at him, their faces as featureless as Bertrand's had been.

His huntsman, Jean-Claude, stood near. He mumbled a formality and his face, like Bertrand's, became distinct. The courtiers might as well have been mannequins.

"Jean-Claude, give me your weapon," Louis said.

He took the gun—one of the new, rifled muskets, not one of the strange scientific weapons that threw lightning or God knew what else at their targets. He had forbidden those on the hunt.

A cry went up as the stag burst into sight. Louis saw it as if through a spyglass, and yet the beast still looked curiously *perfect*. In fact, it resembled a stag he had killed when just a boy, yes, even to that darkening on the shoulder blades. Its eyes were rolling, and two of the hounds virtually hung upon it. Its haunches were soaked in blood.

Fifty paces away the beast knew its mistake and tried to fling itself somewhere, to break through its ring of tormentors. Louis gave it peace with a single lead ball through the heart.

"Why is my sight so strange?" Louis asked the angel later.

It is because I see for you, the angel replied. *Your own eyes are ruined. But I can see through you, through your ears and your skin. Then I paint a sort of picture for you, so that you may see also. You must understand it is only an approximation of sight.*

"It is very strange. Why do some people have faces while others do not?"

When you know them—when you have some memory of their face for me to model them from—then I can paint their faces for you. Otherwise, I do the best I can, Louis."

"Do angels not have eyes like men?" he asked.

Do not presume too much, the angel answered. *You may be the greatest king on earth, but my king is God, and he is yours as well. He has given you for me to watch over, but you may not question me.*

"I am sorry," Louis said, though in his heart he was angered that even an angel might command him.

I will forgive this once. The answer to your question is no. What my angel eyes see, your human soul could not bear. You should appreciate this gift of sight I give you, for in providing it—even in this indirect fashion—I bring myself pain.

"I thank you most humbly," Louis answered. He felt a sudden dread: What the angel had given him, it could take back and, strange though his new vision was, it *was* vision.

Go to the mirror, Louis, for I have something else to show you, the angel said.

Louis obeyed.

"Shit!" he exclaimed, unable to believe what he saw. Staring back at him was Louis XIV. He wore no wig; long, beautiful chestnut curls fell to his shoulders. A darker mustache clung to

his upper lip. His face was smooth. His body was slim, and the stockinged legs bulged with firm, shapely muscle.

He was young again.

15.

Of Secrets

Adrienne wondered if she could catch Fatio if he fainted; he seemed unsteady on his feet as he gawked at the proof she had just handed him. Even Gustavus betrayed a tight little smile of triumph as he peered over Fatio's shoulder at her disguised letter.

"By God," Fatio finally managed, in a strangled voice. "So simple, and yet so—" He whirled upon her. "Who is this Janus?"

Adrienne shrugged. "It came on the second schreiber."

"Really?" Gustavus asked, his eyes glittering. "And this is your first communiqué from this Janus?"

She nodded, feeling the sudden weight of her lie around her neck.

Gustavus grinned savagely at her affirmation, and she felt a sudden unwarranted thrill of fear. How did Gustavus know she was lying?

But he merely clapped Fatio on the shoulder. "Well," he said, "we have our answer, sir, and now we can proceed."

"Yes! Yes!" Fatio replied enthusiastically. "Still, I wonder whom we have to thank."

"I'm sure one of our English colleagues will claim the credit soon enough," Gustavus responded, flicking his gaze to the aetherschreiber. "But let you and I strike while the iron is hot."

"Oh, yes! We can give the king a date, now. That will please him—" He glanced suddenly at Adrienne and then at Nicolas d'Artagnan, standing behind her. Gustavus glared, though she did not need that to know that Fatio had said more than he ought.

A date, Adrienne repeated to herself, walking back toward the aetherschreibers. *Another clue.*

That afternoon, near three, Torcy sent for her. With Nicolas in tow, she met him in the king's antechamber.

"The king has gone to Marly for a few days, at his physician's insistence," Torcy explained to her. "He wishes you to join him there."

"I see," Adrienne said. She had wondered if, in the chaos, Louis had forgotten her. Whereas a few days ago that would have been cause for rejoicing, now she felt relief. Whatever forces were at play, whatever confluence of cabals had swept her up in their plotting certainly did not care what *she* wanted.

The coming storm—whatever its nature—might still break her. But if one had to weather a hurricane, she knew that it was best to be in its eye.

That eye was Louis.

And yet, the thought of being the king's mistress repulsed her more today than it had earlier.

Torcy clearly read the momentary struggle in her features. "Don't wear that long face to Marly," he cautioned. "The king may not be capable of sight—" He hesitated, as if to add something, and then plunged on. "—but he is surrounded by those who are."

"Your pardon," Adrienne said. "I . . . I only hope I can be of some comfort to him."

Torcy nodded diffidently. "I am certain that you can. The king has always been comforted by youth and beauty." He paused for the barest instant, his eyes narrowing their focus. "Have you anything to tell me regarding what we discussed?"

Adrienne shook her head. "I wanted to examine the barge, especially the remains of the lantern, but my bodyguard informed me that it has been incinerated."

"So it has," Torcy confirmed. "Most of the ministers have convinced themselves and the king that this was an English plot. Indeed, one of the Hundred Swiss apprehended an Englishman soon after the fire."

"What made him suspect this Englishman?"

Torcy held up his hands. "The Englishman was carrying a musket. When the guardsman approached to question him, he fired. Actually, he killed one guard."

"But the Englishman did not confess?"

Torcy smiled wryly. "Perhaps to God. The guard arrested him with the point of his smallsword." He reached into a coat pocket. "This is one of his rifle balls," he added, passing it to Adrienne. "Does it tell you anything?" Torcy asked.

"It could be a catalyst," Adrienne finally said. "It would be the simplest way to trigger the lantern into igniting the air. But if a marksman could strike the globe, why not simply shoot the king?"

"There is a plain answer to that," Torcy said, his voice very low. "The king cannot be shot."

"What?"

"He has been protected from bullets," Torcy answered simply.

"Oh." She frowned, wondering precisely how that might be done. Clearly, Torcy was not going to tell her, even if he knew. "In that case, perhaps it *was* an English plot."

"I have no doubt that the English had a hand in this," Torcy replied. "They know that the next king would sue for peace and relinquish much of what we have gained in the last few decades. But I smell a stink in Versailles, Mademoiselle, and it is too grand a stink to be accounted for by one dead Englishman."

The coach bounced violently, and for the third time, Adrienne caught Nicolas glancing quickly away from her, a puzzled, thoughtful expression on his face.

"What is it, Nicolas?" she demanded, irritated. "Why do you keep gawking at me?"

"Your pardon, milady Adrienne," he mumbled.

"Why should you care for my pardon? But if you ask your *question*, I might answer it."

"Question, milady?"

"I am losing patience with all this," she snapped. "The unasked questions, the half-truths, the veiled threats—" She stopped, realizing that speaking thus to one who had Torcy's confidence might not be such an intelligent maneuver.

"Again, milady, my apologies," Nicolas said mildly. "You are quite correct. My question regards honesty," he said, his voice barely audible over the clattering of hooves.

He looked down at the floor of the coach. Finally he cleared his throat. "I just wondered why you hide your gifts, that is all, your knowledge."

"Torcy has spoken to you?"

"A little, but he needed to say nothing. My job is to *watch* you, milady. And though I know nothing of mathematics or science, I am not so dense that I cannot see that you *do*. And yet you hide what you know. You are an educated woman—everyone knows you attended Saint Cyr. Such women are valued, I hear, for their learning."

"Oh, yes," she said, "so long as they learn the *right* things: to make polite conversation, to be cheerful and supportive, to know the New Testament but not the Old, to learn nothing of theology—" What use going on like this to this rustic guard?

Nicolas frowned. "I thought they taught reading and figuring the math, and . . ."

"Reading, yes, but only certain subjects. Mathematics, yes, of the simplest sort but never calculus, never geometry. We were taught to be horrified of science, as if it were sin."

"And yet you learned it."

"Indeed," Adrienne said, chagrined at the way her voice shook. "The king and Madame de Maintenon had the good grace to send me to a school where I learned all that a woman might hope to learn. And what did I do? I betrayed that, Nicolas. Madame de Maintenon would turn in her grave if she ever knew what you know, what Torcy knows."

"And the king?"

She shook her head. "The king thinks me blameless, yet if ever he knew I had betrayed Maintenon and Saint Cyr in such a way, he would be furious."

"And yet you always smile."

"Do I?" She was genuinely astonished.

"Of course. Even when arguing with the marquis de Torcy. Didn't you know this?"

Adrienne blinked, realizing stupidly that she was smiling even now. "I do not notice it," she admitted.

"That makes me sad," Nicolas said.

"Oh?"

"When you smile, it should be because you are joyful."

Adrienne snorted. "A young lady is always joyful," she said. "Serious, dutiful, and joyful."

"Now you make fun of me," Nicolas said.

Adrienne regarded the young man for a long moment. "Do you know," she said after a moment, "that there were supposed to be no dark corners at Saint Cyr? No places for girls to whisper to one another. No places for secrets. Did you ever have secrets as a boy, Nicolas?"

"Of course I did," he replied.

"I believe," Adrienne went on, "that one cannot have a friend if one does not share secrets with him."

"How long were you at Saint Cyr?" the guardsman asked.

"Fourteen years," she replied.

"And you never had a friend?"

She sucked in a deep breath. "Yes, in the end I think I did," she said at last.

He nodded as if he understood. "I am sorry to have troubled you, milady."

"As you suspected, I was troubled before," Adrienne said. "But see here, Nicolas. You have learned a secret about me, and I have learned none about you."

"By your light," he said, "if we share secrets we shall become friends."

"Why, yes," she said.

He smiled. "Well then, I must think a bit, for I wouldn't want to base a friendship on some spuriously chosen secret. It must be a fine one."

He seemed to think for some time, then his gaze found hers again, his eyes like hieroglyph jewels, suddenly full of meaning. She felt a faint warmth in her breast. His lips parted.

At that moment, lightning struck the carriage. The windows shattered inward; she felt a sting on her cheek, and the entire carriage tilted, seemed to leap forward, and then jarred to a halt.

Adrienne found herself crushed against the coach wall by Nicolas, stunned. Then Nicolas was shaking her, his mouth moving frantically, but, though she could hear what he was saying his words made no sense to her. She nodded, hoping he would understand that she was uninjured.

At least, she thought that she was.

The carriage was tilted as if the wheels on one side had been torn from it. Nicolas reached past her and wrenched the door open, producing his pistol and colichemarde as he did so. Outside, Adrienne caught rushed, blurred motion. There was a shot, a tiny little sound, and then another flash of lightning.

Then there was silence.

16.

Lullaby

Ben fit the last bolt into place and stepped back to admire his work. Nodding, he wiped grease on his already ink- and mud-stained breeches. "I don't know if you'll work," he told his invention, "but I like the look of you."

James stepped in from outside, shaking out his greatcoat. "Talking to God again, Ben?" he said. "You can tell him I could do without the rain." He flashed a smile, doffed his hat, and shook that, too.

"I'm done talking to him for the day," Ben said, "but I'll keep it in mind next time we converse. How did it go with the Couranteers?"

"The *other* Couranteers, you mean. We count *you* one, you know."

Ben turned as if examining the press to hide the stupid beam he knew had just crossed his face. "Well, what did they allow?"

"We're all agreed that we'll be damned before letting the ministers tell us what we can and cannot print," James said.

"Relevant choice of words," Ben noted. "But if I'm a Couranteer, I'm in it with you."

"That's good, because if I'm arrested, you must keep up publishing."

"Arrested?" Ben asked, gripping the frame of the press.

"It *is* a possibility," James said. "It has been threatened, though I can scarce imagine what crime they might charge me with that would keep me imprisoned for long."

"What would stop them from arresting me, too?"

"Well, there is the beauty of being an apprentice, Benjamin,"

James said happily, clapping him on the back. "You cannot be arrested for doing what I tell you to do."

"Oh-ho!" said Ben, raising his brows.

"Oh-ho indeed," James repeated. "God's teeth, Ben, what in the name—what the devil is *that*?" James had just noticed his new device.

It resembled a bull's-eye lantern but had what looked like butterfly wings of woven wire unfolded from the sides and thirty small, sharpened graphite rods protruding from the front, where the shutter should be. A wooden grip protruded from the back.

"Is this some sort of weapon like those crafty pistols I've heard of?"

"Sort of," Ben admitted.

"I repeat," James said. "What is it?"

"Just an experiment," Ben said. "I'll explain it after I see if it works or not."

James cocked his head, trying to decide if he should press his younger brother for an explanation. But then he shrugged, went over to the press, and began to wipe it with an oily rag. "What have we got coming in tonight?" he asked.

"Sir Henry's 'Observations of Calcutta,' " Ben replied.

"Good, good," James replied. "His letters always make fine reading. See if you can find some news on the war in Florida," he said. "The war in the South will be on everyone's mind now."

"Do you think the French will win?" Ben asked, trying to keep the tightness from his voice.

James shrugged. "People have been predicting the demise of the French empire for more than a decade now, but they always manage to surprise us. What's your opinion, Ben? This seems to be more a war of science than of men."

"France made the early strides in the application of science to warfare, but now they have fallen behind," Ben replied. "These new guns of Marlborough's pound the French fortresses and have no antidote." *Unless,* he thought sickly, *I have just given them one.* For the more he thought of it, the more certain he was that "F" was French. What had John said about the formula? That it was almost as if it were for bringing two cannonballs in flight together? A picture painted itself in Ben's mind, a battle in which each cannonball fired could be countered in the air. It would change warfare forever. It might bring the French to pre-eminence on the battlefield again.

"Ben?" James was asking. "You have that faraway, stupid look again. Is that what you are working on? Some new weapon for England?"

Ben glanced at the contraption on the table. Was James making fun of him? But he appeared serious.

"Yes," Ben replied, happy that it was not entirely a lie. "Well, more of a defense, really."

James nodded. "We really should talk about taking out patents on these inventions of yours," he muttered.

"Perhaps," Ben replied uncertainly. His mind was still on the eleven-day discrepancy. Could there be *any* other way of accounting for it?

"When all else fails, *ask*," Ben said to himself, staring at the silent schreiber. But *how* to ask? And could he trust their answer? He composed the query in his mind over and over, but no magical solution presented itself.

With the complete punctuality that characterized Sir Henry's correspondence, the schreiber began taking dictation from its cousin in India. Ben watched the paper move without his usual excitement. India, too, was embroiled in the war with the French. What if Calcutta should fall and Sir Henry should die just because a boy in Boston had let his pride and greed for attention blind him to the obvious?

He sent his thanks and the latest news from New England to Sir Henry, and then, hesitantly, reached for his tuning device. Still uncertain what he would write, he moved the tube to the setting he had always assumed was corresponded to a schreiber in Britain. "God will that it is," Ben breathed.

He sat staring for an instant, and then reached for the pen. But before he touched it, it rattled. And then, just above the chime, a red glow appeared. Before he could begin to scream, the glow coalesced into an eye. Then it winked closed again, and the aetherschreiber wrote three words in a scratchy, ungainly hand: *I see you.*

"Why, Benjamin! Come in!" His mother pushed the door wider and gave him a hug. Ben noticed for the first time the lines etching her soft face, the streaks of silver in her auburn hair.

"It's been long enough since we've seen you, Son," she went on.

"I'm sorry, Mother. I've been . . . I've been busy."

"So I hear," she replied. "You and James have created quite a stir. A sermon was preached against you last Sunday—which you would have heard, had you been at church."

Ben returned her hug and looked around the room. For a moment, the aching familiarity of it nearly brought him to tears.

"Ben? Is something wrong?" his mother asked.

He shook his head. "I need to talk to Father," he said. "Is he here?"

"No," she answered him quietly.

He thought he heard disappointment in her voice. Though he loved his mother, he had somehow never found the time to be close to her. He had always imagined that one day he would correct that. He had always imagined there would be time.

"He's gone to Charles Town on business. He won't be home until late tonight, maybe even the morning."

"Oh."

"Have you and James been at each other again?"

"What? Oh, no, we haven't. Actually we've gotten along rather well since we started printing the paper."

"No wonder. You have to stand back-to-back against half the town." She smiled broadly. "That's no matter. I would rather have my sons battling the whole world than fighting each other. It pains your father to see you at each other so." She paused. "It pains him to never see you at the church as well. It makes him think that you have forgotten all that he taught you."

Ben shook his head. "I haven't forgotten. That's why I came to see him. He told me if I was ever unsure I should come and see him." His lip quivered, but he didn't want to cry in front of his mother.

Then, suddenly, her arms were around him again, and she rocked him on his feet, brushing back his hair.

"He'll be back tomorrow," she murmured, "and whatever it is, he'll make it all right."

And for a few moments he believed her. It was the best gift she was capable of giving him.

An hour later, resting on the Long Wharf, he believed no longer. He had counted on his father to help him somehow, but he realized now that this was beyond the older man's power. His father knew little of science and less of whatever sorcery was being practiced against him. Whatever he said, it would be good, solid, common sense.

But Ben was beginning to doubt that there was any room in the world for common sense. Perhaps Sir Isaac Newton had murdered that decades ago and it was only just now starting noticeably to rot.

A sudden, salty breeze buffeted him as he started back toward town. Between him and the shore, a girl of perhaps sixteen sat on the wharf singing, cradling an infant. Her song was plaintive, minor-keyed, rising and falling with the waves that lapped the wharf. The words were clear and somehow chilling, despite the fact that it was obviously a lullaby.

> *"Oh-ho, sleep, my little babe*
> *Oh-ho, sleep, my pretty little colt*
> *Far away my son has gone*
> *They will seek the pretty one*
> *Loo-oohoo, sleep oh sleep*
> *Loo-oohoo, water's deep*
> *Swift thou art and fleet of foot*
> *Thou dost show thy horse's hoof."*

Ben hurried on, fleeing he knew not what. The roofs of Boston, for the first time ever, beckoned him *away* from the sea, back to its solid, land-loving heart.

*   *   *

He walked all over town, from the neck to the millpond, before returning home. Toward evening he felt better, despite the fact that James would be furious at his absence. But the moment had come for him to explain some things to James. He and John had gone too far, boys pretending they were men—worse, *great* men. James might not know what to do, but he had friends in England. If Ben and John had accidentally aided the French surely word could be gotten to someone in London who would know who should be told. With luck, they would not try him and John for treason.

As to that weird, hellish eye, he didn't even want to consider *that* right now.

Just beyond Union Street, Ben saw a familiar silhouette moving through the long shadows that hatched the thorough-fare. Bracewell, riding on a brown mare, turning his head this way and that.

Oh, God, Ben thought. *He's looking for me.* Ben sidled quickly into a narrow lane and then ran. Bracewell was working up Hanover, so Ben planned to double around behind the man, then shoot across to Queen Street and James.

I mustn't panic, Ben told himself. But that was hard. He reached Queen Street and, glancing back, he saw no horse bear-ing down on him, no angry sorcerer. But Queen Street was full of people milling about and shouting. A column of black smoke rose up into the sky. Ben slowed, puzzled.

The smoke came from James' print shop. Someone in the crowd, rushing off, was calling for water.

"Benjamin!" someone shouted. It was Mrs. Sheaf, who owned the school next door. Her eyes were red and tear streaked. "Ben—"
He brushed past her. Thick black smoke was billowing out of the shop. He started toward the door; he had to get the aetherschreiber out, the run of the paper . . .

Two feet inside, the heat smote him. Two men were coming toward him, carrying someone. As he staggered, someone caught him from behind and yanked him out into the street again. He coughed, his head swimming, and sank to the pavement.

"No, no, don't let him see," he heard someone shout.

He turned his head and met James' eyes. They were wide, glassy, still.

Then he was screaming his brother's name again and again.

They let him scream. Soon the buckets were coming, more to keep the fire from spreading to other buildings than to try to save the doomed one.

Bracewell had done this. Forcing his brain to even such an elementary conclusion required hideous effort. Nothing mattered anymore. The aetherschreiber, the French war—it was so stupid that he had been *so* worried about those things, when James had been *dying*, when Bracewell had been *murdering* him.

Why? Why? He thought he had the answer for a second, but then the roof of the shop collapsed, and a billion red demons leaped up toward heaven. He followed those winged little flames and lost the thread of his thought, as somewhere in him—from a deep and ancient place—the animal stirred that cared for nothing but that it should continue to live.

James was dead. If he did not act quickly, he would be dead, too. That was reality. He hadn't worked out the details of *why*, but the animal didn't care. It wanted to run.

Ben rose shakily to his feet, pressing tears from his eyes. Bracewell was probably here, looking for him. Ben cast about him. A few items had been laid on the street nearby, things that someone or other had saved from the burning building: a book, a sheaf of papers, James' coat.

I can use the coat, he thought dully, lifting it.

Underneath was his strange-looking lantern. His head tingled with a sickening surge of hope, anger, and terror. He snatched up the coat and the projector. He looked carefully up and down the street, seeking his foe, his brother's killer, and soon enough found him. Bracewell was still on his horse near the church and square. His face was no more than a shadow, but Ben knew that the manslayer was watching him and waiting.

Ben thought no more, but turned the other way and ran. Though it was impossible, he imagined that he could already hear the hoofbeats coming up behind.

17.

The Korai

Adrienne stared into the pointed metal shaft of the *kraftpistole*. She had never seen one this close, certainly not aimed at her. A part of her considered the terrible weapon, remembering the principles by which it functioned, but much more of her wondered how long she had before lightning snuffed out all of her thought and life.

The man behind the pistol spoke, his voice muffled by the cloth tied over his mouth and jaw. A half mask concealed his nose.

"I am very much afraid, Mademoiselle, that I must ask you to don this." His outstretched hand thrust a black blindfold toward her.

"Nicolas," Adrienne managed. "What have you done to Nicolas?" She could see his body stretched prone on the ground, along with those of the mounted escorts.

"He is alive, as is your coach driver. I am not a murderer, Mademoiselle. Now, please, don the blindfold."

Adrienne shifted her gaze between the unmoving body and the unwavering pistol. She strained to see Nicolas' ribs moving, and fancied—but was not certain—that she did.

"Very well," the man snapped. "Turn around."

She did so, aware that her knees were shaking.

"Stay still." In the next moment the cloth came down across her eyes; the point of the pistol was pressed against her back. *There must be two of them,* she thought, *at least two.* Her captor then knotted the blindfold behind her head.

"There," he said. "Now, take my hand."

She held her hand out and felt his—it was smooth, soft.

153

"I'm going to lift you onto a horse now," he said. "Can you ride?"

"I have ridden, of course," she replied. She felt sick. These men were not bandits, or simple highway thugs: *Kraftpistoles* were very expensive, owned mostly by high-ranking officers and the king's pistoleers. Also, her captor's hands were not the roughened hands of an outlaw. This was a kidnapping.

Someone took hold of her waist and lifted her. "I'm afraid you will not be riding sidesaddle, milady. I regret the indelicacy of the situation, but you must sit astride."

Compliantly, she swung her leg over the saddle. Her narrow skirt shucked up to her thighs as she groped for the pommel.

"Lean back, lady," said a second voice. In the next instant a man's body was in front of her, pressing her almost out of the saddle. "You will have to hold around my waist, lady," said the rider. His accent was precise, Parisian. She had heard the voice before.

When the horse suddenly jerked into motion, she reached around a surprisingly slim, muscular torso, clasping her hands across the buttons of a waistcoat. The horse broke from trot to gallop; the world blurred to a dark cipher of motion and noise. She clung to her enemy, wishing him dead.

She guessed that they had been riding for the better part of the night. Twice the men stopped and fed her, and four times they gave her water. They did not speak again. The air became more chill, and she felt terribly tired. She wondered, again and again, if Nicolas was still alive. It seemed, to her, unlikely.

Day came gradually behind the blindfold, a reddening against her eyelids. By then, she seemed to have become a part of the horse—and of the man. She clung to him as she imagined one might a lover, as if their separate bodies had become a single ferment—horse, man, woman.

She tried several times to get her captor to speak, but he did not respond, perhaps sensing that she recognized his voice. She knew him as the same man who had saved her from the canal.

At last, the horses' hooves clattered upon cobbles. This time when she was helped to dismount she was led indoors, where someone took her hand and directed her, stumbling, down a carpeted corridor.

"Just another moment or two, lady," a woman's voice whispered, heavy with some foreign accent.

"Where am I?" Adrienne choked out. "What has become of me?"

"I am not allowed to answer these questions, lady, only to try and make you comfortable." A door creaked open. A flush of warmth and perfume engulfed her. The air was damp.

The woman untied the blindfold, and for a moment Adrienne felt dizzy and swayed a bit.

She was in a bathhouse, lit only by a few candles. The bath, set into the floor, was filled with hot water.

Adrienne turned to face her escort, a plump woman, probably in her midthirties, in servant's dress.

"Please, milady, have a bath," the woman beseeched.

"I have just been kidnapped," Adrienne said levelly. "I believe my escort was killed. I have been carried on horseback all night. The king was expecting me at Marly." She realized how disjointed this sounded even as she said it.

"I know, Mademoiselle. I can only tell you that you will be well treated here. You will not be harmed."

"I have already been harmed," Adrienne insisted.

The servant looked as if she might cry. "Please," the woman said, "a bath will make you feel better. And I shall fetch you some wine."

Adrienne tried to protest, but the woman began working at the laces of her bodice. Before she knew it, she was resting in the scented water, allowing it to buoy her. When the servant brought her wine, she drank the first cup in two draughts, after which she sipped more carefully.

Oddly enough, the wine seemed to sharpen her senses. She turned to the servant.

"What is your name?" she asked.

"Gabriella," the woman replied.

"Gabriella, tell me why I have been brought here."

"*Signorina,* I don't know," the plump woman answered. "Only Madame knows that."

"Madame?" Adrienne asked rather sharply.

The servant turned quickly away. "Please don't ask me any more," she whispered.

Adrienne closed her eyes, feeling the heat soothe into her bones. "Very well, Gabriella," she sighed. "You have an accent of—is it Tuscany?"

"Yes, Tuscany," Gabriella replied, a hint of surprise in her voice.

"Tell me about Tuscany, then, about your home."

"Well . . ." Gabriella began, uncertainly. "It isn't like France. The sky is bluer, and the cedar trees grow straight up, like towers. We used to . . ." She broke off. "Is this what you mean?" she asked, embarrassed.

"Yes."

"I remember going to pick olives for the Seignior. And there were yellow flowers—I don't know what to call them in French . . ." Her voice lilted on as the wine lulled Adrienne into sleep. She remembered hoping she would not drown.

She awoke in a small, well-appointed room without windows. A demure brown manteau with black ribbons, much as she had worn at Saint Cyr, was laid out on the bed. As she donned it, Gabriella entered, helping her to finish dressing.

"Do I learn why I have been kidnapped now?" she asked.

Gabriella nodded. "This way, milady."

The servant led her down a series of halls, occasionally passing windows through which Adrienne caught glimpses of gardens and rolling countryside, but nothing that really signified where she was. A chateau in the country, any of a thousand such.

She was ushered into a small salon, and there she had reason to bitterly recall Nicolas' observation about her smile. Confronting her captors, who all stood awaiting her, she felt it frozen on her face.

Adrienne dropped a curtsey. "Duchess," she said.

"Oh, well done, Mademoiselle," the duchess of Orléans said. "I would never be so composed after such an ordeal."

"Why have you done this, Duchess?" Adrienne said, her

voice nearly shaking with anger. "What possible use am I to you?"

The duchess of Orléans put her hand to her breast. "My dear, you were abducted, but your kidnappers made the singular mistake of crossing the lands of my brother, the count of Toulouse, whose huntsmen rescued you. Naturally you were brought here, where I happened to be visiting."

"I remember no such a thing," Adrienne said.

The duchess smiled ingratiatingly. "Understandable," she replied, winking. "I have been most rude," she went on. "Let me present my companions, who accompanied me here from Paris: Madame de Castries and Mademoiselle de Crecy."

Adrienne meant to treat the two women with studied indifference, to show no courtesy to her kidnappers. But when Madame de Castries was named, Adrienne blushed and curtsied. It was a name she knew well, a name important to her.

Castries was a tiny, frail woman. Her face was plain; she might have been forty or sixty. In her dark eyes, however, danced sparks of intelligence that only faintly insinuated the intellect Adrienne knew smoldered behind them.

Crecy stood in marked contrast. She was very tall—at least six feet—yet as lovely as a porcelain doll, perhaps twenty-five years in age. Her hair was copper red. Her gray eyes betrayed nothing whatever. Adrienne was powerfully, unaccountably, reminded of Gustavus.

"Now that those pleasantries are behind us," the duchess went on, "shall we take some morning chocolate?"

Adrienne nodded, intent on the equation. She had already solved one part, of course. By the owl on the note, she had known the duchess to be one of the Korai. And of the Korai, Castries was the queen, perhaps the greatest female intellect in France.

The salon was modest. Four chairs clustered around a small card table.

Adrienne hesitated before taking the seat offered her. At Versailles it would be unthinkable for someone of her rank to sit in a chair unless alone; even duchesses usually had to make do with folding stools. Orléans smiled at her reluctance. "Sit dear. Here, for this moment, we are equal."

The chocolate arrived, steaming in ornate cups, and when Gabriella left, she secured the heavy doors.

Then Castries cleared her throat, lifted her cup, and chanted, singsong, *"Chairete, Korai, Athenes therapainai."* It was Greek, meaning *"Hail, Korai, maidens of Athena."*

"Chairete," Adrienne answered with the others, automatically.

"Enthade euthetoumen temeron," Castries went on.

"He glaux, ho drakon, he parthenos," Adrienne finished with the rest. And then, together with Castries, she said, *"What is said here is not repeated."*

Castries smiled and sipped her chocolate. "Now then, Adrienne," she said, "I have heard much of you from our sisters at Saint Cyr. I am pleased to meet you at last."

"And I you, Marquise," Adrienne replied. "Though if I had been asked to come, I would have complied willingly— and without loss of life." She shot what she hoped was an angry glance at the duchess.

The duchess sputtered on her own chocolate. "There has been no loss of life, my dear, I assure you," she insisted, wiping her lips.

"How could you know this for certain?"

The duchess smiled. "The bandits who kidnapped you were questioned. Anyway, Marly has already been contacted; your bodyguard is even now on his way, and you will find that your young guard is intact. But that means our time together, you see, is rather limited."

"Very well," Adrienne replied, "I am listening."

"I take it that you did not realize that the duchess was a member of our sisterhood?" Castries asked.

"I did not," Adrienne confirmed, "until she passed me the symbol of Athena."

"I was not certain you saw it," the duchess said, her brow creasing for the first time, "in the confusion following . . ."

"Madame Duchess," Adrienne said, "whoever was responsible for it, I was kidnapped and manhandled through the night on horseback. I am tired and my skin is bruised, and so you must pardon my candor. The minister, Torcy, suspects that you and the duke might have been responsible for the murder of the dauphin and the attempt upon the king's life. I want to hear from your lips whether this is true or not."

The duchess closed her eyes, and when she opened them they were moist. Her face looked older than her forty-three years. "Despite his flaws, Mademoiselle, the king is my father. And he did what no other king has ever dared to do—he legitimized my brothers and me."

"Yes, which nettles all of France and most especially your husband. It occurs to everyone that with the dauphin dead, the duke of Orléans is next in line, by the law of primogeniture."

"My dear husband has many gifts," the duchess replied, "but ambition is not one of them. He is incapable of the kind of insidious, brilliant plotting of which he has been accused. Regardless, you wanted my vow, not my protestations. I did not plan the massacre you and I were witness to, nor did I know of it. I swear to God, to Jesus, and before all of the sisters of Athena that I and my husband are innocent." She leaned forward, her cup clinking loudly onto the table. "Though should I discover who *was* responsible, he will find that the duchess of Orléans *does* know something about assassinations," she finished savagely.

"Thank you, Madame Duchess. What, then, are we met here to discuss?"

"Why, we are here to discuss *you*, Mademoiselle," Castries answered. "You have recently become a woman of some importance."

"Do you mean the king's interest in me?"

"Among other things," the elder woman said. "First let me confirm that the secret order of Athena has long worked to place a woman in the Academy of Sciences, and you have been placed there. We have also worked to move one near to the king, and *voila*, there you are as well."

"This was your doing?"

"The first—the appointment to the academy—yes, of course. You have Madame Duchess here to thank for that. The second was more providential, but we must make use of it."

"I . . ." Adrienne stumbled. "I do not think I am as close to the king as you may think."

"Oh, no, Mademoiselle," a new voice intruded. "On the contrary, you are much closer than you suspect." Adrienne was startled; despite her striking appearance, the Mademoiselle de Crecy had been so silent that she had faded from notice. But now she had the full attention of everyone.

"What do you mean?" Adrienne asked.

"I mean that you will *marry* him," Crecy said, quite matter-of-factly. "You, Adrienne de Mornay de Montchevreuil, shall be the next queen of France."

18.

Lightning Rod

The shouting of the crowd faded behind him as Ben flew up Treamount and then right onto Beacon Street. Several people hurrying in the other direction stared at him curiously.

"Hey, there, what's on fire?" shouted a man Ben vaguely recognized. Another man he knew—militia captain Samuel Horn—also ran by. Ben wondered if he should seek help. How could Bracewell harm him from jail—or better yet, from the gallows?

But he recalled that horrible eye. He could still see James' eyes, glazed in death, still feel Bracewell's vicelike grip. No, it was leave Boston now or die.

"Leave Boston," he said aloud. Bracewell was going to kill him if he stayed here. Maybe Bracewell would follow him anywhere. And if not Bracewell . . .

He remembered the scrawled note: *I see you.* Bracewell hadn't sent *that*—it had come from France or wherever. And yet, it could not be a coincidence that so soon after the message, Bracewell had reappeared to do murder.

Now he turned right, running across the Common and up around the base of Cotton Hill. Leaving Boston was no easy matter; the town was located on a peninsula connected to the mainland by a narrow isthmus aptly named "the Neck." All Bracewell had to do was wait for him there.

He tried to fix his mind on some plan, separate some strategy out of the whirling images and emotion—something that would save him, bring James back, set everything right. And then it came quite clearly, or part of it anyway: Mr. Dare's boat, which he had used only a few days before, would get him away from

Boston, at least give him time to think. His feet had already turned him in the right direction—around behind the hill, back up along the flats toward Barton's Point.

Behind the hill, the Frenchman's dogs began to bay, howling as they had that morning when he had first been attacked by Bracewell. It was a chilling, angry cry, almost undoglike. In eerie counterpoint, the cry of a whippoorwill warbled from the black tangle of trees ahead, a farewell to the remains of daylight staining the iron gray clouds, a welcome to the moonless night descending. And worst of all came the distinct, if still distant, drumming of hooves.

Running as quickly as he dared, Ben drew James' coat tighter and gripped his device in one hand. His fearful calculations had Bracewell catching him well before he could reach Dare's little quay. Or should he cross the Roxbury Flats, where a horse surely could not follow? In the dark, in the salty marshlands, he might be able to hide.

More likely than not he would drown.

What if he could reach the bluff at West Hill? He changed the course of his flight slightly. Fleeing the city for the wilderness that bordered it suddenly seemed like a stupid idea. But it was too late now. He could only hope that he knew the little-traveled parts of the peninsula better than Bracewell.

Behind him, the dogs bayed louder as, puffing, he ran up the low part of the ridge between Beacon Hill and Cotton Hill. On the top of the ridge, a wind, gathering strength from the endless sea beyond, rushed up to Ben and embraced him. *Flee,* it seemed to urge, *flee.*

A horse whickered. Ben plunged downslope toward the noisome flats, dim puddles of iron stretching to the edge of sight.

Behind him, the hoofbeats grew louder. Ben hit a trough and then was climbing up the lesser slope of West Hill. Glancing back, he saw horse and rider, black against the sky. Flitting orange will-o'-the-wisps described arcs around them.

"Benjamin Franklin!" Bracewell roared.

Ben did not think he could run faster, but he did, charging up the slope. And then he was on the bluff, looking down at the dark nothingness. He hesitated for just an instant too long, lungs burning, feet slipping at the edge of the unseen cliff. He realized stupidly that he still held his device. Lightning struck near, a bright flash and a sound like boards slapping together in his ears. The hair on his nape stood up, and heat blazed close. He shrieked, tripped, fell to his knees, and then all the noises met as the horse pounded to a-halt behind him. Slowly, Ben stood and turned.

Bracewell was watching him, no more than ten paces away. His *kraftpistole*, still glowing red, was pointed at him.

Bracewell chuckled. "Some boys are incorrigible," he said. His eyes glinted beneath the brim of his hat, perhaps catching the glow of the misty phosphorescences flitting about him.

"You killed James," Ben said, surprised to find his voice so strong.

"He would have died anyway, in time," Bracewell said reasonably. "Still, he might have lived out his natural span if he hadn't had the misfortune of being the brother of a boy who doesn't do as he is told."

"I hate you," Ben snarled. "What right have you, to . . . to—"

"To what, Ben? It isn't a matter of rights, you stupid boy, but of *power*. I have the strength to do what must be done, that is all."

"But why? Why?"

"I prefer not to answer that, Ben, for it would be a waste of breath. And then if I told you, I would feel compelled to tell John before I killed him."

"John?" Ben gasped. He had forgotten all about John.

"Of course," Bracewell said, gesturing grandly with the *kraftpistole*. Ben knew his last chance when he saw it. His lantern-like device was already pointed in Bracewell's direction; he raised it and slid the trigger out, a tingle racing up his arm even as he tossed the thing away from him. He closed his eyes and threw himself flat on the ground, but even so he still saw the flash of white flame arcing between the *kraftpistole* and his invention. The horse shrieked.

Ben rolled backward, and space opened up below him as he spun head over foot. He tore through a screen of briars, bounced off the lower slope of the bluff, and then hit something that slammed all of the breath out of him. He tried to draw breath, knowing that he *must* have broken something.

But through the pain he also felt a vicious feeling of triumph. The projector had worked! In his dream Bracewell had carried what Ben guessed to be a *kraftpistole*; if the weapon had been anything else, all of his effort would have been wasted, and he would be lying dead on that bluff. He pulled himself carefully to his feet. Miraculously, a brief inspection seemed to prove nothing was shattered. The smell of burned flesh and hair suddenly reached him.

And then, incredibly, against the faint luminescence of the sky, a lean shape rose up unsteadily.

"Damn you," it gasped distinctly. Bracewell should not be in pain; he should be dead from his weapon's uncontrolled discharge. But Bracewell stood above Ben, and the lean, long claw of his sword snicked from its scabbard.

The bluff was bordered even at high tide by a mucky slope of soil and stones. Ben ran like a mad animal, tripping and falling until his palms were torn, until his knees were battered and bleeding. Before, he had been afraid of death; now he was afraid of something worse, something he could not name. But it stumbled along the ridge behind him, eyes glowing, surrounded by familiar spirits.

The bluff sloped downward, but he seemed to be moving faster than Bracewell. Now the lights of the copper works on Barton's Point made wrinkled footprints of radiance on the Charles River. Halfway to the point was the small quay where he had last left Mr. Dare's boat, just below the man's cottage.

At last Ben reached the boat, beached as he had left it. He fumbled at the rope, cursing the knot and the blood from his hands that slickened it. He could see nothing behind him, but the very darkness felt sharp to him, and he flinched, imagining the long blade sliding into his body.

The rope came loose, and, sobbing, he pushed the boat. It would not move. He stumbled to the stern and began to heave, his feet sucking in and out of the muck.

The boat jolted forward; he redoubled his efforts, and it slid out farther. He kept pulling until he was almost waist deep and felt the keel float free. Splashing around, he threw both arms up over the edge of the boat and tumbled in.

"Who is that down there?" he heard someone shout from up the shore. "Who is that mucking around with my boat?"

Ben glanced up frantically. There was Mr. Dare, a black shadow against the open doorway of his house. In the same instant, Ben saw the pale, flitting lights that accompanied Bracewell.

Words froze in Ben's mouth. There was no time to put up the sail and precious little wind. He grasped one of the oars and fitted it into the lock. The first footstep splashed into the water. Panic took him, and he cried out and began swiping at the water with the single oar.

"Leave my boat alone!" Mr. Dare shouted, as Ben worked frantically to seat the other oar in the lock. The boat suddenly jerked, a pale hand gripping the stern; there, in the darkness, he saw Bracewell's awful eyes. Hardly aware of what he was doing, Ben stood, lifted the free oar, and brought it down on the hand, then swung it again with all of his might and felt it strike Bracewell's head. The man fell away. Ben swung a third time and slapped water, overbalanced, and fell. Only the mast kept him from falling into the bottom of the craft. Breath gurgling in his throat, he locked the oar, sat down, and rowed with all of his strength. As he paddled, he stared frantically back toward shore. Mr. Dare was still shouting from his doorway when something at the water's edge rose to eclipse him.

"Mr. Dare! Flee!" Ben shouted hoarsly, rowing all the harder. He did not slow even when he reached the channel and the current began to carry him along of its own accord. The tide was going out, rushing seaward. Behind him, the lights of Boston—and the dreadful shadows they cast—dwindled.

19.

Dreams of Queens

"Queen?" Adrienne blurted. "That is absurd."

Crecy merely smiled. "You may have heard of our sister, Crecy, and you may not have," Madame de Castries said. "She is one of our secrets. I first met Mademoiselle when she was eight years of age, in 1706. At the time, I was Madame's lady-in-waiting." She indicated the duchess.

"Which was when we became acquainted and I joined the Korai," the duchess put in, casting an admiring glance at Castries.

"Indeed. In that year, the duke, Madame's husband, came home one day with the strangest tale of a little girl who could see into the future."

The duchess interrupted. "My husband is always being fooled by charlatans," she confided. "His interest in both science and the dark arts makes him gullible. He had made the acquaintance of a certain gentleman from Vienna who claimed to see the future in a glass of water." She screwed up her face in distaste. "The duke was at the time having an affair with that whore, La Sery, and they were at her apartment. This magician said he needed an innocent girl to look into the glass." She gestured at Crecy. "Mademoiselle had the poor fortune to be in the charge of the whore at that time."

Castries took the story back up. "The duke had the sense to test the method of the Viennese gentleman. He challenged Demoiselle Crecy to look into the glass and see the nearby apartment of Madame Nancre, and he then sent a man next door to confirm what the little girl had seen—the room's occupants, the position of the furniture, everything. Crecy was correct in all particulars." Castries rubbed her hands absently, as if they pained her. "When this came to my attention, I myself investigated, and quickly discovered that the gentleman from Vienna was indeed a charlatan, but that our dear Crecy here was not. Over the years, her prescience has proven itself infallible. Nine years before the king cheated death by using the Persian elixir, Crecy saw the entire event."

Adrienne had kept her eye on Crecy throughout the strange story, but the young woman betrayed little emotion at this description of her abilities.

"When she was old enough," Castries continued, "she was introduced to our secret order."

Adrienne faced Crecy squarely. "And you have foretold my marriage to the king?"

Crecy nodded. "Yes, Mademoiselle. I have seen the ceremony, seen you standing together before the archbishop. There is no doubt."

"There must be doubt," Adrienne returned furiously. "I might refuse."

Castries stared at her and then grimly shook her head. "You must not refuse, Mademoiselle de Montchevreuil. You must marry the king."

"Why?"

The duchess answered. "Maintenon, as you know, was never one of us," she said. "Indeed, never even knew of us. But my mother, the king's mistress before Maintenon, *was*. When my mother was mistress, the Korai, through her, had his ear—though of course *he* never knew that. Now we do not."

"Is it all so simple?" Adrienne asked. "Is that all that concerns you, having the king's ear? For years I have heard nothing from the Korai, and now you have me kidnapped so that you can tell me I must destroy my life, abandon all that I love, to give you a hand on the throne?"

"You have not heard from us before," Castries retorted, "because this marriage was seen almost two years ago. If there are those who know of the Korai, we did not want them connecting the future queen to us. That is also the reason for your 'abduction.'"

"I would have been subtler, had I the leisure, my dear," the duchess of Orléans interjected. "I had planned a very different meeting. But after the murder of the dauphin and the attempt upon the king's life, it became impossible to approach you without suspicion. And Torcy is suspicious even so, is he not?"

"Torcy knows of my interest in science," Adrienne said, "and that your husband placed me in the Academy of Sciences."

"And what will he do about it?" Castries demanded. "It is not illegal, merely unseemly. Never mind all that," she said. "Know you this, Adrienne; though we did not contact you these past few years, we have done what we could. It was the duchess here who through her husband provided you with your apartments at the king's library and brought you to the notice of Fatio de Duillier."

"So you said," Adrienne retorted weakly, "and yet, you seem to imply that even that was less for me than because you would have me to spy upon him."

"You are being selfish," Crecy said softly in a way that silenced the other women. Adrienne turned once more to regard her remarkable eyes. "There is a blackness descending upon the world, a pall, and you are bound up with it. Do you remember when you first became a Korai, when you were just a girl of nine?"

"I remember," Adrienne retorted. "Did you see that, too?"

Crecy ignored her and went on. "Do you remember our oath? It was not merely an oath to pursue the knowledge our hearts desire, though that was part of it. It was more even than an oath to the other Korai, to help and love our sisters in Athena. There was also a third part, my dear sister. Do you remember what it was?"

Adrienne looked down at her lap. "To *preserve*," she muttered.

"Yes," Crecy agreed. "And yet you seem to remember only the first part of the vow."

"I thought myself abandoned," Adrienne snapped. "I thought I had been excommunicated without ever being told! How could you expect me to hold on to such a vow—" She caught herself. She had not wanted them to see the anger she had nursed for so long.

"And now you know that you were not."

"Now I know only that you need me. You speak of some great darkness, but that means nothing to me. You speak of 'preserving,' yet what am I to preserve?"

"Humanity," Madame de Castries said quite calmly. "Life."

Adrienne found herself at a loss for words for a long, dark moment. "By marrying the king, I preserve humanity?"

"I have not seen it all," Crecy admitted, "only bits and pieces. But that coming darkness comes, to some extent, because *you* opened the door. And you must help to close it."

"This is nonsense," Adrienne blurted. "Excuse me, Madame Marquise, Madame Duchess, but I am a servant of science, of mathematics, and what you speak of here—these are a child's *superstitions,* bogeymen. When did the daughters of Athena lose their faith in science and the masterful God revealed by science and return to the black arts?" She heard her own words, each like a drop of venom flicked from a serpent's fangs. She had found her sisters in Athena, but it seemed her words would quickly drive them away. All humor had drained from the face of the duchess of Orléans, and Castries' features were stone.

Then Castries replied sternly, "You love equations, I know. You trust them. Very well and good. But there are equations in this world so complex that only God can comprehend them, and when we are faced with them, our only tool is intuition. It is my *intuition* that to pass through this darkness, we shall need you at the king's side. Sacrifices must be made," she continued softly. "Marrying the greatest king in the world is not the most painful sacrifice one could render."

Adrienne remembered that being the queen had brought Maintenon misery. Being married to the Sun King was a sentence that Maintenon would not have wished upon any person, despite the fact that she had truly, deeply loved Louis. Adrienne did *not* love Louis.

But Castries was right.

She looked at the waiting women. "I do not know what Fatio is working on, but I shall detail for you what I *do* know, so that perhaps more learned minds than mine may puzzle at it. I believe it is to be some sort of weapon. Is there time for me to write equations for you?"

"I think so," the duchess replied.

"As to the king," Adrienne replied, "if he asks me, I do not see how I can refuse. But I tell you this frankly, my ladies, I will pray every day that he does not ask me."

"You had best pray quickly then," Crecy said, a hint of sorrow in her melodious voice, "for I believe he will ask you tonight."

Adrienne closed her eyes.

"If you can see all of this," Adrienne asked Crecy, "why can't you see what Fatio is working on? Why can't you see what will happen in these dark days you speak of?"

Crecy's lips curled in a vicious smile. "When I was young, I could see what I was asked to see. With each passing year, my mastery grows less certain. It is my curse, now, that I can never see what I want to see. Only what God wishes me to see."

"Or perhaps the devil?" Adrienne returned.

"God or devil," Crecy whispered, "it is always the truth, and it is rarely pleasing."

The carriage from Marly arrived around two hours later, accompanied by thirty of the Hundred Swiss, four pistoleers, and ten mounted carabiners. Adrienne watched them pull into the gates as impassively as she could, concentrating on the details of the entourage so that her gaze would not wander to the pair of corpses laid out in front of the chateau. They were *supposed* to be her kidnappers. One of them was certainly dressed like the man who had threatened her with the *kraftpistole*, but she knew that the body was not his.

At the head of the Hundred Swiss rode Nicolas, his face drawn and doleful. His arm hung in a sling, and he rode unsteadily.

"Milady," he began, as soon as he dismounted, "I can never apologize for allowing your capture." He bowed his head. "I am sorry," he murmured in a tone that wrung her heart. She wondered if he would hate her if he ever discovered that his shame and injury had been incidental details in a grand performance.

"You own no fault in this, sir," she replied loudly so that all could hear. "I would rather that the rogues had murdered me than see such a brave man as you shamed."

"And I would rather have died than that they should have touched you at all," he answered.

Adrienne flashed her smile brightly. "But then who would guard me now, sir?"

He bowed again and escorted her to the carriage, handing his horse to one of the pistoleers.

Once they were both inside, the procession started. Nicolas sat speechless.

"How badly were you hurt?" Adrienne asked after a time.

"I would feel better if I had been hurt more badly." He smiled ruefully. "As it happened, a bullet grazed my shoulder. Then something . . . I don't know. It felt as if all the light were sucked out of my head, and then I knew nothing until I awoke."

"Grazed? Then why do you wear this sling?" Adrienne asked.

"It was the bone that was grazed," Nicolas admitted. He paused. "I hear the king is livid."

"Don't worry, Nicolas, I shall speak for you."

"Lady, I meant only that the king is very worried about you." He looked out the window and said softly, "*Many* were afraid that you might be murdered, or worse."

"Well, I wasn't," Adrienne replied.

The carriage bumped along quietly for a moment, and then Nicolas turned back to her. Something hard and bright glittered in his eyes, something both terrible and wonderful.

"I will only say this, milady," he began, "that if another man lays hand on you without your desiring him to, it will only be because I am dead and God has received me and locked me away so that I cannot throw myself from heaven. I would forsake even salvation to prevent your being accosted again."

"Hush," Adrienne murmured. "Hush, Nicolas." Her gaze locked with his for a long moment, and she felt as if she were falling from a great height.

"You don't understand," he said finally.

"No, Nicolas," she replied. "I think that I do."

It was quite dark when they reached Marly. Adrienne was told that she would be received at the king's bedside before sleep.

Despite his best efforts, Nicolas had fallen asleep in the carriage. Another guard told her later that he had neither slept nor eaten since her abduction.

On the way to the royal chambers she and her escort passed through the great gallery of Marly. She found it carpeted with courtiers, mostly sitting or lying on the floor playing cards. Louis had built Marly for comfort and privacy. And yet Louis could not go anywhere without courtiers. It was as if he did not exist without them.

When the courtiers saw her there was a scattering of congratulations for her "narrow escape." Many of the faces belied the well-wishing, and she realized with a chill that all were now watching her, wondering about her, constructing their schemes around her.

"Thank you," she said, curtseying. "Though I must thank the count of Toulouse and his huntsmen, or I should not stand before you now."

She curtsied again and allowed her escort to take her on to the *coucher*.

Louis lay in bed clothed in a magnificent dressing gown, the covers pulled back to his waist. "My dear Mademoiselle de Montchevreuil," he said, his voice quite strong and clear. "It is so very good to see you alive and well. God will damn me for ever having risked you so. I beg your most humble forgiveness."

"I— You need no forgiveness from me, Your Majesty, for you have not wronged me. And God and your son Toulouse and the guardsmen of your Hundred Swiss have all conspired to keep my body and soul together."

"You were not hurt? They did not harm you in *any* way?"

"In no way other than delaying my arrival at Marly, Majesty," she replied.

"Ah, my dear Adrienne," Louis said. "I am a man and king of all France, and yet you possess more gallantry than I do. It is not meet.

"Sit here," he said, indicating a small stool beside the bed. "I realize that you are tired, but I have something to say to you, something that a few short hours ago I feared I might never be able to say."

"Majesty?"

"So much has gone from my life, Adrienne, so many years since the grand, beautiful days. I thought to return to that, and in some ways I think we must. France must see me as I was, so that France can be what *it* was. Do you understand?"

"I understand, Sire," she replied.

"And yet, I am *not* what I was. Adrienne, I am *better* than what I was then; Maintenon taught me to be better. And though she began as my mistress, she taught me the folly of mistresses." He frowned. "You see, not long ago, I believed that I was about to take a new mistress. I meant to propose this to *you*, Adrienne."

"Me, Sire?"

"Yes, Adrienne. You are so like my Maintenon." He sat up straighter in bed. "You see how I have changed since they killed my dauphin? The fire meant to kill me only awakened the full potency of the Persian elixir. Now that my sight has returned, you see how I have become young again?"

Adrienne felt a sweat form on her brow. The king looked no different than he had when last she had seen him, save that his eyes did not focus. What did he mean?

When she did not answer, he took her hand and patted it. "It is shocking, I'll admit. Though I have felt much younger for many years, I never thought to see again the body and face I had when I was twenty, and yet here it is! This is an age for miracles. And with these new eyes, Adrienne, I see you not as merely another Maintenon. You have a grace and a beauty about you, and you always smile. It would please me, the court, and France, if you would consent to marry me and be my queen. And, as queen, give France a new dauphin."

Adrienne knew that there were tears coursing down her face, but there was nothing she could do about them. She did manage to let no sound escape her. Across the room, Bontemps looked away, his face almost brutalized by sympathy, though whether for her or for the king she could not say.

If Louis noticed her tears, he did not say so, but continued to stare past her, an expectant look on his face. She waited until she was absolutely certain that she could speak without her voice breaking. "Of course, my king," she said. "How could I ever say otherwise?"

But at least, now she was in the eye of the storm.

20.

Teach

Dawn came with no land in sight. Ben rubbed eyes gritty with fatigue but even in full and brilliant morning he saw only the edges of a flat blue plate with him in the center.

The battering of the previous day had sunken cold stones of pain into his muscle and bone. His brain was in worse shape than his body. He had not slept; shock and terror had played themselves over and over in his mind. He could still see them enacting their parts, but he had no tears left to cry, no more prayers.

The endless expanse of sea around him was a wonderful sight. Bracewell could not sneak up on him here—he would be able to see the fiend coming for him for miles. He might not be able to stop him, but at least death would not find him unaware.

It felt to Ben as if he had a hole in his heart, for he couldn't believe James was dead. It made no sense to him: He could *remember* James talking, laughing, scowling. James was *real*, had been real all Ben's life. This nightmare with Bracewell seemed a phantasm. The last few months were the lie, the illusion. James was *real*, and that had to mean *alive*.

But morning made him understand most sharply that he had to return to Boston immediately. James was dead. But what if Bracewell went after his father and mother? What of John Collins? Ben had been the very worst sort of coward, because Bracewell had even *told* him that he would kill John; and he had run anyway to save his own miserable life. He *had* to go back. He rose stiffly and put up the sail.

With no compass and no land in sight, he had not the faintest idea where to point his prow. Probably most directions would take him to land. If he sailed south, he would likely hit Cape Cod. If he sailed west, there would be land. Only eastward was there danger of becoming lost . . .

He knew which way east was! It was a wonder how stupid one could be after a night—two nights, really—without sleep. He went to work setting the sail.

He sat back impatiently, watching for land, noting absently the spangles of sun on the water, the growing warmth of the day, and the gentle rocking of the boat. *How had Bracewell survived?* he wondered. *Kraftpistoles* released a controlled eruption of lux and phlegm, producing a flame much like lightning. His device had been designed to trigger the lux in the metal of the gun to release all at once, randomly rather than directionally. For Bracewell, it should have been like being struck by lightning or worse.

The light on the water seemed to form a pattern. Ben frowned, trying to decipher the heliographic message, blinking often from the glare, each blink longer than the last.

When Ben awoke, it was dark, and thunder stuttered in the distance. Cursing, he sat up, his mind fuzzy. The last he remembered were his eyelids lying like stones, the sun heating them red-hot.

The thunder sounded again, a long stream of concussions echoing across the water. Ben sucked in a few quick breaths, trying to clear his head. He had never managed a boat in a storm, and this craft was not likely to stand a squall even in experienced hands. But a quick survey of the sky showed him stars, bright and clear, and no hint of clouds. But suddenly, off to port, he saw a dozen pinpricks of red light.

And then, a moment later, the rumbling sounded once more, and he understood he had been awakened by cannon fire. Out there in the night, two titans were warring. He saw a jagged slash of light that must be a *kraftpistole* or similar weapon and he watched, fascinated, for at least an hour, trying to imagine the fight. Were they warships of England and France, or were they pirates?

It was only slowly that a chill penetrated his fascination.

Where was he? How long had he slept? What if he had slept for
two days instead of one? He had no way of knowing. His mouth
was dry, and his stomach felt like an empty bag. It *could* have
been two days. Surely Bracewell had either died or killed John
by now. Surely to continue on to Boston was a fool's errand.

But he had to know. He had to return.

He took down the sail, for the night, and shortly after that, the
flame and thunder of the distant battle died down, leaving Ben
alone with his remorse.

A few hours later, daylight brought him considerably more hope,
for land was in sight, probably the cape. He would be able to
find his bearing and work back up the coast to Boston in a day or
so. He raised his sail and began his first tack shoreward.

He had covered only half the distance when the boat thunked
hollowly into something. Ben peered over the bow, and he saw
a halfsubmerged barrel bumping along. The hope of land had
distracted him, he realized, and now he scrutinized the sea.

Flotsam was scattered widely in all directions.

He concluded that one of the ships he had heard warring the
night before must have met its end, for some of the wreckage
seemed to be spars and boards.

When he came nearer to the shore, he saw at least three man
shapes, lying beached among part of a mast and other items he
could not recognize. What if they were alive?

He could hear his father's voice in his heart once more, and
he knew what his father would do. Besides, there might be food
and fresh water and some clue to what ship this had been.

So he put the boat ashore.

The first man was certainly dead: he lay supine, half his face
gone, crabs picking at what remained. These men must all be
dead or they would have made some sign by now. But then he
thought he heard a shout, and he turned to scan the beach.

He saw an arm waving. The arm was attached to a man.

"Hey there!" the man called, weakly. "Boy!"

Ben staggered toward him as quickly as he could.

"Sure it is that God must have sent you," the man said when

Ben drew nearer, "for without you I was surely doomed to die here."

Ben stopped cold in his tracks.

The man—sitting propped against a stone—was enormous, probably the biggest man Ben had ever seen. His shoulders seemed a yard across, and standing he would tower above six feet tall. He probably could not stand, however, for one leg was tied with a rag stained bright red with fresh blood. His black hair hung matted down to the shoulders of his stained white shirt, and his beard—twisted into a dozen or so black-ribboned braids—lay wetly upon his thick chest.

"Have a seat, boy, and tell me your name." He gestured toward a second rock with the pistol gripped in one massive hand. "Or shall I tell you mine first?"

"I know you," Ben said. "Edward Teach. Blackbeard." He began to back away.

"Well, good, so I'm not unknown in these parts. So sit and tell me *your* name. Be a polite lad."

"I think your powder is wet," Ben said quietly.

Blackbeard stopped smiling, and Ben met his gaze. Ben saw his death there, same as he had with Bracewell, but whereas Bracewell had killed James the way one might a flea, Blackbeard's eyes promised something more slow and painful. *From ice to fire,* Ben thought.

"Listen, boy," the pirate said very deliberately. "It may well be that my powder is wet, but it may be that it isn't. Cartridges are waxed, you know, just for this sort of occasion. In any event, let me tell you what will occur here if you do not heed my words this instant. I will pull this trigger. If the pistol does not fire, I will draw my cutlass." He patted the massive sword that lay beside him. "It'll be exceeding painful for me to walk on this leg, but catch you I will, and then I will cut off first your ears, then your feet, and so on. Is that clear?"

Ben wondered if the pirate could make good his threat. It seemed possible. Blackbeard was famous for such feats.

"What do you want?" Ben asked, his voice flat.

"Your name for starters," Teach answered. "And for you to sit."

"I'll sit out of reach of your cutlass, if you don't mind," Ben said. "And my name is Benjamin Franklin."

Blackbeard nodded. "Just sit so as I can see you. You are a cool one for your age, Ben."

"Two days ago my brother was killed. The same man did his level best to kill me. I've been lost at sea, and now I've met the pirate Blackbeard," Ben said. "Just what do you want me to do, sing you an opera?"

Blackbeard blinked at him, then he began to laugh, a coarse snuffling sound that quickly became the roar of a giant.

"Where are you from, Benjamin?" Teach asked finally.

"Boston."

"Ben Franklin from Boston. Ben Frank . . ." He raised his eyes, a hint of incredulity in them. "One of my biographers! I'll be damned."

"I'm sure you will," Ben agreed, reflecting that the single thing he had ever signed his name to should come back thus to haunt him.

Blackbeard laughed again. "Damned fine," he said. "Damned fine." He sat up a little straighter. "Now look, Benjamin, I've taken a liking to you, so I'll tell you how we can help each other. Where is it you want to go?"

"Back to Boston."

"Boston. And you say some fellow is trying to kill you back there?"

"Yes."

"Over what, your smart mouth?"

"That isn't funny," Ben snarled. "He killed my brother. That might not mean a whole lot to the likes of Edward Teach, but it does to me."

"That's the smart mouth I'm talking about," Teach said. "I want you to mind it. Now."

"The hell with you."

The hammer on the pirate's gun snapped down. The flint sparked, and the powder in the pan hissed. That was all.

"Damn. *God*damn," Teach snarled, flinging the pistol at him.

"I told you it was wet," Ben said.

Teach had three holsters strapped across his chest. Two were empty, but he drew a gun from the third. "Let's try that again."

"Wait," Ben said. "Wait. I apologize."

"Apologize to Satan," Teach snapped.

"I just did."

Blackbeard cocked the pistol, eyes smoldering, but then he chuckled. "What do you want, boy?"

"You said we could help each other."

"I did."

"How?"

"I want your boat, and I'm willing to pay you for it, so long as you help me board her."

"You'll slit my throat," Ben said.

"No, I give you my word."

"Well, then you'll break my neck," Ben shot back. "Either way, I'll be dead."

"You seem in a hurry to die," Blackbeard growled, "rushing back to Boston to someone who tried to murder you. What good do you think you can do there?"

"He means to kill a friend of mine."

"Your friend is already dead, if that's the case," Blackbeard said. "Once the officials start looking for who killed your brother, your killer has only a short time. Boston isn't big enough to hide in. He'd finish his business and clear out."

"That's what *you* would do," Ben retorted.

"Lad, I'm not often given to advising the young. But if you come through meeting me still alive—if you can keep me from cutting out that insolent tongue of yours—then you're best advised to pursue some other business, because you will have used up all your luck for ten years. It sounds like your brother has tangled you up in something mean—"

"No. It was I who tangled *him*."

"Well, even worse. If you are the quarry, maybe this fellow would rather chase you than stay to kill your friend. In which case you should lead him far, far away. Now, I'm the fellow can do that for you, see. I can be the man who cuts short this fellow's work, or I can be the one who sets you free of him. Now just tell me which, but don't dither anymore."

Ben looked at the sea. "If I sell you my boat, how will I get anywhere?"

"I'll tell you that, too."

"How much for the boat?"

"Two hundred English pounds."

Ben stared at him. "I don't believe you."

"That fee includes you loading the boat with any provisions—including water—that have washed up here, and it includes you carrying me down to the boat."

"No," Ben said, and then, firmly, "No, *sir*. I'll sell you the boat, and I'll load the provisions. Then I'll cut you a crutch so you can get to the boat. More than that I won't do."

"Agreed. Load up my boat and I'll tell you where to get the money."

"And where to go from here."

"And where to go," Blackbeard replied.

It didn't take very long to load everything useful on the beach into the boat. The heaviest was a half cask of rum, of which Blackbeard demanded a cup the instant Ben found it. He found some ship's provisions. Besides that, there were two crates the pirate insisted on taking with him.

When all was loaded, Ben edged cautiously back toward Teach. The pirate regarded him for a long moment but didn't raise his pistol. "My crutch," he said.

"My money," Ben replied.

The pirate reached into the ample pockets of his gray coat. He withdrew a sack and tossed it at Ben's feet. It jingled. "There, damn you," Teach said.

Ben counted the sterling on the way to the forest edge. It came to just two hundred pounds. Using a jackknife Teach had given him he laboriously cut a sapling with a forked crotch and trimmed it into a rude crutch. He threw it to Blackbeard from fifteen yards away.

"There," he shouted.

Blackbeard nodded, raised his pistol, and pulled the trigger. There was an enormous explosion and a plume of black smoke puffed toward Ben like dragon's breath.

"Double damn!" Blackbeard snarled, as Ben felt his chest and found no wound. "One day they'll make a pistol as can *hit* something."

"The hell with you, Edward Teach!" Ben snapped.

"Don't take it personal, boy." With that, Blackbeard lurched up, with the help of the crutch, and began hopping toward the boat. When the pirate reached the little craft, he turned to shout back at Ben. "Wait till I'm out of sight, then light a fire. If you do it while I'm still in sight, I'll come back and kill you, I swear it."

It seemed possible. He had moved more nimbly on his crutch than Ben had guessed he would.

Watching the sail grow smaller, Ben hoped that the hole he had made in the boat would be slow to show itself. He had stuffed it tight with a plug of hard bread; it wouldn't let water in until the bread had dissolved.

When he couldn't see the sail anymore, he did as Blackbeard had suggested and built a fire with the remaining wood and some deadfall from the forest. He lit it using now-dry powder from the flintlock Blackbeard had flung down. After the fire was going steadily, he watched from the shelter of a large elm, ready to hide deeper in the woods.

Near sundown, he saw the sails of an approaching frigate flying the King's Jack.

"That was clever thinking, I'll be bound," Captain Caldwell told him.

"I saw the battle the night before," Ben explained.

"That was the *Champion*," Caldwell said. "She went down with all hands. We lost them both in the dark and came too late to help." He gritted his teeth. "We'll get Teach, though. Come hell or the deep blue sea, we'll get him."

Ben nodded tiredly.

"Boston lad, eh?" the captain went on. "How do I know you aren't a pirate yourself?" Then he laughed at Ben's expression. Ben found he was quickly tiring of the laughter of seamen. "Never fear, lad," the captain went on. "You don't have the look, the clothes—in short, I believe you. But if you have any idea where Teach was headed . . ."

Ben shrugged. "I hulled his boat, but he may have been able to fix that. He certainly didn't tell me where he was headed."

"No, I shouldn't think he would. Smart thinking, to sabotage his craft. Should make it easier to find him."

"Pardon me, sir," Ben said. "But where will you put in to port next?"

"After we find Teach? Then it's Philadelphia."

"Philadelphia? Not Boston?"

"No, lad, I'm sorry. But you can book passage to Boston easily enough. I can probably find a captain as will do it for free."

"I don't know," Ben said, swallowing hard. "I was leaving Boston anyway. I was headed to Philadelphia to see my uncle and then to England."

"Good lad," Caldwell said. "I may be able to help you there, too."

Four days later, there was still no sign of Blackbeard, and the *Hornbeam* reluctantly put in to Philadelphia. Two days after that, Ben was on a ship bound for England. He did his best to keep thoughts of John Collins, his mother, and his father from his mind. In Boston the best thing he could do was die. In London he could find out what he and John had done to call up the wrath of hell, and maybe he could solve whatever problems the two of them had created.

And though he no longer believed in a God who answers prayers, he still prayed for God to keep his friends and family safe—and he prayed for James, wherever he might be, to forgive him.

Part Two

THE CANNON

1.

City of Science

"There they are, Ben," Robert Nairne observed, thrusting his index finger toward the horizon. "The white cliffs! England at last!"

Ben nodded eagerly and drew in a deep breath, certain that he detected the faint scent of land. Their good ship the *Berkshire* now drew her wake through the straits of Dover, nearing the mouth of the Thames. More ominous was the green line of France in the east, though Ben supposed what he saw was Calais, in British hands at the moment. Unless he *had* inadvertently furnished the French with some new weapon, one which, during his three-month voyage, had allowed them to push Marlborough's troops into the sea. But since the *Berkshire* was equipped with an aetherschreiber and the captain had kept them apprised of most news, he imagined he would have learned of a new French offensive.

"I'd be in love with any land I saw right now," Ben said. "And happy with any sod beneath my feet."

"Let's hear you repeat that in a week," Robert said, shaking back his thick auburn hair. His changeable eyes were green with the sea, or perhaps with the emerald fields peeping over the chalky cliffs. "Three years I've been away this time. I once said I would never miss England, but I repent it all. There's some wonderful wild places on the Earth, Ben, but there's no coast in India nor the South Seas nor the Caribbean as can compare."

Ben shrugged. It was hard not to envy Robert's travels, but at the moment the thought of another ocean voyage did not provoke any excitement in him. For between the destinations there was only the monotonous, endless sea. *Everything* on a long voyage wore out—the wonders of porpoises and flying fish, the novelty of travel. People said the same things over and over again. Fortunately, one of those people had been Robert. The son of a military man, Robert was now, at twenty-one, something of an adventurer, and he had many interesting stories to tell—some probably even true. They had begun swapping pirate stories after Robert had learned of Ben's encounter with Blackbeard, and they had quickly discovered they had many interests in common. Though his scientific book learning was scanty, Robert had a quick grasp of new ideas. Their long days of discussing what could be had kept Ben from dwelling on what had been.

"I've a mind just where we might stay," Robert went on.

"We?"

"Well, certain, if y'd like. I had no mind t' turn you loose in London alone!"

"I'd be happy of a guide and a friend in London," Ben said quickly. "I hear 'tis something bigger than Boston."

"Something bigger? Oh, yes," Robert replied. "London! The best food, the finest entertainments, the sweetest little whores in all the world."

Ben's ears burned a bit. "Well, I've more to do than that sort of thing."

"Oh, but o' course, my young philosopher. You'll be seekin' out those scientific men and whatnot. But I'll wager I can find some time to help y' learn the finer sorts of pleasures."

Ben blushed furiously, both angry and embarrassed.

Robert patted him on the shoulder. "Don't let me devil you, Ben. I just do it for the joy it gives me. But I do mean to show y' London."

"I'll be grateful for it," Ben assured him.

The breeze freshened; a few of the sailors cheered hoarsely, which Ben took for a good sign. By afternoon they had put into the mouth of the Thames. Ben and Robert watched the sun set against land for the first time in more than eighty days.

By dawn, they could make out the gray, bunched houses of Gravesend and the impressive fortress of Tilbury.

The banks of the Thames were verdant, adorned with picturesque villages and fields. Most of the stone buildings in Boston were no older than himself, and he had believed the new church to be grand. Yet in the first two hours that morning he saw two manors thrice as imposing as even the Faneuil mansion back home. And this was the *countryside*. What would London be like?

He had always thought that James had exaggerated the provincial nature of Boston, but Ben began to fear just the opposite. He was suddenly grateful that he had met Robert.

He realized his fingers were fidgeting, as if impatiently awaiting the chance to open a present. No trepidation could overshadow the waxing excitement in his breast.

They had to drop anchor nearly a league from London, as it turned out, when the tide receded. Ben's fidgeting increased five-fold, for even from there, the London skyline was visible, and it was unbelievable indeed. It compassed the whole of the northern and eastern horizon, its buildings so legion that Ben could sort little sense into them. Only the church steeples gave him any notion of scale, thrusting into the lavender dusk like the sharp silhouettes of twenty or more fingers pointing the way to God. Twenty gesturing preachers in a crowd of thousands, packed shoulder to shoulder.

Among these giants stood a titan, the majestic domed profile that Robert identified as Saint Paul's Cathedral. Closer by, the right bank of the Thames was betowered by the hulking shadows of windmills; five of the monstrous engines were in sight, their great wheels creaking in the evening breeze.

When night fell, it did not fall uniformly. The sky north of them glowed. It was unnatural, in its own way the strangest thing Ben had ever seen, including the sorceries of Bracewell.

A thought came to him then: This invasion of light was what Bracewell sought to prevent. Perhaps he feared that every town would become as London, banishing night's dark mantle and perhaps robbing darker things than night of *their* strength as well.

"Amazin', i'nit?" Robert said from the nearby rail. "Even a few years ago, when I was a boy, 'tweren't as much light as this." He looked speculatively at Ben. "Let's you and me take a boat and row up to the city. We can be there in under two hours."

"Steal?" Ben replied, raising his fist to his chest as if horrified. "Heavens, no. We could just *borrow* one, though . . ."

Behind them, the lights of the *Berkshire* were lost among those of the thousand or so other boats. This near the city, the river itself was a town. Merchantmen and frigates were its churches, masts thrusting up like steeples. Steam barges and pleasure craft were its gaily adorned missions; houseboats and smallboats the common dwellings. As they moved through this floating village toward the greater brightness of the city, conversations waxed and waned around them, snatches of Dutch, French, Spanish, and languages that Ben could not even begin to guess at.

"What'll we tell 'em when we land at the Tower?" Ben asked Robert as he pulled on the oars.

"That'll be no problem. They'll just assume we got permission to come ashore. By the time anyone tells 'em different, you and I will be to Fleet Street. And after all, there's no harm done; the cap'n'll get his boat back from the Tower—it has the *Berkshire* written on it, plain as day."

"Good enough," Ben replied.

At about an hour before midnight Benjamin Franklin first set foot in the City of Science. Above him loomed the Tower of London—castle, prison, mint—an ancient medieval edifice resplendent with alchemical lanterns.

Beyond was an endless sea of stone and light, a million-strong tide of humanity, that Ben had to navigate to a single man: Sir Isaac Newton.

2.

Menagerie

The beast slammed into the bars with such force that they screeched in their sockets. Fatio gave a little gasp and hopped back, but the king stood impassively, watching the huge animal.

"It looks like a cow," Louis complained.

It did *not* look like a cow to Adrienne. No cow Adrienne had ever seen possessed shaggy fur and a mountainous hump of muscle above its shoulders, nor stood near five feet *at* the shoulder. And no cow expressed such utter rage at its captivity as to shatter its horns against adamantium bars.

"What is it called, Sire?" Fatio asked.

"A boeuf-a-l'eau," Louis replied, disappointment still edging his voice. "I am told they are quite dangerous." He turned his still blind-seeming eyes toward them and shrugged. "But to me it looks like a cow."

Louis gestured them on. "Come and see my lion. I acquired it some years ago, and *it* at least, is quite impressive."

The lion, actually, was rather old and bony. The wildness in its eyes had dimmed to a memory. In a horrible way, the lion reminded Adrienne of Maintenon in her last days.

How long before *she* reached that state? What did the king see when he looked at *her*? That anomalous vision that perceived a cow in a raging monster and a rampant lion in this shrunken kitten—what did it see in *her*? Whatever he looked at, whomever he was making love to, it was not her.

Her throat tightened, but she was nearly past the grief of her lost virginity. She might have resisted the king longer, she knew, but why delay the inevitable? Why risk his displeasure?

191

Madame de Maintenon had taught her that one should not expect too much from the carnal act. And yet she had hoped that Maintenon was wrong. She hoped when Louis came to her—for he had once been a famous lover—that she might gain something to compensate for what she lost.

But Louis was old and fat, and she had discovered no undreamed-of ecstasy but only a form of revulsion that she had never known.

She tried to comfort herself that she was serving a higher purpose, but in her honest moments she knew that was not why she was marrying the king. She did not believe in the prophecies of Crecy, or in the Korai—for they saw her only as an instrument. No, she had taken Torcy at his word: she became queen because she feared being a pawn more.

"Come, my dear," Louis said, "these are mere samples of what you shall see in the menagerie proper." The king, Fatio, and the rest of the retinue had moved on. She joined them and caught Nicolas watching her, an expression of concern upon his face. She flashed him a wide smile.

I should ask the king for a different guard, she thought, for perhaps the hundredth time. But three months ago she had begged Louis to retain Nicolas, despite his failure to prevent her abduction. He had been in a generous mood after her acceptance of his marriage proposal and so had agreed. She was selfish to keep him near, but it would be harder to send him away.

"Well, de Duillier," the king said as they walked along to the next beast, "may I plan my wedding now?"

"Indeed, Majesty," Fatio replied, his voice bubbly. "The completion of our project can be named to the day."

Louis nodded, his face nearly as radiant as the Apollo he thought himself to be. "This is wonderful news, my good fellow. Please pass on my compliments to your staff." He paused to glance at Adrienne. "And accept my apologies for stealing away its loveliest member."

"You rescued her only from dreariness, Sire," Fatio said.

They finished their tour of the menagerie at the Triannon Palace and then returned to Versailles on foot. On the way, Fatio made the mistake of venturing a few questions about the war against England and her allies, which the king dismissed brusquely, despite his obvious good cheer. Back at Versailles, Louis kissed Adrienne, sent her back to her rooms, and then swept Fatio along to a closed meeting with his ministers.

Her suite had become her sanctuary. Not for her body, of course—the ornate doors could not protect her from the King's lechery—but for her mind. Alone there, she could take pen and ink and contemplate the hidden places in her soul where the king could never go—and conceal the written evidence of her explorations with comparative ease.

That evening, however, she found little comfort as she pored over the results of three months' work. Her attempts to discern the purpose of Fatio's project had not met with complete success, so she had diverted herself with her own speculations. She designed a craft for flying to the moon and painstakingly calculated its trajectory, then recalculated voyages to Jupiter and Saturn. Improving upon Janus' formula, she outlined the basics of a "universal" aetherschreiber that would carry the voice and image of its operator. Other, less pertinent theoretical explorations had yielded a mirror that could "remember" what it reflected for an indefinite time and other, sillier things. But she could neither perform experiments to bear out her calculations nor publish her hypotheses. The only positive result she could perceive from her efforts was her certainty that Fatio was not laboring at any of *these* projects. "Newton's own cannon," he'd said. What could that mean?

If only she had her copy of the *Principia* she might be able to find a clue.

So she sat, considering burning her calculations when she heard a scratch at the door. Sighing, she hid her papers in Maintenon's old secret drawer and called out, "Come in."

She found herself confronting the tall form of Crecy.

"Hello, Mademoiselle," Crecy said. "We have not met. My name is Veronique de Crecy. I am to be your lady-in-waiting."

"What?" she demanded. Why was this woman pretending not to know her?

And then she realized a guard stood no more than twenty

paces away. When the tale of her abduction and "rescue" had been told by the duchess, Crecy must have been left out of it.

"May I come in?"

Once the door was closed, Crecy favored her with a small smile. "You understand, of course."

"Of course. My lady-in-waiting? How did you manage this?"

"I did *not* manage it. Madame de Castries did and at some risk. It was, however, thought to be best."

"And why would anyone think that? I have no love for you, Mademoiselle. It was your prophecy—and the unbelievable superstition of our sisterhood—that placed me in these straits."

An opalescent fire flickered in Crecy's smoky eyes. "Surely you don't believe that. Certainly you do not think Castries is superstitious."

Adrienne slumped into a chair. She pointedly did not invite the redhead to sit, but to her annoyance Crecy did so anyway.

"She has shown me no formula to explain your supposed prophetic powers. She has offered me no proof or principle. She demands that I accept you on faith, when only God should be accepted so!"

"And yet you do."

"No, Mademoiselle, I do *not*. I have done what Castries asked of me, only because I have no one. Because I could think of nothing better to do."

"And that is why I am here," Crecy said, her tone softer, less imperious. "Look, I have brought you something."

Adrienne reluctantly accepted the package Crecy bore, but once the wrapping was removed, she could not repress her delight.

"The revised *Principia Mathematica*," she gasped. "And the *Corrections of Planetary Motions*."

"I knew that you would have a difficult time obtaining such books," Crecy explained. "I will bring you new volumes whenever possible. The Korai have opened their libraries to you."

"Mademoiselle . . . thank you," she finished woodenly.

After a moment Crecy spoke again, almost shyly. "I have always admired your work, you know," she said. "Even your first paper, 'On the Likelihood of a Seventh Planet,' displayed a rare sort of genius. How old were you when you wrote that?"

"Fifteen," Adrienne murmured. "I had to compose it at night, in secret. One of the other girls informed on me, and the matrons thought I must be writing love letters."

"What happened?"

"Nothing. One of the Blacks was a Korai, and she warned me. That night I stayed up writing, but they found me copying devotions. In fact, it was that 'piety' that first brought me to the attention of Madame de Maintenon."

"This Black—she was the one who introduced you to the order?"

Adrienne nodded. "Yes." She frowned. "Now she pretends not to know me."

Crecy knelt before Adrienne and took her hand. "I am sorry, Mademoiselle, for your pain. I am here now to try and make amends. I realize that you do not trust my prophecies. But I beg you to forget that and let me be your friend, your confidante. I can deliver your letters—past Torcy—publish your works in the inner circle, bring you scientific correspondence. I can be your link to the Korai, Mademoiselle, if you will only let us back into your heart and life." She squeezed Adrienne's hand and lowered her head.

"It is not so simple," Adrienne said, inexplicably blushing. "I trusted the Korai as I never trusted anyone. I trusted my mentor at Saint Cyr. I thought she loved me, and yet at a word from Castries, that love evaporated."

Crecy rose, her expression enigmatic. "Your friend was a weakling, then," she said. "For it is not in the power of anyone to command love."

"I think perhaps I am near to going mad with no friend in the palace. But someone cannot merely proclaim herself my friend," she said, in a voice so cold it surprised her. "She must prove herself."

"Perhaps that is why you have no one," Crecy remarked. "But I understand you. In the meantime—as you come to realize that I *am* your friend—I can do things for you. I have spoken to your guard—"

"Nicolas?"

"Oh, *Nicolas* is it?"

"It is just an arrangement we have," Adrienne explained, "to call each other by our Christian names. No one does that in Versailles."

Crecy shrugged. "So I think you *do* have at least one friend here. But it is not so much the guard himself who concerns me as what he tells me about you: That you do nothing but mope about your rooms and wait for the king to call or come to you."

"What else is there?" Adrienne snapped. "I have my work still. I have been trying to determine what de Duillier is up to."

Crecy shrugged. "You have the whole of France at your feet. Make the most of it."

Adrienne frowned. "I don't know what you mean."

Crecy's smile suddenly had something of the cat about it. "Then you *do* need my counsel, Mademoiselle. I can help you find out what secret experiment Fatio de Duillier is engaged in," Crecy said, her eyes dancing with mischief. "Listen to me, and in two days' time we shall know all."

"Through your sorcery?" Adrienne asked sarcastically, unwilling to admit how intrigued she was by the offer.

"Not mine alone," she replied, strolling toward the window, blinking against the sunlight. "No, we shall need a bit of *your* sorcery, too, Mademoiselle." She turned back. For an instant, Adrienne thought a small red spark flashed in her eyes.

"Tell me more," Adrienne said.

3.

Coffeehouse

"Will y' be needin' more coffee, sir?" a young woman asked. Ben looked up from his paper into a wide, warm pair of brown eyes and honey yellow hair. If he allowed his eyes to stray again he would notice her dangerously low-cut bodice, the spray of freckles below her throat. He concentrated instead on her smile, which seemed lavish considering that she was only offering to refill his coffee bowl.

"Um . . . yes, please," he said.

"I've not seen y' in here before," she murmured, tipping the pot so that its aromatic contents gurgled into his empty cup.

"I've never been here," he admitted. "I'm waiting for a friend of mine."

"A *him*?" she mused. Ben glanced up at her, startled.

"Um, yes," he replied stupidly.

"Y' know," she said, confidentially, "I pride myself on bein' capable of placin' a man's home by his speech. Those that's from Islington talks in one way, them from Cotswald another. But *your* tongue baffles me. You *are* an Englishman, and yet . . ."

"I'm . . . I'm from the Colonies," Ben explained, wondering exactly what he had done to draw her attention and hoping he could do more of it. Around him, the clinking of china, the low mutter of men discussing politics or reading their papers aloud to one another receded. The air—fragrant with smoke from half a dozen long-stemmed pipes and the fire in the poorly vented hearth—suddenly seemed rather rarefied.

"The Colonies!" she exclaimed. "Are they's full of wild Indians as they say?"

197

This had gone beyond passing comment, Ben realized. This young woman actually *wanted* to talk to him.

"You see Indians in Boston now and then," he replied. "And those as ally with the French are wild enough, I suppose." He sipped the coffee and wondered where Robert was; he was very late.

"I see," she said. "And what brings such a likely lad across the deep to the city, 'f I may ask?"

How would Robert reply to that? How would he fan this little flame of interest? "I . . . well, I can't say," he managed at last. "It's a secret sort of thing."

"More an' more fascinatin'," she said. "Mr. . . . ?"

"Oh!" Ben stood so quickly he nearly upset his coffee. "My apologies. My name is Benjamin Franklin." He gave an awkward little bow.

She curtsied, giving him a good view of her abundant assets. "Sarah Elizabeth Chant at y'r service."

Ben felt his face glowing as brightly as a beacon, but he reached for her hand in an attempt to be gallant. When she saw that he meant to kiss it, however, she gently disengaged.

"Sir," she protested, her eyes dancing merrily, " 'tis clear that y've not been in London fer very long, or y' would know how t' greet a lady." And with that she took a single step, and planted a warm, quick kiss on his lips that sent a rush of sparks dancing down his chest. Then she winked at him, picked up the silver decanter, and moved on.

Ben quickly sat back on his bench, staring furiously at his copy of the *Mercury*—unable to read a single word.

Of course, he *did* know by now that kissing on the lips was as common as a handshake in London. He had always supposed that it would be pleasant to kiss a woman, but the reality was powerfully better than imagining.

Which was why, he mused, experimental philosophy was superior to mere conceptual philosophy. Actually *doing* something almost always produced unexpected results.

In this case, the result was that he could not bring himself to think of a single other thing than Sarah Elizabeth Chant without *intense* effort.

Which was too bad, because he had much to think about. In the ten days since he had arrived in London, he had addressed no fewer than three letters to Sir Isaac Newton but had gotten no answer, though his last letter had been quite candid about his concern over a French conspiracy of some sort.

Perhaps Newton was out of town or ill. Perhaps Ben's letters were being intercepted by the like of Bracewell, whatever the hell Bracewell's like *was*.

He quelled a growing feeling of desperation. The French— or whoever had already had months to perfect whatever weapon he had helped them to create—did not need more time while he waited to be noticed by Newton. To make matters worse, Blackbeard's two hundred pounds were spending themselves pretty quickly, and though he and Robert had managed to find a cheap place to stay, neither had a job.

An hour later, Robert had still not put in his appearance, and Ben was beginning to feel ridiculous when Sarah came by with more coffee.

"Y'r friend is very late," she said softly.

"Yes. I suppose he has been held up." *Probably in some sort of trouble, knowing Robert,* he privately reflected.

"Well, p'raps I can impose a favor upon you, Benjamin Franklin of Boston."

"Of course," he replied.

"My job is done this hour, an' a girl on the streets alone is a sure target for scoundrels. I was wonderin' if you might not care to escort me to my apartment."

Ben's mouth felt very dry. "Of course," he said.

"And your friend?"

Ben shrugged. "I've waited for him often enough. He can wait for me."

"Good man," she replied.

Outside, Ben drew in a deep breath of the night air as Sarah took his arm.

"Such a beautiful city," he mumbled. The coffeehouse was just off of Fleet Piazza, a beautiful, spacious yard paved in gray stone. In the center a trio of alabaster mermaids conspired to raise a jet of water high into the air. Streetlights illumined red brick buildings framing the square.

"Which way?" he said, stupidly, a brew of fear, hope, and desire churning in his belly.

"Not far," Sarah said, cinching her arm more tightly into his own. "I live above Corbie Lane, just outside of the city."

"Oh. Shall we go, then?" He tried to keep the anxious tone from his voice, but his words had an unnatural ring. He was grateful that she seemed to be ignoring his unease as they followed Fleet Street west from the piazza and in a few moments reached the edge of the city of London.

When James and others in Boston had spoken of the oldest section of London as "the city" he had believed it to be a sort of pretension, the way North- and Southenders in Boston referred to their own respective parts of the town as the "real" Boston. But the city of London was another lesson in the truth produced by experience, for it proved itself very real when one encountered its border. Where the city ended, so did reason and order. The broad, straight-paved streets and radial piazzas, the mathematical gridwork of neat, clean, orderly ways, suddenly twisted into a mass of tangled, narrow, dark tracks, as cryptic as the labyrinth of a minotaur—and often as dangerous.

Fleet Street itself narrowed dramatically, from ninety feet wide to less than half that. They turned up Corbie Lane, and their footfalls became the dominant sound, accompanied, Ben fancied, by the thumping of his heart.

All of a sudden Sarah was pressed against him, her mouth covering his, her hand guiding his to her bodice, and he was abruptly in the heart of sweetness and mystery, of hunger and delight. His other hand was somehow directed to push up under Sarah's skirt, to the warm flesh above her stockings.

It was agony when she suddenly pushed him back, but he went, distantly ashamed of panting like an old dog.

"Come along," she whispered, tugging at his hand.

"Wait," he said. "I . . . are you . . ."

"A whore? Of course, silly. Do y' care?"

"I . . ." Truth to tell, he didn't, his tongue still tasting the sweetness of hers, his hands still tingling.

"I serve coffee at the Arabian Coffeehouse," Sarah said, a hint of pique in her voice. "What did you expect that I was?"

"I . . . look here, we have coffeehouses in Boston, and the servers there are not . . ."

"Y' really didn't know, did you?" Sarah said. "What a babe y' are, Benjamin Franklin! Next time," she advised, "look at the sign. If it has upon't a woman's arm or hand, y' can be sure to be served more th'n coffee if y' desire it."

"At . . . at what price?"

Sarah smiled sardonically and pressed back against him. Beneath her dress she was solid, warm. "Well, y' *do* want me then. Are y' virgin, my American gentleman?" And she kissed him again. Then she moved her lips up to his ear and whispered, "F'r a virgin, I charge but ten shillings."

Ben had begun to change his mind, but with her melted against him, ten shillings seemed more than a bargain. "You'll have to show me what to do," Ben murmured.

"So ten shillings it is," Sarah replied. "That'll be no chore at all, sir," and once more tugged at his hand. "It's just up this flight of steps where my bed is."

He followed along, the humming of his blood in his ears obliterating the sound of footsteps coming behind.

4.

Masque

Adrienne critically regarded the three gentlemen facing her. On her left stood one as straight and tall as an Italian cedar, somewhat slender, one hand rakishly on the hilt of his smallsword, the other straightening his bronze-embroidered waistcoat. Beneath a beaver tricorn and periwig, a black mask with a hooked nose covered all but his sardonic smile.

The gentleman on the right was almost as tall as the first, though his shoulders were broader. He seemed ill at ease in his vermilion coat and chocolate waistcoat. His mask was small, with a buffoonish round nose picked in silver scale.

But the fellow between them commanded most of Adrienne's attention. A head shorter than the other two, he wore an old-fashioned felt hat with an enormous ostrich plume, brim cocked at the side like a musketeer's of the last century. A gold waistcoat overlapped indigo knee breeches, and his greatcoat was a deep brown faced with blue and gold. His little mustache and beard looked, to her, ridiculous beneath the huge-nosed scarlet mask he had affected.

"This will never work," she groaned at the mirror. "I will never pass for a man."

"Nonsense," said the first gentleman—who was, of course, Mademoiselle Crecy. "You look the true image of a chevalier."

Nicolas nodded his head.

"Besides," Crecy went on, "it does not matter if from your voice and mannerisms someone guesses you are a woman. It is not so important that we disguise *what* you are as *who* you are. And I assure you, you do not resemble Adrienne de Mornay de Montchevreuil in the slightest."

"There is truth in that." Nicolas sighed. "But if we are found out, if the king should discover my part in this—"

"How ungallant," Crecy interrupted. "Since when do the Hundred Swiss care for personal safety?"

Adrienne could see Nicolas blushing furiously below his mask, and found herself confused. She wanted Nicolas to push his point—that this masquerade was bound to end in disaster for them. But now that Crecy mentioned it, it *did* seem ungallant for her guardian to balk at accompanying her.

"How much worse for you if we had eluded you rather than asking you to accompany us," Adrienne said, and understood that, almost without meaning to, she had now committed herself to Crecy's plan. Yes, the devil with it. If this silly costume could help her get the secret of Fatio's experiments, it was worth the risk.

"I hope no one challenges me to a duel," Adrienne remarked, patting the hilt of her mostly ornamental sword. "I have not the faintest idea how to use this."

"Nor do most who wear them," Crecy replied.

Nicolas sighed heavily. "I know who shall do the dueling when it comes to it."

Adrienne felt a brief flare of anger. Maintenon was right; men promised much but little could be expected of them. After all, had Nicolas not sworn to her that no man would ever touch her again if she did not desire it? And yet *one* man did. Should it matter that it was the king? Of course she had never actually *told* Nicolas that she did not desire the king's embrace . . .

But he should know.

"Well," Crecy said, "shall we go? Our carriage awaits us."

"Where did you tell the king we were going?" Adrienne asked.

"I did not, of course, speak to the king," Crecy told her, "but his valet gave him to understand that you were not feeling well. The word is that you are visiting Montchevreuil for a breath of country air. And so you shall." She winked.

Adrienne plucked thoughtfully at her glued-on beard. They had ridden from Versailles as if heading out into the country, stopping covertly here at Triannon to don their garb. Were there any flaws in their story? Probably, but it was not important.

Adrienne wondered if she would enjoy being a man for a night. To her surprise she realized that despite her misgivings she felt a certain excitement, a kind of devilish joy. She recalled how Ninon de Lenclos had once dressed as an officer, complete to guns and sword, to pursue on horseback her lover of the month. She was playing such a scene, something that would have provoked disdain from Maintenon but that made her feel—for the first time in months—young, hopeful. Alive.

After months in the country, the trip to the palace through Paris was something of a shock. Versailles, Marly, Triannon, Fountainbleu—the palaces the king frequented were all reflections of Louis' fancy and fantasy.

Paris was real—and frightening. The sullen faces were more hostile than ever. One person even threw a rock at their carriage. When they at last reached the Palais Royal, it loomed over them, an ancient and potent mistress who would not be neglected forever. Louis believed that the heart of France was where *he* was; the Palais Royal quietly pronounced that a lie.

Inside, Paris and its ragged masses were again forgotten. Glowing ephemeral things bobbed in the air, luminescent dandelion puffs dancing to a brittle elfin music. Water jetting from the mouth of a triton fountain became ice and shattered back into its basin as squealing courtiers plunged their hands into the shards. Where Louis used science to re-create the grandeur of his past, the duke of Orléans delighted in the toys it could produce. Adrienne found herself intrigued and saddened by this waste of scientific effort and talent.

Crecy presented their invitation. The three of them moved onto the floor, where dancing had already begun. Hundreds of people danced, overlooked the dancing from the gallery above, or stood milling about. Glimpses of side chambers showed courtiers at cards or billiards. All wore fantastic masks, many in the Venetian carnival style, many more outrageous.

"And now?" she asked Crecy as they made their way through the crowd, beginning to relax. Though she had identified several men she knew to be of the king's secret police, her worries about being noticed in such an immense crowd were fast fading. Indeed, they would be lucky to find Fatio in such a swarm.

"Now, enjoy yourself," Crecy remarked. "Let me do the work."

"Enjoy myself?" Adrienne protested, but at precisely that moment an arm slipped through her own.

"Dance with me, Monsieur," a delighted voice lisped into her ear. The music had just changed to a minuet, and Adrienne found herself staring into a delicate black mask that made no real effort to hide the duchess of Orléans.

"No!" Adrienne said, trying to pull away.

"My dear, don't cause a commotion! Dance with me!"

"Someone will notice. The police!"

"They will only notice if you do *not* dance," the duchess insisted.

In a moment she was in the line, and the duchess was smiling across the floor at her as the first couple began the stately minuet.

"My God, I can't believe it," Adrienne gasped, stumbling into the courtyard with the duchess. Adrienne realized she was more than slightly intoxicated. She had never drunk brandy before. How could she have known it would be so much stronger than wine? She finished what was in her cup as the duchess poured her a bit more.

"Such a wonderful partner, sir," the duchess complimented, curtseying. "You should dance more often."

"Indeed," Adrienne said. After that first dance with the duchess she realized that people really *did* believe her to be a man. She realized further that she was not the only person clothed contrary to her sex; more than one man was dressed as a woman. Adrienne knew that the transvestites had been cast out of Versailles nearly twenty years before, but it had never occurred to her to wonder where they had gone.

Apparently the court of the duke of Orléans was one place, which was fitting since the duke's father, Louis' brother, had been the beloved lord of such men.

"What are you thinking, dear?" the duchess asked, leaning against one of the white pillars that supported the inner eaves of the palace. "Your face grew long. And you seemed to be enjoying yourself a moment ago."

"I was. It's only . . . This thing the Korai have asked of me—to be the king's mistress and marry him—it is a very hard thing."

"Marriage is often hard."

"I know. But the king is . . ." She frowned. "I'm drunk."

"Not drunk enough, I think," the duchess remarked, pouring her another finger of brandy.

"No, I can't."

"No, you *must*," the duchess insisted. "For your own good."

Adrienne took the newly filled glass, stared at it, and then took another sip. "He is *old*," she said at last. "And mad."

The duchess took her hand and squeezed it. "Never say that, dear," she chided, gently.

"You have not been with him. You have not *lain* with him. He believes himself to be young!"

"Poor dear," the duchess sighed. Then she brightened, and Adrienne now recognized the future of her own smile—as false as the masks they both wore. "You must learn what all of us at court learned, Adrienne—to gather your pleasures while you can. You must dance, and you must take lovers, and you must be happy when you are able, or you will wither."

"Those aren't the things that make me happy," Adrienne said.

"Of course they are, dear. Look at how much fun you have had tonight. And how *many* things you have not tried. A lover for instance."

"I couldn't," Adrienne said. "I won't. And what would be the use? What point of lying with *another* man?"

"My dear," the duchess said, "you must not think that all men are the *same* in that respect. There are some with whom you might enjoy it quite a lot. That handsome young guard, for instance."

"No, I don't think so," Adrienne replied, though she had a sudden image of Nicolas and knew that she lied. "Thank you for your concern, but I cannot listen to you in this matter."

"Dear, you are *young*. You have a body with every part of it at its height. Do not waste that, for you will not be young for very long, I assure you. Not in Versailles, you won't be." She put her arm around Adrienne's shoulder. "See what you are doing right now, worrying about things you can't help? You are wasting the pleasure you could be having now by contemplating miseries yet unborn. You are an intelligent woman, Mademoiselle, when it comes to the science, but in this you are a stupid girl. Come, drink your brandy. We have a card game to attend."

By the time they reached the card game, Adrienne was having trouble standing steadily.

She frowned. She had missed something. She was being introduced to someone.

In a sharp wave of clarity she realized that it was *Fatio* she was being introduced to. The mathematician wore a small mask across his eyes only—his own nose was more impressive than any carved impostor.

"It is no matter, sir," Fatio said, bowing from his seat, apparently responding to her failure to acknowledge him. Was she *that* obviously drunk? "I am also in my cups tonight," he went on. "It is good to meet the baron."

Baron? Oh yes, she was supposed to be an Austrian, was she not, with little command of French? Baron von Klimmer, or some such nonsense.

"And I, you," she said. Crecy was there, she saw, as well as several men and women she did not know. Crecy was carrying out the introductions as well as dealing the cards. Adrienne was sure she gasped aloud. Crecy had unbuttoned her waistcoat and shirt, leaving no doubt whatever that she was *not* a man. Fatio's face was flushed, and Adrienne suddenly realized that Crecy's hand was beneath the table.

"Please take a seat, sir," Fatio said magnanimously. "Play a hand of *reversi*."

Adrienne sat, stupefied in more ways than one.

"Monsieur de Duillier is a famous mathematician," Crecy remarked, addressing the duchess. Adrienne blinked, for Crecy pitched her voice low like a man, and recognition struck her like lightning.

Crecy! It had been *Crecy* at the canal, *Crecy* who was her kidnapper, not a man at all.

The room spun. And she must pay attention, for Fatio was speaking.

"Not so famous," Fatio demurred. Both Crecy's hands had reappeared, and cards were sliding across the table. Adrienne stared at them stupidly, realizing Crecy had been dealing her cards for some time. Her scalp tingled, recalling the hours on horseback, the violent intimacy.

Confession. Tomorrow she must go to confession.

She squeezed her eyes shut, but the darkness behind them was cyclonic. *Pay attention!*

"No, do not pretend," Crecy replied to Fatio. "We have all heard of your fabulous invention, the one which will sweep our enemies into the sea."

"Oh, I shouldn't talk about *that*," Fatio murmured, swallowing more of whatever was in his cup.

"But of course not," the duchess interrupted. "It is a state secret, I should think."

"The king . . ." Fatio said, slurring badly, "the king frightens me. I am not afraid to admit it. But I will please him! I will please them all, and then they will see!"

"What will they see, sir?" Adrienne blurted.

For an instant Fatio's clouded eyes sharpened. "Do I . . . do I *know* you, sir?" he asked.

"But of course, my dear," Crecy interposed. "You were just introduced."

"Oh. Yes, of course. What will they see? They will see that I understand Newton better than anyone. That no one grasps his equations as *I* do. They will see—" He grinned drunkenly and went on. "—they will see that Lead and Tin have not gobbled all their children. They will see the dogs of Iron sent baying by their master in toward Earth! They will see the ellipsis straighten. They will see the *cannon*, by God! Look to the west on October twenty-fourth, my friends. You will *see* something then!"

"I'm sure we shall," Crecy said, hand beneath the table again.

"No, they will," Fatio insisted. "*He* will."

"The king?" the duchess asked.

Fatio laughed. "Yes, yes, the king: the king of science, the king of calculus!"

"Newton?" Adrienne asked suddenly.

"You see?" Fatio nearly shrieked. "The baron knows! But now they shall know me! I shall steal a cannonball from God's own arsenal and *smite* him with it."

"Using what powder, sir?" Adrienne managed.

Fatio laughed again, and nearly choked as he finished his glass.

"Gravity, of course," he snapped, and then, looking down at his cards, he smiled. "No, I have said too much. The time will come."

But Adrienne knew. Now she *knew*, and she had been stupid not to know all along. But her mind had not been able to conceive of something so monstrous, not coming from sweet, sympathetic Fatio. But it was true.

She had long known of his obsession with Newton, his thirst for validation and revenge. But she had never suspected that he was willing to kill a million people or more to quench that thirst.

October twenty-fourth. Her wedding day.

Adrienne bolted up from the table and fled to the yard, and then things became very confused. Somehow her feet missed the ground, and she sprawled on the green.

"Monster!" she shouted. "The king is a monster!"

Behind her eyelids the ocean of space surged, whirled, sucked all into the spiral dance, but she saw what Fatio meant, saw the comet plucked from its path and sent hurling toward Earth. Because Louis told him to. Louis, the monster.

She struggled to her feet as the courtyard seemed to dim, flatten, recede. Was everyone staring at her? Were they laughing? A frowning face bent near, and she recognized the blurred features of the police lieutenant she had seen earlier.

"Sir?" he asked.

"You have to stop him," Adrienne managed. "The dogs of iron . . ."

And then her mouth spoke on as her mind went elsewhere, sinking into the cold depths of space, darkness, forgetfulness.

5.

Hermes

Ben lay on the narrow bed and wondered at the perfection of the universe. Sarah's apartment was pitch dark, but his palm smoothed over the flawless curve of her thigh, the divine junction of thigh and hip, the convex miracle of her belly. Surely there was no more marvelous thing in creation than her body, her lips, her hair.

Making love was nothing at all as he had imagined it. He thought it would be an ethereal sort of thing, a sublime embrace. That's how the books he had read had spoken of it. Instead, it was a damp, musky, salty, *awkward* business.

He loved it. Better, he felt not the slightest bit of guilt.

"Thank you," he said, surprised that he could even speak, that God hadn't stolen that to compensate him for what he had just gained.

"Ben . . ." Sarah began, and then stopped. He wished he could see her face.

"Yes? Sarah?" Her name sounded perfect, too.

"Ben, y' should go."

"Why?"

"Because y'r a nice young fellow." She sighed. "Because y' weren't mean or rough." She chuckled throatily. "Because y' give me the money first. Now, please, leave while y' can."

Ben's spine prickled, despite the lethargic warmth that seemed to insulate it. "Am I in danger?" he whispered.

"Yes."

He began patting around, feeling for his clothes. "I've been stupid, haven't I?" he muttered.

"Just naïve," she answered, a bit wistfully. "Now go. I'm surprised y' made it this long."

"Can I have another kiss?" He decided he could button the waistcoat later.

"For another shilling."

Ben quickly counted out five, and she kissed him warmly on the lips.

"There. Now go, y' butter-head."

He went down the dark, dank stairwell, through the heavy battered door, out onto the cold cobbles of the street.

He made three steps before a hand fell on his shoulder.

"See here," a voice rasped, "what'v ye been up to doin'?"

Ben jerked away so violently that he completely lost balance and stumbled wildly backward—hitting something warm and soft. Something that grunted.

"Here," the voice said. "Ben, it's me!"

Looking up in the dim light he could just make out Robert's grinning face.

Ben rolled away from whomever he had fallen on. "Who's that?" he gasped when he could find the spare breath.

"That's the fellow as was gonna slit y'r throat and drop you in the Thames," Robert remarked nonchalantly.

"Let's get out of here," Ben gulped. "Please. Now."

"As you command," Robert said sardonically, sweeping off his hat in a mock bow.

Ben didn't speak again until they had reached Fleet Street and the relative comfort of the streetlights and midnight traffic.

"Where were you? Why didn't you meet me at the coffee-house? And why didn't you *tell* me about such coffeehouses?"

"Would you have gone?"

Ben grabbed Robert by the lapels of his worn brown coat. "You *planned* it! Left me sitting in there *knowing* what would happen."

"Oh, is that so?" Robert asked, scratching his head thoughtfully. "Well, I suppose it _could_ be."

"And what about the throat cutter?"

"That's why I was down the street the whole time, watchin'

fer y' ta *go* with one of 'em. Damn, but you took your time about gettin' interested."

"I didn't *know*."

"For such a bright lad, the obvious has a way of eludin' you."

Ben wondered if he should be angry or grateful. He finally settled on saying nothing at all.

Another week passed, and Ben began to despair of ever hearing from Newton. He spent his time trying to reconstruct the essentials of the formula he and John Collins had composed, enlarging upon it where he could. Much to Robert's chagrin, he also spent a significant portion of his remaining money on a copy of the *Principia* to refresh his memory, determined that when he did meet the great man at last, he would not appear completely foolish.

He sought employment as well, but with no success. Fortunately Robert managed to get a job driving a locomotive, one of the noisy steam-driven machines that rattled in and out of London hauling cargo overland. Robert was sufficiently grateful to Ben for sharing his money in renting the apartment and feeding them for the first few weeks that he was willing to support Ben for a time in compensation. Indeed, Robert still owed him a bit more than twenty pounds.

He consoled himself with the knowledge—gleaned from daily papers in less adventurous coffeehouses—that the war against France was going no worse, and in fact, that gains were being made on the continent. James the Pretender, with French support, was still holding Scotland, but there was no evidence of any terrible new weapon.

"This whole business with the Pretender seems absurd to me," he told Robert one day when, lacking anything better to do, he had gone along on the locomotive ride out to Northampton. The carriage they rode in perched atop the water tank, a riveted steel cylinder about the size of a horse. The source of motion was a steam engine whose massive pistons cranked equally gargantuan wheels. Nestled into the steam engine one could just see the torus and cylinder of the fervefactum that boiled the water, and behind the carriage rose the funnel-shaped device that separated water from the air to keep the tank full. He delighted in the machine. It was a joy to behold science in motion, to see theory in practice; but it was better still to ride on a great, steam-snorting beast.

"What's to understand?" Robert asked. "James claims that the British throne is his, and the House of Hanover claim that it is theirs. So they fight."

"Yes, but the issue is really one of religion, true? James is a Catholic, otherwise *everyone* would acknowledge him as king."

"Yes, of course," Robert affirmed. "And George is a Protestant."

"It seems so silly—all this fighting and killing over religion."

"What they fight and kill over is *power*, Ben. Religion's just the clothes they dress it in whilst they do it. If they were all atheists, there'd still be a war. That's the real way of the world."

"Then I suppose George imports his troops from Holland and Bavaria because he likes the cut and color of their uniforms, rather than because he fears some of his own British soldiers might have Jacobite hearts."

Robert shrugged. "I don't say as some people might not feel religion is worth fightin' over. It's them that kings and ministers send out whilst they smoke their pipes and make shake with their mistresses. But mark, that's not the same motives as drives the engines of George or James or Walpole."

"I am fortunate to have such a wise counselor," Ben returned sarcastically. But he chewed over what Robert had said for the rest of the trip and found that it had the flavor of the wider world he had begun to taste.

The run to Northampton took most of the day, and when Ben returned he was dead tired from having helped load and unload several tons of grain. He wilted onto one of the two wooden chairs in their sparsely furnished room.

He had just closed his eyes for an instant, wondering which tavern they would go to for supper, when something tapped him on the head. He opened his eyes and found himself staring at a letter addressed to him.

"Must've been brought while we were out," Robert told him.

Ben fumbled at the seal. His eyes darted to the signature at the bottom; when he saw it, he sucked in a disappointed breath.

The letter was signed "Hermes." Who in the devil was Hermes? And then he realized that it was, like Janus, a pen name. More puzzled than ever, he turned his attention to the text.

To the honorable Janus:
Allow me to make apologies for my master, the illustrious Sir Isaac Newton. He is presently engag'd in activities of high import which require his entire devotion and energies. Your persistent letters, however, have made themselves known to Sir Isaac, and he has instruct'd me—a pupil of his—to make your acquaintance. Consequently, it is my pleasure to invite you to a meeting of a scientific club. You may present yourself at the Grecian Coffeehouse in Devereaux Court, the Strand, on September the fifth, at six hours past noon. Myself and the other members of our society await your presence with great anticipation.

Your humble servant,
Hermes.

Two days later, with a lump of anticipation large enough to choke on lodged in his throat, wearing a new coat and waistcoat bought with his last pound and shilling, Ben Franklin walked up the Strand, past the Sommerset and Essex houses and the grand old college of the Temple. Hackneys and sedan chairs hurried up and down the street, bearing bewigged and be-powdered gentlemen and ladies. Footmen hurried after their masters, liveried and plumed, and girls walked in groups along the sidewalk admiring the wares of hawkers and shopkeepers. The Strand was like a river of bright jewels, not certain which way it should flow.

Ben took no real note of this colorful flood of humanity around him. He saw only one thing; the right turn that wound into Devereaux Court, and above it the sign of the Grecian Coffeehouse, growing larger and more legible with each step.

The time was five hours and fifty minutes past noon.

6.

Disclosures

"Awaken, O beauty in the tower," urged a most unpleasant voice.

Everything was unpleasant: the sickening motion of the carriage; her swollen, papery tongue; the eye-pricking darts of the rising sun. She felt as if she had been drowned in brandy and resurrected in some pagan underworld. What exactly had happened last night?

"I wasn't asleep," Adrienne growled at Crecy, who was shaking her arm.

"My pardon," Crecy returned. "What I mean to say is, you must get out of the carriage."

"What? Why?" For it was clear that they had not reached Versailles. Adrienne saw nothing but trees through either window.

"Because," Crecy explained, "Nicolas and I are about to sink it into a lake."

Adrienne blinked. She allowed Crecy to lead her out of the carriage. Her legs seemed nerveless, but she was soon seated against the rough bark of an elm.

"Stay there," Crecy commanded.

Adrienne squinted at her surroundings. Nature's architecture surrounded them, colonnades of oak and ash supporting green arches above, where unseen birds piped and chattered cheerfully. Perhaps five paces away she could see the lake Crecy spoke of. A pond, really, but it looked deep. They were on a bluff some thirty feet above it.

Meanwhile, Nicolas was unharnessing the horses. Now and then he lifted his head and scanned the woods.

Adrienne digested her situation and found that it gave her

heartburn. She had been drunk, drunk right out of her silly mind. The duchess had done it to her, feeding her glass after glass of brandy, but she should have known better. She remembered meeting Fatio. Fatio had been even drunker than she, she guessed, and he had confessed . . .

Now she remembered.

"We have to return to Versailles," she said weakly and then again, with all of the strength she could command. "We *must* return to Versailles."

"I assure you that is what we are trying to do."

"You don't understand," Adrienne said. "Fatio, his formula! It's designed to—"

"Wait!" Crecy entreated, throwing a saddle over one of the horses. Where had she gotten a saddle? "Let me see if I can guess. Fatio's formula will kill *millions* of people. It's a *horror*, a *monstrosity*. The king is the *devil himself* for approving its use. Does that hit the mark?" Crecy delivered the lines like a melodramatic actor, grasping at her chest as if rending her garment.

"Veronique, I demand that you still your tongue!" Nicolas shouted. "It isn't her fault!"

"Not her fault that she was drunk? That she ran screaming about death and destruction and the king's moral character all through the Palais Royal? Well, tell me then, Monsieur Hundred Swiss, whom shall we blame?"

"Nicolas, is that true?" Adrienne gasped.

Nicolas would not meet her eyes, but he nodded reluctantly.

"Oh, no. My disguise?"

"We did our best," Crecy answered. "We kept you between us, shouting drunkenly ourselves to try and drown you out. We kept your wig and mustache on."

"Fatio?"

"Fatio found his rest about the same time you took ill. I doubt that he will remember much of what he said, though someone might tell him."

"And why do we sink the carriage?"

"I'll explain in a moment," Nicolas said. "Crecy, if you don't mind?"

Adrienne watched impatiently as Crecy and Nicolas grunted and shoved the massive carriage toward the edge. It seemed to her that they should not be able to move it, but a moment or two later the carriage tumbled over. The lake kissed it with watery lips and then sucked it down.

"Now, we should be gone," Crecy recommended. "Adrienne, can you ride?"

Adrienne wondered if she meant at all or at the moment, but she merely nodded, rising unsteadily to her feet. Nicolas held the reins of a golden stallion out to her. It was bridled and saddled, not one of the carriage horses. Two similar mounts awaited Crecy and Nicolas.

"Where did these come from?" Adrienne asked as she put her foot in the stirrup.

"We took them from the men d'Artagnan, here, killed," Crecy replied, tersely.

Adrienne's jaw dropped, and she swung about to regard Nicolas. "What is happening?" she asked.

"Let's go. I'll tell you as we ride."

Adrienne mounted. Her horse moved off at a fast walk.

"We shall have to make more speed soon," Crecy informed her. "You see, Demoiselle, we have something of a trick to accomplish, your guardian and I. We must not only return you to Versailles alive, but we must return you without anyone knowing that you were in Paris. We three rogues—" She gestured at the three of them. "—must vanish as if we have never been."

"Why?"

"Because, my dear, I fear you will be killed if we do not."

"By the king?"

"No, the king would be very upset, but he would not kill you. There are those, though," Crecy said, "who would be perfectly happy if millions of human beings died."

"What do you mean?"

"I cannot tell you that yet. But you must tell me, Adrienne. What was it you suddenly understood about Fatio's formula?"

"I don't know if I can trust you," she finally said after a pause.

"*You* trust *me*?" Crecy said, her voice quite cold. "Do you know what d'Artagnan and I have risked for *you*?"

"I know that you risk yourselves. I don't know why, or that it is for *me*. I don't know you at all, Mademoiselle Crecy, save that in each instance I have been involved with you, I have spent altogether too much time on horseback."

"What do you mean?" Crecy asked.

"You know very well what I mean, Monsieur Brigand."

Crecy clicked her tongue and looked up at the sky. "So you guessed *that*?"

"I didn't until yesterday. When you were pretending to be a man, I recognized you."

"Brilliant, Mademoiselle," Crecy said.

"That isn't all," Adrienne continued. "On the horse was not the first time I ever heard your voice. You were also the guard who fished me out of the Grand Canal when the barge was set afire."

"Now your story becomes more fantastic," Crecy remarked.

"Nevertheless, I believe that you have masqueraded as a man and become one of the Hundred Swiss—perhaps with some help from my good friend Nicolas here."

Nicolas opened his mouth to protest, but Adrienne held up her hand. "It was entirely too simple for Crecy to bring you into this mad scheme. You know that since the 'kidnapping,' the king has misliked me traveling alone or with a single guard, and yet you allowed it."

Nicolas colored but held her gaze. "I have done what I thought was best," he answered stubbornly.

"Oh? And was it best when you allowed me to be kidnapped?"

She had been guessing about that part, but their reactions confirmed it.

"Yes, I see it now," she continued. "A prearranged kidnapping, one in which no one would be killed. You, Nicolas, only pretended to be hurt while Crecy—and who else was it, Count Toulouse himself?—rode off with me."

"You omit one important detail," Crecy riposted. "D'Artagnan here had a musket ball in his shoulder."

"Did he?"

"Enough, Veronique," Nicolas replied. "It is no use."

"No, Nicolas," Crecy objected, some real heat entering her voice at last. She turned on Adrienne. "He shot himself after we left, to prevent suspicion, to protect *you*."

Adrienne nearly faltered at that, but she pressed on. "I don't see how I have been *protected* by that," Adrienne retorted. "But even assuming I have, you understand if I wonder what your motives are."

"Perhaps we are both deeply smitten by you, Mademoiselle, and have followed you about to keep you from harm. And see how you repay us." Crecy uttered a pacific little laugh and shook her head.

Adrienne felt her face burn. "Don't ridicule me," she demanded. "Give me a reason to trust you. Give me *someone* to trust!"

But at that, the two exchanged glances as if trying to communicate by silent parley and decide how to respond. That meant that they were both most likely interpreting someone else's commands.

"I only wanted you to know that I know," Adrienne explained, "so that you will not both think me an utter fool. And if you are taking me somewhere to sink me like that carriage, you will do so knowing that I was not entirely ignorant of my fate."

Nicolas turned wide, shocked eyes on her. "Whatever else you believe," he gasped, "do not think I could do you any *harm*!"

"How touching," Crecy declared, and then added more soberly, "but of course the same is true of me, my dear."

And then, suddenly, she drew a pistol. "Nicolas, did you—"

"Yes," he said grimly, "I hear them, too." He readied a short carbine musket designed for firing from horseback. A thrill of fear swept through Adrienne—she almost believed they were about to shoot *her*—but now she heard the baying of hounds.

"Who hunts us?" she asked.

"Any number of people," Nicolas replied. "The secret police came after us last night, but I killed them. I don't know who these are." He urged his horse over toward her, opened his coat, and pulled a weapon from a pocket. "Take this," he said. "Go with Crecy. If you are beset, aim and pull the trigger. Make certain that Crecy is nowhere in front of you."

The pistol he handed her was huge. It had a normal-seeming flintlock, but the barrel flared to more than an inch in diameter toward the end.

"Where are you going?"

"Hunting." He dropped his voice. "Adrienne, I am sorry for the lies between us. Sometimes a man has many duties to choose between. Sometimes he does not make the right choices." He paused, and his eyes hardened. "Crecy is half right," he whispered harshly, "for I do love you."

"I don't know what you want," she moaned, but the sudden concussion of joy and terror shook her to the bone. He had said it, and now she could no longer pretend.

Nicolas had already turned his mount, was already galloping away.

"Come," Crecy said, riding up alongside. "Come now if you want to survive this."

"Nicolas . . ."

"If anyone can live through what he is about to attempt, believe me, it is Nicolas," Crecy said. "You don't know him like I do. But if he dies, we must make it worth the sacrifice. *Now.*"

Perhaps five minutes later, she heard shots in the distance, little snapping sounds like ice breaking. She gripped the pistol in her hand, trying to recall if she had ever even held one before; she *knew* that she had never fired one.

She wondered where they were. What would she do if both Nicolas and Crecy were killed?

It would be her fault. If not for her drunken babbling, the plan would have been perfect.

"Head down," Crecy shouted suddenly, and her pistol barked. Something whined by Adrienne's ear, and then she heard a second muffled boom. Ahead, four riders emerged from a blind of trees; one hung almost comically to his horse's mane, his chin and neck scarlet. A second was holstering a smoking carbine and drawing his sword, and the other two commenced to charge. She had time to absorb that they wore the uniform of the Gray Musketeers as she awkwardly raised her pistol.

7.

The Newtonians

To first appearances, the Grecian was a coffeehouse like other coffeehouses—well, like other *respectable* ones.

At first Ben merely stood inside the doorway. The Grecian was crowded, its long tables packed with gentlemen dressed from the height of fashion to near rags. Ben slowly picked through the crowd with an eager gaze, hoping he might recognize some famous philosopher. To his disappointment, though he fancied he saw many faces of great intelligence and wit, none spurred recognition.

How was he to know this Hermes? How was Hermes to know him? He had deliberately omitted any mention of his age in all of his letters, figuring that Sir Isaac would not eagerly greet a young boy. If Hermes had an eye out for him, he was probably not looking for a boy.

He went through the room again, and this time his eye picked out a single table at which only a few people sat, one of whom was a woman—a rare sight in *real* coffeehouses, especially when they were young and pretty.

This woman *was* pretty—and exotic as well. She wore her own hair, which was very black. Her skin was pale, her eyes slanted and almond shaped. Her red lips wore a sort of permanent pout below an upturned nose that might almost be thought of as impish if her demeanor were not so regal. She might have been any age between sixteen and thirty-six. She was speaking, and the others at the table—four men in their twenties—listened, enthralled.

Ben noticed an empty space on a nearby bench. If nothing

else, he decided, he would go and see what this strange, lovely creature was saying.

"Our institute is not so grand," she said in an accent Ben could not place, "and yet we have made progress in attracting scholars."

"Yes," one of the men answered in a French accent, "I'm certain that Herr Leibniz was a great prize. I wonder if he had any luck instituting the social reforms he aspired to?" His sarcasm was evident; his lips seemed frozen in a perpetual smirk. Though Ben had no great love for Leibniz and his philosophies, there was something so self-satisfied about the man's criticism that he bridled a bit.

The woman was affected in the same way. "Sir," she said, "your contempt of Leibniz's philosophies is well known, but whatever you may think of him, he was a man of science, and his students are not necessarily hampered by his faults. It is true that he took his position in my lord's court in hopes of implementing certain policies. I assure you, Tsar Peter was well aware of that. But I argue that his wish to reform humanity was no stranger than Sir Isaac's latest . . . obsession."

"Here, here," seconded another fellow in a solid British drawl. Unlike the rest, he affected a large wig that seemed to swallow his small, plump face. Ben barely noticed, for he had just understood two things: The woman was Russian, and they spoke of Sir Isaac almost as if they knew him. Could one of these men— or even the woman—be Hermes? He took up a newspaper and tried to appear to scrutinize it, but he found himself glancing up often.

The Smirker favored the Wig with a slightly disdainful glance. "Come now," he said, rather patronizingly. "Sir Isaac has shown us a world of order, of poetic precision. His method has dissected light and matter and mathematics from Leibniz's mysticism. Do you truly hold that Newton's interest in history and the ancients is on par with Leibniz's absurd notion that we live in the best of all possible worlds?"

The woman frowned. "I believe that you are deliberately misrepresenting the late doctor," she said, "and just as deliberately you are ignoring the theological arcanery of Sir Isaac's latest efforts."

"He is old," the Smirker said, "and his thoughts turn to the religion of his youth. I can forgive him that."

"Oh, 'tis passing fair *generous* of you to cede him that!" snapped a third man, who sat across the table from the woman. He spoke in a crisp and unmistakable Scottish burr, which perfectly suited his square, studious face and curly brown hair. " 'Tis more than presumptuous of *any* of you t' guess at what the great man is aboot. He ha' applied mathematical tools to the understandin' o' alchemy, physics, and thaumaturgy. What makes you so *certain* that he will fail t' apply the same methods t' history?"

"Oh, pish, Maclaurin," the Wig snorted. "You don't really believe that. And this outlandish obsession of his has cost the Royal Society dearly. Parliament and the king want science and weaponry for the war, not chronologies and bizarre arguments about the science of Babylon. That's a large part of what has put us in our present position!"

"Sir Isaac is uncomfortable aboot producin' more devices for killing," Maclaurin said quietly. "It ha' nothing at all to do wi' his present endeavors."

"We'll see what use those scruples are against the bloody French," the Wig retorted, and then, suddenly realizing his blunder, glanced sidewise at the Smirker. "Ah . . . no offense intended, sir."

The fourth man—whose back was to Ben, so that he could only make out his blondish mane—held up his hand placatingly. "Let's have none of that between us," he entreated. "As philosophers, we should be above this nonsense. In any event, let us not forget our good guest from the continent is exiled by the Sun King."

"Indeed," the Frenchman agreed. "And you all know that I find England a more enlightened place than the stifling court of Apollo. Still, I *would* remind you that this war cannot be placed entirely at the Sun King's door."

"I agree with Mr. Stirling. Let's not argue politics," the woman broke back in.

"Yes," Maclaurin agreed. "And meantime, has anyone spotted our friend Janus?"

Ben could not help starting at that, and he blushed furiously when he realized that the woman's exotic eyes were narrowing to focus on him.

"Why, yes," she replied. "I believe I have."

"Not that *boy*," the Wig grunted.

A strange kind of calm followed Ben's initial embarrassment. He did not know what to say to them, but nevertheless he stood and approached their table.

His voice felt remarkably firm when he said, "I am Janus." He stuck out his hand toward Maclaurin, the nearest.

"G'drot me," the Wig swore. "We've been convened by a *boy*. How do you like that?"

"Are you *really*?" the Smirker asked. *He* merely seemed amused.

"Which one of you gentlemen—or lady—is Hermes?" Ben asked. His hand remained out.

The Wig snapped, "Come, my friends, this is absurd."

Ben dropped his hand and stood bolt upright, throwing his shoulders back. "Gentlemen and lady, I urge you to hear me out. If you dismiss me on account of my age without at least listening to me, you will show yourselves not simply neglectful, but—you will pardon me—stupid."

The Frenchman's eyebrows sprang up like surprised frogs. The others simply stared.

Maclaurin broke the silence and reached out his hand. Ben shook it. "How old are y', lad?" he asked.

"Fourteen, sir," Ben replied.

"Tell me, Giles," Maclaurin said, without shifting his thoughtful regard from Ben's face. "Do y' know how old I was when I wrote my thesis at Edinburgh?"

The Wig—whose name was apparently "Giles"—rapped the table impatiently. "What has *that* to do with anything?"

"I was fifteen," Maclaurin replied.

"Yes," drawled the Smirker, eyes merry, "and I was but twelve when the great Ninon de Lenclos wrote a provision for me in her will—solely on account of my poetry. Some of us bloom at an early age, Mr. Heath."

The Wig sent the Frenchman a vitriolic glance, but said nothing.

"Have a seat, my boy," Maclaurin said. "We ha' things to discuss."

A boy in an apron brought more coffee while the group digested Ben's presence silently. Then to his vast surprise, the woman reached over and patted his hand. His skin seemed to tingle where she touched it.

Maclaurin—who despite initial appearances seemed to be presiding over the group—cleared his throat. "Well, shall we continue t' call you Janus? Janus, let me introduce you to the members of our little club—at least those as are present. The lady is Vasilisa Karevna, an envoy from the court of Tsar Peter of Russia.

"Our French companion is François Arouet," Maclaurin went on, indicating the Smirker.

The Frenchman frowned, though his eyes counterfeited his anger. "As you prefer 'Janus'—a nom de plume—I prefer 'Voltaire.' "

"Sir," Ben said, bowing.

"Our doubtful companion is Giles Heath."

Heath glared at Ben's outstretched hand, and then touched it, briefly and laconically, a frustrating parody of a handshake.

"James Stirling." The fourth man—the one whose back had been to him before—nodded at Ben when introduced. He had spindly brows that seemed forever arched in surprise, a crooked nose that must have once been broken, and green eyes.

"I myself am Colin Maclaurin," the Scotsman finished.

"I am pleased to meet you all," Ben said gravely.

"Likewise," Maclaurin replied. "Now, suppose y' explain to us why y' indicated nothing of your age when you wrote to Sir Isaac."

"I didn't think he would see me," Ben answered. "And I believe that it is very *important* that he see me."

"This may be as close as y' get," Maclaurin cautioned, "so speak well."

"My name is Benjamin Franklin," Ben said. "I was born and

raised in Boston, Massachusetts. I came to England to see Sir Isaac Newton because I think I have done a very bad thing and because someone is trying to kill me. What else would you care to know?" He stopped. He could tell from the way they stared at him that he had at least succeeded in capturing their attention.

Maclaurin blinked, and Voltaire breathed a little chuckle.

"Suppose y' start at the beginning," Maclaurin said. "I've seen your formula—if it *is* yours—and it contains a spore of brilliance. Certain that it is a new thing, wi' many uses. Wi'out that, we would never have seen you at all. So start you at the beginning, and tell us everything important."

They were all waiting now. Even Heath seemed willing to be convinced. The presence of "Voltaire" worried him—he might be a spy—but he had already proclaimed his separation from France, and the others seemed to trust him. It was time to drop his mask completely. He could not barter with Maclaurin and his friends; not yet, at any rate.

"It began," he said quietly, "when I was ten years old . . ."

"That is *something* of a story. You really met this Blackbeard? I should like to hear more," Voltaire exclaimed after Ben was finished. "By God, if you are not telling the truth, you are pursuing the wrong calling, my friend. You should become a writer!"

"François," Maclaurin said, a bit impatiently.

"And you have these notes—the communiqués that you now believe to be French?"

"No. I had to leave them in Boston. But I can remember the gist of them."

"And your only proof that this was part of some French plot was the use of the popish calendar?"

"Someone tried to kill him," Vasilisa reminded them. "Just as—"

"Hush ye, Vasilisa," Maclaurin thundered. The Russian narrowed her eyes angrily, but she closed her mouth.

"Colin, there's no need to snap at Vasilisa. It's not as if it is a *secret*," Heath remonstrated.

"Just . . . let's do one thing at a time," Maclaurin said, clearly near the end of his patience. "The question is, How the hell did they find you in America? How did they know where you were?"

"I was just thinking," Vasilisa murmured, "that if a new affinity can be established, as Benjamin did with his aetherschreiber, then surely an aethercompass could point out its physical direction."

"Oh, aye, but still, t' turn a crude direction into a *street* address . . ." Maclaurin scratched his chin.

"I've never heard of an aethercompass," Ben admitted, "but Bracewell already had his eye on me and John well before I made the tunable schreiber. If Bracewell had something to do with this 'F,' or Minerva, or whomever, then they could have contacted *him* through a different schreiber. He might keep one where he stays. Then he might have just added things up."

"This is a *fairy* story," Heath exploded. "I don't know what he's after, but there's none of this he couldn't have heard eavesdropping at the right window—or hell, he may have sat next to us in here an 'undred times before today."

"There is the equation," Maclaurin reminded him. "Mr. Franklin's explanation of its origins seems likely enough. We can build a device such as he describes and prove that part of his story."

"Well, to be accurate," Stirling added, in his soft voice, "that would prove only that Mr. Franklin had seen such a device. Whom do we know in Boston who could confirm some of these other assertions?"

"I ha' a friend there," Maclaurin answered. "For the moment, young Franklin, I see no reason not t' take you at your word. If the rest are willing, I'd like to bring you to our laboratories tomorrow and begin work reconstructing the particulars of the formula. It is probably nothing—this fear you have of a French weapon—but we shall see."

"The academy? Will I meet Sir Isaac?"

A general murmur ran around the table.

"Tha' 'tis entirely possible and entirely *impossible* to predict," Maclaurin replied. "Y' see, when we wrote that note to you we told you something of a lie."

"A lie?"

Maclaurin nodded. "Sir Isaac di'na tell us to contact you. In fact, he never read your letters."

"None of us has spoken to him in better than a month," Heath put in. "He has locked himself in his house and will speak to no one."

"Why?"

Heath shrugged. "Who the hell can tell, with Newton? But there are reasons enough."

"What do you mean?"

They all looked at him for a moment, and then Maclaurin sighed heavily. "Technically speaking, only Mr. Heath and myself are Newton's students, and I ha' been so for only a year. Vasilisa here has met him once, but the academy voted to take her as a guest. Voltaire—"

"I am a sort of hanger-on," Voltaire confided.

"And Mr. Stirling is more a student of Edmund Halley, the royal astronomer, than he is of Sir Isaac."

"I see," Ben said. He recalled that Maclaurin had spoken of their "club," and it suddenly occurred to him that such young people were unlikely to be part of Newton's inner circle—or even particularly important in the Royal Society.

"No, I doubt that y' do," Maclaurin replied, his voice grave and sinking low. "One year ago the Royal Society boasted fifty-seven members. Today—with the possible exception of Sir Isaac—those of us at this table and two friends who couldn't be here today are all that remain. The seven of us *are* the Royal Society."

8.

Children of Lead and Tin

Adrienne pulled the trigger. The weapon shrieked and jerked like a living thing, tearing from her fingers. At the same moment, her horse stumbled. Two of their attackers, along with their horses, were thrashing on the ground, smoking. The nearby trees were smoking as well, their leaves stripped as if by a flaming sirocco. Her horse dropped like a stringless puppet, and she hurled forward over its neck.

Tasting blood in her mouth, she shook her head to clear it as another pistol shot echoed off through the surrounding hills. Painfully, she drew her legs up beneath her, hoping nothing was broken, remaining in a crouch.

Her horse lay a few feet away, one side of its head stripped down to charred and pitted bone. One eye remained, staring dully at her.

I did that, she thought. What kind of weapon had Nicolas given her? Not a *kraftpistole*—at least not the standard sort.

Now she heard steel ringing and rose up slowly.

Only one of the musketeers remained, but he was beating his sword against Crecy's. Adrienne cast wildly about, searching for some weapon, some way of helping her. Then she realized it was not Crecy fighting for her life: It was the musketeer.

Both used nearly identical straight-bladed broadswords, the sort soldiers used. Adrienne had tried to lift one once and found it a challenge. In Crecy's hands it whipped about like a wand. Both fists clenched on the weapon, Crecy hammered thunderstrokes upon her opponent, cut and cut and cut. The musketeer fell back before her, eyes wide with terror and disbelief. He was bleeding already from two wounds, one on the cheek, another on his thigh.

Crecy was playing with him, a weird little smile on her face, her eyes distant. As Adrienne watched, the redhead batted the man's weapon aside again and sliced him on the shoulder. He stumbled back, and this time she waited for him to recover.

The musketeer was not a young man—he was perhaps thirty-five. He gritted a painful smile and threw down his sword.

"You've entertained yourself enough with me," he snarled. "God have mercy on my soul, for I will not fight another moment against a witch like you."

"As you will," Crecy said, and plunged her weapon into his heart. The musketeer flinched at the last moment and cried out. His body jerked at the blade in it, as if his chest might spit it back out. His arms flapped, and then he died.

"Are you wounded?" Crecy asked Adrienne, wiping her blade on the dead man's cloak.

"No."

Crecy surveyed the scene, clucking when her gaze fell on Adrienne's horse. "Should have warned you about that, I suppose," she commented dryly.

"You killed him," Adrienne said, still not believing what she had just seen.

"Did I?" Crecy murmured. "Come here for a moment, Mademoiselle." She took Adrienne's arm; her fingers bit like five blunt teeth. When Adrienne understood where she was being led she tried to struggle, but Crecy had no mercy.

"Who killed *them*?" she demanded.

Actually, one of the men was not dead; he was feebly beating one hand against the ground, breath rasping in short gasps.

"Well?" Crecy snapped.

"I did," Adrienne answered faintly. The scent of charred flesh was strong, and she remembered the heaps of dead on the barge.

"You did," Crecy affirmed. She reached down and cupped Adrienne's face in both palms. "Hold this tight in your heart, Adrienne. They would have killed *you*. That was their intention. Instead you killed them—you. Not some army, not some executioner, not some bodyguard."

Adrienne watched the man's feeble movements. "Can we help him?"

"Yes. Do you want to watch?"

"I can't."

"Turn around then." Crecy leaned down and kissed her on the forehead, then turned her gently away from the dying man. An instant later, the labored breathing ceased.

"Now come on. We still have several miles to go."

Adrienne proved incapable of managing either of the spirited mounts that survived the fight and so again clung to Crecy on a galloping horse. This time, however, she did not resist holding tightly; she *needed* the feel of a human body against her own.

She wished Crecy were Nicolas. Crecy's body was lean and hard, much as she had imagined Nicolas' might be. Holding Crecy now felt like salvation, like hope, though she knew she should be frightened of the woman and her strange powers. She felt Crecy's heartbeat, and she felt *life* there.

Nevertheless, she would rather it was Nicolas, his life, his heart. His last words to her thudded in her pulse and hissed in with each breath. She had never loved before. She could not, could not love Nicolas. Not now. It made no *sense*.

"How did you do that, Crecy?" she called through the wind, hoping in conversation to escape the thoughts and images rattling around in the coffin of her skull.

"Do what?" Crecy asked.

"Best a musketeer at swordplay."

"It is something I have learned, that is all."

"But how? Where? And your strength—"

"It is more than natural, yes," Crecy replied, half turning. "Does this surprise you?" She laughed, deep in her throat. "Men are always surprised, too, when I turn my edge on them."

"But how came you—"

"I have always possessed it, always nurtured it. It is another of my gifts."

"You seem to have a great many gifts," Adrienne muttered.

"They are not without their price," Crecy replied. There was something final in the way she said it.

Adrienne reluctantly took the hint. "Can you tell me where we are going?" she asked.

"One of the duke's houses," Crecy answered. "There we have an entourage to accompany you back to Versailles. They will all swear that you have been in the country."

"What is this, Crecy? What schemes am I involved in?"

"I'm not altogether certain," Crecy replied. "I will tell you what I can."

"Do you know who tried to kill the king?"

"No." But did she hesitate a bare instant? How would Adrienne know if Crecy lied?

They broke from the forest and entered a region of hilly fields. The sky had clouded, and sparse dapples of sunlight seemed like the footprints of an angel on the waving green wheat.

She wondered if Nicolas were still alive. Surely he would have caught up with them by now.

"You could have gotten Fatio to say what he said without me," Adrienne said. "Why did you need me?"

"You were the only one who could interpret what he said, ask the right *second* question. Also—" Crecy paused. "—you must know that I *never* suspected that this outing of ours would put you in such grave danger. If I had known that, I would not have even suggested it. I thought . . ."

"What?"

"I thought you might actually enjoy it. I thought you *needed* some diversion."

"Why do you care what I need?"

Crecy was silent for so long that Adrienne believed that she had ignored the question. Finally, however, she slowed the horse to a walk—its coat was foamy—and began speaking once more.

"For you," Crecy said, "it has only been a short time since we met. For me, I have seen you many times, Mademoiselle, in dreams and visions. I have known us as friends, in the future. I feel what I *shall* feel. Does that make sense?"

"This is real, then, this 'sight' of yours? And what you see always comes true?"

"To be frank, I cannot say that what I see is *always* true. But it is certainly very often true."

"If you are less than certain, why do you insist that I marry the king?"

"The truth is—" But then Crecy stopped again. "I'm sorry, Adrienne, but I cannot tell you that. I have sworn an oath."

That sounded final, but Adrienne was unwilling to stop talking without learning *something*. "Then tell me this," she appealed. "You spoke of a great catastrophe coming. What do you see?"

"The apocalypse: storms of flame, walls of water, flood, famine, plague."

"And in the sky? Do you see anything in the sky?"

"Yes. A comet, another omen of disaster."

"This comet: did it rest in the sky or move?"

"It moved swiftly."

Adrienne sighed. "Then you have known the answer all along, Mademoiselle."

"No. Seeing and knowing are different things. Can you explain my vision?"

"When I came to work with Fatio, he had already completed a calculation of two trajectories, but he was searching for a way of attracting the two bodies to each other so that their trajectories would intersect. For one of the bodies he had a very precise harmonic equation; for the other he had none. To attract two bodies, you must know their harmonic natures and then you must build a sort of bridge between them. We call this *mediation*."

"But if you do not know the nature of both bodies you cannot create a mediator," Crecy interjected.

"Precisely, and that was the problem for Fatio. However, during that time, I intercepted a strange communication from someone calling himself Janus who had been eavesdropping on our aetherschreiber conversations."

"I didn't think that was possible."

"It wasn't, and for the same reason; the mediation between

the two chimes of matched aetherschreibers is so specific that it only bridges between them. But this Janus had solved that problem, thus enabling us to see the way clear to solve Fatio's problem of attracting bodies."

"This equation from Janus, then—it allowed you to read the nature of the second body?"

"Not at all, though I think that may be what *Janus* thought. But what his equation really does is to allow us to quickly and exhaustively create the whole range of possible mediators between the two bodies. When the correct one is applied, it should immediately become obvious through counter-resonance."

"I see that. What I don't quite see is how this creates a weapon, though it raises some interesting possibilities."

"Last night, Fatio mentioned 'Lead' and 'Tin' eating their children. He was using alchemical parlance. *Lead* is the planet Saturn, and *Tin* is Jupiter. By their children he means comets."

"Comets?"

"Planets have elliptical orbits tending toward circular. Comets have very *narrow* elliptical orbits. They approach the sun very nearly and then retreat to the nothingness out beyond Saturn. It has been guessed that the great attraction of the large planets likely pulls some comets into them—they thus 'eat their children,' as Saturn did in Roman myth."

"So one of these bodies in the equation is a comet?"

"Yes. Or something like a comet. He also babbled of the 'dogs of Iron.' By *Iron* I suppose him to mean the planet Mars."

"Mars? *War* dogs, then?"

Adrienne shrugged. "The language of alchemy is more poetic than exact. But there has been some suggestion that there are dark comets between the orbits of Mars and Jupiter. If the gravity of Mars perturbed one of these comets, it might be 'sent baying in' toward the sun and thus Earth. In any event, it is clear that one of the objects in the equation is a celestial body, like a planet but smaller. The body was of *unknown* affinity."

"Why unknown?"

"Because no one knows what comets are composed of. We can make guesses, but that is all."

"Then the known body? The other moving object?"

"Why, *Earth,* of course," Adrienne replied. "And more specifically, London."

9.

The Royal Society

Maclaurin gave him a moment for that to sink in by signaling the server to pour them more coffee. Ben surveyed the others for some confirmation of the Scotsman's bizarre assertion.

"You think I have not a capful of wit?" Ben finally asked. "Why tell me such a thing—to see how gullible I might be?"

"There's too much salt in this boy," Heath muttered acidly. "He might be most useful to us as bacon."

But Voltaire and Vasilisa both grinned at his impertinence, and he knew he had won headway in that quarter.

Maclaurin stared at him, a perplexed scowl on his face. "Now why in th' hell would I do *that*?"

"Do you mean to say you are in earnest? What has become of the Royal Society?" Ben asked.

"It's not the least thing that Parliament has dissolved it," Vasilisa said.

"Replaced it, rather," Maclaurin clarified. "Our charter has been revoked."

"Why?"

Maclaurin sighed and scratched his chin. "The reasons given are many and complicated, but when the broth is boiled down, what's left is three things. First, the king and Parliament want killin' magics, and Sir Isaac won't give them any more. Second, Sir Isaac ha' made a number of enemies of late of a purely personal nature—but nothing stays purely personal in politics. Third . . . well, as I intimated earlier, Sir Isaac ha' not been entirely well."

"Not well?"

"And that is *all* you will hear on this subject for the moment, sir," Maclaurin said firmly. "So just leave it at that."

Ben nodded thoughtfully. "You said something about the society being replaced . . ."

To Ben's surprise Heath answered his unspoken question.

"The London Philosophical Society," he said, "received our charter. Many of our number defected to them."

"Muttering, chanting Rosicrucians," Voltaire opined with a sort of languid vindictiveness. "Superstitious, churchish pretenders . . ."

"So you see, Ben," Maclaurin said, sipping his coffee and speaking loudly enough to drown out Voltaire's continued muttering, "when I told you that there were many who wished to join our ranks, I lied. You're the most likely candidate we've had in a month." Ben felt a little flare of hope, but the rest of them either chuckled or smiled. Now they *were* playing with him.

"There's also the other matter . . ." Vasilisa began.

Maclaurin nodded. "We'll ha' t' talk a few things out in private, Benjamin, now that we've heard your story. Come around Crane Court aboot noon, day after tomorrow. Do y' know the place?"

"Yes, sir!" Ben replied. "But if the Royal Academy is dissolved—"

"The charter is dissolved, true enough, and our funds cut off. But the laboratories and halls at Crane Court are *ours*. Sir Isaac bought them outright, years ago. Now go on. We'll see you Thursday."

Ben stood awkwardly and then bowed. "Thank you all for your time," he said.

The miracle was that he survived the walk home. A locomotive might have come up from behind without his noticing. At one point he was sent reeling against a wall by the burly bearers of a sedan chair, and he didn't even bother to curse after them, he was so deep in thought.

The dissolution of the Royal Society was an unexpected development, but he quickly saw that it presented him with an opportunity. The older, more famous philosophers would probably have paid him little mind. But these Newtonians were not unlike his brother's Couranteers back in Boston. They were young, full of wit and sarcasm, ready to fight the Crown or anyone else for what they wanted.

Remembrance of the Couranteers summoned his brother's ghost, however, and from Charing Cross on, he returned to the guilt he thought he had buried on the long sea voyage. The worst was not James. The problem was John Collins, who might be alive and might not.

He knew he should write him, but he remembered Bracewell. If Bracewell knew where he was, he would come for him, Ben was certain of that. Could he find him in London? Yes, because he would know where to look—Crane Court.

Which was where he was going the day after tomorrow. The thought brought a little chill.

As ridiculous as the notion was, once it entered his head, he could not force it away. He wasn't able to sleep until Robert returned sometime after midnight, staggering and reeking of gin.

The next day, Ben took himself down to a bookstore he had noticed—The Archimedes Glass and Bookshop—and bought two books with money Robert reluctantly paid him. The first was *Occult Philosophy* by Cornelius Agrippa, a general text on magic written in prescientific times. It was concerned somewhat with fantastic beings—demons and the like. He felt ashamed to spend good money on such rubbish, but no more scientific book had given him any clue to Bracewell's weird nature. And Bracewell was *real*, his abilities and strange companions were *real*. If scientific philosophy did not account for such beings, perhaps occult philosophy did.

Another book caught his eye—a thin chapbook entitled *The Secret Commonwealth* by a Reverend Kirk with a "studious" note by a T. Deitz. He pulled it down and thumbed through it.

A line on the first page caught his attention:

. . . are said to be of a midle nature betwixt man and Angell (as were daemons thought to be of old); of intelligent Studious Spirits, and light changable bodies (Lik those called

Astrall) somewhat of the nature of a condens'd cloud, and best seen in twighlight.

The words "condensed cloud" brought the image of Brace-well's familiar—or whatever it was—vividly to mind.

He read the entire book on the way home. That night he slept dreamlessly, the inchoate terror held at bay by the beginnings of a hypothesis.

Despite his worries, he reached Crane Court without anything unusual happening. The court itself was so narrow as to be almost a lane, a canyon with four stories of handsome red brick for walls. A fifth floor of a darker, almost black brick surmounted the older building. From his narrow prospect, Ben could just make out what appeared to be a hemisphere on the roof. Was it an observatory?

He was surprised to be greeted by Vasilisa at the door.

"Good day, Benjamin," the Russian said. She wore an indigo dress with black lace, the cut of which seemed somehow Oriental. He felt an embarrassing rush of desire for her that he hoped did not show.

"Good day," he said.

"The others aren't here yet," she informed him. "They all have their own homes, but I stay here."

"I'm a little early," he admitted. "I suppose I'm overeager."

"Believe me, I understand," Vasilisa told him, casually linking her arm with his. "Imagine how *I* felt. A poor girl from Kiev, reading what bits and pieces of Sir Isaac's work I could get. I never in all of my life dared hope that I might *come* here and meet him, work with his students." She smiled, and Ben was gloriously aware of her arm in his, of the occasional pressure of her hip against his own.

Don't be stupid, he thought. He had seen how all of the other men—especially Voltaire—watched Vasilisa. They were all infatuated with her. Perhaps she was even involved with one of them. What could she ever see in a boy?

"This is one of the meeting halls," she said, gesturing through an open set of double doors at a spacious room. Ben gazed in with a certain awe. Who had spoken in that room—Boyle? Huygens? Of course, Newton himself had, and his presence made itself known in a pair of portraits.

"Come here," Vasilisa urged, tugging on his arm. "When I first saw this, I thought I would faint."

Ben didn't come near fainting when they reached the next room, but he did grin ear to ear.

"An orrery," he gasped. "I've never really seen one."

"I love just to watch it move." Vasilisa sighed.

For a long moment, the only sound in the room was the clicking of clockwork.

The sun in the center of the orrery glowed with a gentle radiance, save where it was marred by darker spots. Ben felt a little thrill at such accuracy. Nearest the sun raced Mercury, a grayish sphere, its orbital movement visible. Next out was Venus, then their own Earth, Mars, and finally the giant globes of Jupiter and Saturn. Earth's moon was present, as were the moons of the larger planets.

Ben had seen drawings of such models of the solar system before, but in those, the bodies were supported by armatures. Here, all floated freely, as the glowing stone had floated above Bracewell's head.

"Most remarkable," Ben breathed. Then a thought struck him.

"Where is the clockwork I hear? What drives these around?"

Vasilisa smiled and pointed up to the ceiling. There, behind a plate of glass, a mass of gears clucked and clattered.

"The planets are attuned to those rods, which attract them just enough so that they do not fall. Their spin and orbit is imparted internally—each orb has been taught to spin of its own accord."

"It's unbelievable. Who built this?"

"James did, for Newton and Halley."

"James? The quiet one?"

"Quiet but brilliant. I'm told he did not sleep for five days, working out just the basics of this."

"And it is accurate? The movements are all correct?"

"Not perfect, but the corrections required are so tiny that it can run for months without need of adjusting, at least when it is running at 'real' speed. Right now it's going about triple the speed of the true solar system: Colin and James are trying to place more bodies into the structure."

"What do you mean?"

"This isn't a toy," Vasilisa replied. "We use it to experiment with the motions of bodies. These, for instance." She gently relinquished her hold on him and strode over to the orrery.

"Of course the size of the orbs is proportionally too large for the distance between them," she explained, "else the planets would be too small to see. But all of that can be corrected for. Now, see this?"

She pointed to something Ben had not noticed before: a marble-sized object suspended in air near Saturn but too far away to be one of the moons.

"A comet?" he asked.

"Oh, wonderfully done," Vasilisa said.

Ben walked around the orrery now, frowning. "Why, there's another," he muttered, "and another. And there, between Jupiter and Mars, a whole belt of them."

"Actually, those seem different," Vasilisa remarked, stepping in toward Mars. "See, these have more circular orbits, like the planets. The comets and black comets stream in elliptically."

"Black comets?"

"They do not develop tails of flame as comets do." She dimpled. "They cannot be seen through a telescope."

Ben gestured vaguely around him. "Then how—" he began.

"A new device," she said. "You will not have heard of it. But these comets are the least of things. Much more major additions will have to be made to the orrery than that!"

"What? What are you saying?"

"Too much," Vasilisa said. "I should wait for Mr. Maclaurin to explain all this to you. I have been a bit impertinent, I'm afraid."

"Well, finish explaining about the uses of this," Ben pursued stubbornly.

Vasilisa nodded. "I don't see the harm in that," she admitted. "As you probably know, each heavenly body has some small effect on every other. The gravity of Jupiter bends slightly the orbit of Mars, and so on. The motion of no one planet can be calculated without reference to another."

"Yes, that I understand," Ben said.

"Well, then, taking into account everything we know, we make this orrery and set it running, and we find that in a short time it deviates from reality. Do you see what that means?"

"It means that there are unseen bodies amongst the seen," Ben replied. When Vasilisa beamed at his answer, he felt a surge of satisfaction.

"Of course. So we try to account for them by adding things. We can test our hypothesis here until we have a model of the solar system that runs precisely correctly. Then we shall know we have it right."

"But you imply that you have some other way of detecting these unseen bodies."

"I did, didn't I?" Vasilisa grinned. "But you have dragged enough from me today. Let us retire to a sitting room and have some chocolate. It will be our secret that I showed you this in advance."

Ben agreed, finding that he liked sharing secrets with Vasilisa.

They were halfway through a cup of chocolate when Maclaurin and Heath arrived.

"Already here, eh?" Maclaurin said when he saw Ben. "Have you been makin' too free of our secrets, Vasilisa?"

"Colin, you astonish me," Vasilisa demurred.

"Oh, certain," Maclaurin said. "Well, whatever. Finish up, me boy, for you've much work to do."

"Work?"

"Aye. Didn't you come here in hopes of 'prenticing to Sir Isaac?"

"I . . . ah—" Ben started.

"Well, with luck, all of us students together might add up to a single Newton."

Ben stared at the Scot, wondering if he was really saying what he seemed to be saying.

"We've agreed," Maclaurin explained, slowly, as if to a dim-wit. "You can be 'prentice to us all."

* * *

Ben soon discovered that being an apprentice to philosophers was much the same as being any other sort of apprentice; it mostly involved doing the boring, menial tasks that the adepts did not themselves care to do. His first day he washed glassware, swept floors, brought water and coffee. But he got to see three of the laboratories and wonder at the alchemical and philosophical devices that filled them, and even if he had not, his moment that morning with Vasilisa and the orrery would have paid for all of his work.

After a week of sweeping and washing and answering the door, he was no longer certain. He finally confronted Maclaurin about it.

"I'm supposed to be an apprentice, and yet I'm not learning anything," he grumbled. "Or being paid, for that matter."

"Didn't I tell you?" Maclaurin said, taking a bench and rubbing his eyes. "Tomorrow you'll build us one of your aetherschreibers. Besides that, the library and the little laboratory are open to you, should you wish to use them." He paused briefly. "We've not much to pay you with, but you can take a room here, just as Vasilisa has."

"I . . . well, the thing is, I'm sharing a house with a friend of mine. I'm expected to help with the rent there." And yet the thought of actually living here, of having every spare moment to spend with whatever experiments he might conceive . . . "I'll think about it," he finished.

"I can't say I blame you," Robert said quietly. "These new friends of yours must be a hell of a lot more interestin' than a footpad like me."

"It's not *that*, Robin. It's that they've nothing to *pay* me with but the room. And I've nothing to pay you with for this one."

"I still owe you a few pounds. Besides, I can get you on as an adjustant on a locomotive," Robert replied.

"By my reckoning you've paid me in full," Ben said. "If it weren't for you, I'd probably be dead several times by now."

Robert nodded absently. "The thing is, Ben," he said, "I'm in a bit of a spot. I had some ill luck at the gambling tables the other night. I'm more than a little in debt. I was truly hoping you would take the locomotive job and stay here until I can settle up and start paying rent again."

A sort of sinking feeling had begun in Ben's belly. He owed Robert a lot, he supposed.

But not that much.

"Robin," he said, "I . . . your gambling and drinking are your affairs. I don't mean that to sound harsh. You're the best friend I have in London. If I had more money to lend, I would. But I *have* to do this 'prenticeship. It's what I came to London *for*."

"That's odd," Robert remarked somewhat coldly. "I had the idea that you came here because you were *fleeing* Boston. How many debts did you leave behind there?"

Ben's face flushed hot, and he stared hard at the floor.

"I thought I could count on you," Robert said softly, "but I should know by now that Robert Nairne must count only on Robert Nairne."

Ben had no answer for that.

Ben moved to Crane Court the next day. The whole scientific world lay before him.

10.

Sin

Louis arose, leaving Adrienne drenched in their commingled sweat. She drew the sheet up over her nakedness. Pressing the linen against her face, she blotted the tears there, knowing that if Louis could not hear her cry, he would not know of it. Whatever sorcery gave him vision would not show him tears.

I am becoming the ghost of Maintenon, she thought.

Tonight her body actually hurt. The king was never brutal, but she still bore the bruises from today's adventures, and the dull ache that followed sex was like a key that unlocked those other pains.

No word had yet been heard from Nicolas, and that was a whole different species of pain.

Crecy and she had reached the country home that had been their destination, where Adrienne had been bathed and dressed in proper women's fashion. She had then returned to Versailles as if nothing had happened. Bontemps himself had greeted her, asking no unusual questions, and that evening she had played cards with the king and Torcy. Torcy told her of the strange trio who had invaded the masque of the duke of Orléans and slain a number of musketeers, but he did so without irony. The king had quite casually asked about Nicolas, and she had lied, saying that she had released him for two days to visit a cousin in Paris. It had already occurred to her that the king and his minister might know exactly where Nicolas was, but if so she was probably already doomed. At the king's suggestion, she had returned to her rooms early, and he had come to her shortly thereafter.

She wished she could peel off her body like a soiled dress and throw it on a trash heap, but the best she could do was to hide it from her sight. It had been bad enough that her flesh had been dirtied without the sacrament of marriage. Now she knew she had been whore to the bringer of the apocalypse. Nothing could cleanse the stench of monster from her.

It was lying there, weeping for dead Nicolas and her own dead soul, that she began to understand what her remaining purpose was.

She, Adrienne, would kill the king.

Who else could do it? Who else could have him alone and naked, without his protections against bullets and daggers?

She might already have waited too long. If Nicolas had been killed, if the musketeers had his body . . .

But Louis, who had just lain with her, could not suspect much unless, in his madness, he thought himself invulnerable.

The outer door creaked open again. "I've ordered you a bath," Crecy's voice said gently, after a moment.

Adrienne didn't answer, but presently she heard maids bringing in hot water and pouring it into her tub in the adjoining room. When Crecy had helped her into the hot, scented water, she felt better, especially when the other's immensely strong fingers began stroking her shoulders. As the knots in her neck and back were kneaded loose, she considered again how she might murder the king. Feeling the strength of Crecy's fingers, she wondered if Crecy and the Korai had always known that it would come to this, if their plan was to kill Louis XIV all along.

It seemed reasonable, but she could not work up the anger that she should. After all, *someone* had to stop him.

"Is this too hard?" Crecy asked.

"No." She paused. "May I call you Veronique? Now that I no longer have Nicolas . . ." she started, but on his name she choked and began to whimper.

"I had uncharitable thoughts about you the other night, Cre— *Veronique*."

"You would not be the first, Adrienne," Crecy answered.

"I thought you a whore for using your body to extort information from Fatio."

Crecy's hands paused, then resumed their work. "Perhaps I

was," Crecy replied. "I did not have to use very *much* of my body. I did not fuck him, Adrienne, but I *would* have, to learn what we learned."

"You see, I would not have," Adrienne said bitterly, "though I would let a king fuck me because I have been told to do so. Doing what you did would not have been *passive* enough for me."

"Don't speak of yourself so," Crecy admonished. "It is difficult enough to survive the humiliations heaped upon you by others without adding your own."

"Is it easy for you?" Adrienne asked. "Do you enjoy it?"

"Do you mean sex?" Crecy asked.

"I suppose. Did you enjoy seducing Fatio?"

Crecy chuckled throatily. "I suppose I did—it is a feeling of power, to see men become helpless. Fatio was not much of a challenge."

"I used to enjoy my power over him," Adrienne admitted, "though I was never so bold as you. I only smiled, only implied possibilities. I was jealous of you, I think."

"Jealous?"

"Stupid, isn't it? It's just that I never conquered much, Veronique, and you so quickly overran my possession."

"Some would consider the king a great prize," Crecy pointed out softly.

Adrienne stiffened. "*I* did not do that," she said. "Can't you see that with your prescience? The king's love is for some creature of his mind that I have the poor fortune to resemble."

"I said 'some,' Adrienne. *I* do not envy you—your pain is too apparent. I wish I could extricate you from this mess, for I know that I am in large measure responsible."

"No," Adrienne averred, "you may have seen it, but you did not bring it about. I thought that I would be the queen, and powerful. I thought the king might—that I might even enjoy . . ." She sighed. "I betrayed myself."

"You are very young," Crecy said. "You must want many things you are told you should not have. Such conflict makes one stupid."

"I suppose. I suppose that I thought with the king, it would not be sin."

"*Pfah*. Sin. There is your problem, Adrienne. Have not your researches shown you that the universe has no need of God?"

"Perhaps *I* have need of God," Adrienne answered shakily.

"Weakness."

"What would you know of weakness?" Adrienne asked. "You, who do as you please, who hold a man's position in the Hundred Swiss, who wield a sword like Roland or Oliver?"

Crecy laughed. "You admire this?"

"I have always wanted . . ." Adrienne stopped. "Castries was right," she went on. "I have always sought some middle path between marriage and the convent."

"Yes, yes, that is clear," Crecy said. "But I tell you again, your agony is in the *contradiction*. You want the fruits of the life of Ninon, but you insist on the principles of Madame de Maintenon. As if *she* had principles."

"What? What slander is this? I *knew* Maintenon, I saw her piety—"

"You saw her in the prison she built for herself, but she was not always thus. Let me tell you a story, Adrienne. It begins many years ago. Maintenon was Ninon's pupil in love and life. She married the cripple Scarron, who was Ninon's dearest friend. Does this sound like a lie yet?"

"No," Adrienne whispered.

"Scarron was worthless for the lusts of a young beauty like Maintenon. Ninon passed her hand-me-downs to Maintenon. Ninon lent them a room for their lovemaking. And Ninon and Maintenon shared the same bed for some three months."

A terrible little thrill jolted through Adrienne's belly. "Are you saying . . ."

"I leave it for you," Crecy replied, her mouth quite near Adrienne's ear, so that her breath touched it with warmth. "In the end, Maintenon had another sort of ambition than Ninon. Ninon wanted nothing more than to lead life on her own terms, beholden to no one. Maintenon craved riches and power. When she managed to become governess of the king's bastards by Montespan, she saw her chance. She saw the king had begun to feel the guilt of his many sins. And so, to win him, she put on the mask of piety. And she succeeded, replacing Montespan as mistress. When the queen died, she replaced her, too. The woman you knew, Adrienne, was a woman whose mask had become glued to her face."

Crecy fell silent, and Adrienne stared up at the baroquely patterned ceiling. She felt sick, but it was a new sort of sickness. It was true, she knew it.

"Why do you tell me this?"

"I told you," Crecy said quietly. "One day we shall be friends. I want to save you, Adrienne, from Maintenon's fate. You wear a mask, but it has not yet become fixed."

"Then you should not have told the Korai of your vision," she replied.

"That would not have saved you, only prolonged your silly illusion. Maintenon's so-called morality is what keeps us chained, Adrienne. You cannot be her and Ninon at once."

Adrienne wiped her eyes of tears she had not even realized were present and felt a sudden strength, as if something wobbly within her were suddenly unshakable. "Come where I can see you, Veronique. Sit on that stool, please."

Crecy did so.

"You are very convincing," Adrienne told her, "though I know you lie to me often. But you are right; I have been playing at the wrong game and losing. Torcy once wondered whether I was a queen or a pawn, and I vowed to be a queen. I failed because I did not understand that the queen is as lacking in free will as the pawn. What I wish now is to be neither. I wish to move the pieces myself."

"I understand you," Crecy replied, a suspicion of a grin brightening her features.

"Good. I do not know what your obligations to the duchess and the Korai are, Veronique. Frankly I do not care what they are, so long as they do not impede my own designs. Some things need doing, and I would prefer help in doing them. These things are very dangerous. Will you help me?"

Crecy's smile vanished. She stood up from her stool. For the first time since they had met, Crecy looked eager.

"There you are!" she exclaimed. "The woman I have seen in

visions, the woman I hoped you to be. Command me. I am yours."

"Do not mock me," warned Adrienne.

"Adrienne, I do not mock you. This is not sarcasm. I am giving you what pledge I can."

"What does 'what pledge I can' mean?" Adrienne asked.

"I cannot lay aside any earlier oaths, but henceforth I will make no new promises without your permission."

Adrienne reached for the towel, staring at this strange woman. What new ploy was this? "Do not say these things if you do not mean them," she cautioned.

"I do not."

"Then here is what we must do first, tonight."

The trouble with sneaking about Versailles at night was that it was as bright as it was during the day. Lanterns of fanciful design lined the halls—nymphs with glowing eyes and mouths, sun standards, seraphim with wings like slivers of moon. Guarding the stair ahead of her was a golden Michael with flaming sword. She wondered briefly how the uneven fluttering of his lantern-sword had been produced. In stockinged feet she glided past the archangel, down the stairs.

A rustle of skirts and the clatter of shoes on marble followed, and Crecy stood beside her.

"Well?" Adrienne whispered. They were in the part of the chateau where older ministers and household servants had their lodgings. Most were asleep or in the fashionable salons of Paris or flattering some member of royalty.

"He is distracted," Crecy assured her, speaking of the guard who had taken Nicolas' place in front of Adrienne's door. "For an hour or so, anyway." She smiled. "One of the kitchen girls owes me a favor.

"Worry not," Crecy added. "This one had an itch to scratch anyway. *She* will not suffer, I promise."

"Very well. The laboratory will be guarded as well."

"And that is what *I* am for, is it not?" Crecy asked.

Adrienne did not answer, but Crecy kissed her on the cheek and started ahead.

Adrienne stood at the head of the stairway and waited, until she heard whispered conversation, and then more dubious sounds, down the corridor. She edged up and peered down the hall.

Crecy was leading the guard away by the hand; the young man was kissing her neck playfully. They vanished around a corner.

So simple. She wondered if she could unlearn this use of people when everything was over.

Of course, when everything was over, she would doubtless be dangling from a gallows.

Her key still fit the laboratory lock. She opened the door gently and then shut it behind her and locked it again.

She found the papers she sought, copying the parts of the formula she did not already know. She no longer needed the broad outlines. In fact, looking at Fatio's final calculations, she saw that she could have even suggested improvements. She understood this city-killing spell now; what she wanted were the specifics.

She found them. She also found a sheaf of papers with odd, stippled patterns on them, as if they had been smudged by dirty fingers. A closer examination revealed that the patterns had been burnt on.

The comet's mass and dimensions and gross composition— the alchemical symbol for iron in greatest proportion—were recorded. A rough sphere of iron half a league in diameter was going to hit London. How fast would it be moving? Did it matter?

Something nagged her that it did, so she found that, too, and wrote it down.

She didn't have to check the date when it would strike London. That she knew already.

Now there was one more thing, perhaps the most important. She rapped very lightly on the door of Fatio's bedchamber.

If a kitchen girl and Crecy could do it, so could she. She closed her eyes, preparing what she would say.

But no answer came, so she tried the handle and found the door was unlocked. She glanced in.

The bedchamber was lit by a half-shuttered lantern but Fatio was out. He could return anytime. Her heart was thumping, but she knew she only needed a few moments to commit the treason she planned. Where was his aetherschreiber?

She found it immediately. It was a very old one, probably one of the first fifty made, sitting on a little stand in the corner.

Removing the lid, she found that spiders had made a home within; cities of silk tore as she readied the device for use. When Fatio went to use it next, he would know that someone else had.

She was dreadfully aware of the clock ticking by the night-stand as she lay paper in the machine.

She began to write. If this machine's mate was not there, if it was not wound, her labors would be for nothing.

She was not finished when she heard the outer door open. Condensing as much as she could, she hurried through for-mulae, omitting explanatory text, knowing that if this machine had its mate where she thought it did, a longer explanation was not necessary. It had to be with Newton himself. Given Fatio's betrayed love and his sick pride, it could not be otherwise.

Someone fumbled at Fatio's chamber door.

No time to remove the paper. She wrote the last line and quickly placed the lid on the machine. Just as Fatio stumbled into the chamber, she dashed into the open closet.

She was not quick enough, and Fatio glimpsed her. He looked puzzled, then laughed.

He was very, very drunk. He tried to get his breeches off and fell on the floor, then he whimpered a bit before rising un-steadily and flopping across the bed.

After Adrienne counted a hundred breaths and he hadn't moved, she slipped out of the closet and removed the paper from the schreiber.

Once back in the laboratory she moved to one of the win-dows that opened onto a broad ledge. She planned to walk along it until she reached an outside stairway. She could then reenter the chateau as if she had merely gone out for some air.

The window creaked as it opened, and suddenly all of the hairs on Adrienne's neck stood up. The pane before her red-dened with reflected light. She turned, and her heart seemed to stop in her chest.

Drifting toward her from the center of the room was a cloud of smoke and flame with a single glowing orb that resembled a huge eye.

11.

Newton

"Don't get stupid, Ben, I need you payin' attention," Maclaurin snapped, interrupting Ben's speculations.

"Maybe if I understood what we were doing," Ben grumbled.

"I'll explain in a moment," Maclaurin said. "For now just keep up wi' me. This all must be performed wi' in a certain short period of time."

Ben did as he was told, though he continued to eye the telescope speculatively.

If it even *was* a telescope. What kind of telescope could you use at *midday*? What was Maclaurin looking at?

He should have learned by now that the mathematician—or whatever he was—did not give answers readily. He preferred Ben to *deduce* what he was about.

A click sounded, and Maclaurin quickly handed him another plate. It was about a foot square and seemed to be made of rusty iron. Handling had shown Ben it was some nonferrous metal— he suspected zinc—with a fine emulsion of rust on one side. Following Maclaurin's instructions, Ben laid a piece of paper on the plate, clipped a frame onto it that held the paper tight against the metal, and dusted it with iron powder. Then he blew to clear it, revealing swirling patterns that resembled fingerprints. Next he removed a similar plate—on which he had put paper about a minute ago—from a boxy device. This plate was warm. He placed the new plate into the box and pulled the handle. The machine hissed. Meantime, he unclipped the frame from the earlier plate and brushed off the filings. The patterns remained on the paper, apparently burned there.

This was the sixteenth such sheet, and he numbered it accordingly.

Maclaurin, during all of this, had shifted the telescope a few degrees. He depressed a switch, and another plate came out. Ben handed him the old one and began the process once more.

"This would be easier if there were more than three plates," Ben remarked.

"Yes. But those things are expensive," Maclaurin explained. "Hang on, now, just a few more to go. We ha' to make all of these as close together as we can."

A quarter of an hour later, the philosopher stepped away from the telescope. "Let's see what we got," he said.

Ben finished up the last sheet, then brought it over to where Maclaurin was spreading the rest out on a table, overlapping them a bit. Ben noticed that the sheets matched at the edges, and together they formed a *large* image.

"Well?" Maclaurin said expectantly.

"Ah . . . it looks a little like star patterns or something, but the sizes are all wrong."

"What do ya mean?"

"I mean that stars don't vary that much in size. Here's one the size of a shilling and another no larger than a pinhead. Besides, it's daylight . . . Wait, I see. This telescope doesn't look at light at all, does it?"

Maclaurin grinned broadly and slapped him on the back. "Good lad! Would it help if I called it an affinascope?"

"Yes," Ben replied immediately.

"Explain, then."

Ben felt a rising tide of excitement lifting the words out of him. "The scope registers the proportionate pull of gravity of different celestial bodies. You must have a mercuric translator that transforms the gravitic harmonics into magnetism. That, in turn, writes patterns on the rust. The patterns hold the iron dust in similar patterns when I sprinkle it on, and that gets burned on the paper. This *is* a star chart, but it indicates the *mass* of the stars."

"Aye!" Maclaurin confirmed. "Though I must correct you in one particular; what you see here are not stars, but planets, moons, and comets." He stabbed at the largest mark. "This is Jupiter, and these—" He pointed in turn at seven smaller blobs. "—are its moons."

"I thought Jupiter had four moons."

"Haven't you looked at the orrery?"

"Yes. I meant to ask about the extra moon, but I assumed that it had been discovered recently."

"Indeed. By Edwin and I. And now we can add two more!" he crowed. "Things too small to see wi' an optical telescope are easily found wi' the affinascope. Of course, we *knew* they were there already—this is only the proof."

"How did you know?"

"Remember Newton's laws of harmonic affinity? Attraction is a function of the generality of the affinity and the distance. In the case of gravity 'tis a simple matter of mass and the inverse square of the distance. Wi' more specific affinities, the proportion changes so that the attraction is stronger over longer distances."

"Yes, I understand all of that."

"Well, that means one orbiting body will skew the orbit of another, if it's close enough and massive enough. We could tell, for instance, that Ganymede's orbit was perturbed in a way that Jupiter, the sun, and the moons we know could'na account for. Ipso facto, there must be other moons. And there they are!" He gestured wildly at the sheets.

Maclaurin tousled Ben's hair and then began searching about for paper and pen. "You've been a great help," he said. "Why na' go an see if one o' the others has some use for you now?"

"What of these?" he asked of a handful of sheets that had not been spread.

"Och! I forgot! Those need to be run over to Sir Isaac's place right away. I dunno what they are, to tell you the truth. He just sent a message to look at such and such a place in the sky and compose some affinagraphs. Best run those now, Ben. This is the first any of us have heard from him in an age, and 'twould be impertinent to keep him waitin'."

"But I don't know where Sir Isaac lives."

"It's on Saint Martin's Lane, near Leicester Fields."

"Ah . . . what should I say when I see him?"

"Oh, I don't think you'll *see* him, lad. Just give the papers to his niece, Mrs. Barton."

"We'll see," Ben replied.

Ben's first impression was red, and so was his second. The rug was red; the chairs were red; the walls were red.

After red, he noticed the portraits. He counted five paintings: Sir Isaac draped in the gowns of the Trinity Lucasian professor, periwig on his head; Sir Isaac holding a copy of his *Principia*, gazing abstractedly at the universe; Sir Isaac with his own, sparse gray hair, dignified, one fierce dark eye fixed toward the artist . . . There were busts, too. All of these depicted him *old*. He was vague in some, haughty in others, but in all he bore a frown, ranging from a small puckering between his nose to a full-out glower.

Ben noticed, somewhat abstractedly, that his palms were damp. How many times had he imagined meeting Newton? He had even written out one of the speeches he had hoped to give by way of introducing himself. He realized that he had imagined that the old man would greet him like a soul mate, a long-lost grandson. But no such grandfatherly man gazed down at him.

Mrs. Barton—an attractive, fortyish woman—let him gaze, open-mouthed. She must be used to the reaction.

"You say you come from the Colonies," she said, offering Ben a chair.

Ben paused, distracted by a sort of pinging noise issuing from behind a heavy wooden door. "Yes, I was born in Boston Town, in Massachusetts."

"Massachusetts," she repeated. "What a mouthful, eh? My brother used to write me, and I could never pronounce those American names to my friends. I had to show them the letters."

"Your brother traveled in America?"

"He died there, unfortunately," Mrs. Barton replied.

The pinging was getting louder. Mrs. Barton followed Ben's glance to the closed door and sighed. "Well, if you have brought those things for him . . ."

"I was given to understand," Ben quickly lied, "that I was to deliver them to him personally."

Mrs. Barton gazed at him thoughtfully for a moment. "I rather doubt that."

Ben pursed his lips, and then nodded slightly. "I'm sorry. But won't you see if he will receive me?"

"He won't," she told him.

"Tell him it is 'Janus' calling."

"Very well. It won't hurt to try. Wait a moment."

Her skirts whisked briskly as she went to the door and rapped. The pinging stopped.

"Sir Isaac," she called through the door, "a young man has brought you something from Colin Maclaurin. He wishes to speak with you, if you have a moment. He says that it is Janus come to call."

"Send him in." The voice did not sound old, as Ben had expected, but it did sound like the voice of the portraits. Distracted, as if he could spare only a small part of himself to speak.

The room beyond the door was red, too, but it was dark. In the murk Ben made out books, glassware, a furnace, calipers and other measures, and a thousand things he couldn't recognize, including what looked like a sort of step pyramid built of wire and metal plates.

"I've changed my mind. Leave it on the table." The speaker was a vague shadow seated in a darkened alcove all the way across the room.

"Sir?"

"Leave it on the end table. And go away." Ben saw the table he meant and put the papers on it with trembling fingers. He hesitated, trying to think of what to say. "Sir . . ." he began, with not the slightest notion what his next words would be.

"Wait. Wait." The shadow seemed to shift. Ben paused obediently.

"What are they saying about me?" the voice demanded.

"Ah . . . who, sir?"

"Flamsteed. Locke. De Duillier. All of them."

"Sir, I . . . *John Locke*?"

"Yes. What has my *'friend'* Locke been saying about me? He tried to poison me, you know."

Ben wasn't certain, but he thought that John Locke had been dead for at least a decade now. He couldn't say that, could he? What *could* he say?

Fortunately, Newton rushed on. "Well, *I* have heard from de Duillier. Tell him I am not pleased, not at all."

"Yes, sir."

There was a long pause, then Sir Isaac spoke again, in quite another tone. "You're that boy from America? The one who improved the aetherschreiber? Janus?"

"Yes, sir. Benjamin Franklin, sir," he replied, shocked. He started forward, more or less without thinking. "And if I might say so, a great admirer—"

"No!" Newton snapped. "No, stay there. Come no closer." Ben froze in place as Newton continued. "I am stalking the Green Lyon again," Newton explained in a harsh whisper. "It would be unwise of you to approach. Tell Maclaurin that I thank him. Come back in . . . three days, do you hear?"

"Yes, sir," Ben acknowledged.

"And tell that lecher Voltaire to stay away from my niece!"

Ben nodded.

"Very well. Leave now."

His mouth dry, Ben backed through and closed the door.

Mrs. Barton lay a hand on his shoulder. "Would you care for a dram of brandy, Mr. Franklin?" she asked sweetly.

"I . . . I think so," he answered weakly. "That would be much appreciated."

12.

In the Maze

For perhaps ten heartbeats Adrienne stared at the eye, frozen by the same instinct that took hold when one saw a snake: to stay still lest it strike. The thing did not resemble a serpent, of course, at least not overtly, but its sheer alienness—coupled with the overwhelming sensation that it was a *living* thing—created a snakelike impression.

The only sound in the room was her own ragged breathing.

And then a key scraping into the outside lock jarred her from her paralysis, and she darted out the window and onto the ledge. She inched along, her skirts hissing against the stone, wondering if she could survive a two-story fall. Casting a fearful glance over her shoulder, she saw the thing drift languidly out the window. It seemed in no apparent hurry to catch her, but skeleton fingers spidered up her spine. She walked faster, but her feet tripped over themselves.

Suddenly there was nothing supporting her, and her arms were beating crazily against air. Then she felt scratched by a thousand daggers, her skirts and bodice tearing.

The ground caught her like the blow of a fist, stole her breath and would not give it back. Stunned, with bright spots dancing before her eyes, she felt suddenly lifted by a strong pair of arms. Whoever it was began to run, cradling her against a muscular torso. She saw Versailles receding and looked toward the open window of Fatio's laboratory. The red thing hovered in the window, limning a human form: *Gustavus.*

And in that same moment, she realized who was carrying her.

"Nicolas!" she gasped.

"Shh. Just a few moments more."

"I can run."

He loped across the grounds, bearing her as if she were weightless. He ran where night had spilled her dark milk, avoiding the lanterns that illuminated the pathways, the colonnades, the monuments to himself Louis might wish to see when he gazed from his window. Nicolas shifted her somewhat, and she reached around his shoulders, gripping tight. Above, the horns of the crescent moon reached out to embrace Jupiter, all the argenteyed gods of heaven looking on.

Which of those bright points above was the ammunition for the cannon? Which was the chariot of death?

Suddenly hedges enclosed them in walls high and dark; Nicolas brushed against them. At last his breath was beginning to sound labored.

"Please," she said. "I'm not hurt."

"It was a long fall," he whispered.

"I'm not hurt," she insisted. "I must have landed in a bush."

He came to a stop and slowly, carefully set her on her feet. Her arms seemed welded around his neck and came away sluggishly.

"Sit," he whispered, and suddenly there was a pistol in his hand. He jogged back a few feet, made a satisfied noise, and returned to her.

"If you can walk, we should move a little farther. I know the way through."

"Is this the labyrinth?" Adrienne asked.

"Yes. We should stay here a bit, until the dogs stop barking and the guards relax. What in the world were you doing?" His eyes blazed with concern.

"Nicolas, you're alive," she said.

"Why, yes," he replied.

"I . . . Crecy and I believed you dead."

"I had to make a longer detour than I would have liked," he explained. "I was out of ammunition, my sword was broken, and one of them still had a *kraftpistole*. I led him a merry chase before he got careless. What about the two of you?"

"I had to use the gun you gave me. What kind of gun was that? It killed my horse. And then Crecy killed a man with her sword, and we thought you were dead . . ." She felt very stupid. Her voice seemed to be talking entirely without her.

"I should have warned you about the gun. It shoots a spray of molten silver . . ."

He said something else, but she wasn't listening. The blood was roaring in her ears as she screwed up her courage.

She meant it to be a long, passionate kiss, but at the last moment her courage failed, and it was a quick one. His mouth tasted cool and salty, and he grunted in surprise. Just as she was feeling foolish, his lips came back to her, and she got the kiss she had meant to give.

"None of it is random," she told him a little later. They lay on their backs, she in the crook of his arm, watching the stars. She felt a contentment that she knew could not last.

"It looks that way," he said. "My grandmama used to say that two angels once argued over a strand of jewels and broke the thread that held them. But I've heard philosophers speak of the harmony of the spheres. I never really knew what it meant."

"Should I explain?" She sighed.

"I might not understand."

"You would, but I won't bore you—"

"You could never bore me."

"—bore you with the dry details. What do you see when you look up into the night sky?"

"The same as what I see when I look at you," he replied. "Beauty. God's beautiful universe."

"Me, too. And every way I look at it—with a telescope or through a mathematical lens or like this beside you—each prospect only adds new sorts of beauty. The same laws of nature that produce the music of a flute or a harp govern the motions of the stars. It makes my heart sing to think about it."

He was silent for a moment and then said, "I love you, Adrienne de Mornay de Montchevreuil."

She kissed his cheek. "I'm glad you are alive, Nicolas." She wanted to say much more. She wanted to tell him how he had changed her from dead to living in only a few moments, but she kissed him instead, delighting in the roughness of his jaw, the warmth of his breath.

When they parted again, he sat up and spoke seriously, gripping her by the shoulders. "Adrienne, we should leave here tonight."

"Where would we go?"

"Anywhere. Austria, Acadia, Louisiana. We cannot stay here."

Adrienne closed her eyes. "If only you had said this two months ago, Nicolas."

"Why not now? I know you don't love the king."

Adrienne almost choked. "Love him?" she said, hearing her voice flatten. "No. But I cannot leave yet, Nicolas."

"Do you love *me*, Adrienne? You did not say so."

"I think I do, Nicolas," she replied softly. "My lips like the touch of yours. My body likes your hands upon it. I think one day I would like . . . to make love to a man I *did* love. I think that is you. But I cannot be certain until some important things have ceased to demand my attention."

"Adrienne, if you stay here . . . You are engaged to the king."

"I may have to marry him. I don't want to, Nicolas, but things have gone beyond allowing me to choose what I want. Millions of lives are at stake."

"I don't understand."

"I will explain it to you later, Nicolas. Now I want you to kiss me again; hold me some more. Give me some of your courage. And later . . ."

"I cannot cuckold the king," Nicolas breathed. "If you marry him, I will—"

At that moment came the faint sound of feet upon the grass, and a tall shadow moved against the stars.

"How lovely to see you alive, Nicolas," Crecy's voice said. "I see you have Mademoiselle well in hand. But if the two of you don't mind, I think it would be best for us all if we returned to our rooms before dawn."

Nicolas reluctantly slipped off to where the Hundred Swiss had their lodging while Crecy and Adrienne entered by one of the few unguarded ways. Adrienne hid most of her torn gown with Crecy's shawl.

The guard at Adrienne's door started when he saw the two of them. "Miladies," he gasped, "I did not—"

"You did not see us go out because we *did* not go out, Alexander," Crecy finished for him.

The guard's face waxed scarlet. "Whatever you wish," he mumbled.

"How gallant. I hope you were as thoughtful of Marie's needs."

The guard's expression promised that she had made her point clear.

Helen was asleep in a chair in the antechamber and roused muzzily when the door opened.

"Mademoiselle," she murmured.

"Helen, go to your chamber and sleep properly. My presence was again requested by the king."

"Yes, Mademoiselle."

When they were alone, Crecy helped her undress.

"I am so *tired*." She sighed.

"The devil!" Crecy said, examining Adrienne's stockings. "No grass stains! Now there's a trick I've never learned."

Adrienne giggled. Her blood felt as if it were fizzing like champagne. Outside, the sky was already gray, the morning star a bright spark.

"We didn't do *that*," she said shyly. "He just kissed me."

"Didn't he even *try*?"

Adrienne laughed. "I suppose he did, but he was very polite. He let me have what I wanted and asked for nothing." She noticed Crecy's skeptical smile. "No, really," she went on. "I know it's stupid, Veronique. I've been with the king many times. But in this way, I'm still a virgin. Does that make any sense at all?"

Crecy's expression softened. "Yes, it makes sense. And if it is of any consequence, *I* still regard you as a virgin."

Adrienne studied Crecy carefully for any signs of mockery. "Thank you," she said.

"You are the only woman in Versailles who would thank me for such an accusation. Nevertheless, you are welcome. Now, not to say that your little encounter with Nicolas would not have made all of our efforts worthwhile, but did you—"

"Oh! I found it in his room, just as I thought I might."

"How did you know?"

"Do you remember at the party in Paris, the way Fatio went on about Newton? Once Fatio and Newton were very close. The impression I get of Sir Isaac is that he is a very cold man with few friends. But I think Fatio was his friend."

"Do you think they were lovers?"

Adrienne paused, embarrassed that she had considered that already. "No. But Crecy, there is something to your question. These two men were once dear to each other, that is clear. Yet they have not spoken in twenty years. All this time, I think that Fatio has been trying to win back Newton's heart, and I think that his love has turned to venom. He has created a weapon that will kill everyone in London, using Newton's own theories to do so."

"And that is why you suspected he has a way of communicating with Sir Isaac."

"Yes. He wants him to *know*, Veronique. Maybe not until the comet is plummeting to Earth. Or maybe he means Sir Isaac to flee London and truly *understand* what he has wrought. But a man like Fatio lives for the praise of others. For Fatio, this would have all been for naught if Newton were to die without knowing who had killed him."

"And so?"

"And so I sent a message to Newton. Fatio will discover this when he tries to send his own, I think. Also, Veronique, something *saw* me in the laboratory."

Crecy narrowed her eyes. "Some*thing*?"

"Yes, a sort of cloud with a red spot in the center, like an eye."

A tremor seemed to pass across Crecy's face, an unguarded instant of some emotion Adrienne had never seen her or anyone express. Then Crecy's face hardened to porcelain again, perfect and smooth. Had that been fear? Despair?

Whatever else it had been, it had been recognition.

"What? Veronique, what was it? You *know*."

Crecy shook her head, but Adrienne grabbed the other woman's wrist. "Veronique, there may be things you are sworn not to tell me. I accept that, even though I don't like it. You say that in the future we will be friends. But if you and Nicolas are not my friends *now*, then I have none. I know both of you have secrets from me. Both of you have some goal involving me of which I am unaware. I know this, and yet I need—" Tears threatened to clot her throat, but she swallowed them. As she continued, her tone remained as cool and controlled as Crecy's. "You must trust me. You have helped me solve one equation. Now help me solve the one in which I am a variable."

"There are still things I cannot tell you," Crecy cautioned. "But ask me now what you most want to know. Understand, it is not *you* I do not trust, Adrienne, but *myself*."

"Do not dare to play games, Veronique. I need answers *now*."

"It is not a game," Crecy replied. "Did someone see you? Besides your big red eye?"

"Gustavus might have."

"Gustavus? Have I met this man?"

"No. He is Fatio's assistant. He was not at the masque at the Palais Royal—or if he was, we did not see him."

"Assistant. Damn. I should have known."

"Veronique—"

"Adrienne, what is your question?"

"I want to know what that *thing* was."

Crecy looked away. "You have chosen the worst question," she said. "To see one of them is one thing. That they can forgive. But if one such as *you* knows about them— Adrienne, I already fear for your life. Do not make me triple my fear."

"Trust me," Adrienne said. "If doom finds me, let it not find me in ignorance."

Crecy reached to stroke Adrienne's chin. For a strange moment, she thought Crecy would kiss her, but she did not. "I will tell you what I know," she said. "But I promise you, you will not like it."

13.

Vasilisa

Vasilisa's throaty accent at his shoulder was a shock, coming unannounced by footsteps. Ben jerked as if stung, involuntarily slamming his book in the process.

Throaty her accent might be, but her laughter was silver chimes. Ben blushed furiously as he turned to find her framed by the door to his room, beautiful as always. Today her dress was pure London, an azure skirt and loose, low-cut blouse that revealed the hollow beneath her throat and just a hint of . . .

"I didn't mean to frighten you," she explained.

"Ah," Ben replied, feeling stupid. "No, it's just that when I read—"

"The storm of words smothers all other sounds. Yes, I know that feeling well. What *is* that you're reading?"

"Oh, it's nothing," Ben said quickly, but Vasilisa was already frowning a bit at the title.

"The *Daemonicum*?" she asked. "What are you doing reading such a silly book?"

"I got it from the society's library," he replied defensively.

"Well, it's still silly," Vasilisa maintained. "At least you'd best not let Colin or James—or especially Mr. Heath—see you with that."

"Why?"

"Demonology is a favorite topic with the Philosophical Society right now. It's all the rage." She rolled her eyes and then showed him a sliver of smile. "I came to see if you might accompany me to a tavern for a bite to eat."

"What of Mr. Voltaire?"

Vasilisa blinked. "What about him?"

Ben suddenly felt that he had committed a colossal blunder. "Well, I don't know . . . I thought that you and he . . . ate . . . ah, dinner together."

Vasilisa burst out laughing, and Ben felt his face redden. "You mean you heard us in my room the other night. Why, Benjamin, how rude!"

Ben was certain that his head would simply catch fire and burn to a cinder. He wished it would, in fact. "Well, no, I didn't *hear* anything, I just thought . . ."

"It's no matter, Benjamin. With just the two of us staying here, there can be few secrets of that sort between us. Monsieur Voltaire did *'dine'* with me a night or two, but he and I are very . . . um, *casual* friends. I don't know where he is tonight. He's probably at one of those coffeehouses with his literary friends." She paused and assumed a bit more gravity. "What passed between Voltaire and me—I don't mind *you* knowing, Ben, but it's not something I wish generally spoken of."

"Oh, yes, of course," Ben replied. "Discretion is my watchword."

Vasilisa's brow puckered in a tiny frown. "You don't think worse of me now, do you, Ben?"

Ben wasn't sure precisely what to think. He had never known a woman so bold about such things—except Sarah, who was a whore. To know a woman who sought sex for the same reasons as a man—well, Robert had spoken of such things, but Ben had begun to despair of ever meeting such a woman.

All that went through his head, but what he *said* was, "Of course not, miss."

"Come, Ben, call me Vasilisa. And let's go to a tavern, for if you aren't hungry, *I* could devour a bear."

Once the roast was in front of him, Ben found that he did, indeed, have an appetite. It might have been the walk that did it. Vasilisa wished to eat at a tavern in "the city," and so they had made their way up Fleet Street and across the canal. Then again, it might be the glass of dry Portuguese wine glowing in his belly, and the Russian's flattering attention.

Another thing he liked about Vasilisa: She didn't let food get in the way of conversation. To Ben, conversation was what was enjoyable about a meal—it was the only time you could get people still long enough to pursue a topic in any depth. And even though he was thousands of miles from the table he was brought up at, dining in a grand tavern in the heart of the City of Science with a woman from *Russia*, it reminded him of his childhood and of his father in the most pleasant way possible.

"I'm glad that you met him," Vasilisa was saying around mouthfuls of roast beef. "Even if you never meet him again, it is something to tell your children and *their* children about."

"Yes," Ben agreed. "I can tell them that I met Sir Isaac Newton after he became senile and *mad*."

"Who has more right to go mad?" Vasilisa asked. "Never has there been a more brilliant man. The memory of my own meeting with Newton—even given his state of mind—is something I will always cherish.

"Tell me why you were really reading that book, Ben," Vasilisa insisted, pouring them each another glass of wine and then signaling to the server. When he came she placed three shillings in his hand. "Another bottle of the Portuguese, please," she said. When the server was gone, she arched her brows at Ben. "Well?" she asked.

"You remember my story? The man Bracewell?"

"Yes. The one you believed to be a sorcerer."

"Vasilisa, I left two things out of my story. I thought you would all think me stupid. Maybe you will, if I tell you."

"Well, we should find out," she murmured. "Here, drink your wine to give you courage!" and she swallowed more of her own.

I'm going to regret this, Ben thought. But he followed her example.

"Now tell me what you didn't tell us before, and I'll promise not to think you stupid."

Ben drank some more of the wine, and then he told her about Bracewell's strange familiar, about the similar eye that had appeared above the aetherschreiber. She did not laugh at him or call him stupid; she watched him with utter fascination.

"Now I see," she said. "You are not the first to witness such things, you know."

"I'm not?" he asked.

"No. In my country, there are many such things. Witches keep them at their beck and call. I am a philosopher, like you, Benjamin, but even I believe I have seen these things." She lowered her voice further. "Even here in London. Before it dissolved, certain members of the Royal Society died mysteriously. They say lights such as you describe were seen nearby."

"But they cannot be . . . I mean, there must be some explanation," he said.

"Yes, I agree. Think of this, Benjamin. For many years the mechanical philosophy of Descartes was the prevailing truth, was it not? The belief that every action of every material in the universe was caused by the impact of one particle against another. You have seen those absurd diagrams that explain magnetism by postulating a plethora of screw-shaped particles *turning* their way around a magnet, attaching themselves to iron and dragging it in like gear teeth?"

Ben could not help but laugh. He remembered those diagrams, and thinking back on them, they did seem *extremely* absurd.

"Fifty years ago, no philosopher in his right mind would dare to postulate unseen, occult forces working between matter, and yet Sir Isaac not only dared theorize this, but proved it and then *harnessed* those forces. It was his willingness to explore what the prevailing philosophies dismissed as superstition that brought about the new science."

"Yes. Yes! So you're saying—" Ben was *sure* he was following this.

"Maclaurin and the others would be quick to dispute what I'm about to say," Vasilisa continued, "but I think you will see my point, Ben. Perhaps *Newtonians* have too quickly invented their own orthodoxy when they refuse to consider these genies, these angels and devils that haunt the places of darkness and of light. Were the Greeks merely fools to speak of gods and spirits? Was my grandmother an idiot to leave milk out for the *domovoi*? Here is a whole realm of phenomena that science will not attempt to speak to."

"I found one book," Ben said. "It's an essay called *The Se-*

cret Commonwealth in two parts, one by this Kirk fellow and another by Mr. Deitz, a commentary on the first part. He speculates about Leibniz and his monads—"

"Yes, yes," Vasilisa said enthusiastically. "I freely admit that in many ways Leibniz was the worst sort of Cartesian, and yet at the same time he considered the possibility that *sentience* might exist in the aether—"

"That's what I'm thinking!" Ben noticed that he was waving wildly as he interrupted Vasilisa. Tides of wine seemed to be rising and ebbing in his head, but here was someone he could finally tell his thoughts to. "It seems to me—well, I mean, I read this, but it makes sense to me—that if there is a great chain of being, from the lowest to the highest—"

"As Browne discussed, for instance."

"Yes!" Ben agreed. "Shur Thomash Browne." He grinned and giggled at his slurring. "If this chain leads up through animalcules and insects and frogs and dogs, and so on to us, and if above us there are the angels and finally God—well, what if we're about *midway* up, instead of close to the top? I mean, why couldn't there be as many kinds of creatures between us and God as there are between animalcules and us?"

"No reason at all," Vasilisa said, pouring more wine.

Ben awoke curled against something warm, his nose pressed into a head of dark hair. He felt an instant of panic, but then he began to remember. He remembered her kissing him good night—and that it went on and on. That she had laughed a lot. That she had sung something in Russian afterward.

Now what should he do? She was still asleep. He was surprised that he felt so good. He was theoretically acquainted with hangovers from observing first James and later Robert.

It was difficult to draw his eyes away from Vasilisa, who was naked and mostly uncovered. Last night it had been dark, but today his *eyes* could appreciate her lithe limbs, her pale skin. He frowned and looked more closely. She had scars, too, on her back and arms and legs. He wondered how she had gotten them.

Already his heart was beginning to ache. Why had she made

love to him? Because she had been drunk, and he had been there. But *not* because she was in love with a fourteen-year-old boy.

Unfortunately, he was totally, completely in love with Vasilisa Karevna.

It got worse as the day went along. He managed to rise without disturbing her, dressed, and went for a morning walk. He feared being alone with her, feared what she would say. Or would she say *anything*? She might pretend it had never happened. He couldn't decide if that would be best or worst.

When he got back a few hours later, Maclaurin and Heath were already there, but Vasilisa—both to his sorrow and relief—was not.

"There y' are, Ben," the Scot said. "How would y' like to take notes at a meetin'?"

"Sir?"

"Dr. Edmund Halley is in the meetin' room. We were aboot to speak to him on Sir Isaac's behalf. I canna find Vasilisa anywhere, and James is late."

"Halley?"

"Yes, yes, but you mustn't gape," Heath hissed. "And don't forget, he is the *enemy* now."

"That is such an unfortunate thing to say," a rich baritone voice complained from behind them. Heath—who rarely was flustered by anything—suddenly turned red. Ben turned to see a man of perhaps sixty, broad-faced, determined about the eyes.

"Dr. Halley," he said, "I'm sorry, I only meant—"

"I know what you meant, sir," Halley replied. "And I consider it a terrible shame. It may be that the Crown and Sir Isaac have a quarrel of sorts, but I have been his truest friend since before you were *born*, young man. I *financed* his first *Principia*."

"Dr. Halley," Maclaurin conciliated, "please know that all of us have nothing but the greatest respect for you. I urge you to have a seat while we prepare some coffee."

"What, so I can be further slandered behind my back?"

"I only meant," Heath went on evenly, "that you are a competing philosophical society."

"Philosophers should not compete," Halley replied. "They

should work together. They should pool their knowledge into oceans rather than divide it into rivulets. I have invited you all to join the London Philosophical Society; that invitation is still open."

"And appreciatin' it we are," Maclaurin answered. "But until Sir Isaac—"

Halley placed his hand on Maclaurin's shoulder in what appeared to be a friendly gesture. "Sir Isaac has had *episodes* like this before," Halley said, "but this one has been longer and more painful than most. It torments me to speak of it, but his correspondence with me has been quite . . . irrational. He has walked out onto a narrow limb, my worthy colleagues, and as his friends we should coax him off it."

"I don' pretend to know what Sir Isaac requires," Maclaurin stiffly replied. "If you would, please?" He gestured toward the meeting room.

Halley puffed out a breath, and it seemed some of his pomposity stole out with it. "No, my friends, I wish I had time for your company. I do miss it—especially my wayward student James. I had hoped to see him, at least. No, I am here in my official capacity as the royal astronomer."

Neither Maclaurin nor Heath responded, and after an instant Halley coughed. "You understand," he explained hesitantly, "this request does not have its origin with me."

Heath continued glaring, and even Maclaurin's mouth was tight. Once more, Halley sighed and went on. "I thought you deserved to hear directly from me: I must formally request the transfer of the orrery to the new observatory at the palace."

14.

Magic Mirror

"Genies, fey, familiar spirits? Why do you tell me such fairy tales?" Adrienne snapped in annoyance.

"Oh, indeed? Is the Holy Bible a fairy tale, with its cherubim and seraphim? Did the great philosophers of antiquity tell fairy tales when they spoke of gods and elementals?"

"Very well, then, Crecy, what do you know of these supposed creatures besides hearsay?"

"I have seen them, as you have. I have conversed with them."

"*Conversed* with them? How did you speak to them?"

"Through my visions," Crecy replied, "and in dreams. And over the aetherschreiber."

"The aetherschreiber?"

"Yes."

Adrienne closed her eyes. "I'm too tired to think about this."

"You saw one, Adrienne. What did you think it was?"

Adrienne sighed. "Exactly what you say. My grandfather used to tell me stories of such creatures. But as a philosopher—"

"I am not a philosopher," Crecy said, "but I thought a philosopher's vocation is to explain all phenomena, rather than selecting only those most amenable to scientific explanation."

"I am a mathematician, mostly," Adrienne said. "I have no starting place for an equation to account for a *succube* or *feu follets*."

"Well, then," Crecy said, "you shall be a pioneer."

"I do not *wish*—" She stopped, clenched her teeth, and began again. "What *are* they?"

"They are creatures, like you and me."

"What I saw was *not* like you and me."

"Not in form. Not inside, either. I only mean that they have thought, will, and desire."

"And what do they desire?"

"Like us, they desire many things."

Adrienne closed her eyes. "In this matter of the king, the comet, Fatio, *you*, *me*—" She ceased when she realized she was shouting and then more quietly finished. "What do they want with us?"

Crecy smiled thinly. "I cannot say for certain, but they mean us no good, I think."

Adrienne nodded, studying Crecy's face. "The instant I begin to trust you, you prove yourself untrustworthy, Veronique. You are not telling me all you know."

"I am telling you all I can, for the moment."

She began removing her petticoats. "As you say, then. I'm going to sleep. There is no telling when the king will make some demand of me."

"Sleep well," Crecy said, "and dream of Nicolas rather than genies. Sleep in peace."

She felt suddenly shy. "I will try," she said.

But as Adrienne closed her eyes, she saw a comet, a million corpses, and a floating red eye.

"If it pleases Your Majesty," Fatio de Duillier said, nervously fingering the long lacy cuff of one sleeve, "we have brought you a present."

Louis smiled thinly as he shrugged off his gold damask dressing gown, which Bontemps took before presenting him with waistcoat, coat, and breeches.

"Yes, those will do," he told his valet. To Fatio he said, "A present is all very well, but I called you here to discuss another matter."

"Sire," Fatio replied, faintly.

"Who is this with you?"

"May I present to Your Majesty Gustavus von Trecht of Livonia."

"Ah, your assistant. But of course I have heard of you. Be assured that a measure of the delight I feel for the success of your project is reserved for you." It had taken Louis a moment to understand what was so odd about von Trecht, but now he had it. When he met someone new, his magical sight had a tendency to render them vaguely. Occasionally they would resemble someone from his youth, especially if their voice or accent had a familiar ring. But this Livonian had neither a face he recognized nor one without character; it was rendered in detail, from his bloodless smile to the small scar on his right cheek. Curious.

Now von Trecht bowed.

Louis cleared his throat and went on. "However, I'm afraid that you also share, by that same association, my ire. Word has come to me, Monsieur de Duillier, of your disgraceful behavior at the Palais Royal, and most especially of your ill-considered rantings."

Fatio drooped like a plucked morning glory. "Your pardon, Majesty," he moaned. "I allowed myself to be ill-advised."

"As I understand it, you allowed yourself to become drunk, after which you engaged with transvestites and began to blabber about the coming destruction of London!" Louis had purposefully allowed his voice to rise.

"I have no defense, Your Majesty."

"And where were you during this, Monsieur?" he demanded of von Trecht.

"If it pleases Your Majesty, I was in my quarters, reading."

"Sire, he was in no way responsible for my—"

"Monsieur, I will ask your opinion when I require it," Louis told him. "Now. You both have been assigned guards, of course, and my police are always watchful of danger to you. But from now until the time that London lies in ruins, neither of you will leave Versailles. And if, Monsieur de Duillier, your drunken rantings have informed the English of our plans, and if they rally their magus, Newton, to cast a counterspell so London *never* lies in ruins, then you shall never leave Versailles."

"I assure Your Majesty that I let nothing slip of importance."

"The spies to whom you let it slip were obviously of a contrary opinion," Louis replied sourly.

"Spies?"

"Your transvestite friends. My police and musketeers tried to restrain them and were slain most foully. We have not apprehended them. My valet—" He nodded toward the impassive Bontemps. "—and my foreign minister, Torcy, both agree with me that this sort of desperation might indicate that they did *indeed* believe that they obtained worthwhile intelligence."

"If I may, Your Majesty," von Trecht said, "if I were a spy and found out, I would flee to keep my neck from the rope, whether I had intelligence or not. And I understand that one of these transvestites was also somewhat drunk. Such is hardly the behavior of a professional spy."

"What, then, do *you* suggest, sir?"

"I have not been at court long, Sire, and my knowledge of it is limited. But many courtiers seem—if I may be so bold—rather childish. Perhaps this was some prank gone awry."

"Pranks do not often end in murder, but your point is taken," Louis replied, unconvinced. He agreed with von Trecht's thinking on one important point: These spies were most likely French.

"Permit me to observe," ventured de Duillier, "that no matter how indiscreet I may have been, even if I went to Sir Isaac or King George today and laid the whole plan before them there is still naught that they could do."

"Why? It is a full twenty days until this fabulous stone from heaven falls upon London. Why could the British magi not unspell your spell?"

"The stone, my lord, is already falling, traveling much faster than any bullet or cannonball. And our stone continues to gather speed. No force on heaven or earth can deflect it far enough to save London."

"*You* deflected it, with *your* spell. Why can't the English do the same?"

"They haven't time. We aimed our cannon, so to speak, months ago, when it could be aimed. The stone was moving a great deal more slowly then. My spell made it sociable to London. Even if this sociability were negated—and honestly, Sire, neither I nor my colleagues overseas have any idea how that could be done—the relentless mechanics of gravity would continue our work. Even if the stone could be slowed or deflected, it would only miss London by leagues—not enough distance to make any difference."

"What do you mean? You've said nothing of missing. How can a miss of leagues be of no importance?"

"Sire, this weapon will cause a great deal of destruction. It will level not only what it strikes but anything for—oh, six or seven leagues."

"What of our allies in Scotland? James?"

"Like us, I believe he will see a very spectacular sight, but will experience no ill effects."

"You are quite certain?"

"Gustavus, here, has worked out the parameters of destruction. Though I have not yet looked over his work, I am entirely confident of his figures."

"Very well. Write all of this up for Bontemps and Torcy. We shall want to make certain that anyone valuable to us is outside the range of this weapon of yours. How far do you think will be safe?"

"Gustavus?" Fatio asked.

"Ten leagues should suffice," von Trecht replied. "Though fifteen might be safer."

"I thought one might be closer," Louis said. "What will we see from here?"

"Sire, that is what our present to you concerns."

"What is that?"

"It is a mirror Monsieur von Trecht invented. Quite ingenious, I should say myself." As he spoke, he worked the cloth off of the large rectangle the two had brought with them. It *was* a sort of mirror. Louis smiled. Though he looked every morning, it still delighted him to see his new, almost black mustache, the dapper figure he cut in his gold and sapphire flowered coat and waistcoat with its scarlet trim, his handsome face beneath flowing dark curls.

"I have arranged a demonstration, Sire," von Trecht said.

The mirror seemed to shiver, and then it became like an open window. Louis fancied he felt a breeze blowing from the blue sky pictured there.

That sky was challenged by the silhouette of a city, proud spires thrusting up, the arch of some titanic dome rearing . . .

"London," he breathed. "That is London! You have built me a spyglass just like my nurse used to tell me of so long ago." In the foreground of the picture, a row of trees bent in the wind, leaves fluttering like butterflies. It was unbelievable. "Show me something else."

"Unlike the mirrors in the stories you speak of, this one can look at only one place—where its mate rests. It is much like an aetherschreiber in that particular."

"Does that mean that someone there can see me?"

"Yes, Sire. But you would see them standing there peering at you, and you could cover the glass if you wished. That is nothing to worry about. The other mirror is in the keeping of one of our Jacobite confederates, hidden so it looks out the window of an uninhabited tower. Only by flying could anyone reach it to look through. When our friend leaves London for his own safety, he will leave the mirror there, so that you can perceive firsthand what occurs." Fatio cleared his throat and then continued, "I only wish that the picture were clearer."

"What do you mean? If it were any clearer, I would be there! This is a most wonderful invention. My dear sirs, you have both moved many paces toward redemption."

Fatio nodded vigorously. "I suppose it is my eyes that are not so clear," he murmured and then bowed.

After they left, Louis spent a long moment gazing through the mirror at that great imperial city, and for the first time he felt a trace of sadness that it must be destroyed. But it was a trace only; English guns were even now pounding on the fortresses of France in more countries than he cared to think, and redcoats trampled vineyards beneath their boots deep within France herself. In challenging the Sun, they had condemned themselves. And though the Sun might *feel* pity, he was not *moved* by it, but only by the remorseless clockwork of the heavens.

15.

The Aegis

When Halley was gone, Maclaurin left word that they should all meet at the Grecian Coffeehouse and then retired angrily to his room, leaving Ben the task of watching for the other members of the society.

So Ben sat outside on the marble stoop, trying to read but instead finding himself distracted by the memory of Vasilisa and the giddy mixture of feelings it brought. What in the world would he say to her when she arrived?

His heart skipped when he noticed someone turning into the court, but it was James Stirling.

"Good morning, Benjamin," Stirling greeted him, removing his hat and wiping back his rather damp hair. "Why so doleful?"

"Mr. Maclaurin wants us all to meet at the Grecian at four o'clock this afternoon."

Stirling frowned. "On account of some serious business, by your face. What could be *so* serious?"

"Dr. Halley came by," Ben quietly explained. "He wants the orrery taken to the new observatory."

"The orrery . . ." Stirling frowned. "I hadn't thought of that."

"Mr. Maclaurin and Mr. Heath were too upset to talk about it," Ben continued. "Can Halley really take the orrery from us?"

"Well, it probably was someone else's idea," Stirling mused, "someone in the palace, maybe the king himself." His eyes narrowed thoughtfully. "They do have a case," he decided. "The orrery was built with the king's funds. In a strict legal sense, I suppose it belongs to the Crown."

"But *you* built it, didn't you?"

Stirling shook his head distractedly. "That's an exaggeration," he said. "Many contributed to creating the orrery. Mr. Maclaurin and Mrs. Karevna and I contributed the most, I suppose—besides Newton, of course, whose idea and plan it was."

"Va— I mean, Mrs. Karevna didn't tell me she worked on the orrery."

"We all did. That's why the Philosophical Society wants it, I'm sure—to strike at us for having the impertinence to continue on. They won't *use* it for anything except to impress visiting dignitaries. Damn, I'll bet Maclaurin *is* upset." He paused. "Has anyone got word to Newton? He's the only one who could do anything."

"Oh, God," Ben exclaimed. "I was supposed to see him today."

Stirling raised his eyebrows. "Really. On whose invitation?"

Ben briefly outlined his last visit to Newton's house while the other man shook his head knowingly.

"It may not do much to the good," Stirling said when Ben was done, "but you should try to explain to him about the orrery."

"I will. Mr. Stirling, why are Sir Isaac and Dr. Halley at odds? I thought they were friends."

"I don't know that they were ever friends, really. They've made use of one another all their lives, but that is hardly the same thing. And Sir Isaac always came away the better for that trade. Halley financed the first publication of the *Principia*, for instance. Many say that without him, the name of Newton would still be obscure, for in those early days Sir Isaac was something of a hermit, not given to pursuing publication. Despite all of that, Newton seems to have forgotten the debt. Years ago, a word from him could have established Dr. Halley at Trinity College, but Newton never recommended him. Still, until the split of the societies, Halley was always firmly in Newton's camp."

"What changed that?"

"Some difference of opinion—I don't know what, exactly.

Sir Isaac can be a difficult man to get along with. I came here from Venice to study with *him*, but after proposing me as a fellow of the society, he seemed to forget I existed—"

"You're from Venice?" Ben interrupted.

"Oh, no, no. I had to go to Venice for political reasons. I was branded a Jacobite, and so my opportunities were suddenly abroad."

"Are you a Jacobite?"

Stirling smiled. "A bold lad, you. I'm no Catholic, nor, I suppose, am I a Protestant. But I would rather see a Stuart on the throne. Did you know that King George speaks no English? What sort of king is that for a country to have?"

"A Protestant one for a Protestant country, I suppose," Ben replied.

"What nonsense. What difference does it make?"

Ben knew all the arguments, but he found himself agreeing with Stirling. "Well, I don't really know," he confessed. "I suppose I just said that for argument's sake."

Stirling smiled. "Save that for Voltaire. I've got better things to do than to argue politics, and worse things to worry about."

"Worries like the assassins coming after you?" Ben asked.

Stirling's reaction was an unpleasant surprise. "Where the hell did you hear that?" he demanded, uncharacteristically sharply.

"I . . . some of the others, I suppose. I thought they were joking."

"Oh, no. They are not joking and they should not be so free with such private information. Assassins have indeed been paid to undo me, though I doubt that they've followed me here. But if I ever go back to Venice, I'll not be long on two legs."

"Really? What business have Venetian assassins with you?"

Stirling—whom Ben had thought the quietest, most inoffensive of the group—smiled, and suddenly Ben saw something still and dangerous in him, a sort of determination that required no blustering or bragging. This was the sort of man who could design something as fantastic as the orrery and then pretend his was the smallest part.

"I'll tell you some other time," he promised, "though I think you will be disappointed. When were you to see Sir Isaac?"

"In an hour."

"You should go on, then. Maclaurin charged you with finding everyone?"

"Yes."

"Who remains?"

"Voltaire and Mrs. Karevna."

Stirling quirked his mouth. "Silver-tongued French devil. Ah, well." He clapped Ben's shoulder. "You go conclude your business with Sir Isaac. I'll find those two."

Ben nodded and hurried off, feeling thrice a fool and wondering if the pain he felt at the mention of Voltaire and Vasilisa together was written as plain on his face as on his heart.

Mrs. Barton was on her way out when Ben reached Newton's house. A hackney carriage waited at the street, horses stamping restlessly.

"Oh, good, there you are," Mrs. Barton said. "My uncle is expecting you. I have some business to attend." Then she departed in the carriage.

Left before Newton's open door, Ben knocked hesitantly and when no answer came, stepped gingerly inside.

The door to the study—or laboratory—was ajar.

"Sir Isaac?" he called. "Sir, it's Benjamin Franklin."

No answer, but he noticed a smell wafting through the door, something like tincture of iodine and something like that which had lingered after Bracewell fired his *kraftpistole*. The hairs on his neck pricked up, and he inched toward the door and peeked through.

The study was now brightly lit. Books littered the floor and sprawled upon two wooden tables. The odd pyramid of metal and wire was now glowing, a red so deep as to seem almost black. On top of the pyramid shivered a sort of hollow sphere of sparks, scintillating in all the colors of the spectrum, from violet at the pole farthest from the pyramid to red nearest it. A jolt of horror went through him when he recognized what floated *inside* of the sphere: a red eye like the one that had accompanied Bracewell.

Nearby stood a human shape, but Ben could not *focus* on it. From the corner of his eye, he got small impressions of a red coat, dark hair or wig in disarray, a penetrating hazel eye turned toward him. But when he looked at it full on, he only became dizzy and saw nothing.

"Come in," the nothing said in Newton's voice.

Ben slammed the door closed and lurched back four paces, breathing hard. What in the name of God had he fallen into?

His panic followed him outside, into the natural light of day, his mind spinning. What had he seen—or not seen? Nothing that made sense to his brain.

Thirty paces from the house he stopped, keeping his eyes focused on the door, trying hard to *think*. How could he run away now, when he was so close?

He took three deep breaths. These people were no better than him, just older and more learned. What man ever achieved anything without courage?

Eyes fixed on the door, he walked back toward the house.

"Sir Isaac," he said, keeping his voice level.

"What do you want?" the voice snapped. Ben turned to look. Newton was there, but Ben's eyes would not converge, would not let him *see*. He swallowed and said, "I'm Benjamin Franklin. You told me to come here today."

"Franklin, is it? The fellow who tuned an aetherschreiber?"

"Yes, sir." Since he couldn't focus on Newton, he looked at the eye again. He remembered the message from his aetherschreiber—*I see you*—and shuddered.

"A useful equation," Newton went on, as if they were merely two gentlemen discussing things, as if he, Newton, had not become some sort of illusion, some twist of air. "Somewhat crude, but I should like to include a note on it in my new draft of the *Principia*."

"That would be a great honor," Ben said faintly. This might not be Newton at all. For all he knew, it was Bracewell or Beelzebub.

Newton must have noticed him staring at the eye, for he was

just able to make out the magus waving an arm toward the pyramid and the thing upon it.

"Have no worry about the malakus," Newton said. "It is harmless at the moment, unable even to communicate with its kind."

"Its kind?"

"The rest of the malakim. Do you know of them?"

"I have seen such a thing as this," Ben said. "I did not know what it was called."

"The ancients called them many things. To Moses and Solomon they were the malakim, and so I call them that." The blurry figure eased down onto a bench. "Do you know much about history, Mr. Franklin?"

"Not as much as I would like," Ben admitted.

"Science has begun to neglect history," Newton told him. "This is a shame, because anything we discover today—Boyle's perfections upon alchemy, Harvey and his anatomy, even my own work—is all merely reinvention of what the ancients knew."

"The Greeks, you mean?" Ben asked tentatively when Newton paused. The fact that the eye had a name suggested a reasonable explanation, suggested science, suggested that this all might make sense after all.

"To some extent the early Greeks. Do you know who Hermes Trismegistus was?"

"Legend has it that he was the founder of alchemy."

"Not entirely true, but he was a great man, so great that the Greeks made him a god. So did the Egyptians, who named him Thoth, as the Romans named him Mercurius. But even Hermes had only scraps of what Adam acquired when he ate of the Tree, of what Moses had when he stood upon the mountain— or even of what they taught in the colleges of Nineveh and Ur of the Chaldees. It is only now that we begin to return toward that more perfect knowledge. Ironic."

"Ironic, sir?"

"Yes. It makes me wonder what scientific discoveries might have been made in Sodom and Gomorrah, just on the eve of *their* doom.

"In any event," Newton went on more distractedly, "you asked about the Greeks. Pythagoras and Plato, I think, had a good enough knowledge of the science I have rediscovered, but they made the mistake of enshrining it in mystical symbol. Aristotle and his Peripatetic followers failed to understand that, and their stupidity drew a shade over knowledge that has lasted more than two millennia."

Ben was having a difficult time following this. He did not possess enough knowledge to evaluate what Newton said, and trying to speak to this spectral image, this optical impossibility—

Optical. Newton's earliest treatise had been on optics.

He realized that Newton had paused, and almost without thinking, Ben took his chance. "Sir, this malakus—"

"You *have* seen one before, haven't you?" Newton asked.

"A man tried to kill me. He *did* kill my brother. One of these malakim was with him."

"With him? Bound up like this?"

"No, sir. Floating behind him in a big cloud."

"Floating . . . Was this man a philosopher?"

"I thought him a warlock," Ben said, "but I only *know* that he was a murderer."

Newton laughed, a dry, harsh laugh. "This one was sent to murder me. Until recently, I knew not by whom. I suspected many." His voice dropped somewhat. "I fear I have been ill. When one gets old . . ."

Ben remembered what Stirling had said. This might be the only chance he got to introduce the subject of the orrery. "Sir, James Stirling asked that I speak to you on behalf of the society. The—"

"That's why I wear the aegis," Newton interrupted. "It protects me from many sorts of assassination."

Ben stopped, frustrated. He wasn't being listened to. Not that he wasn't interested in this aegis, which he took to be the cause of Newton's unorthodox appearance.

"Sir, I really must tell you something."

"Eh? Then *tell* me, boy. What do you want me to do, applaud each new word so as to encourage you to go on to the next?"

Not interrupting me would do nicely, Ben thought. But he began again anyway, telling Newton about Halley's visit, about the demand for the orrery.

"Very well," the philosopher said. "I will save my lecture on the ancients for another time. But while I have been locked in here with them, I have learned some things. You see my captive malakus and the aegis I wear. I have not been idle or completely mad. Tell them all this, Mr. Franklin. I choose you to be my messenger because you are new; you are the only one I do not suspect." He stood and walked toward Ben, who found he had to close his eyes to keep from wobbling.

A warm, smooth hand took his own.

"Unclench your fingers and take this," the magus said.

Something round and cool was pressed into his palm.

"Take this with you. One of you will understand what to do with it. Now turn around and go out. Wait to open your eyes until you turn, or you may lose your balance."

"Yes, sir."

"Thank you, Mr. Franklin. I will see you again. But next time I will visit the society at Crane Court."

"When shall we expect you, sir?"

"You will not, I hope," Newton replied.

"What of the orrery?"

"The wheels of the court move slowly. I shall register an objection by letter today. That will slow things a week or so."

"Can't we stop them from taking it?"

"No. But it doesn't matter."

"Sir?"

"It doesn't matter," Newton bellowed. *"Now go!"*

Ben met the others at the Grecian at twenty after four—a bit late. They sat at the same table in nearly the same places as when he had first seen them.

"Well, here approaches the apprentice," Voltaire called out, raising his bowl of coffee.

"Have a seat, Ben," Maclaurin said. "Since you are informed of the situation, I've told the rest."

"What will Newton do?" Heath demanded. "You did speak to him, didn't you?"

"Yes," Ben answered. "He said that he was going to send a letter of protest today."

"Did he?" Maclaurin asked. "He seemed . . . *lucid*, then?"

"More so than when last we spoke," Ben said cautiously. "Still, he said the orrery doesn't matter—that he will see that we keep it another week or so, but that after that he didn't care."

"Why another week?" Vasilisa asked.

Ben threw up his hands. "He didn't say. He talked about history and creatures he called malakim—"

"Malakim?" Voltaire interrupted. "A Hebrew word for angels or genies or what have you."

Vasilisa's gaze flicked to Ben, and for an instant his heart-sickness was forgotten as he remembered their conversation about such creatures. And was he imagining it, or did he see a warning there also?

"Sir Isaac often riddles at such things," Stirling said. "He believes such references in the Bible and other ancient books to be ciphers of a sort, cryptic ways of speaking of natural law. For him, malakim might mean the heavenly bodies or the forces that govern such bodies."

Ben remembered that thing atop the pyramid and knew that Stirling was wrong, but Vasilisa's implied warning had its effect, and he swallowed the explanation of what he had witnessed.

"You know," Voltaire said, "I once knew a fellow who claimed to have seen an angel. A pious fellow who never failed to repent after taking a mistress or losing at cards. He had discovered the key to opening the mind, you see—as an alchemist opens metal—and his elixir was, I believe, of one third brandy, a second part arak, another third wine—and a fourth third more brandy—"

"Voltaire, dear, does this story have a point?" Vasilisa asked.

"Only," Voltaire said, "that we are taking this perhaps too seriously."

"Which 'this' would that be?" Heath snapped. "Our orrery being stolen or our mentor and benefactor being mad?"

Voltaire regarded Heath levelly and said, "This angel came

to my friend. He had six wings, but no head nor ass nor genitalia, and he resembled nothing at all, and he glowed like a lantern. He told my friend not to despair, because all was for the best. 'Horses are made to be ridden,' it said, 'and so you ride them. Feet are made to wear boots, and so you have boots. You were made to contain vast quantities of wine and to empty your pockets and consort with the meanest of women, and you are admirably good at it. So have pity on yourself and cease basting in guilt!' "

"And what became of your friend?" Stirling asked.

"Oh, well, a few days after his celestial visitation, he was quite enthusiastically investigating the inner workings of a certain lady when her husband arrived home. My friend explained to the husband that married men were admirably suited to be cuckolded, that he had done his job quite well, and that he should be proud to be a part of such a lovely and orderly universe."

"To which the husband replied?" Vasilisa asked.

"With a musket ball. The postscript is that skulls are wonderfully suited to being perforated by musket balls."

"And this Aesop's fable tells us what?" Maclaurin asked.

"My friends, I only suggest that the usefulness of our philosophies is limited by our own powers of reason and sense. As I have admitted, I am no scientific man. But we cannot judge such as Newton on such scanty evidence as we have before us. What is mad is to think that because his behaviors seem to suit our image of madness, we are right."

"But the orrery!" Heath groaned.

"There *is* more," Ben said.

"Oh?" Maclaurin and then the rest turned back to him.

"Three things more. First, he said to tell you he has not been idle. He has invented a number of things. One was something he called an aegis. It made him appear blurry, hard to look at—"

"The aegis is a sort of impenetrable armor the goddess Athena wore," Voltaire volunteered.

"Go on, Ben," Maclaurin encouraged.

"He believes that someone is trying to kill him." *As someone tried to kill me,* he understood suddenly. *What do he and I have in common?*

"Someone?" Stirling asked.

"Yes. He apparently once suspected everyone, but now—you must all forgive me, he *told* me to say this—he says to tell you all he knows now who it is."

There was a general uproar, but Vasilisa banged on the table with her fist, silencing them. "Wait," she said. "Benjamin, is that exactly how he said it?"

Ben thought about it. "I don't think so."

"He did not imply that it was one of us?"

"Oh. Why no, I suppose he didn't. It's just from the way he was going on, I thought—"

"Think carefully," Maclaurin said. "Don't let anyone lead you on. Did he imply that he suspects one of us of trying to murder him?"

Ben closed his eyes, relived the conversation as best he could. "No. He once suspected all of you, and Halley, and Flamsteed and John Locke—"

"Those last two are dead," Heath growled. "Mad!"

"He said himself he had been ill," Ben told them, "but now he seems to think he is well again."

"To his health, then," Voltaire said, lifting his bowl. The others imitated him a bit distractedly.

"There was one more thing, Ben?" Maclaurin inquired.

"Yes. This." He withdrew the sphere from his pocket and handed it to Maclaurin.

"He said that one of us would know what to do with it."

Maclaurin gave the object a long, thoughtful look. It was no larger than a marble but was oblong. Ben had examined it closely on the walk to the Grecian. Inscribed on its metallic surface were seven sets of three digits, each punctuated by an alchemical symbol, and a single set of two digits set apart in a square.

Each of the philosophers examined the object in turn, as Ben watched their faces carefully.

"Do any of you know what it is?" Ben asked, as Stirling, the last, turned it over in his palm.

Each answered in the negative.

"Well," Ben said, trying as best he could to quash the flood of self-satisfaction that seemed to expand in his chest like a new heart, "*I* do."

16.

Maneuvers

Adrienne woke with a start as her sedan chair thumped suddenly to the ground. She blinked at the scene before her, trying to recall where she was. To her left, a number of men and women were dismounting. To her right was the king in his sedan chair, waving for her attention. He let down the window, signaling for her to do the same.

"I shall be commanding a regiment personally," he informed her, smiled, and then signaled his bearers to pick up and move on down the hill.

A vast meadow spread out before them. On the field marched two armies.

Yes, she remembered now. She had managed four hours of sleep before the king had sent for her. On a whim, he had decided to recreate one of the more famous early battles of the war. Once she might have thought such a spectacle interesting; now it seemed perverse. Her sedan chair was stiflingly hot. She signed for her servants to open the door.

The king was halfway down the hill, his chair and bearers looking like a fat, gilded beetle.

Standing was better; a breeze soughed through the elm, oak, and maple along the ridge of the hill. The court began entrenching itself around her, their servants spreading blankets, opening wine, and erecting tents and sunshades.

"Shall we set out your tabouret, Mademoiselle?" Helen asked.

"No, thank you, Helen. I should like to walk along toward the forest a bit. If you could inform the guard?" Then, not waiting for them, she began to stroll that way.

She could not keep Crecy's pronouncements out of her mind.

If the creatures of tale and legend had some scientific basis, then what was it? The stories she remembered often took place in deep forests. Auberon and his fey followers held court in sunless places. But what *she* had seen had been in *Versailles*, and it had been a thing of fire and air. Could life be built of such insubstantial stuff? Could such animalcules as could be seen through microscopes form into something like that?

Four Swiss Guards ran to catch up with her, and Nicolas, who was among them, shot her a dour look. The sight of him cheered her a bit.

Then she noticed that Torcy was on a path to intersect her, one guardsman and a young valet coming close behind.

"Good morning, dear Demoiselle," he greeted her, kissing her hand. "I notice that you seek a somewhat different perspective on the king's battle. See, he has just reached his command."

Adrienne followed Torcy's indicating finger, and there Louis was, stepping out of his chair. When one was near Louis, he seemed a giant, towering above all others. At several hundred yards, he could be seen for what he was: a short fat man. For a score of heartbeats, she pitied him. He was so convinced of his youth and health, so sure that she must find him as beautiful as he had once been, the man shown in glorious portraits. From her present view, he looked so vulnerable . . .

And then he *moved*. There was something so unlovable, so unsympathetic about his calculated, pompous motions that she almost shuddered.

She had almost forgotten that Torcy was there. "I am sorry, sir," she told him. "My mind wanders a bit today."

"Understandable," he said. "Considering."

"Considering?"

He smiled his wolfish smile. "I wonder if our servants might spread a blanket for us? I could then explain to you the maneuvers on the field." He gracefully twisted his hand to indicate the "armies" below, but she had a chill feeling that he meant a different field, different maneuvers.

"That sounds lovely," she said.

Within moments, a small pavilion had been erected for them,

as down below the flam of drums and the wild piping of haut-
boys signaled the battle had begun. Two lines of infantry advanced, and suddenly smoke bloomed from their rifles. The
enfeebled bark of gunfire reached them a moment later, as if
from a world away.

"Watch for the Light Horse to sweep in from the side in a few
moments," Torcy commented.

"Very well."

Torcy waved the servants away.

"You have been a very busy young woman."

"My wedding is approaching."

"Yes, which is why I found it odd that you should be engaging in such precocious adventures, my dear. Posing as an
Austrian baron? Breaking into Monsieur de Duillier's rooms?"

Adrienne knew she was still smiling. Aside from a small
chill, she felt fine, her thinking seemed clear.

"What evidence do you have for these accusations, Monsieur?" she asked sweetly.

He reached into his coat pocket and withdrew a bundle of letters. "These are the signed accounts of witnesses: guards who
were bribed, servants who witnessed certain things. A number
of people can swear that both you and your lady-in-waiting
were at the Palais Royal. One of my agents followed you to de
Duillier's apartments."

Adrienne stared intently at the field. Horsemen in blue and
gray uniforms were closing in upon one of the lines of infantry,
but suddenly their horses were shying from a string of explo-
sions; from the body of the infantry had stepped a group of tall,
lanky men wearing floppy, unbrimmed hats. They had muskets
slung on their backs, but they were hurling something.

"Grenadiers," Torcy clarified.

"They have strange hats."

"If they wore brims, they would knock their hats off when
they unslung their muskets. I notice that you make no attempt to
deny my accusations."

"I do not *dignify* your accusations," Adrienne replied.

"I prefer to think that even after all you have been through—
after all of the poor judgment you have exercised and the evil

influences that have beset you—that you still prefer not to dissemble."

"You are free to believe that."

"Mademoiselle, I have not passed on what I know to the king, or Bontemps, or anyone else."

Adrienne turned to face the minister. "And what could *that* possibly mean?"

"It means, Mademoiselle, that I would like your cooperation in a certain matter."

"Well," Adrienne said, in as pleasant a tone as she could muster, "I would not think that the marquis of Torcy would be second in anything, but I have been proved wrong, for anything you might want of me, someone else has already inquired after. You wish my virginity? Oh, I *am* sorry, but the king has taken that. You wish my soul? A pity, for it has been purchased. Surely not my heart, for as you know, that is not mine to give. But if you want to fuck what has already been used, I can accommodate you. If you wish to rent a share of a soul already transacted to others, by all means, lease it. My heart, I fear, I have no control of, but I am certain that I can act the part of a lover well enough."

Her tirade caught Torcy off guard, but he quickly recovered. "This talk of a heart," Torcy mused. "There are some things I have failed to learn after all. You have been unfaithful to the king?"

Adrienne, preparing another verbal sally, stopped in astonishment. How could Torcy know the details of her adventures and not know—

Ah.

"Never mind that," Torcy said. "I do not care about such things. What I want—" Tears were trickling from the stern minister's eyes. Adrienne stared at him, unbelieving. "What I want," he whispered, "is for you to kill the king."

For a quarter of an hour, neither of them spoke. Adrienne watched the weird ballet below them.

"Is it so orderly in reality?" she asked finally.

"No," Torcy answered huskily. "In reality there is much

screaming, chaos, and confusion. Men with holes in their heads do not know it and grin at their comrades, believing that they have survived the battle. The field stinks, for men foul themselves as they die, and open entrails have their own diverse odors. No, war is nothing like what you see before you now, my dear."

She nodded. "You have lost many who were beloved to you in the wars?"

"Mademoiselle, you cast your line, but it will catch no fish. It is sufficient that I have decided—much against my heart, entirely against my honor—that Louis XIV has reigned too long. If he rules another year, France will be ruined."

"You were behind the attack on the barge? That was why the barge was burned before I could examine it."

"*No!*" he snapped, and then repeated more quietly, "no. Then I was as I seemed: the king's minister and friend. It was your observations that led me to the real culprits. No, *that* plot was engineered by the Korai."

Adrienne stiffened, but he waved his hand. "I care not if a group of women form some Rosicrucian cabal. I have known of them for some time. I never cared until they became active in politics. You led me to them, my dear, but when I found them I was . . . persuaded."

"The duchess *swore* to me—"

"The duchess is an admirable woman and well suited to lying, but she did not lie to you. The assassination attempt was planned and carried out without her knowledge. Madame Castries, as I am sure you know, is the brain behind that feminine body."

"And when you learned this?"

"At the time I was shocked, and I would have seen all of you hanged. Now . . ." His eyes went a little distant. "Now I grow older. Do you understand what will become of France after that *thing* of de Duillier's strikes London? No civilized country in the world will stand with us. Mademoiselle, I have seen things, heard the king say things . . ." He looked weary enough to die. "He is no longer Louis," he said. "I know my king, and that man down there is not he. You, of all people, should know that."

"Regicide will not stop the comet."

"No, but it might undo some of the worst damage. If Louis is dead, we can end the war. France and Spain will be divided, a peace can be drawn up, and the new king can distance himself from the affair. It will be bad, but if Louis is still alive—"

"Then he may do it again. And again, and again, until all of Europe bows before him."

"Ridiculous. Until some enemy sorcerer lays waste to France with an even more destructive spell. And this weapon of de Duillier's is not like a cannon, as you well know. It cannot be fired at will, but only when the heavens provide ammunition. Even I see that."

"And who will you support as king?"

"Orléans, of course. Maine is a bastard, and France will not have him."

"And how is it that you need me, sir?" she asked. "Why must I help you to slay my husband-to-be?"

"Mademoiselle, the king cannot be slain under most circumstances. He wears ensorceled clothing, and there are *things* that seem to watch him."

"Things?"

"Demons, I believe. Serpents from the pit."

"So he must be naked? Why not when he is changing in his own bedchamber?"

"Bontemps would rather see France rise in flames than betray the king."

"Some would say the same of you."

"And once they would have been right. But times and people change. I only ask you to think on it."

"No, you ask much more than that," Adrienne said. "Else why inform me of all the crimes you could charge me with, if you wished?"

"If I must coerce, I will. But in truth, I wanted you only to know that our interests coincide, and that I am not your persecutor."

"No? And yet I feel enormously persecuted, Marquis. How can that be?"

"It is the king who despoils you, Adrienne. It is the king you must be free of."

Below, the battle seemed to be concluding; the bodies of men were scattered on the green field. There was no blood.

"Do you leave me a choice?"

"I wish to, but I cannot. If you refuse, I must try to kill the king anyway, and I will probably fail. Mademoiselle, the worst thing that can happen to you is that I fail and have pity on you. Then you will have to marry the king. You will have to become another Maintenon, without possessing her fortitude and lack of imagination. Better by far if my evidence were to come to light, for then you would probably be cloistered in some distant convent, where your life would be more pleasant. No, think of my blackmail evidence as proof that you were forced into my mad scheme if it should fail. I can remove from my documents any mention of the Korai, if you wish. In short, I will assert myself as sole author of all events. But to secure these things, you must help me."

"What will become of me afterward?" she asked.

"You will quit France, if you wish. You can vanish, and in the new regime you will be forgotten. I can secure you a position in Florence, Venice, Vienna—someplace you can pursue your studies."

Now the king was climbing back into his sedan chair. All traces of her earlier compassion were gone. Torcy was right. Louis must die. She did not trust the minister, but that was beside the point. If this was a trap, it had been set and baited too well.

And she knew a thing or two the foreign minister did not, things that might make all of the difference or none at all. She smiled brightly at Torcy. "Tell me what I must do," she said, "and I will do it."

Torcy grimaced. "It is more complicated than that," he said. "I told you the king was protected."

"You implied I need only have him naked, away from Bontemps."

"I am afraid that I hedged. I wanted to persuade you before I told everything."

"I see."

"As I said, he is protected. I do not know how far that protection extends."

"Do you mean you do not know *how* to kill him?"

"Yes, Mademoiselle, that is exactly what I am saying. When fully dressed he wears certain garments that repel bullets and render neutral the energies of such weapons as *kraftpistoles*."

"He does not wear them with me."

"I'm sure he doesn't. Neither was he wearing them when the barge was attacked. It was a whim of his to leave them off. He felt that it disturbed the lines of his costume."

"Then there is something else."

"Yes, there is." Reaching into an inner pocket of his coat, he withdrew a small book and passed it to her. "You will find what details I know in there. I am not a magus, Demoiselle. I know poison has no effect upon the king. He may, indeed, be immortal. We can only pray that he is not, and *I* can only pray that you can find the solution to France's dilemma."

Adrienne took the book without hesitation and opened it to the first page. It was a notebook, unsigned, scrawled in a tight but clear hand. *Notes to the Experiments Concerning the Persian Elixir of Mehemet Mira Bey, or the Elixir of Life,* it read.

"The elixir that saved his life?"

"Yes. The king's piety was always mostly an affectation, you know, but he once had enough sense not to defy God's will with some diabolical liqueur. Would that he had retained it for another hour that day in Marly. He would have died honorably. Instead, he has damned himself and France, and now I, too, face the flames of hell."

"Well, sir," Adrienne said sardonically, "I will meet you there, I suppose. Perhaps you will be Lucifer's minister."

"I fear I already am," Torcy said.

17.

The Orrery

"Of course!" Maclaurin muttered, as he and the rest followed Ben into the orrery room. "How stupid of me!"

"How stupid of *all* of us," Heath added, "except for Ben."

"I had more time to think about it," Ben said, but he was secretly pleased at Heath's left-handed praise.

"But the alchemical symbols . . ." Voltaire muttered.

"Ciphers, again," Stirling said suddenly. "They don't represent the elements—but the *planets*."

"Yes, yes," Maclaurin agreed. "And the groups of numbers represent coordinates in three dimensions."

"It's an addition to the orrery," Vasilisa exclaimed. "But what, a new planet?"

They were all crowded around Ben, gazing at the oblong object. "No. It's a comet or some similar body," Stirling answered. "Its orbit must be built into it, like the models already in the orrery. The coordinates are so we can insert it at the proper point."

"And this numeral set here tells us what date to set the orrery *at* when we insert it," Maclaurin went on excitedly. "You see, Jove must be in this position, and Mars in this— Stirling?"

"Right away." The astronomer extracted a key from his pocket and crossed the room. There he unlocked a cabinet Ben had never seen opened. Inside, mounted on a hardwood board, were a number of polished brass wheels.

"I need people to stand at the predicted positions," he said. "Ben, you be Mars; Maclaurin, Jupiter; Vasilisa, I think you would fit Venus nicely—"

"Mercury for me, then," Voltaire cheerfully volunteered.

"How do I know where to stand?" Ben asked.

"The first coordinate refers to the position out along the plane from the sun. Those are marked on the floor."

Ben saw a series of concentric circles traced on the tile and wondered why he had never before noticed them. He supposed it was because the floating spheres themselves were so captivating.

"The second number refers to the rays coming out from the sun, in degrees. That places you at the right spot along the orbital path. We have to use both, of course, because the planets don't follow truly circular orbits, though our coordinate system does."

"I see." Though he had guessed what the numbers represented, he had never had the orrery system explained to him. He didn't ask about the third number: That would represent the distance above or below the imaginary plane of the solar system, drawn through the sun's equator.

He found his spot and stood there, noticing that Mars was nearly across the room from him. Vasilisa, Voltaire, Maclaurin, and Heath ranged out to complete the system, Heath playing Saturn. Ben noticed that Heath was nearest to him.

"Now, mind being hit!" Stirling cautioned.

The planets slowed and stopped, and as Ben watched, excited and bemused, reversed their courses.

"I've been running it ahead, to check some calculations I made on Jupiter's moons," Stirling explained. "I'll have to run it back a few years."

Voltaire gave a little yelp as Mercury fairly whizzed by him, hurtling back along its mayfly years. Vasilisa waved Venus by her with a laugh. The others were in no danger; even at this accelerated speed, the planets from Earth outward moved sluggishly, Saturn and Jupiter crawling like twin hour hands.

It took a fair half an hour, but at last Ben stepped aside and let Mars take his place.

"This looks right," Maclaurin said, "or near enough."

"Saturn isn't quite right," Heath complained. The ringed planet was still half a foot from him.

"Saturn is never quite right," Stirling said. "I've said more than once that that French philosopher was correct in predicting a seventh planet. It shouldn't matter, though. Newton's object will be inserted—" He walked out across the now stationary orrery, eyes on the floor markings. He hesitated a moment, held the egg-shaped object up, and released it. "—here."

It remained there. Vasilisa applauded delightedly, and Ben released the breath he had been holding. How angry they would have been if he had been wrong.

"Now, if everyone will step off the floor," Stirling entreated, returning to the cabinet.

Ben backed to the edge of the room. The marble-sized sphere, unconcerned with the effects of gravity, continued to hover just inside the orbit of Mars.

"When was this?" Vasilisa asked. "When was this alignment represented?"

"A few months ago," Stirling told her. As he said this, the planets began rotating again, very, very slowly.

"That's at real speed," Stirling said. "But I'm certain that Sir Isaac must have wanted us to see the motion of this new object, so I will quicken it."

"Why did he go to all of this trouble?" Maclaurin wondered. "He must have found this comet using the affinascope. It must be small indeed. Why not simply calculate its orbit and send us the projection?"

"It must be something he wants us to *see*," Vasilisa offered. "Something interesting."

"I'm moving it up so that a minute equals a day," Stirling said.

Now the Earth and most of the other planets were spinning on their axes quite visibly, and Mercury and the moons of the larger planets began to inch noticeably around their orbits. Ben kept his eye on Newton's spheroid. "It's moving," he whispered.

Maclaurin moved nearer, fixing a critical eye upon it. "Yes, the orbit must be highly elliptical. See how it plummets sunward? And my God, the speed! It must be traversing a thousand miles per minute!"

"And accelerating, of course," Heath added.

In five minutes—five days to the orrery—the thing had moved an astonishing distance.

Vasilisa saw it first. *"Matka Bozhye,"* she muttered. "See? See?"

For another instant, Ben did not, but then he got it.

"Oh, shit," Maclaurin swore.

They continued to watch for the next quarter of an hour, but by then they all knew. When the object bumped into the model of the Earth with a metallic *ping*, none of them were surprised.

"There is still one inscription unaccounted for," Maclaurin said. He had just retrieved the model and was looking it over more thoroughly. "Just two numbers, and no symbols at all—nine and zero."

That nagged something in Ben's head, but he could not remember what.

"It's the object's dimensions," Stirling offered.

"Possible." Maclaurin shrugged. "Though how can something ha' a dimension of zero? In any event, I'm goin' up t' the observatory. I want t' ken if that thing is really out there or if this is all some part of Sir Isaac's illness. Heath, would you assist?"

"Of course. Stirling?"

The astronomer shook his head. "I need to consider this. Perhaps if we tell Halley—"

"Halley? Are you daft?"

"No one knows more about comets and their kin," Stirling replied stubbornly.

"James, I do' na' ha' the power to forbid you, but I beg you not to tell Halley of this until we ha' better proof and can substantiate that Sir Isaac made the discovery. One thing we do' na' need in the present climate is another priority dispute."

"Halley would never—"

"I know that, but Sir Isaac must na' get it into his head that even the possibility exists."

"Consider, also," Voltaire inserted, "that since this discovery represents a potential danger to the Crown, this information may actually aid Halley and his cronies in impounding the orrery—and perhaps the affinascope, too."

"Pardon me," Vasilisa said, her voice rising from the back of the room, "but isn't it more important that Earth is soon to be bombarded by a comet? I for one would like to contact my embassy and warn them."

"Warn them?" Heath said. "Warn them of what? Such bodies strike the Earth every day."

"This one appears considerably larger than most, Heath."

"But of course the simulacrum is exaggerated in size."

"Yes, still, it must be quite large. Suppose it were a few hundred thousand feet in diameter? Such a mass, with the velocity it has—"

"I know that. But we know that only the tiniest part of our planet is inhabited. The odds that this comet will strike anyplace of import are passing small."

"That may be," Maclaurin interceded, "and the orrery is too crude a device to show us where it will strike. But a few hours with the affinascope, and a bit of time calculating, and I'm sure I can discover where it will fall to within a gross region, anyway. Shouldn't you wait at least for that, Vasilisa, to avoid alarming your people?"

Vasilisa, for the first time since Ben had met her, looked somewhat dour. "I will wait a day, no longer. Colin, this comet will fall in less than a week!"

"I ken that. Heath is probably right, however. This is likely t' be an event of stupendous scientific consequence, but of little danger, save to perhaps some unlucky savages in South America or the Islands of Solomon."

Vasilisa seemed unconvinced, though she finally nodded. "Very well," she replied. "I'm going for a walk."

"Vasilisa, please—"

"Ben will accompany me," she snapped, "to assure that I do not act the spy."

Maclaurin sighed. "Do' na' be absurd, Vasilisa. Of course we trust you."

"Of course. Nevertheless, Benjamin, if you would not mind?"

To Ben's relief, Vasilisa didn't walk even generally west—toward the foreign embassies—but turned pointedly east and south into the city.

For five minutes or so, neither of them said anything.

"Take my arm, Ben," Vasilisa requested softly. He offered it, though it felt stiff, tightened by the knotted muscles in his chest and stomach.

"Do you have any questions about last night, Ben?" Vasilisa asked him.

"Why did it happen, Mrs. Karevna?" he asked.

"I think you can safely call me Vasilisa, now," she said. "It happened, Ben, because I like you, and because we had been drinking, and because I like that sort of thing."

"Why me, then? Why not Voltaire or some other, some older—"

"Is that your worry, your age? Ben, in my country men younger than you fight in the army. In yours, too, I think." Ahead, through the lane, the blue expanse of the Thames winked a million sun-glitter eyes at them. "That wasn't fair, was it?" Vasilisa sighed. "The fact is you *are* young, though not so much younger than me as you might think. Voltaire is considerably schooled in the ways of love. That is attractive at times, but it also makes him . . . um, perfunctory. You weren't perfunctory, Ben."

"Or very skilled, either. You're saying you made love to me because I *am* a novice?"

"Look at it this way, dear. You must learn from someone. And I enjoy teaching sometimes. Also—" He felt her stiffen a bit. "Let's just say that I am choosy. I have had very bad luck with men in the past, Ben."

"Your scars—"

"I will not speak of that," she said, and for an instant she seemed icy cold.

"So you thought I was harmless, too," Ben murmured.

"Harmless? No. No man is harmless. Gentle, caring—yes. And if I can teach you to make love in that way—teach you to love women without hurting them—then both of our sexes gain. And when you find your true love—" But then she must have felt him tremble. She stopped walking. They had reached the Grand Terrace on the river. Below them the Thames extended, at least a hundred small craft bobbing on its surface.

"No, I am not she," she said softly to his unspoken thought, and kissed him on the lips. He knew his face showed his anguish. He wanted to beg her to love him.

"You take it all too seriously," she said. "One day you will look back and remember how much fun it was."

"Actually, that's part of my concern," Ben replied, trying on a little smile. "I remember too *little* of it."

She gave his arm a playful squeeze. "Well, if you can adopt a more casual attitude, perhaps we can see what we can do about that. But if I find that I'm making you more unhappy . . .

"Come, let's walk up the terrace," she said.

They had come onto the terrace near the mouth of the Fleet Canal. Facing the river, the walls and towers of the Temple college rose on their left, a little city all its own. To their right, along the curve of the river stood the ancient sentinel of the Tower, where Ben had first set foot in London. The terrace was a broad quay that ran more than a mile, punctuated by stairs descending to the water where boats might dock. The stone-paved terrace itself was crowded with the gaily dressed well-to-do on outings, with fishermen and gypsies, with beggars and hawkers. A single breath tasted salt from the distant sea, fish spoiling in the afternoon sun, tobacco, pastries, shellfish, and the underlying stench of sewage.

They strolled toward the Tower, though Ben guessed they had no destination.

"That was clever of you, deciphering Newton's riddle."

"It was simple enough. Any one of you would have figured it out if I hadn't."

"That's entirely beside the point. You have many talents, Ben. Have you thought of attending college?"

Ben grinned wryly. "There is only the matter of money," he said. "My father wished that I should attend a college back in America, but that was never to be, I think."

"You don't talk much about your family in America."

Ben heaved a sigh. "I try not to think of them."

"Were they so bad?"

"No, I love them very much. But I betrayed them, abandoned them."

"It seems to me you had good reason."

"I can put any face on it I want, but when my life was threatened, I fled."

"It must be more complicated than you paint it. Before this man threatened your life—before your brother was killed—didn't you already wish your liberty?"

When he didn't respond she continued. "It was that way with me. I was born in a place where no woman could ever be more than a wife and mother. I always wanted more—to see the world, to learn things. But it was impossible."

"Impossible? But here you are."

"Yes, here I am," she mused. "And yet it was impossible. I had to die before my life could begin."

"Die? What does that mean, Vasilisa?"

"It isn't important—a story for another time. I, too, left much behind me to be here, but this is where people like you and I must be. We are not like ordinary people, any more than Newton is, or Maclaurin." She chuckled. "Oh, I don't mean to say that I'm a genius like they are—"

"I *do* know what you mean. I would have never found what I wanted in Boston."

"Have you found it here?"

"Yes. Yes, but still . . ."

"Still what?"

"I put them out of my mind. It's as if the ship that brought me from America was taking me across the river of the dead. That's how I tried to think of it—as an irrevocable decision. Onboard ship when I stood looking at the sea, I only looked east. I begged the captain to let me look at his charts, and I explored all the world on them, from India to Cathay—but the maps of America I left furled." He shook his head. "Mostly I looked at the charts of the coastline of England, at—" He stopped abruptly.

"What is it?" Vasilisa asked. "Are you faint?"

"Not faint," he croaked, "but I have to sit down."

"Why?"

He shook free of her and found an empty bench, sank onto it. He looked up at the sky, which suddenly seemed too close, more menacing than the sword of Damocles.

"Those other numbers," he said. "I know what they are."

"What?"

"London. In the new system, the latitude and the longitude."

He looked around him, as if in a dream. A dandy swaggered by, sword wagging like a tail. At the base of the steps, a little boy in a blue coat and tricorn exhorted his toy boat to fire its cannon.

"What are you saying? Are you saying that the comet will strike *London*?"

"That's what Newton was trying to tell us. Oh, God, that's why he went on about Sodom and Gomorrah."

"How can it be?"

"It can't be. It's just numbers, just an equation, just philosophical nonsense." He closed his eyes, trying to think, trying to find some other answer.

When he opened them, Vasilisa was gone, vanished into the crowd. Of course she had gone, to warn her countrymen. That was where her real allegiance was. Newton's words came back to him then, and he understood two things with perfect clarity. The first was that the old man really was mad, mad beyond anyone's worst nightmares. The second was that he could trust none of the Newtonians—not Maclaurin, not Vasilisa, no one. He was alone.

18.

The Elixir of Life

Summer marched into October undeterred by the usual logic of the seasons as Adrienne studied the notebook, such a Mediterranean heat settling upon the land as normally confined itself to August and the south. When she went out, she was accosted by sunlight that crushed her as if it had weight.

Her rooms were hot but not intolerable, a dark cave where she pored over the notebook Torcy had given her. When reading it, she took no notice of the heat, so cold and passionless was its tale of horror. It was the story of a young servant named Martin. She read it with a sick fascination; a year before she would not have been able to read it at all. As all reading should, it brought questions to mind.

"What can you tell me of Mehemet Mira Bey?" Adrienne asked Crecy one day. They sat beneath an awning on the roof of the chateau, each holding a cup of orange sherbet that melted much faster than they could finish it.

"I saw him," Crecy remarked, "several times, in fact. He called upon my mistress La Sery at least once. She was intrigued by his foreignness, at first. She found him disappointing, ultimately."

"What was he like?"

Crecy shrugged. "A Persian. He spoke little French and dressed abominably. He was a fraud, you know."

"What do you mean? The king received him as an ambassador."

Crecy tipped her sherbet bowl and chased a dollop with her spoon. "The king was dying," she explained. "I heard it told that his ministers—especially Pontchartrain—wished to give their dying king one last chance to play the grand monarch."

"You were there?"

"It was the most incredible thing I ever saw. Of course, I was eighteen and easily impressed. The whole court was resplendent, but the *king* had every diamond in the treasury sewn onto his coat. He could barely walk in it."

"All that for a fraud?"

"All of that for the *king*. That was when France still loved him."

Adrienne recalled Torcy's tortured face when he spoke of the king's earlier brush with death. Yes, it *would* have been better if he had died then.

"Who was Monsieur Bey really, then?"

"He really *was* a Persian, if that's what you mean. Why are you interested in events five years gone?"

"This Persian gave the king an elixir of life."

Crecy smiled. "I remember. That and a lot of worthless baubles. Pontchartrain and the others might have done a better job of making him seem like the real representative of an Oriental potentate, I think. But the elixir worked, I suppose, so clearly the Persian was more than what he seemed."

"Clearly. What became of him?"

"He stayed around the court, taking every scrap of food, wine, and courtesy he could get. He remained for the most part of a year before he was finally deported." She grinned. "Clearly the hospitality here was better than what he was used to at home. The best part was the souvenir he took with him."

"That being?"

"When his things were loaded upon his ship, the inspectors found one rather large chest he would not allow them to open. He screeched and caterwauled that it contained books sacred to his prophet, Mohammed, and that infidels might not lay eyes upon them."

Adrienne leaned forward with interest. "What manner of books?"

Crecy's eyes sparkled devilishly.

"It was but a single tome entitled, the *duchess d'Espinay*."

"What?" Adrienne asked.

"It was a *duchess*. It seems she had become pregnant by the ambassador and inclined toward life in a more Oriental clime.

Really! Madame de Maintenon slighted your education if she never told you that story!" She laughed, but stopped when she saw that Adrienne was not amused. "What is it?"

"The man sounds as if he was nothing but a swindler, a charlatan, a kidnapper. And yet he brought the elixir of life."

"Have some imagination, Adrienne. If he could steal a duchess, he could steal an elixir from some great Egyptian magus, could he not?"

"I suppose."

Crecy shrugged. "Perhaps the elixir *itself* was fraudulent. Perhaps the king recovered on his own."

"No, the elixir was real,". Adrienne answered. "Some of the philosophers tried it on someone else before they tried it on the king."

"Naturally. It might have been poison."

"Yes. They gave it to a young man who was dying of consumption. It saved him."

"I see." Crecy's eyes narrowed a bit.

"Not only that, but as it turned out, it conferred other lasting benefits. When he was kicked by a horse onto a sharp stake, it impaled him, but he did not die."

"This is more fascinating than my story. Go on."

"This young man was of mean birth. The physicians gave it out that he had died, and they took him to the laboratories of the Academy of Sciences. There they tried to kill him in every way imaginable. Though many of their methods reduced him to a wretched state, he never died."

"What became of him?"

"I suppose he is there yet. He went mad, and the physicians lost interest in him."

"How do you know this?" Crecy asked, wide-eyed.

Adrienne lifted the notebook from her skirt and handed it across the table.

"Torcy gave me this," she said.

"What is it?"

"The notes of one of the physicians I just spoke of, and of an alchemist who worked with him. Notes of their experimentation upon 'Martin.' "

"Why in the name of God did Torcy give you that?"

"Because I am to kill the king for him," Adrienne said simply. "No, do not act surprised, Crecy, please."

"I won't. I wasn't sure he had yet approached you."

"So Torcy told the truth. It *was* the Korai who engineered the attack upon the barge."

"It was. I was there to see to it that you survived, Adrienne."

"And to cause the explosion."

"That, too. You amaze me."

"Why? Because I can see what even a child can see?"

Crecy shook her head. "No. Everyone else believed that it was the Englishman and his magic musket. Even the Englishman believed it."

"Yes, until Nicolas killed him."

Crecy actually gasped and touched her hand to her breast. "Incredible," she murmured.

"Ridiculous. That was the easiest part. Once I suspected that the Englishman was a ruse, I asked discreet questions of the stablemaster. Torcy had told me that the murderer was killed by a guard of the Hundred Swiss: Nicolas knew where the Englishman would go because he was part of the plot. Admit it."

"I am sworn not to speak of that, and yet the theory seems quite logical."

"I am sure it does. How long has Nicolas been one of the Korai?"

"He is not one of us. Only a woman can be one of us. But his mother . . ."

"No, don't tell me. Castries?"

"Yes. He is a bastard; she went to Florence to have him. Few know. His father, d'Artagnan, raised him."

"Well, then, I wonder if his mother knows he is also a spy for Torcy?"

Crecy frowned and was silent for a moment, and then she said, "He is, isn't he? But I didn't see it either. I doubt that Castries knows."

"Never fear," Adrienne remarked, "I shall ask him."

* * *

Nicolas made no attempt to deny the accusation. Instead, he bowed his head, removed his hat, and lowered himself onto the bench. A faint wind lisped through the high leaves of the trees, but here, among their straight boles, it was still.

"You must understand," he said very quietly, "that I did what I had to do."

Adrienne, standing, crossed her arms across her breast and stared at him, silently daring him to raise his gaze to meet hers. "And how is that, Nicolas? How is it that what you 'had to do' was betray me? You say that you love me."

He looked up at the ancient red marble of the pavilion, the grape vines crawling from the forest to swallow it, the tiny chapel nearby.

"Believe me or not," he said. "But I brought you here to tell you. If you had not confronted me—"

"I am certain you speak the truth," she retorted. "For I am infallible regarding you, am I not? You have played me like a harp, Nicolas. You have plucked my strings, and I have sung your tune. But I—" Her breath caught. This wasn't going as she wished.

At last, his dark eyes focused on her, wells of remorse, and she faltered. "I meant to tell you," he repeated. "I had to report to Torcy. If I had not, someone else would have, and then he would no longer trust me. And he must trust me when I betray him. Adrienne, look to your heart. You know I love you."

"My heart? My heart is an imbecile. There is nothing trustworthy about my heart. And what do you mean, betray Torcy? What—" Hot tears streamed down her face, but her voice stayed steady.

"Come here," he said almost harshly, his long frame unfolding. In four steps he had reached her, taken her arm in a grip almost too tight. She jerked violently, but his grasp remained secure.

"Come," he said more softly and tugged her toward the little chapel.

"I found this place long ago," he told her. "I think it must have been here even before Louis XIII built the first Versailles. No one else comes here."

They now stood just within the dimness of the building. Nicolas withdrew a small, glowing stone from his pocket, and the single room grew visible.

Inside was a small, austere altar and crucifix. In the right-hand corner there was a pile of blankets, leather packs, a musket.

"Nicolas? What is this?"

"We are leaving Versailles," he said, "today. Now. I have the things there that we need—forged documents, supplies, everything."

"Why?"

"Torcy knows you will fail to kill the king," Nicolas hissed. "He hopes your attempt will drive him mad or some such. Torcy is desperate, Adrienne, and he does not care what becomes of you. I do."

"How long have you planned this?"

"Since first I met you, I think," he replied. "I hope that in time you will understand. I hope you will forgive me."

She took his head in both hands and kissed him, burying her lips against his. He was a furnace, a portal to flame and alchemical mystery, to immolation. She sought more and more, until in the end they slipped together onto the chapel floor, bodies gripping tighter than hands enfisted until they reached the physical limits of human embrace, went a pace farther, and finally collapsed back into space and time, exhausted.

Lying there, counting his ribs, she laughed and kissed him with lips still salty from tears.

"What?" he panted.

She gestured at the crucifix. "I suppose now that I am damned beyond redemption," she said. "But I love you, Nicolas d'Artagnan."

"Then you will go with me?"

"No," she said. "No, but afterward . . ."

He reached his hand up to her lips, and she kissed the tips of his fingers. "There will be no afterward," he said. "Not if you try to kill the king. You will not survive, Adrienne."

"Yes, I will, Nicolas, and then we shall away together. Not before."

"Adrienne—"

"Shhh. You asked me to forgive you. So I shall, my sweet, but you must abide my wishes. For a change, we must do as I say." She hesitated. "It tempts me, Nicolas, but I must do this."

His tender gaze turned somewhat stony, but at last he nodded.

"Good," she said. "Now—" She gently disentangled from his embrace and stood naked in the dark chapel, feeling instantly shy. Ruefully she picked through her clothes. "It was here somewhere," she said. "Ah!" She brought forth a folded note. "Take this to Torcy and tell him I need this made."

Nicolas sat up, leaned back on his elbows, and after a moment surrendered a little half-smile. "Give me a kiss first, and I will consider it."

She did, and thus another half hour passed before they emerged from the chapel, Adrienne inspecting her clothing for damage. Most of it was unseen, and Adrienne thought how pleased Crecy would be at the state of her stockings.

19.

Traitor

Ben pounded on the door, his fist driven by a rising sense of desperation. "Robin!" he shouted. "Please, open up!"

Something rattled beyond the portal; someone cursed. Finally came the scratch of the bolt drawing, and the door opened a crack.

"Damn," Robert muttered from within. "I was wonderin' when you'd be back." Even through the narrow gap, Ben caught the faint juniper stench of gin. "What th' hell do y' want?"

"It's important, Robin. Let me in, please."

Robert grunted and pushed the door open, stumbled back into the apartment. "Lost my job," he explained. "Not that I expect you t' care. What did y' come back for, t' press the debt I owe you?"

"You don't owe me any debts, Robin. It's I who owe you."

"That's a fine thing to *say*," Robert grumbled. "But y' must want something. You didn't come back here out of friendship."

"I *did*."

"Hum. So will y' visit Boston next, an' y'r friends there?"

Ben felt he could hardly breathe. "Look, Robin, I can't explain it," he gasped, not sure what he was saying. "I seem to have a knack of putting people out of my mind. When I think about it, it grieves me, but not so much as I *do* anything about it. I don't know why I'm that way."

Robert arched an eyebrow and then traced the sign of the cross. "Well, my son," he muttered sarcastically, "now that I've heard your confession—"

"Dammit, Rob, I've come back to save your life!" Ben shouted.

"Dammit, dammit . . ." His pulse was rushing in his ears. He seemed to be outside himself, watching some sort of poorly written comedy. As his knees buckled and he sank to the floor, he thought what a pity it was that theatrics were so often substituted for wit.

He came to with Robert flicking beer into his face. "No water," the older man said gruffly. It seemed like an apology. "I shouldn't have given you such a hard time for doin' what I myself have done a thousand times. Hell, Ben, you don't know how often I thought about taking your money and just leavin' you." He grinned toothily. "I s'pose it's like with a woman. No matter how often y' think a' leavin' *them*, when you find *they've* gone and left *you*, it grieves you. Now. Suppose you trace back a few steps and tell me what got you so upset."

Ben still felt faint. His skin had a sort of papery feel, and his mouth was dry. "Give me a cup of that beer," he gasped.

It was small beer, weak and cidery, but it wet his tongue and lips and made him feel a bit better.

"This will sound mad, Robin, but you have to believe what I say."

"Go on."

"In less than a week, London's going to be annihilated, and I'm to blame."

Robert blinked, but otherwise his expression didn't change. "Go on," he said.

"I know it sounds mad," Ben repeated, and told him the story. In his mind, it had acquired a sort of *crystalline* structure, all of the elements coming together at once—not unlike how he had seen the way to tune an aetherschreiber. His correspondence with the unknown philosophers; their calculations of trajectories and their search for a way of altering those trajectories. Then Newton's cryptic model, and finally, all at once, the two mysteries meeting.

"I gave them the key," he finished. "I made it possible."

Robert pushed his fingers through his copper-tinged hair and sighed. "You want me to believe that the French king has summoned down a comet from the heavens t' smite London? Jesus and Mary! This thing you're after telling me . . ." He waved his hands despairingly.

"I know. But it's true."

"Why tell me? Tell your fine scientific friends! Tell the king!"

"I'm telling you because I want you to leave London and save your life."

"That's it?"

"No. I also needed to tell someone I trust. In case something happens to me."

"*Now* what are y' going on about? No more of your mysterious talk, Benjamin Franklin. Everything plain!"

"I don't know. Just a feeling. All the way back in Boston, Bracewell *knew*. He *knew* that I had gained some information about this plot. I don't know how—maybe some way of tracing the aetheric path back to my schreiber—"

"I thought he threatened y' before y' made the schreiber."

"That was on general principles. But after I wrote to the French philosophers, all hell broke loose. Don't you see? He's connected to all of this. Now Maclaurin and Vasilisa—all of us—we all know about the comet. And they must *know* we know."

"Because you think there's an Englishman informing."

"Yes."

"Aye. Because the transactions were in English and Latin. So even if the magi behind all of this are French—"

"They certainly had help from here. They would have had to, to aim the comet so precisely. Robin, they had to tune the comet to harmonize with London."

"What about this other society, the Philosophical Society? Might they be the villains?"

"Maybe. But I think I know who the traitor is, Robert."

Ben finished the mug of beer in one long draught and set the cup down. "I think it's Sir Isaac himself."

"Sir Isaac?" Robert turned incredulous eyes upon Ben.

"Hear me out."

"I'm listening."

"One. Sir Isaac has ample reason to be angry at the Crown—"

"This isn't the Crown, Ben. 'Tis the city of London and a million souls!"

"Two," Ben continued stubbornly, "he could be deranged. All of his disciples think he is and have therefore either quit the Royal Society—which I remind you has been dissolved—or have stuck with him from loyalty. I have met him, and he hardly impressed me as sane."

"Three?"

"Three, he made the model—"

"Which goes against your case. Why would he arrange all this and then warn his disciples?"

"You just said it, Robert. He's warning the only people he still cares about."

"And the only people who could cast some counterspell."

"It doesn't work like that. Even if we had all his notes and all the French notes, we would still have to *construct* a counterspell. That would be the work of months, not a week. And even if we had an equation to divert this comet—and the apparatus to implement it, which I can't even begin to imagine—it's still *too late*." His voice rose to a nearly hysterical shout.

"You don't know that fer sure," Robert said.

"No, I don't, but it's damn probably the truth."

"Well, y' should be finding out, not cracking y'r teeth here with me."

"I wanted you to know. I left one friend to die. I won't do it to another."

Robert covered his eyes with his palm. "I wish I were more completely sober," he said, "for heaven help me, I'm starting to believe you."

"Then you'll leave London?"

"A week, eh?"

"Yes. Unless Newton intentionally lied. But by the time I get back, Maclaurin will have checked this all astronomically."

"Well then, let's go see him."

Ben stared. *"Us?"*

"Aye. I'm no philosopher, but it sounds as if y'r worried about physical danger—that this Bracewell or some wild Frenchman or even Newton will attack you. That is something I know how t' handle. I'll bodyguard the whole lot of you."

"That's a generous offer," Ben said quietly. "But Sir Isaac has philosophical weapons and protections. I'm far from certain—"

"Ben," Robert interposed, "I'm at home in a lot of cities, but London has a special place in my heart. I'd rather not see her buried under this big rock of yours. Just let me get my sword and pistol."

"You have weapons?"

"Always, milad. I'll clean up and escort y' back t' Crane Court. And then we'll see what other philosophic heads might have t' say about all this."

Returning to Crane Court, Ben had to admit that having Robert with him did lend a certain feeling of security, with his confident swagger and his sword.

It gave him enough peace of mind to think, to wonder where Vasilisa was, and he reluctantly considered the possibility that she might be involved in the foreign plot. After all, his assumption that the philosophers on the other end of his aetherschreiber were French was a purely circumstantial one.

"Robert, do you know which calendar the Russians use?"

Robert uttered a guttural chuckle. "What a question."

"That means no?"

"That means no," he affirmed. "Russia I've never been to."

Ben decided to let the matter drop. His suspicions about Vasilisa were probably groundless. A much more likely candidate for traitor *within* the group was Voltaire, who—not being a philosopher—had a rather thin excuse for always being present.

"This is the place," Ben told Robert as they came up on Crane Court. By now it was quite dark between the street lanterns, but the windows of the former Royal Society were lit from within.

"Let me do the introductions," Ben said. "For now you are a cousin of mine from Philadelphia."

"Y'r facility with deception is developing quite nicely, Ben," Robert whispered.

"Thank you," he replied as he opened the door.

In the shocked pause that followed, Robert was the first to react, his hand snaking toward the pistol at his belt. Ben was still a statue.

"No, no!" shouted Bracewell from where he sat in the hall, two pistols trained on the door.

Robert did not pause. In an instant he was standing behind Ben, arm straight out as a ramrod over Ben's right shoulder. If he pulled the trigger, the pan would spark right at Ben's cheek. Ben closed his eyes, waiting for the thunder.

It did not come. Instead, Bracewell chuckled and held his own weapons steady.

It *was* Bracewell. He wore an eye patch, and his generous wig could not entirely hide the stippling of scar tissue on his face and neck. Of his two weapons, one seemed a normal flint-lock, while the other had three small barrels clustered together. The latter Bracewell gripped in a metallic hand, much too skeletal to be a gauntlet. He wore his uniform jacket, a black waistcoat, and a surfeit of lace about his neck.

"Well, Ben, well met. But I would advise that you have your ape-man lower his pistol, or I shall be forced to shoot through you to kill him."

"I'm willin' to bet that Ben's body will stop y'r ball," Robert said. "I'm just wondering where I oughta open a hole in *you*."

Two more men entered from the hall, each armed with *kraftpistoles*.

"What's this?" one of them asked Bracewell, raising his own weapon.

"A silly situation," Bracewell explained.

"You haven't fired yet, so it can't be all that silly," Ben managed.

"Oh, but I *will* fire," Bracewell said. "It would be more convenient for me if you were to live a bit longer, that is all. But I assure you, rather than let you escape again, I will kill you. There are three of us." This last to Robert.

"I don't care about the other two," Robert clarified. "It's you I plan t' kill."

"Do we know each other, sir?"

"I don't think so," Robert said, "and I would certainly remember a face such as yours."

"Tish," Bracewell said. "You can do better than that, I expect, if you wish to insult me. Ben, where did you find such a droll acquaintance? Quite unlike that other fellow—what was his name? John. Yes, John."

"What did you do to John?"

"Why, I'm not obliged to tell you that," Bracewell said. "Though if you ask nicely—and have this good fellow point his gun elsewhere—I might."

"Robert—" Ben began.

"No," Robert said evenly. "Whatever happened t' y'r friend is over and done. I don't know this fellow's game, but I do know that if I put this here pistol down, you and I are both dead men fer sure."

"You are dead men no matter what. Though I would prefer Ben live long enough to see what he has accomplished." Bracewell still hadn't moved a muscle below his neck.

"Sir?" one of the men said. Ben thought he might have a French accent.

"We have time—a few moments, at least. You see, Ben, in the end I am delighted that you failed to heed my friendly advice regarding the scientific. If you had, certain acquaintances of mine might still be frustrated. It was necessary to kill you afterward, of course, but you eluded me. Very clever."

"Why are you bothering with this now?" Ben asked. "We found your plan out too late."

"That may or may not be so," Bracewell said. "When I came upon Maclaurin, he was hard at work on a counter formula. You see, as we expected— Oh, hello, James."

James Stirling had just entered the room. "Mother of God, Bracewell, what's going on here?" he said, eyes darting about at all the gun barrels.

"Well, you neglected to inform me that young Ben here had a watchdog."

"I don't know this man. Ben, step inside. Tell that man to put down his gun."

"You!" Ben said.

"Ben, where is Vasilisa?"

"Safe, I hope. She left after I—" He shut his mouth stubbornly.

"Ah. You worked it out," Stirling smiled.

"But you knew all along."

Stirling's face changed. A kind of concern had overwritten his normally bland expression, but now his lips parted in a grin that showed teeth. "And you *announced* yourself to me. Didn't it occur to you that when you used your schreiber to send your brilliant little communiqué to F that *two* machines would receive the message? F's and the one that his was originally paired with? For better than two months I fretted about who the hell Janus could be, and then here you appear, with your notes to Newton, right here in London. Janus! I still didn't believe it could be that simple—that you were just a boy who blundered into the situation. I imagined some crafty, unseen opponent, a brilliant tactician, using you as his pawn. You scared the hell out of me, Ben, especially when you and Newton started having your little meetings. I had to keep Bracewell off you until I was certain, and that wasn't easy at all, I promise you."

"It's true," Bracewell replied.

"You've been here this whole time?"

"No, of course not. I only arrived a short time ago, really. Still, it has seemed quite a long time. I *do* hold grudges."

"You were trying to *kill* me."

"Yes, and you should have cooperated," Bracewell replied.

"My arm's getting tired," Robert grunted.

"I don't know who you are," Stirling called to Robert, "but if you back out of the door and leave, no one will hinder you. Keep your gun."

Ben blinked and then tried to hold his face steady. Something was coming up the hall behind Stirling, something wavering, hard to focus upon.

"Generous as a whore on Sunday, an't you?" Robert sneered.

"We have to get them out of the doorway," Stirling sighed. "Else Vasilisa will see—"

Suddenly the atmosphere above Bracewell's head condensed, gathered substance, and a red flame lit within it as it darted toward the shimmering in the hall. Bracewell cried out, and his head snapped around to follow his familiar. Ben heard a hiss at his ear, screamed as flame licked his cheek. His voice was drowned by the air breaking, and smoke stole his vision.

20.

The Face of Thetis

In the Grotto of Thetis, Adrienne met Torcy as if by accident, finding him already there as she escaped the fearsome eye of the sun into its cool interior. Aquamarine light rippled gently from the ceiling and floor, making it seem possible that this *was* the dwelling place of the sea goddess Thetis, mother of Achilles, comforter of the resting sun. Beneath three darker arches in the grotto, statues of the goddess and her nymphs clustered around the weary Apollo and his steeds.

"Are you alone?" Torcy asked.

"No. Nicolas is just outside, watching for us."

"Good. My own servants are at a discreet distance. Have you been in this grotto since its construction?"

"No. It has only been finished for a month, and as you know, I have been otherwise occupied."

"This is the second Grotto of Thetis, you know. The first was torn down forty years ago to make way for the Northern wing."

"I don't believe I *did* know that," she replied.

"You should inspect it closely. You may not get another chance."

His words prickled in her ears, but she obeyed him and walked quietly over to the statues.

Apollo was Louis, of course. The statue of Thetis bore her *own* face.

"Oh, my God," she whispered.

"Yes," Torcy said. "I asked you to meet me here to give you a last chance. I cannot have you failing at the crucial instant. You see how the king adores you? Can you still help slay him?"

"I won't falter," she answered. "I can't."

"Then we proceed," Torcy said, "for your method worked."

"Worked? What do you mean?" But she already understood.

"You knew I would test it," Torcy replied quietly. "It was a mercy, really. Poor Martin was entirely mad. He had to be moved from his own shit—"

"By God, tell me no more," Adrienne snapped. She had never seen Martin and had tried not to think of him as a human being, and now she had *killed* him, a boy whose only crime had been to be ill at the wrong time.

"Come. His suffering has ended. Ours has just begun." He handed her a wrapped package. "This is the device," he said. "Have a care with it: There is no time to build another."

"What night?" she asked instead.

"Tomorrow night, I think. Nicolas will know to come for me when he arrives. You must wait—"

"I know what to do," she said.

Back in her room, she unpacked the device in front of Crecy. "If something happens to me, *you* must know how to use it," she explained.

"It doesn't *look* like a weapon," Crecy observed.

It was a translucent crystal cube, impaled by a key. Inside, a few gears could be seen, along with a looped silver tube that also projected several inches from the surface. Near this was a hemispherical depression large enough to accommodate the small silver orb that rested nearby. This second piece had a diameter of perhaps an inch.

"It's not a weapon exactly. It will neutralize the effects of the so-called elixir of life."

"So-called?"

Adrienne nodded. "Given all of the effects of the elixir on body and soul, I expected a complex formula. Consider what it has done: It cured the king of advanced gangrene and the gout; it restored his eyesight; it protected him from incineration by a discharge of energy."

"Could not all of these things be accomplished by augmenting some natural healing virtue of the body?"

"What I understand is that these results weren't caused by

the direct action of the elixir, since it is composed of only two things: water and a fine suspension of philosopher's mercury."

Crecy stared at her for a moment. "I'm afraid I don't see the significance of that."

"Philosopher's mercury is highly resonant with aether. It mediates between physical vibrations and aetheric ones. It is the key element in the aetherschreiber, transforming the motions of the pen into aetheric vibrations and then back again."

Crecy nodded. "And if one ingests philosopher's mercury?"

Adrienne held up her hands. "I would have predicted that it would pass through the system, but it remains lodged in the body. Or at least this was the case with Martin. The result, somehow, is that those who drink this potion become like the chime of an aetherschreiber."

"You mean to say— You mean that—"

"The king has been healed by someone elsewhere, his body manipulated by something or someone else."

"Do you see who looks out of the king's eyes, whom he mutters to in the night, who sends him vigor when he should be dead?"

"No. This is all a surprise to me."

"What my device does is to search out the harmonic upon which the king resonates and interrupt it."

"Thus cutting him off from this force that animates him?"

"Yes. While he is thus separated, he is susceptible to ordinary means of—" She paused, her throat constricting, unwilling actually to pronounce the words.

"I will do the killing," Crecy promised. "I will not have you bloody your hands."

Adrienne laughed harshly. "My hands will never be clean, Veronique. The king is merely an epilogue to my novel of death. I will have murdered a million souls."

"Surely murder implies some intent," Crecy protested.

Adrienne flopped into a chair. "If I inadvertently brought about the death of a single person, you would admit that I must accept some fractional blame?"

Crecy shrugged.

"Let us be absurd," Adrienne continued, "and assume that

hell's tithe for such manslaughter is only a thousandth of what it exacts for a cold-blooded murder. A million such deaths still add up to the murder of a thousand innocents—not counting the men I slew in the forest."

Crecy shook her head wonderingly. "You are the only person I know who would resort to mathematics to enhance her sense of guilt. I bow to you: You are the queen of blame."

"I accept the title," Adrienne said lightly. If her calculations were true, and she was already a killer many times over, then why did she feel so sickened at the prospect of killing the king?

Because whatever sort of monster he was, he loved her and he trusted her. Was it possible that Crecy was right that "murder" was defined by premeditative choice?

Then Fatio and the king were the guiltiest of all, for they had plotted to cause death on an unbelievable scale.

Versailles grew more beautiful each day, Louis reflected. In the past months, Versailles had become as he had always envisioned it, the perfect palace of the sun. And in two days, the flaming chariot of the sun was coming, and it would deliver his name to the heavens. He would reign a hundred years, and no one would ever forget him.

And the angel had promised him he would have a new heir—his true child—a miracle and the lord of all that France should be.

God had even given him a chance to smite his tormentor, Marlborough. In two days, Marlborough would know who was king of France, and he would despair.

So Louis thought as he walked the deserted length of the Hall of Mirrors, where soon he would be made a husband again before all of the world, so all would know his child.

He flushed, and passion stirred in him. His flesh began to ache for Adrienne's embrace, his heart for the adoration of her smile. Still, he was master of himself. He did not hurry his pace, but went circuitously to her rooms through the War chamber where his own statue rode horseback, through the chamber of Apollo. His passion and need grew as he toured the chambers of Mars, Mercury, and Venus before—at last—he took himself down the Marble Staircase to where Adrienne awaited.

"Hello, my dear," he said as he entered, posing to display his excellent calves and gracious bearing to their best advantage.

"Sire," she replied.

"One last time you shall be my mistress, and after that only my queen."

She smiled at him, a glowing, brilliant smile, more dazzling than any lover he had ever had—yet somehow a combination of them all. Smiling tenderly, he began to undress her.

It isn't real, Adrienne told herself, as the king undid her bodice. Tonight she prayed more desperately for unreality than ever. It was almost as if her lovemaking with Nicolas had cleansed her body so Louis could degrade it afresh. She tried to wrap herself in her accustomed numbness. She tried to review the plan in her head, but her thoughts would not stay focused. She cringed at the smoothness of the sheets, the touch of the king's fingers, his choking perfume. She remembered her first time in bed with him, the awe and terror, and it came again, redoubled.

He disgusts me. I loathe him. He deserves to die. She needed anger, revulsion, pain, but she couldn't find them. As he moved upon her, she began to sob.

Louis froze. His blind gaze sought hers in the lamplight, searching for something it could not see. His face was *so* old, so drawn, as ecstasy fled it and a troubled look replaced it. For the first time in her life she saw Louis as an old, sick man, as much a victim as she.

No. He had doomed a million people.

Or had he?

"Adrienne? Are you weeping?"

But now her mind *had* found a focus.

"Adrienne, please," the king begged.

She sobbed, her body contorted by her grief, but her brain raced. The patterns of numbers and symbols burst into her mind fully formed.

"There is still time," she gasped.

"Time? Time?"

"My lord, it can be stopped. I can stop it."

He rose up above her, face puzzled.

"A million people, my king. I know you as Maintenon knew you. Think, please. She could not have borne this. *You* cannot bear it, though you think you can."

"Who told you this?" he asked slowly. "Did that idiot Fatio tell you?"

"No. No—"

"You presume?" Louis shouted suddenly. He grabbed her roughly by the arm, and suddenly fear surged through her. His strength was not that of an eighty-two-year-old man; his fingers bit like iron.

"Who betrayed me?"

"Sire," she moaned, reaching to touch his face, "*listen* to me."

He closed his eyes for a moment, and then he said, in a perfectly reasonable tone, "It will save France, Adrienne. That is all I care for."

"It will destroy France, Sire. This comet is far more powerful than you have been led to believe—"

He snarled, tightening his grip again. "You presume too much, I say again! How dare you speak of these things!"

He twisted her arm nearly out of its socket, and she screamed. His mouth opened in astonishment and dismay, and a tear started from his eye. "Mademoiselle, forgive me," he whispered.

Before she could reply, a red tongue licked out of the king's chest, wagged at her, and was gone. He croaked, then jerked his arms wildly, releasing her. She shrieked and propelled herself onto the marble floor.

The king tried to reseize her, but Crecy, who stood behind him, sword in hand, ran him through again.

"God damn your soul," she swore.

"Do not touch me!" He gasped, blood bubbling in his throat. "For the love of God keep back from me! I am the king! Guards!"

"Adrienne!" Crecy snarled. "Your device!"

But Adrienne was paralyzed. Blood was everywhere—in her hair, spattered on her breasts.

"Mademoiselle!" Louis implored, reaching for her again. "Tell them I am the king!"

Crecy slashed the back of Louis' neck, but her sword shattered.

"Adrienne!" Crecy shouted. A black angel appeared, wrapping the king in its wings. The window exploded, and through it blew a gale of smoke and dancing balls of flame. In their midst stood Gustavus, a hideous expression on his alabaster face, a *kraftpistole* clenched in either fist.

21.

Magus

Ben clawed at the floor with his fingers, hoping somehow to dig into the earth itself. He thought he heard more gunfire, but one whole side of his head thudded.

Trembling, he raised up his eyes. Robert was some ten feet away, back against a wall, his sword up. He seemed to be staring at him. One of the two men who had been with Bracewell lay on the floor, belly up, breath coming in choppy whistles, blowing bubbles of blood. The other man was still on his feet, a short, heavy sword in his hands. He held it shakily, pointed at a man Ben did not recognize.

He was perhaps twenty years old. His face was sardonic, with a cleft and thrusting chin. His lips were thin, compressed in pain, and he was frowning. But his *eyes* smoldered with a fierce, even manic intelligence. Ben had seen those eyes before, that frown. He wore a scarlet coat and waistcoat; blood visible on his white shirt and cravat. He clutched his shoulder where his wound seemed to be, but remained on his feet, glaring at Stirling.

"Don't move, Ben," a ragged voice said. Ben turned.

Bracewell was on the floor, back propped against the wall. One hand was pressed against his sternum, blood streaming between his fingers. His metal hand held a pistol less than a foot from Ben's nose, hammer cocked. Bracewell's eyelids fluttered in pain, but they never narrowed farther than to slits.

"What now?" Ben asked him quietly.

"Now? Now?" Bracewell panted. He frowned as if that were the most perplexing question in the world.

"Close that door," Stirling ordered.

"I'll cut down the first man who comes near the door," Robert snapped.

Stirling looked confused. His pistol was trained on the red-clad newcomer, who, despite his wound and lack of weapons, somehow seemed capable of doing damage.

Ben realized that Bracewell's familiar was nowhere to be seen. He also wondered what had happened to the wheezing man, whose wound was much too large to have been made by Robert's pistol.

"Close the door, Guillaume," Stirling repeated. Guillaume, apparently Bracewell's man, looked doubtfully at the tip of Robert's sword.

"No," Guillaume said. "I don't think I will. You have the pistol—you deal with him."

Suddenly, Stirling struck the red-clad man in the face with the butt of his pistol. The fellow gasped, head slamming against the wall. Blood started from his nose.

"Who the hell *are* you?" Stirling demanded, a tinge of hysteria in his voice. Ben suspected that some part of Stirling knew, just as he did, exactly who the man was.

"Close the door, or I'll kill Ben," Bracewell gurgled, blood leaking out of his mouth.

"Ben," Robert said, "his pistol is empty."

Bracewell's eyebrows went up as he and Ben simultaneously glanced at the empty powder pan. Bracewell cursed and swung the barrel at Ben's face. The pain was brilliant, like fireworks exploding. Ben hit Bracewell hard in the face. He swung again and again, as Bracewell squirmed, arms up to fend off the blows. Ben fell against him, and now they were hammering their forearms and elbows together in an attempt to hit each other. Bracewell was *wounded*, damn him. The pain in Ben's hands was severe, but he didn't *care* if he smashed all of his fingers—this was Bracewell, his nightmare, his brother's murderer. Suddenly, he found that he had hold of an ear, and he yanked and yanked.

And then a blow from nowhere, driving into his belly. His body no longer obeyed him, trying to curl up into a ball, and a steel claw was fastened on his neck, starting to cut through. All he could see was Bracewell's face, nose bleeding, eyepatch ripped away to reveal an empty, whitened socket, his other eye a hellish flame of malice. Then half Bracewell's head was gone, and Ben was falling, the claw still around his throat.

He tore it away frantically, and kicked across the floor. Wiping blood and brains from his face, sobbing and gasping for air, Ben tasted the gore on his lips and was violently sick.

When next he lifted his head, it was to meet Vasilisa's concerned gaze.

"God damn you, Stirling," Heath said, holding a rag to the oozing wound on his forehead. "Why?"

Heath and Voltaire had both been found bound and gagged in the orrery room. The Frenchman had some cuts and scrapes, but Heath had received a nasty blow to the head.

Stirling didn't answer but glared defiantly at them. His hands were tied behind his chair, and two of Vasilisa's guards stood nearby armed with pistols. Vasilisa was playing surgeon to the man in the red coat who lay on the table of the meeting room. She had just dug the ball out of his shoulder and was now bandaging the cauterized wound.

Robert and Voltaire clumped back into the room. "Maclaurin is dead," Voltaire said in the most subdued tone Ben had ever heard him use.

"Stirling and his comrades were going to kill us all." Vasilisa said icily, "I think you owe us an explanation, James."

"I answer to no one, least of all some Russian bitch," James replied.

The Russian guard struck Stirling so hard with the back of his hand that the chair nearly rocked over.

"Misha!" Vasilisa snapped.

"There are four more of them," the man on the table groaned.

"At your house?" Vasilisa asked, and Ben felt a glow of pride. "Yes."

Vasilisa snapped a few words to her two guards. They left the room. "They will do what they can, quietly," Vasilisa assured them.

"Just the two of them?" Voltaire asked.

"No. I left ten more outside."

"Vasilisa, I had no idea."

She frowned. "My dear Voltaire, you know I was Tsar Peter's envoy to the Royal Society. Did you think he would give me no access to my embassy's resources?"

"I want to know what was going on here," Heath interrupted. "Who were those men, James, and what do you have to do with them? And who is *he*?"

He thrust his finger toward the red-coated man, who had managed to drag himself to sit on the edge of the table. Beads of sweat stood out on his face, and pain still twisted his features, but he managed to grin briefly when he looked at Heath. "Mr. Heath," he said quietly, "I am insulted, for we have met on several occasions. I am Sir Isaac Newton, of course."

The dumbfounded silence that followed made it clear that only Ben and Vasilisa had guessed.

"Sir Isaac? But how can that be? You—" But Heath *believed*; Ben could see that much.

"I am an old man? Quite right. But I told your young friend here, Benjamin, I had not been idle."

"An elixir of life?" Vasilisa said. "Or is this some illusory seeming?"

"No, it's real enough. The cost was my sanity for a time. Or perhaps—" He wrinkled his brow. "—perhaps I had already gone mad when I invented it."

Ben found that he could not contain his impatience. "The *comet*," he blurted out.

"I'm sorry to have been so cryptic," Newton said, "but I trusted none of you. I wanted to see how each of you reacted when my model was placed in the orrery."

"You were *there*?" Heath gasped.

"Wearing the aegis," Newton confirmed. "It can be adjusted to render one nearly invisible."

"Well, you smoked the snake from his hole," Voltaire declared, with a poisonous glance at Stirling.

"How did you know?" Stirling asked.

"About the plot? My first hint of it was Mr. Franklin's letter, but I was deep in my . . . depression . . . at that time. Still, I recalled it a short while ago, when I received a most unusual aether-schreiber message." He set his feet gingerly on the floor, managed the few steps to one of the chairs, and slid into it. "It came on a machine I have not used in many years, the mate to which I didn't even know still existed. A gift to a friend and student of mine, long ago. But the message was signed *Minerva*."

Ben started. "Minerva," he repeated, under his breath.

"This message was part equation and part warning. It seems that this former student of mine—" Here he paused, as if the wound in his shoulder had begun to throb with sharper, unexpected pain. "It seems," he began again, "that the French king had managed to attract some philosophers of real talent. As Mr. Franklin guessed, it is they who have summoned this stone from heaven—this cannonball, as Minerva called it—to fall upon London. Minerva suggested that the French philosophers had English accomplices. I saw immediately that it had to be one or all of *you*. The orrery and the affinascope were both necessary to make the initial calculations. What I didn't know—still don't know—is how James could so betray his country."

"Perhaps," Vasilisa murmured, "we can question him more thoroughly later."

"When I asked about the comet," Ben clarified, "I meant how can we *stop* it? What can we do?"

"I have a few ideas," Newton said cautiously. "To tell you the truth, I have little faith in them, but they must be tried." He cleared his throat, closed his eyes, and settled deeper into the chair. "Yes, in truth, I think we will fail, though I am fully prepared to stay here with the orrery and the observatory—"

"Sir," Voltaire said gently, "Stirling and his cronies have destroyed both."

Newton blinked, and for a moment his face slackened into utter defeat. "Well, that is even worse, but I must try. I still wish your help, of course."

"London must be evacuated," Heath said, voicing what all of them knew.

"Of course," Newton agreed. "In an hour or two I will seek an audience with the king—"

"And what?" Vasilisa interrupted. "Tell him you are Sir Isaac

Newton? He will not believe you! He may even have you arrested. Certainly when the massacre here becomes known, some of us will be taken into custody. Do any of you wish to be locked in a prison cell, vainly trying to explain to your idiot captors that a celestial body is soon to settle your case? And what if you manage to convince the king to order an evacuation? Do you suppose that it will be peaceful? Looters will sack the city, mobs will riot, philosophers will be burned like witches."

"Vasilisa, what are you suggesting?" Ben asked.

"That we all leave, right now. Take Maclaurin's notes, and this murderer here. Don't you understand? If this weapon can be used once, it can be used again. London in a few days—then Saint Petersburg, Amsterdam, Vienna. We have to develop a countermeasure. Sir Isaac and Benjamin *must* escape London—preferably with the rest of us."

"And you can provide this escape?" Voltaire asked.

"I know of a locomotive ship that can leave within the hour."

"Young lady," Newton began, "I understand your concern, but when the time comes, I, and whoever remains with me, *will* escape the devastation."

Vasilisa chewed her lip for an instant, and then her regard met Ben's. He almost gasped, for he saw only bleakness and determination there.

"In that case," she replied softly, "I must insist. I have your best interests—and the interests of the world—at heart, and I also have the men and guns with me to implement my will. Sir Isaac, Mr. Franklin, Mr. Heath, Voltaire, and you . . ."

"Robert Nairne," Robert clarified.

"All of you are *invited* to be my guests. I will insist only on Sir Isaac and Benjamin. The rest of you will be free to go once we are on board the ship. Heath, if you wish, you may begin warning Londoners about their fate."

Heath didn't say anything. He just stared at Vasilisa.

"Don't do this, Vasilisa," Ben said, "please."

"Dear boy, it is for the best. You will see. A philosopher with your potential will be denied nothing in Saint Petersburg."

"Unless, perhaps, *freedom* counts as something," Voltaire said.

"What is freedom to such men as Sir Isaac?" Vasilisa snapped.

"Sir Isaac, have you not been prisoned all of your life, hemmed in by fools? Have you ever been a free man, able to do anything whatsoever?"

"You play at semantics," Voltaire accused.

"My sweet Voltaire," Vasilisa said, "you have pleased me often and dearly these past months. Do not make it necessary to have you killed. I would not enjoy it, but I always do what is necessary."

As you did with me, Ben thought, with sinking heart. *I was in love with you.* Was she so coldhearted as to have made love to him only in the hopes that she might later gain some advantage from it? Looking at her now, he knew she was.

"Mr. Franklin?" Sir Isaac said. "What do you say?"

"I say that if we resist Vasilisa, we will lose. Over and above that, she makes sense."

"Good boy, Benjamin," Vasilisa said.

You wait, Ben thought. *Keep thinking I love you, that you have me at your beck and call. One day—when it will do some good—this dog will turn on you.*

"Very well," Sir Isaac said. "But there are some things I will need from my house."

"Sit still, please," Vasilisa said. "Where is this aegis you spoke of?"

"It was destroyed when Bracewell's malakus attacked me."

"Where are its remains?"

"It was built into my coat."

"Make a list of your needs. I cannot risk you alone with your things. You might have another of these invisibility cloaks about. Ben and my men will pack what you need. And now, if all of you gentlemen will accompany me to the docks—"

"I wish to remain," Voltaire said. "I will not let an entire city perish without warning it."

"I also," Heath added.

"As you wish," Vasilisa said, "but you still must board my boat. We will put you out in the Thames in a rowboat once we are under way."

22.

Bridges

Crecy reacted instantly, hurling the hilt of her sword at Gustavus. It struck him between the eyes, and his right-hand pistol roared. The tall redhead bounded toward him with catlike speed. From somewhere she had produced a dagger, and Gustavus barely got his arm in front of his face fast enough for *it* to receive the point instead of his eye.

Adrienne was still blinking at the sudden appearance of the angel, a creature of wings and shadow but no discernible human features. With a sudden grim determination, she crawled across the blood-soaked bed toward the crystal cube that lay on the end table. Behind her, glass and porcelain shattered as Crecy and Gustavus exchanged blows. Where in heaven or hell was Nicolas?

She pressed a tiny stud on the cube, and it clucked softly, producing a low, melodious note that began to rise in pitch. When the pitch stopped climbing, it would be time to place the sphere in its socket.

Crecy and Gustavus slammed into a floor-length mirror, limbs writhing together, eyes flashing like red flames. Then they parted, Crecy's head snapping back as Gustavus caught the point of her chin with his fist. She sprawled roughly to the floor, and the Livonian paused to wrench her knife from his belly before rising, breath rasping horribly in his throat. His eyes, as red as Satan's, met Adrienne's, and she wondered if she weren't already in hell.

"Bitch," Gustavus coldly swore. "Do you think to ruin our plans so easily?"

"Whose plans?" Adrienne managed, suddenly hearing the frantic pounding on the outer door.

Gustavus laughed and, brandishing the knife, limped toward Crecy.

The door burst open, and four of the Hundred Swiss rushed in, pistols and blades drawn.

Thunder cracked as pistols fired, and then a cone of flame engulfed two of the guards. They fell, howling. Adrienne spun, confused. She could not hear the rising tone from her cube: The gunfire had nearly deafened her.

Gustavus faced the remaining guards, a broadsword in hand.

"They mean to kill the king!" he snarled at the guards. "You fools, can't you see? They are assassinating the king!"

The guards hesitated only for a moment, for to them the situation must have seemed obvious.

They charged Gustavus, and they died. He cut one's leg from below him and gutted the second man with the return stroke.

Then Nicolas stepped in through the shattered window, face as merciless as death, a pistol in each hand, and shot Gustavus in the back. The Livonian screamed, turned, and raised his sword. Nicolas shot him in the face with his second weapon, and the blond man crumpled to the marble.

For an instant they all stood looking at one another; Crecy rising shakily to her feet, Nicolas with his two smoking weapons, Adrienne panting, huddled against a wall, the cube and crystal clutched in her hands. Then Nicolas crossed the room in two bounds and wrapped his arms around her. "I'm sorry. I'm sorry," he gasped, hugging her, kissing her hair. "I saw him coming toward the window—" He seemed suddenly to understand that she was naked, and cast about as if to find her something to wear.

"Oh, my sweet God," he said, as he noticed the blood, then the angel.

The angel had said nothing, done nothing except to enfold the king and contemplate them with luminescent eyes. Its eyes were the king's—the king's new eyes had been angel eyes all along. In a day of horrors, *that* was somehow the most horrible.

As if it were a world away, Adrienne suddenly noticed the sound of a single note from the cube: Her hearing had returned. Her device at last matched the king's harmonic.

"Farewell, my lord," she said, socketing the sphere. It incandesced as the catalyst triggered aetheric vibrations matched to the king. The angel thinned like lifting fog, so that Louis' naked form was visible again. He groaned, hands cupped uselessly over his wounds.

Faster than a bee's wing, the sublimating angel flew at her, and she had an impression of something mothlike. A black sickle or talon or *something* cut through the air toward her. Nicolas leapt between them, but the inky blade passed through his body as if he weren't there and bit painlessly through her own head.

And agony blinded her as the cube became molten in her fist.

She came back to consciousness borne between Crecy and Nicolas, hurtling through a nightmare of gaping courtiers, painted ceilings, marble floors, and flashes of red that were probably sparks of pain somehow running up from her hand to her brain. She gaped down at her body. The hand that hurt looked not much like a hand at all but like some sort of twisted, blackened—

No. Save that for later.

"Where are we going?" she panted.

"A carriage. The marquis promised me a carriage," Nicolas said.

"No! No, we can't leave!"

"She's out of her head," Crecy said. "Look at her hand."

"No. Listen to me." She had to make them understand. "I can *stop* it—the comet. I know how to stop it."

They had passed out of Versailles now, into night air that was yet torpid. Stars blazed above, and a dry breeze was blowing with a taste upon it like hot iron.

"Adrienne," Crecy said, "if we go back, we will be arrested and killed. Do you understand? We tried to kill the king and failed. We can't go back."

"*I* will then," she said, trying to pull away from them, but they easily overpowered her.

"They may already be after us," Nicolas said. "More guards had already arrived, but with all of the bodies it was confusing. The courtiers will remember us and report where we went."

Adrienne realized that she wore a dressing gown that was thoroughly spattered with blood.

Her head was clearing, and agony was sharpening her mind. The pain was all in her wrist. The hand itself was without feeling of any sort.

The three of them approached the carriage. Adrienne relaxed, as if submitting to their judgment, but when she felt their grips loosen, she shoved them away and ran.

She made it perhaps three yards and then sprawled.

"Stupid girl!" Crecy shouted. "Come on! There is nothing you can do here! If you truly know how to stop the comet, then do it elsewhere!"

"I need Fatio's laboratory!"

"Then it cannot be done. Adrienne, it *cannot* be done! But if you live to work elsewhere, you can—"

"What? What can I do? Reverse the course of time?"

Then Nicolas clasped her tightly from behind, and they forced her into the carriage.

She found herself crushed against Torcy.

"For God's sake, get in and stop screaming," he snapped.

"We failed," Nicolas told him.

"Yes," Torcy responded dryly, "I rather thought it went badly by the looks of you. Did you at least wound him?"

Nicolas slammed the door of the carriage, and it lurched to a start. "He was wounded."

"Didn't your device work?" Torcy asked. "It worked on Martin."

"I—I didn't use it," Adrienne admitted.

"Yes, she did," Crecy contradicted.

"I didn't use it in time. Torcy, I know how to stop the comet! I was trying to tell the king, trying to convince him."

"Oh, God," Torcy murmured tiredly. "For nothing. All for nothing."

"She *did* use it," Crecy repeated. "Belatedly, but she used it."

"It was that thing, that specter," Nicolas explained. "It struck her hand."

"It struck you, too," Adrienne said. "No, it struck the cube. I never considered that what I could attack through the aether might attack back. Stupid."

"Which means it *couldn't* have worked," Crecy pressed.

"Perhaps," Adrienne agreed wearily.

Near daylight, the carriage creaked to a stop. Torcy got out, brushed at his breeches, and straightened his wig and hat.

"I bid you *adieu*," he said. "The coach will take you to a small village in the Midi. There you will be given horses, provisions, and false documents so that you can cross into Switzerland. I have provided a map, that you may seek out an old friend of mine."

"Mademoiselle needs a surgeon," Crecy said.

"There will be one in the village. Beware of large towns and guardposts—Bontemps will have sent word ahead by aetherschreiber. The whole of France will be watching for you."

Adrienne tried to answer, but she felt feverish, lightheaded. The pain in her wrist was nearly intolerable.

"Won't you be accompanying us, sir?" Crecy asked for her.

Torcy smiled grimly. "I have betrayed my king and thus the Colberts. I have tried to save France and failed her, too. But I shall not leave her."

"You are a true gentleman, sir," Crecy said, and she rose and kissed him on the cheek.

"Thank you, Mademoiselle," he replied. "And good fortune to you both. A small distance behind us is a bridge. My men and I will destroy it, which should break the trail of pursuit long enough for you to lose yourselves in the countryside. It is the last favor I can grant you." With that he nodded and was gone.

Adrienne counted ten men accompanying him, all in the uniform of the Black Musketeers. Then she noticed the expression of resolve on Nicolas' face.

"No," she said, with as much force as she could manage.

"I'll come back if I can," he said. "I do love you."

She reached for him, but it was with the wrong hand, and when she caught the smell of her ruined appendage, she nearly fainted again.

"Crecy, stop him," she pleaded.

"Torcy will need every man at the bridge. I should go, too."

"She needs you, Crecy," Nicolas said. "And of the two of us, you are better suited to protect her in the days to come."

"Sadly, I agree," Crecy said, her voice quavering slightly. "Take care, my friend."

"Nicolas," Adrienne said as he began stepping from the carriage.

He stopped and closed his eyes. "Yes," he said, with visible effort.

"I love you. Please . . ."

He shook his head again, eyes still closed. "I will return," he said.

And with that he ran from the carriage. A few moments later, it rocked into motion again.

"I think I should wrap your hand," Crecy said after a moment.

"Let it be. I don't care."

"Adrienne, let the men kill themselves in foolish heroics. We shall survive, you and I. I will take care of you."

"I love him, Veronique."

"I know. But as I told you once before, if anyone can survive . . ."

"Can you *see* it, Veronique? Can you see what happens?"

Crecy took her under her arm, stroking her hair with her free hand. "If you wish," she said.

"Do it."

Torcy sat his horse as Nicolas and the sapper planted the charges beneath the bridge. The morning had broken fine and cool, real autumn at last. The tall trees shivered at the belated chill, releasing a thousand leaves to become boats on the surface of the river.

"The charge may not be sufficient," the sapper called up, his dark face pinched in concern.

Torcy shrugged. "That is as it must be, then. Do your best."

Nicolas stuck his head from under the bridge. "It *has* to be enough. We have to *stop* them."

Torcy rolled his eyes. "Come here, Nicolas."

Nicolas complied, his face set in worried but determined lines. Torcy regarded him as he approached. "Why didn't you tell me that you had fallen in love with this woman?" he finally asked.

"It was not your affair."

"No, apparently it was *your* affair. You and I have worked together for several years, Nicolas, and I have never seen your judgment so clouded."

Nicolas waved his hand impatiently. "My judgment is sound," he snapped. "And I have served you well."

"You did not kill the king."

"It was beyond our ability. Some . . . *thing* . . . protects him."

"Very well," Torcy said. "If your judgment is sound, then ride on and leave this business of the bridge to me."

"You need my help to stop them," Nicolas insisted.

"No, you see? This is what I meant about your judgment, Nicolas. If the charge is powerful enough, the king's men will be stopped. If it is not, they will not. What else can be done?"

Nicolas frowned in sudden understanding. "You don't *care* if you stop them."

Torcy allowed himself a smile. "No, I do not. I do not play 'Horatius on the Bridge' for the benefit of your love, Nicolas, but so that I will be remembered as a man who died well. Do you understand?"

Nicolas licked his lips. "There is no need for you to die at all."

"Bah. Nicolas, I have lived my whole life for the king and for France. I know what the Bastille is like, and I will not retire there. My country and king—whatever else they think of me— will know my death was honorable. But there is no need for *you* to stay, my friend."

"I've always been loyal to you, Father," Nicolas returned.

"You've been a good son; d'Artagnan raised you well. I'm proud of you. Now, go!"

At that moment a shout went up from Torcy's musketeers across the bridge as they fell into a double line, muskets raised. Good men, those, for he now saw what they faced.

At least a hundred of the Royal Horse thundered toward them. Torcy indulged himself in a moment of pride; he was a

Colbert, still, a man to be reckoned with. He deserved a hundred horse at the very least.

"Shit!" Nicolas swore, and raced to his horse and weapons.

"Ride on, Nicolas, I beg you," Torcy shouted.

"The fuse isn't laid."

"It matters not. Ride on, Son." Then he winced as the first fusillade of shots rang, fired by his own men, eight muskets cracking in near unison. They began reloading as the second row fired.

The response from the Horse was a hailstorm. Three of his men went down, and carbine balls sang into the woods all around Torcy and Nicolas. Nicolas dropped to his knee, cocked his musket, and shot. Torcy shrugged and pulled out one of his own pistols, a wonderful weapon that had been his uncle's—a gift from the king.

Nicolas changed guns; taking up his carbine he fired that, too.

The second volley from the Horse finished Torcy's musketeers. The body of the sapper fell into the river, felled by a marksman or an unlucky bullet. The fuse was still not lit.

"Shoot the charge," Nicolas told him steadily, gesturing right. "If you move that way, you can see it. Shoot it." He leapt up, drawing his *kraftpistole* and colichemarde, and ran across the bridge.

Torcy watched him go, reflecting that Nicolas did not understand aesthetics. He intended to meet his killers standing squarely on the bridge, pistol cocked, defiant to the end.

The Horse had no intention of engaging Nicolas; they had all dismounted, forming a wall of muzzles. When Nicolas was halfway across the bridge, they fired.

Nicolas spun, and Torcy felt something brush one shoulder and something else slap him in the gut. He looked down in astonishment at his swiftly reddening shirt.

"Damn," he said.

Nicolas fired the *kraftpistole*, and the reddish bolt jetted out far enough to touch the outer ranks of gunmen. Five of them pitched to the ground. Nicolas shouted something, raising his sword, as Torcy braced for the next volley. Instead, the captain of the Horse stepped from ranks, his own weapon drawn in salute. Nicolas, swaying somewhat, raised his blade to a guard position.

Good for him! He had offended the Horse and bought his love a few more moments. It ruined Torcy's own plan, of course—by the time the Horse came across the bridge he would have lost too much blood to meet them defiantly. He sighed. Nicolas had been a good son. He deserved his father's help.

Torcy staggered to the side of the bridge, squinting so as to see the keg of powder, looking back to follow how Nicolas was doing, an unaccustomed and unwelcome pride swelling in his chest.

Nicolas had no feeling in his left arm, but then, he did not need his left arm. What he *needed* was more blood in his body to replace what leaked from his several musket wounds.

A man in the uniform of an officer saluted him.

"I am Captain Cleves. Lay down your sword and you will be treated honorably," he promised.

"One captain to another," Nicolas panted. "If you will agree to wait here, with your troops, for one hour, I will surrender my arms."

"In an hour you will be dead of your wounds," Cleves pointed out. "If you surrender now, I can have a surgeon tend to you."

"Give me your bound word, and I *will* surrender now."

Cleves hesitated for an instant, and then said, "I must be truthful. Only your courage and my honor prevents me from having my men cut you down as you stand. You and your companions attacked the *king*, Monsieur!"

"Has the king been so good to you? I know what the household troops think of the king. Those men lying dead there were musketeers, all devoted to France. How many more of you will lay down your lives for a bewitched king?"

"My duty is clear. Your words do not confuse me."

"I, myself, saw the devil that possesses him," Nicolas snapped. He was rewarded by a general murmuring among the men.

"Surrender and you can relate the tale."

Nicolas sighed heavily. "You are a man of honor, sir. You

could have had my sword with a simple lie. The man is rare, these days, who has such scruples."

"I prefer to believe you wrong," Cleves replied.

"En garde," Nicolas replied, "before I bleed to death."

Cleves beat a few times at his blade experimentally, nimbly shortening and lengthening the distance between. Nicolas held his ground, treating the feints as what they were, until Cleves suddenly lunged. Nicolas deflected the spearing blade and riposted in a low line toward his opponent's crotch. Cleves dropped his wrist and parried, but Nicolas had already disengaged, ghosting away from the hastily intervened weapon, darting up toward the captain's throat. Cleves stumbled back, and Nicolas bounded forward to follow his advantage. Unfortunately, his left leg was numb, and he went down on one knee. Cleves did not hesitate— everyone in the guards knew that Nicolas had never lost a duel. His point darted down. Nicolas' left arm was numb, but it could yet move. He got it up in time, gratified that the only feeling was a dull shock as the blade buried itself in bone. His own return thrust was merciful, straight into the heart. Cleves sobbed and fell.

Nicolas climbed unsteadily to his feet.

"Next, if you please," he panted.

Across the river, Torcy had decided that it was best to be very close to the charge. A pistol could miss at half a dozen paces, especially when one was shaking as he was, but it would not miss at a foot. He stopped ten paces away because he could still see Nicolas fighting. He watched until the boy had won, nodding his head. Then he took the last few steps and placed the muzzle of his weapon against the wooden cask.

"I commend myself to thee, Lord," he said. "Let you judge me, and no other." He hesitated a second longer. "I loved you, my king," he whispered. "Only because I loved you did I . . ." Then he tightened his lips. How stupid that death made men maudlin. He squeezed the trigger.

Nicolas didn't really *hear* the explosion so much as feel it. He surged into motion, running with what little energy remained in him, diving into the river. The water felt good, and he thought for an ecstatic moment that everything would be well. He put all of his will into swimming.

Then he saw the bridge, as he came up for air. Wreathed in black smoke, it still stood.

Then he felt something like goats dancing on his back, and the water closed again over his head. As he sank, he wondered at the red shroud enfolding him, like the cloak of a cardinal.

"He's dead," Crecy said softly.

Adrienne didn't even nod. She had no tears or grief left. Her body throbbed in time to the pulse in her arm. "You say that they didn't destroy the bridge?" she asked Crecy.

"No. It stands."

"They will catch us in a few hours then?"

"Much more quickly than that," Crecy corrected.

"Our driver will go on without us?"

"Yes."

"Well, then," Adrienne said, "we should disembark, and let them chase an empty carriage for a time. We have traveled in the woods before, you and I."

"You aren't up to it. Your hand . . ."

"I am not up to a hundred years in the Bastille either," Adrienne replied.

"I can make certain that neither of us suffers that fate," Crecy promised.

"No. I don't want to die. I have things to do."

Crecy's face was always hard to read, but Adrienne thought she saw a certain pride dawn on her features.

"Very well," she agreed. "We shall walk."

23.

Cannon

Clouds hung against the evening sky like the rotted tatters of a shroud on murky water. Ben gazed miserably at them.

"How will it appear, I wonder?" Vasilisa asked, just a few feet down the rail from him.

"Now you're the philosopher again, observing phenomena, rather than the tyrant," he grunted. "I wonder how you shall feel about the deaths of a million people."

"Just as you will, Ben. For most of them I will feel only a sort of abstract horror. When I think of those whom I met and knew—" She raised her hands helplessly. "—I will pray or pretend that they were some of the lucky ones Mr. Heath and Voltaire managed to convince to flee. And I will miss London."

"We might have saved it."

"I do not think so," Vasilisa replied. "In your heart, I know that you are grateful for my actions. You have been saved, and the moral burden was shouldered by someone else. You can pretend to yourself that you would have rather been there with Heath and Voltaire, trying your best till the end."

Ben had a sick spot in him that knew she was right.

"It should be any time now," Sir Isaac, his arm in a sling, said, coming up behind them. His eyes had a haunted quality, as if he had already seen something terrible.

"Perhaps we won't *see* anything," Vasilisa said. "We have, after all, put near three hundred miles between ourselves and London."

"Are we on deep waters then?" Sir Isaac asked abstractly, eyes fixed on the southern skies.

"Passing deep," Vasilisa answered.

"That is well, I suppose," Sir Isaac murmured.

Ben noticed Vasilisa's puzzled frown, but though he didn't understand the great magus' statement, he had very little curiosity left.

"How big did you say this rock was?" Robert asked. In many ways, he seemed most subdued of all.

"A mile or so in diameter," Sir Isaac replied. "Maybe more, maybe less."

"I should think we shan't see a thing," said Robert.

"No, I think we *shall*."

Stirling was on deck, hands and feet in chains, staring south with a grim intensity.

"Will you enjoy it, Stirling?" Ben asked brusquely. "Will it give you joy?"

"Not joy," Stirling answered, "but satisfaction. Peace, perhaps."

"Your sickness is deeper than mine ever was," Sir Isaac said, his voice almost inaudible, "and yet I am as much to blame. If I had not let myself slip away, I could have stopped this."

"How?"

"I'm not certain. But God would not allow the creation of such a thing and not provide for its destruction as well."

Something high above caught Ben's attention.

"There," Vasilisa shouted.

Far above the southern horizon was a kernel of brilliant light, brighter than any star Ben had ever seen. It moved slowly toward the horizon, passing behind a cloud.

The cloud fluoresced, and quickly the light in the south flared. The comet itself appeared again, pipe-shaped. In a moment, it became so bright that it could not be looked at.

Stirling was the only one to speak. His face was nearly argent in the unholy, bluish light.

"Oh, God!" he said.

Ben's hands trembled violently at the rail. When Vasilisa's hand found his, he gripped it without thinking.

The new sun set.

It rose again, fifty times as large, a dome of purest white, and all the south was white. Everyone around him was screaming as the scene rippled, and then suddenly the light was replaced by a black tower, rising without end, reaching for the darkening heavens.

Louis XIV sat in the Hall of Mirrors, surrounded by his court. He wore the diamond- and emerald-crusted coat he had planned to be married in. The rest of his court was as splendid.

His armchair rested on a dais, and his children sat or stood around him. In addition to them was Fatio de Duillier, his face grave and troubled.

"When will it begin?" he asked de Duillier, switching his gaze from the London-facing windows of the Hall of Mirrors to the smaller glass that rested before him.

"Very soon, Majesty, though I warn you, we may see little or nothing at this distance. You should keep your eye firmly on your mirror."

Louis quelched the frown that threatened. This was the moment, the moment when France would at last understand, when his court would love him again.

A general gasp went up from the courtiers, then scattered applause.

"What is it?"

"The sky, Sire," Fatio replied. "Do you see? I was wrong, it *is* visible."

Louis stared through the vast windows of the hall at the darkened sky. "I see nothing," he snapped. But his court clearly did, for their astonished sounds continued to wax.

You cannot see it because I cannot, the angel told him. *Or, I should say, I see it but not in terms you would comprehend. I can only translate images that both of us have. You have no image for this.*

"Show me anyway," Louis snapped petulantly.

If you wish. But you should watch in the mirror instead. But at Your Majesty's insistence . . .

Suddenly the sky changed. It became something more like a taste or a sensation than sight, and yet he could perceive a monstrous thing, a hole in the sky, a phantom's eye.

"Stop! Stop!" he managed. The sky became again a flat pane across the heavens.

"Sire?" Fatio and several others said at once.

"Nothing!" he snapped, and then forced himself to relax. Act the king. *Be* the king. This must be his greatest performance, his finest moment.

His breathing smoothed out, and then he noticed something new in his magic glass.

London had begun to glow, the sunset shadows of its cathedrals washed away by light.

Loud cheers and thunderous applause went up all around him.

"What? What?" Louis asked.

"The comet passed beyond the horizon, Majesty, but it was quite spectacular in the end. It lit up the entire sky like summer lightning."

I really can't see, Louis thought. *I am blind.*

I have helped you as I could, the angel told him. *I have helped you act the king, this one last time.*

"Last?" Louis whispered, suddenly afraid.

When the comet strikes London, I shall have to depart from you for a time.

"Why?"

When you throw a pebble in a pond, it sends out ripples. The ripples the comet will send out affect angels of my sort so as to make us ill. I shall be forced to leave you. I only remain now so that you can see your triumph. I have grown attached to you, great king, and it amuses me to please you.

Louis absorbed that for a moment. London was nearly white now. He could make out a sliver of the Thames, burning like the surface of the sun.

"I will be blind again?"

As you said, you have been blind since the attack on the barge. But you have put on the best of faces. You have behaved nobly. You are the king.

"I am the king," Louis assured himself. He let his face relax into a smile.

London grew suddenly dark. *I adjust the light so you can see, so it will not be intolerably bright,* the angel explained. Louis opened his mouth to ask what that meant, when suddenly even the darkened city was once again bathed in light. A huge ball of fire had appeared beyond London, filling half the sky. Fatio had missed! But before that dismay could even register, London was gone. For less than a second there was a confused impression of flame and wind—and then the mirror went silvery.

Farewell, my king, he heard, and then *everything* went dark. He heard Fatio shriek, and instantly there were hands upon him everywhere.

"His wounds!" Someone screamed, "Oh God, the blood!"

He no longer cared. He felt heavy, as if he were sinking into the earth.

"Thank you," he told the angel, though he knew it was gone. And yet, he could see in the mirror of his mind, he could remember things. He was again ten years old, holding little Phillipe under his arm, telling him it would all be well.

"Will it?" Phillipe asked.

"Of course. Because God loves us. And you will be well because *I* love *you.* Because you are my brother, and I am king."

He remembered how sadly Phillipe had looked at him then as he said, voice quavering, "I love you, too, Louis. That's why I'm sorry you have to be the king."

He understood Phillipe, and so he smiled as sleep claimed him. It had been so long since he could rest.

One quarter hour later, the sky began raining burning stones. The more jaded of the court applauded again, for the shower of stars was more beautiful than the first had been. When the nine windows of the Great Hall shattered and swept through them as a wind of glass, they ceased applauding.

Adrienne did not witness the flame in the sky. She lay on a mattress stuffed with leaves, twisting in a fever, as Crecy and an old peasant woman tried to quench the fire burning inside her.

"I never dreamed . . ." Stirling groaned. The black column had become a mushroom, still climbing, filling more and more of the sky.

The air suddenly slapped Ben in the face. The paddle wheeler creaked in complaint as shards of heaven fell from above.

"Look!" Vasilisa shouted, waving her arm wildly at the sea. Near the horizon, Ben could make out a plume of steam rising. Its size was impossible to estimate. The sailors, howling, pointed out two more.

"Do you comprehend what you have done, you fool?" Newton asked Stirling.

Stirling jerked his head about. "I . . . how could I . . ." He hadn't found his words when the noise came. It sounded like a thousand cannon firing fifty miles away, a groaning, rumbling noise. To Ben it was a million people screaming.

"You and your French allies have obliterated a good deal more than London. Did you never calculate the precise consequences of your actions?"

"Of course I did! I just didn't understand! Numbers like that have no sense to them!"

"If they were too vast for you to grasp, didn't you reckon that the effects might be so, too?"

But Stirling had no time to answer, for the Russian in the crow's nest began yelling.

Ben realized then that he was still gripping Vasilisa's hand. "What?" he asked.

She pointed south. "The wave," she said simply.

It looked like no wave Ben had ever seen. It was really more a fantastic swell, a bulge in the water four yards high, sweeping toward them with abnormal speed. The line of it stretched off to the limits of vision on each side. West, toward England, it seemed larger, and there Ben could see foam churning at its crest.

Vasilisa let go of his hand and began to run across the deck, shouting something in Russian.

The ship, broadside to the immense swell, lifted up and tilted. The deck flew from beneath Ben's feet, and for a long moment he hung suspended in the new, nightmare world of black clouds, shooting stars, and impossible waves. Then the deck found him again, dealt him a welcoming blow that left him with a twisted ankle and the taste of blood in his mouth and nostrils.

The deck was nearly perpendicular. Ben skipped down it like

a stone across a pond, hit the rail, flew again, and the sea sucked him in. He shouted and fought; the wave seemed to go on to the ends of the Earth. Ben was a good swimmer, better than anyone he knew in Boston. He had felt the pull of the Charles River and on one occasion had wrestled a bit with an undertow in the sea. He had never felt anything remotely like this, this Neptune's fist that had hold of him. His only fortune was that he was on the trailing side of it, that it was gradually outdistancing him.

After the first panicked moment or so, the pressure eased, and he began to think he might live. Swimming on his back, he made out the vague hulk of the ship framed by its lights: He thought it was still on its side, perhaps a hundred yards away.

He began to shout. There was still a current, a powerful one, but its speed had diminished so that it was no worse than being in the channel of a swift river. However, a black night was also rapidly falling, as clouds of growing size and density whipped by overhead with unreal speed, suffocating what remained of day. South was a wall of jet, lit only by sparks of hellfire, the hoofprints of dancing devils in God's stolen sky. An occasional sound like a cannon being fired boomed across the waters.

It began to rain, huge hot drops of salty, gritty rain, and then he lost even the lights of the ship. He ceased his efforts to stroke toward it then, for he quickly lost his sense of direction. Instead he concentrated on keeping afloat. That was far from easy; the rain came so thickly it seemed a solid sheet, leaving little more air to breathe above the sea than below it. Hail or perhaps rocks were mixed in it, and they tore mercilessly at him.

In less than half an hour, despite his best efforts, his limbs and lungs began to fail him. The sea, remorseless, swept him along.

24.

The Night-Dark Day

Ben felt the first sting of water in his lungs and found a feeble strength he was unaware he possessed. His arms and legs thrashed at the sea mindlessly, hatefully. Shouting at the top of his lungs, he swallowed a mouthful of water with every cry.

But the black water did not even pay him the honor of mockery. He was mere flotsam. His rage began to dwindle, and with it his hopes of living.

Jewels suddenly sparkled in the air, were gone, shone again to his right.

Jewels? It had rained fire and stone and salt water, and now burning jewels?

Then his weary brain understood, and he began shouting again, waving one of his arms wildly.

"Damn lucky you are, Ben," Robert shouted above the rain as Ben collapsed onto the floor of the dinghy. "We might have been twenty feet from you and not known you were there if not for your screaming."

"I saw the lantern light," Ben explained. "But you must have been close."

"We set out for you when we still had a little dayglow. But that was some time ago."

Sir Isaac sat silently, water pouring from each corner of his hat, his mind clearly focused elsewhere. Ben hoped he hadn't gone mad again. Aside from the three of them, there was no one else in the boat.

"Vasilisa?" he asked.

"I don't know, lad. I think the ship went down. I'm sorry."

"Maybe in the morning—"

"In the morning we shan't be here," Sir Isaac said calmly.

"Sir?"

Newton only smiled, but Robert poked his finger at a large copper globe that shared the lifeboat with them. It was perhaps two feet in diameter. Six cables were fastened to a large eyehook at one of its poles. The other ends of the cables were attached to various parts of the dinghy.

"Are we ready then?" Newton asked. Robert shrugged. Ben didn't have the strength to ask any more questions.

Newton reached over and did something to the sphere. "Mind the cables," he said.

Ben was hardly listening. The sphere had begun to shine faintly red, and more importantly, it had begun to rise. It floated straight up until all of the cables were taut. And it *continued up*! The cables hummed in the high wind as they took on the boat's weight, and then suddenly they were rocking airborne.

That swinging sensation was Ben's only clue that they were flying. Otherwise, the boat was still a small island of light in a stygian sea: Raindrops were still the only vista, and though the occasional flare of lightning opened the sky a bit wider, it still seemed closed.

"Are we still rising?" Ben asked after a time.

"Yes," Newton replied. "I'd like to be above the clouds, above the rain."

"Above the rain?" Ben weighed these words for madness but kept his judgments in abeyance. He was, after all, flying in a boat. He wondered what a cloud would smell like.

Finally the rain stopped, and the wind did take on a peculiar smell: sharp, chemical, *burned*. Mixed currents of hot and cold air touched them. They were enclosed by an eerie silence, the only sounds their own breathing, the whisper of winds in the cables, and an occasional distant rumble of thunder.

"Oh, God," Robert said, "look!"

Below them, Ben saw lightning brightening the heart of one cloud, and then another. The endless mass beneath them seemed like some vast organism, its internal organs luminescing now and then, shining through its convoluted skin. The clouds were hundreds of feet below.

Tremulously, Ben turned his gaze upward. "If we have risen above the clouds," he asked, "shouldn't we see stars?"

But there were no stars, only the arcane radiance of the sphere that bore them. Ben felt a tickle of horror when he understood that the luminescence was patterned. The once-solid globe now seemed translucent, an egg held up to a candle, its yolk bright, an eye straining to peer through a cataract.

Ben slept briefly and restlessly in the damp bottom of the boat, his mind racing despite his weariness. He had just dozed for a second time when he saw new light.

"The moon but not stars," Robert murmured beside him. "How very odd."

The rising orb was ruddy and huge, spreading its light liberally upon the clouds below. In the dim luminescence, Ben could still see no end to them, a vast desert of mist.

"That's a bright moon," Robert remarked, his voice unsteady. Sir Isaac, nearby, snored a noncommittal reply.

Ben stared in momentary incomprehension. "No craters," he said. "No man in the moon. Robert, that isn't the moon. That's the sun."

"The sun? But the sky is still so dark. It's so pale!"

At noon, it was brighter than the full moon, but one could still stare at it for a few moments without looking away. The sky was amber, shaded to a vile brown at the horizon. Newton, now awake, sighed.

"We have made the world different," he said. "We can only hope God will forgive us."

"I don't understand," Robert admitted tightly. "I'm no philosopher, I . . . Couldn't this be the end? Armageddon?"

Newton kept looking thoughtfully at the sun. "My researches into history suggest that the last days are not upon us yet," he answered. "But it could be. In a few days we shall know. Mr. Nairne, you are in good company, for I don't understand these things we see much better than you do—nor, I suspect, does Mr. Franklin. But I will tell you this. If this is *not* the time foretold in

the Revelation of John, it is a time of testing nevertheless. It is a
time to use the minds God gave us, to decipher the phenomena
around us. Most especially, we must stop this from ever happening again."

"Again?"

"If one madman can call a comet from the sky, so can another. I mean to make certain that it cannot be done again. Mr.
Franklin, I am sore in need of an amanuensis, a laboratory aide,
a collaborator. In short, sir, I need an apprentice. May I interest
you in the position?"

Newton's offer held only a vague hope of accomplishing too
little too late, but it held the only hope that Ben saw left anywhere in the world.

"Yes," he finally replied, not from eagerness or innocence, but
from the beginnings of something wiser. "Yes, sir, I am interested."

Adrienne woke to the tattoo of rain on a tile roof and tried to reconstruct from scant, disordered memories where she was.

Her last clear recollection was of fleeing through the woods
with Crecy, of a throbbing pain in her wrist.

She raised her right hand and for a crazy second nearly
laughed, because it looked so *odd* to have an arm ending in a
wrist. She touched the clean bandage gingerly and was rewarded with pain.

She remembered fevered dreams of a filthy cottage, but now
she lay in a large, comfortable bed in a small room. Outside a
cracked window, the rain poured in a solid sheet. A faint sul-
phury odor wafted in from the open window, infusing the damp,
metallic scent of rain.

She tried to rise and quickly discovered that she was too
weak for that yet, and worse, she had a sudden, vicious bout of
nausea. Fortunately, the chamber pot was on the side of the bed.

The noise of her being sick brought motion outside, and the
door creaked open. Crecy entered, clad in a loose brown manteau somewhat short for her height.

"So!" Crecy said, kneeling nearby with a damp rag. "You're
awake. How do you feel?"

"Veronique, where am I? How many days have passed?"

Crecy touched Adrienne's forehead lightly. "You have been very ill," she said. "I thought you would die. You may have noticed your hand."

"Yes."

"It's been more than a week since we fled Versailles. You remember that?"

"Very well. And Nicolas . . ."

"Good. Then I don't have to explain." She hesitated a moment and then added, "I *am* sorry, you know."

"It was my fault. If I hadn't hesitated—"

"Then you would merely have lost your hand sooner," Crecy finished. "Enough of that. We have other worries, and I will need you attentive to them, not frozen considering the past."

"Other worries?"

"I'll get to that. When we fled the carriage, you didn't get far. I found a woodcutter and his wife; she had some knowledge of herbs and poultices. Your hand had to be removed."

"The pursuit?"

Crecy smiled grimly. "The next day, Newton's cannon fired, and the pursuit seems to have quite forgotten us."

"Truly?"

"Adrienne, the western sky lit up like midday, and then stones began to fall. Some of them were aflame, and the woods caught fire. A few hours after that, the sun was blotted out."

"Blotted out?"

"By black clouds. It's been raining the most part of every day since, and the rain smells foul. I took you from the woodcutter's place to higher ground, for the lowlands are all flooding. I killed a gentleman and his driver, stole his carriage, and brought us here."

"Where? Whose house is this?"

"Madame Alaran, one of the Korai. She received us, but we cannot stay here long. Her servants and tenants all think that the world has ended, and her fields are drowning." She smiled sardonically. "Some of this is to our advantage. Many roads are washed out between here and Versailles. It will make our flight easier."

Adrienne remembered her own calculation of the impact of the comet.

"I never saw all this," she muttered.

"No matter," Crecy said softly, "I did. It isn't the end of the world, I assure you. But it will be a very dark time, and you and I must leave France as soon as possible, while you are still well able to travel."

"What do you mean?"

"I mean that you are with child, my dear," Crecy replied.

She stood in the ruins of Versailles and knew that she dreamed or that somehow Crecy had given her the second sight, for she understood that she also remained in bed. Most of the great mansion still stood, but its windows were shattered, and the pounding of rain filled the empty halls like the sound of God's tears.

Through the downpour, she walked to the Grotto of Thetis, and there, with a mixture of pity and triumph, she regarded Louis' face on Apollo, the eyes now altered somehow so that the stone registered not a dread, sovereign gaze, but the sad eyes of a little child betrayed.

Her own face looked different, too. Older, and with something in the curve of the lips—something disturbing but not immediately recognizable.

Pain throbbed in her wrist, and it seemed now that she remembered why she was here. Approaching her statue, she gazed more closely, her eyes microscopes looking deeper and deeper until she spied the atoms that made it, the mathematical prisons that gave them form. She smiled and then laughed at the beauty of it.

Still smiling, she reached with her good hand and broke the stone wrist of Thetis, pressed the hard marble hand to her own stump. And then she wrote an equation the like of which had never been written before. She wrote it not with pen and ink but with atoms, the way God writes.

And then, dream or vision, it faded. She forgot much on waking, and forgot more each moment thereafter. But when she woke, she had two hands again.

Epilogue

The Angel of Kings

Peter Alexeevich, emperor of all the Russias, Livonia, Karelia, and Sweden, paced through the rooms of his modest Summer Palace like a caged tiger. At forty-eight, his tall frame trembled with the pent-up energies of a younger man, a man used to action and presently denied it.

How could he act when he knew nothing? Oh, he had a few reports, but most aetherschreibers seemed to have stopped working. He knew, at least, that the spectacular sights in the western and southern heavens of two nights ago, the subsequent darkening of the sun, and now the unseasonable storms rolling in from the west were small things compared to the cataclysms in the rest of Europe. Of two score ambassadors, merchants, and spies in the Netherlands, only one had so far contacted him, a short, panicked note that raved of fire from the heavens and the waves flowing over the dikes. Amsterdam, that most incomparable of cities, had been reclaimed by the sea. In France, the Sun King was dead, and all was chaos. There was no word from London. It was as if every agent in England had vanished.

Whatever horror had been visited upon his western neighbors had thus far spared Russia. *Thus* far.

He stalked into his turning room. He glanced at the yard-wide dials on the wall, which registered the time and—through clever devices upon the roof—the direction of the wind and its force. Today, the dials told him the wind blew from the west, and it blew with great strength.

After a time, he found himself outside, gazing at the weird sky and the defiant, proud thrust of Saint Petersburg against the uncanny yellow clouds. Thus far, no damage had come to his

365

beautiful city: The water had risen slightly in the mouth of the Neva, but not so much as to drown anything. He felt, as he often did, a great swell of pride at his city—*his* city—which less than two decades ago had been a marsh without even a village to mark it. Now it was his capital, a bustling metropolis with more than forty thousand buildings designed by the greatest architects of Italy, France, and the Netherlands. A bright, shining, *new* city for the new age of the Russian Empire and of the world.

What threatened it? What should he be doing? His eyes searched the skies for an answer and found none. With a low growl he stalked off to see his philosophers again, but they had no clear answers. Finally, he went to Trinity Square, paused long enough to bestow one twitchy smile on the three-room cabin he had built and dwelt in so long ago, now dwarfed by great stone façades. Many thought it odd that Peter's subordinates had grander palaces than the tsar himself, but to Peter *his* palaces were Russia and Saint Petersburg. He preferred the airy Summer Palace with its fourteen rooms or Mon Plaisir, which was hardly bigger, where he could sit with his telescope and watch the ships, where he could enjoy his few precious moments alone with Catherine.

He entered the Four Frigates Tavern and was welcomed by the crowd with cheers. His searching gaze quickly found the French and Dutch ambassadors sitting with their staffs at opposite ends of the room. They greeted him wanly; they were well into their cups, and most had streaks of tears on their cheeks.

"Bring vodka and brandy!" Peter shouted. A profound silence settled on the usually noisy crowd as Peter positioned himself near the center of the room, downed his first glass, refilled, and then raised his voice again. "My friends, something terrible has happened, and we do not yet know the nature or the extent of it. God willing, we will soon. We have heard awful reports that our neighbors and brethren in the west have suffered terrible catastrophes. I wish to raise a glass in their honor, and in prayer for those who have died. We have heard Amsterdam has been inundated, but I give you the *Dutch*, gentlemen, and I tell you that in Holland, the sea never wins! If waves lie on that great city, it will be a short-lived victory for the sea!" He raised his glass in salute, and there was a ragged cheer. The Dutchmen's eyes told him that he had touched them to the core.

His blood liked the feel of brandy in it, and he raised a fresh glass for a second toast. "And to my French friends, please know that my sympathies are with you as well. Russia stands ready to give her aid if it is needed." He looked around. "And have my English friends any news?" he asked, but the Englishmen, grim faced, had no answer.

They all huddled there in the Four Frigates as the sky grew darker and colder, holding their grief and worry at bay with strong drink and brave words. And at last, beneath a lightless sky, Peter made his way back home and sought his bed.

And there he had a dream.

He was ten years old, shivering in a dark place. His mother, Natalya, crouched nearby. He could make out little of her face, but he remembered it as he had last seen it: stoic, brave, determined. Hours ago—when they had faced the mob of Strelitzi soldiers with their muskets, pikes, and axes—her grip on his hand had been tight, but her voice had been strong.

The Strelitzi, it seemed, had gone mad. The Strelitzi, who had been the personal guard of the tsar and his family since the time of Ivan the Terrible, now ran riot in the narrow, dark maze of the Kremlin itself, *hunting* the royal family, killing and looting, as Peter and his mother and his brother, Ivan, hid in a darkened banquet hall.

If I live, Peter thought, *the Strelitzi shall pay for this. One day they shall know the judgment of a tsar.*

The Kremlin, the palace of his father, had become a nightmare, a dark warren full of rats.

Late in the night, when she thought he was asleep, his mother rose to leave.

"Mother?" he whispered.

"I must know what is happening," she told him, stroking his head. "Stay here and watch Ivan. Be very quiet."

"They might kill you, too," Peter moaned.

"That would be going too far," she said. "Even the Strelitzi would not dare go that far. They will not kill me, Peter. Now be a good boy and stay here. Ivan needs you."

Peter glanced at the sleeping form of his older half brother Ivan and nodded. Ivan was weak of body and spirit, nearly blind, and scarcely capable of comprehensible speech. "I will watch him," he promised.

Some time later, Peter heard men singing in the halls and saw a yellow light approaching. Peter felt as if he could not breathe, and began to shake as his courage failed him. He saw, in the light of a flickering torch, the bearded face of one of the Strelitzi, spattered with blood, grinning like a wolf.

The torch was thrust into the banquet hall.

"Might be some silver in there," someone said.

"Might be," said another.

"Isn't that where the tsaritsa was holed up, a while back? Goddamn Naryshkins! Do you hear me in there? Goddamn Naryshkins!"

Peter felt as if he were underwater, with no place to get air. What could he do?

Then something soft and dark wrapped around him, something comforting. He couldn't see the Strelitzi anymore, but he didn't fear them, either.

"*Nyet*, see," one said. "Nobody here. It's empty now."

After a time they went away.

"Who are you?" Peter whispered, for he understood someone was there. He had been having this dream for many years. But this time in his dreams there was *something*, something dark and strong, a protector he had never really had.

"I am here to help you, Peter Alexeevich," the darkness whispered. "For there are angels who protect kings, and I am such a one."

JONATHAN CARROLL

White Apples

TOR

A captivating and constantly surprising tale of life, death, and the realm in-between.

Vincent Ettrich, an engaging philanderer, discovers that he has died and come back to life – but he has no idea why, or any memory of the experience. Beset by peculiar omens and strange characters, including a talking rat, he gradually discovers that he was deliberately brought back by his one true love, Isabelle, because she is pregnant with their son – a child who, if correctly raised, will play a crucial role in saving the cosmic mosaic that is the universe.

But to be brought up right, he must be educated by his own father. Specifically, he must be taught what Ettrich learned on the 'other side'– if only Ettrich himself can remember it!

Tempting and provocative, *White Apples* is forbidden fruit plucked straight from the orchard of Jonathan Carroll's abundant and legendary imagination.

'I envy anyone who has yet to enjoy the sexy, eerie and addictive novels of Jonathan Carroll. They are delicious treats – with devilish tricks inside them'
Washington Post

'Can create an entire world in three paragraphs, and that world is unlike anything I have ever read in my life'
Pat Conroy

JEFFREY FORD

The Physiognomy

TOR

Winner of the 1998 World Fantasy Award

A prestigious novel of literary fantasy and disturbing imagination.

The nightmare metropolis called the Well-Built City exists because a satanic genius Drachton Below, the Master, wished it so. And few within its confines hold the power of Physiognomist Cley. With scalpels, callipers and the other instruments of his science, Cley can divine good and evil, determine character and intelligence, uncover dark secrets, and foretell a person's destiny.

But now the Master has sent the great physiognomist out of the City on a seemingly trivial assignment in the rural hinterland where, removed from Below's omnipresent scrutiny, even the most loyal servant of logic can fall prey to seductions of the flesh and spirit.

And in this unfamiliar place, possessing terrors uniquely its own, await stark revelations that could shatter Cley's perceptions of himself, his profession and his ordered world.

'Ford writes equally well about the scientific cult of precision
and the acceptance of ambiguity'
New York Times

JACQUELINE CAREY

Kushiel's Dart

TOR

A massive fantasy tale about the violent death of an old age and the birth of a new one. Here is a novel of grandeur, luxuriance, sacrifice, betrayal and deeply laid conspiracies.

Born with a scarlet mote in her left eye, Phèdre nó Delaunay is sold into indentured servitude as a child. When her bond is purchased by an enigmatic nobleman, she is trained in history, theology, politics, foreign languages and the arts of pleasure. Above all, she learns the ability to observe, remember and analyse. An exquisite courtesan, yet a talented spy, she may seem an unlikely heroine . . . but when Phèdre stumbles upon a plot threatening her homeland, Terre d'Ange, she has no choice but to act.

Betrayed into captivity in the barbarous northland of Skaldia, and accompanied only by a disdainful young warrior-priest, Phèdre makes a harrowing escape and an even more harrowing journey, to return to her people and deliver them a warning of the impending invasion. And that proves only the first step in a quest that will take her to the edge of despair and beyond.

'A very sophisticated fantasy, intricately plotted and a fascinating read'
Robert Jordan

OTHER PAN BOOKS
AVAILABLE FROM PAN MACMILLAN

JEFFREY FORD
THE PHYSIOGNOMY   0 330 41319 8   £6.99

JACQUELINE CAREY
KUSHIEL'S DART   0 330 49374 4   £7.99

MICHAEL DE LARRABEITI
THE BORIBLE TRILOGY   0 330 49085 0   £8.99

JONATHAN CARROLL
WHITE APPLES   0 330 49274 8   £6.99

All Pan Macmillan titles can be ordered from our website,
www.panmacmillan.com, or from your local bookshop
and are also available by post from:

Bookpost, PO Box 29, Douglas, Isle of Man IM99 1BQ
Credit cards accepted. For details:
Telephone: 01624 677237
Fax: 01624 670923
E-mail: bookshop@enterprise.net
www.bookpost.co.uk

Free postage and packing in the United Kingdom

Prices shown above were correct at the time of going to press.
Pan Macmillan reserve the right to show new retail prices on covers
which may differ from those previously advertised in the text
or elsewhere.